CLASSIC EU[ROPEAN]
SHORT STORIES

CLASSIC EUROPEAN SHORT STORIES

Edited by

Robert Beum

Sherwood Sugden & Company
PUBLISHERS

1117 Eighth Street, La Salle, Illinois 61301

ACKNOWLEDGMENTS

The editor and publisher are grateful to the following publishers, agents, authors, and translators, for permission to reprint certain stories in the present volume:

The estate of Aylmer Maude—for "God Sees the Truth but Waits," by Leo Tolstoi, translated by Aylmer Maude.

The estate of A. E. Chamot—for "The Sentry," by Nikolai Leskov, translated by A. E. Chamot, copyright © 1922.

The estate of Clara Bell—for "The Red Inn," by Honoré de Balzac, translated by Clara Bell.

The estates of Ivan Bunin and Helen Matheson—for "Sunstroke," by Ivan Bunin, translated by Helen Matheson.

The Bobbs-Merrill Company, Inc. and Peter Owen Ltd.—for "Dawn" and "The Bracelet," by Colette, from *The Other Woman*, by Colette, translated by Margaret Crosland, copyright© 1972, reprinted with permission of The Bobbs-Merrill Company, Inc. and Peter Owen Ltd., London.

Farrar, Straus and Giroux, Inc.—for "The Little Boullioux Girl," by Colette, translated by Una Vicenzo Trowbridge and Enid McCleod, copyright 1953 by Farrar, Straus and Young (now Farrar, Straus and Giroux, Inc.).

Alfred A. Knopf, Inc., Jonathan Cape Ltd., and the estate of Elizabeth Bowen—for "Tears, Idle Tears," by Elizabeth Bowen, from *Look at All Those Roses*, copyright © 1941.

The editor is indebted to Sherwood Sugden not only for helpful suggestions about selections and textual points but also for that necessity of authors and editors, encouragement; to Marynel Young for constantly valuable counsel and assistance, especially on selections and on translations from the French; to Brendan O'Grady of The University of Prince Edward Island; and to The University of Nebraska—Lincoln, The University of Saskatchewan, and St. Thomas More College, Saskatoon, for the use of library facilities and for assistance in research.

9JB0018401

ISBN 0-89385-025-X

First Edition

Sherwood Sugden & Company, Publishers
1117 Eighth Street
La Salle, Illinois 61301

Contents

To the Reader

Early or late, many readers come to prefer European stories to all others. The reason may have something to do with one of the most striking facts of European civilization: cultural richness. Europe is the old *World, and time means layers of change—depth, richness. Immensely diversified through military and cultural invasions, the area that extends eastward from the British Isles to Russia is also relatively small, and that smallness, forcing peoples of quite different traditions and habits to remain aware of one another, has furnished writers with breadth of vision and a considerable range in portraying the forms and spirit of peoples, places, and events.*

Three, at least, of Europe's military and cultural invasions have been crucial for its literature.

Teaching organization, order, unity, the Romans provided a heritage of structure for all the arts. And in the days of its most vigorous colonizing, Rome also carried, wherever it went, something of the Greek legacy to which the Empire had long since become indebted.

More directly from the Greeks came an intensification of interest in the very thing literature is all about: human experience—highly valued, closely observed, faithfully rendered. Within the Hellenic genius was something else immensely serviceable to literature: an unprecedented aesthetic and contemplative development, balancing the claims of sensibility and sense, creating an ideal not just of finish or perfection, but of harmony, "unity of being." Though in certain ways the arts and ideals of the Middle Ages developed along lines rather different from the Graeco-Roman, the latter had already done much to shape the medieval civilizational force itself—Christianity. And the advent of the Renaissance meant of course a second wave of Graeco-Roman influence, a reinvigoration of humanism and classicism.

In its own right, Christianity encouraged the development of moral sensitivity and moral individuation: through its doctrine of personal salvation and personal responsibility grounded in free will, it supplied the individual with the necessary motive force lacking in the Socratic injunction Know thyself. *Modern psychology of character in literature develops directly out of the Greek and Christian exploration of moral constitution. And in realms by no means limited to the moral, Christianity, as Paul Valéry puts it, "educated and stimulated millions of minds . . . made them act and react through centuries" by proposing "the subtlest, most important, and even most fertile problems to the mind."*

If time means change and diversity, it also means tradition, stability, continuities—for the individual, an inspiriting and also settling sense of belonging to something meaningful because rooted; a certain confidence, a relative lack of anxiety about roles and values. Such feelings are propitious for literature, at least for literature that isn't crippled by fear of affirmation. "The art of literary expression," Arthur Waugh reminds us, "invites enthusiasms, and prospers under their influence, while it withers and desiccates under the spirit of indecision." Despair and deep-running anxiety are enervating; but writing, especially over the long haul, requires ambition and a certain belief in the value of what one is writing—in its value as contribution, not just as self-therapy; and no contribution is discoverable in the thesis or implication that experience is unintelligible or unmeaningful. More therapeutic for the writer than significant for the reader, the typical product of nihilistic inspiration is not what one treasures for rereading or for handing over to one's children when they reach a certain age. At their best, existential Angst *and the spirit of* nada *produce gloom but not tragedy; power, sometimes, but not the joy that begets and binds the generations.*

Old Europe also implies the land: the soil, as way of life, wealth, and symbol. The European sensibility, the European habit of mind, developed from an agrarian, not an urban-industrial basis. Great literature implies reality; for us, the first reality is nature, "creator and destroyer"; "ancient, cosmopolitan, feudal, agrarian" Europe knew nature in all its aspects, and the writers appropriated its universality as fact and as symbol of unequalled power and richness. Land and landedness were the bastions, too, of a religion beneficent to writers because it was equally aware of God as mystery and poetry and as ethical imperative. The religion sanctioned what agrarian life usually enjoins: creative poverty, a way of life that, providing few passive amusements and no mass communications, forced the individual to create out of his own imagination—forced him, in other words, into being rather than into having, into deep engagement with experience valued for its spontaneity and creativity.

In the political sphere, old Europe's concept of "right order" provided a check upon mankind's tendency to become completely caught up in practical materialism. The hierarchic and aristocratic orientation of the anciens régimes quite naturally encouraged people to think that the ultimate standards of reference ought to be not those of economic ambition and the marketplace but those of temple and tower. "Arrogance and hatred are the wares/Peddled in the thoroughfares," Yeats says, and the lines have more than color. The truth of the soul, without which there is "no health" in us or in literature, is seldom spoken there and more seldom heard above the traffic.

Of course the New World itself is the creation of European mind and energy; but a creation it was, not just an extension—it was, in short, both recent and different. Historically, its emergence coincided with radical transformations in the European cultural fabric itself: the ascendancy of the commercial classes and, predictable consequence, the rise of an unprecedented materialism; the advent of an anti-sensuous, anti-imaginative individualism intent upon shattering not only traditional—that is, universally meaningful—symbolisms but the tie with the land itself; and domination of the intelligentsia by the skepticism and parvenu optimism of the Enlightenment.

If artistic creation depends on spontaneous imagination and the spirit of play, rather than on appetite and calculation; if literature thrives on innocence, wonder, and ideality, and not on the preoccupations of commerce and bureaucracy, then the Old World was providentially equipped to produce literature in the first place—the genuine article, rather than the narrower thing, the pseudo-literature that would flourish later as an instrument of escape, titillation, and politicization, *in a spiritually shrunken age when even the materialism had generally become passive and lacking in distinction and glamour. And, in the second place, the physical and cultural conditions were right for the proliferation of work that was not only genuine but also technically proficient, evocative, and masterfully ambient.*

Reflecting the beginnings of radical cultural change, fiction was the last literary genre to come fully into its own; and short fiction—the short novel and short story—representing partly a literary accommodation to the increasing tempo of modern life, with its greater impatience, shorter attention-span, and impressionistic habits, was the latest comer of all. The novel, made into a tradition by Fielding, Smollett, Scott, Austen, Stendhal, and Goethe, had been triumphant for about a half-century before the likes of Hoffmann, Storm, von Kleist, Poe, Nodier, Balzac, and Mérimée opened up the fabulous mines of short fiction. For us their era, in fact that whole chromatic era between the early 1800s and the First World War, has a special fascination. Not all was the back-breaking labor and wretched poverty that capitalists and mainstream socialists alike portray. People lived then, as Barbara Tuchman says, "with greater magnificence, extravagance and elegance; more careless ease, more gaiety, more pleasure in each other's company and conversation" and with "less sufferance of mediocrity, more dignity in work, more delight in nature, more zest." Intellectually, imaginatively, and spiritually vigorous, the stories reflect the milieu. Transmuting the élan of a vanished epoch into vibrant art, they live on to minister to an era perhaps less affirmative, less living, but hardly less in need of their life-enhancing power.

Collected here are twenty stories that have in common that power, that special kind of excellence the condition européen *once made possible in life and art.*

Diverse in themes, techniques, textures, and lengths, the stories appeal to catholic taste and make no plea for any specific worldview, theory of fiction, or mode of interpretation. Nor are they offered as works that promote social consciousness, equality, international unity, or economic development. The present editor's faith is a simple one: whatever gives pleasure to the imagination is its own reward; and if, at the same time, that pleasure is intimately bound up with the exploration or affirmation of life in its variety and depth, so much the better.

The main criterion for selection has been the story's ability to explore the truths of personal experience richly, openly, and with con-

summmate artistry. That ability implies, of course, a sense of wonder—derives from it and encourages it in ourselves. Amidst their differences, all the writers included here seem to have agreed with G. K. Chesterton, echoing Longinus, that "The dignity of the artist lies in his duty of keeping awake the sense of wonder in the world."

The need for such a collection as this may be very simply stated: the demand is perennial but the market now offers little to meet it. Though there is no evidence that the classic short stories of nineteenth-century Europe are any less highly regarded than ever, they are simply not being made available. The new anthologies, overemphasizing novelty and oversimplifying the concept of relevance, go with the trends and the untried. Bringing several of the classics back into circulation, the present book at the same time takes advantage of the opportunity to present some tales that have never received the attention they deserve. Among them are Stevenson's "Olalla" and Pouvillon's "Duck Shooting."

Individuation is the hallmark of genius, and the stories gathered here were created in the age of individuality par excellence. They cry out to be unencumbered by the usual critical and historical labels and classifications. In this collection all such have been avoided. Nor has any attempt been made to select stories because they are distinctly representative of the writer or of the various intellectual movements and schools of fiction that arose or developed in the nineteenth and early twentieth centuries.

The anti-historical and generally pragmatic and anti-intellectual bias of most contemporary education has created a special stumbling block for readers: European literature has always been vigorously allusive, both to its present and its thick-layered past. Provision has been made. In the present book, developed headnotes introduce each writer, and brief notes on the individual stories identify historical persons, places, dates, events, and foreign phrases.

Robert Louis Stevenson

1850—1894

Stevenson was born and reared in Edinburgh, where he studied engineering and then law, and then, to the chagrin of his practical-minded father, abandoned both, permanently, for letters. Eventually, because of tuberculosis, he also had to abandon his wet, chilly homeland, a deep source of spiritual strength. Even so it was only with great difficulty that he managed to stretch out his years to forty-four. The salubrious climate of Samoa, where he settled in 1890 with his wife Fanny Osbourne, gave him less than five more years and imposed the loneliness of self-exile. But neither loneliness nor ruined lungs hurt his literary productivity or its quality. On the whole, in fact, the fiction he wrote at Vailima (his estate at Apia) is both deeper and richer in compassionate humanity than his earlier and to this day better-known work such as Treasure Island, Kidnapped (David Balfour)*, and* Dr. Jekkyl and Mr. Hyde. *(The immense and lasting popularity of these and of* A Child's Garden of Verses *has long kept Stevenson a victim of that critical snobbery which interprets, quite uncritically, popularity to indicate that which is not worth the sophisticated reader's time.) Four, at least, of the late works are far more than islands nights' entertainments. The long story "The Beach of Falesá" (1893) is a narrative and linguistic* tour de force *and marries Stevenson's expected adventure and suspense with an unexpected and perfectly executed realism. Two full-length novels,* The Wrecker *(1892) and* The Ebb-Tide *(1894), deserve to be ranked along with*

Joseph Conrad's better efforts and should be allowed to modify the prevalent notion that Stevenson is more masterful in shorter fiction than in the full-dress novel.

A lifelong admirer of Hazlitt, Stevenson is also, of course, an essayist of the first rank. His essay "Pulvis et Umbra" ("Dust and Shadows") is often singled out as the most powerful short essay ever written in the grand manner. It is in any event an accurate statement of Stevenson's ambivalent outlook, which was bleak in its conclusions but game, undaunted, and perhaps secretly hopeful in its spirit. In all, Stevenson produced ten volumes of essays. There were also four volumes of poetry, but Stevenson, like Oscar Wilde, put most of his best poetry into his prose. It is not "purple patch" or even, in the usual sense, "poetic" prose: it remains genuine prose, flexible, modern in its own way, and does not lapse into affectation or meter; but underneath *its allegiance is to the traditional impulses of poetry.*

As G. K. Chesterton says, Stevenson underwent a "reaction into adventure." He was the enemy of inaction, of all unnecessary or self-indulgent withdrawal and reclusiveness. He even championed conversation as a form of action, an engagement that teaches generosity, forcing the ego to give and take and not skulk away. Emphasis on gusto and adventure was also Stevenson's scrappy answer to the enervating self-consciousness of hyperintellectualism, to the "end of the century" malaise, and to the contagion of ennui spreading from the intellectual nihilism and futilitarianism of the late nineteenth century. Walter Allen said that Stevenson "successfully married Flaubert to Dumas"; that is, high artistry and intellectual depth to a penchant for adventure and spirited play.

The concept of adventure is central to an understanding of the particular kind of fiction Stevenson consistently wrote: romance. Stevenson regarded this earlier-evolved form as superior to the "realism" or "naturalism" that had triumphed (especially with the intelligentsia) in his own era. Romance preserves the interests of poetry even when the outward clothing has changed to prose. Symbolism rather than reportorialism; the impulse to set a limit to minutiae and to reduce meaning to its dramatic and symbolic essence, and to stay in touch with the largest and most universal issues; to locate and strike through to the primordial—to the archetypes in the collective unconscious, as Jung put it; this is the region of romance, and the highway or seaway that leads to it is called adventure. There is also the adventure of words. Stevenson's brilliant sallies, his crispness and freshness, are the perfect complement of his narrative substance.

Olalla

Robert Louis Stevenson

"Now," said the doctor, "my part is done, and, I may say, with some vanity, well done. It remains only to get you out of this cold and poisonous city, and to give you two months of a pure air and an easy conscience. The last is your affair. To the first I think I can help you. It falls indeed rather oddly; it was but the other day the Padre came in from the country; and as he and I are old friends, although of contrary professions, he applied to me in a matter of distress among some of his parishioners. This was a family—but you are ignorant of Spain, and even the names of our grandees are hardly known to you; suffice it, then, that they were once great people, and are now fallen to the brink of destitution. Nothing now belongs to them but the residencia, and certain leagues of desert mountain, in the greater part of which not even a goat could support life. But the house is a fine old place, and stands at a great height among the hills, and most salubriously; and I had no sooner heard my friend's tale, than I remembered you. I told him I had a wounded officer, wounded in the good cause, who was now able to make a change; and I proposed that his friends should take you for a lodger. Instantly the Padre's face grew dark, as I had maliciously foreseen it would. It was out of the question, he said. Then let them starve, said I, for I have no sympathy with tatterdemalion pride. Thereupon we separated, not very content with one another; but yesterday, to my wonder, the Padre returned and made a submission: the difficulty, he said, he had found upon enquiry to be less than he had feared; or, in other words, these proud people had put their pride in their pocket. I closed with the offer; and, subject to your approval, I have taken rooms for you in the residencia. The air of these mountains will renew your blood; and the quiet in which you will there live is worth all the medicines in the world."

"Doctor," said I, "you have been throughout my good angel, and your advice is a command. But tell me, if you please, something of the family with which I am to reside."

"I am coming to that," replied my friend; "and, indeed, there is a difficulty in the way. These beggars are, as I have said, of very high descent and swollen with the most baseless vanity; they have lived for some generations in a growing isolation, drawing away, on either hand, from the rich who had now become too high for them, and from the poor, whom they still regarded as too low; and even to-day, when poverty forces them to unfasten their door to a guest, they cannot do so without a most ungracious stipulation. You are to remain, they say, a stranger; they will give you attendance, but they refuse from the first the idea of the smallest intimacy."

I will not deny that I was piqued, and perhaps the feeling strengthened my desire to go, for I was confident that I could break down that barrier if I desired. "There is nothing offensive in such a stipulation," said I; "and I even sympathise with the feeling that inspired it."

"It is true they have never seen you," returned the doctor politely; "and if they knew you were the handsomest and the most pleasant man that ever came from England (where I am told that handsome men are common, but pleasant ones not so much so), they would doubtless make you welcome with a better grace. But since you take the thing so well, it matters not. To me, indeed, it seems discourteous. But you will find yourself the gainer. The family will not much tempt you. A mother, a son, and a daughter; an old woman said to be halfwitted, a country lout, and a country girl, who stands very high with her confessor, and is, therefore," chuckled the physician, "most likely plain; there is not much in that to attract the fancy of a dashing officer."

"And yet you say they are high-born," I objected.

"Well, as to that, I should distinguish," returned the doctor. "The mother is; not so the children. The mother was the last representative of a princely stock, degenerate both in parts and fortune. Her father was not only poor, he was mad: and the girl ran wild about the residencia till his death. Then, much of the fortune having died with him, and the family being quite extinct, the girl ran wilder than ever, until at last she married, Heaven knows whom, a muleteer some say, others a smuggler; while there are some who uphold there was no marriage at all, and that Felipe and Olalla are bastards. The union, such as it was, was tragically dissolved some years ago; but they live in such seclusion, and the country at that time was in so much disorder, that the precise manner of the man's end is known only to the priest—if even to him."

"I begin to think I shall have strange experiences," said I.

"I would not romance, if I were you," replied the doctor; "you will find, I fear, a very grovelling and commonplace reality. Felipe, for instance, I have seen. And what am I to say? He is very rustic, very cunning, very loutish, and, I should say, an innocent; the others are probably to match. No, no, señor commandante, you must seek congenial society among the great sights of our mountains; and in these at least, if you are at all a lover of the works of nature, I promise you will not be disappointed."

The next day Felipe came for me in a rough country cart, drawn by a mule; and a little before the stroke of noon, after I had said farewell to the doctor, the innkeeper, and different good souls who had befriended me during my sickness, we set forth out of the city by the Eastern gate, and began to ascend into the Sierra. I had been so long a prisoner, since I was left behind for dying after the loss of the convoy, that the mere smell of the earth set me smiling. The country through which we went was wild and rocky, partially covered with rough woods, now of the cork-tree, and now of the great Spanish chestnut, and frequently intersected by the beds of mountain torrents. The sun shone, the wind rustled joyously; and we had advanced some miles, and the city had already shrunk into an inconsiderable knoll upon the plain behind us, before my attention began to be diverted to the companion of my drive. To the eye, he seemed but a diminutive, loutish, well-made country lad, such as the doctor had described, mighty quick and active, but devoid of any culture; and this first impression was with most observers final. What began to strike me was his familiar, chattering talk; so strangely inconsistent with the terms on which I was to be received; and partly from his imperfect enunciation, partly from the sprightly incoherence of the matter, so very difficult to follow clearly without an effort of the mind. It is true I had before talked with persons of a similar mental constitution; persons who seemed to live (as he did) by the senses, taken and possessed by the visual object of the moment and unable to discharge their minds of that impression. His seemed to me (as I sat, distantly giving ear) a kind of conversation proper to drivers, who pass much of their time in a great vacancy of the intellect and threading the sights of a familiar country. But this was not the case of Felipe; by his own account, he was a home-keeper; "I wish I was there now," he said; and then spying a tree by the wayside, he broke off to tell me that he had once seen a crow among its branches.

"A crow?" I repeated, struck by the ineptitude of the remark, and thinking I had heard imperfectly.

But by this time he was already filled with a new idea; hearkening with a rapt intentness, his head on one side, his face puckered; and he struck me rudely, to make me hold my peace. Then he smiled and shook his head.

"What did you hear?" I asked.

"O, it is all right," he said; and began encouraging his mule with cries that echoed unhumanly up the mountain walls.

I looked at him more closely. He was superlatively well-built, light, and lithe and strong; he was well-featured; his yellow eyes were very large, though, perhaps, not very expressive; take him altogether, he was a pleasant-looking lad, and I had no fault to find with him, beyond that he was of a dusky hue, and inclined to hairyness; two characteristics that I disliked. It was his mind that puzzled, and yet attracted me. The doctor's phrase—an innocent—came back to me; and I was wondering if that were, after all, the true description, when the road began to go down into the narrow and naked chasm of a torrent. The waters thundered tumultuously in the bottom; and the ravine was filled full of the sound, the thin spray, and the claps of wind, that accompanied their descent. The scene was certainly impressive; but the road was in that part very securely walled in; the mule went steadily forward; and I was astonished to perceive the paleness of terror in the face of my companion. The voice of that wild river was inconstant, now sinking lower as if in weariness, now doubling its hoarse tones; momentary freshets seemed to swell its volume, sweeping down the gorge, raving and booming against the barrier walls; and I observed it was at each of these accessions to the clamour, that my driver more particularly winced and blanched. Some thoughts of Scottish superstition and the river Kelpie passed across my mind; I wondered if perchance the like were prevalent in that part of Spain; and turning to Felipe, sought to draw him out.

"What is the matter?" I asked.

"O, I am afraid," he replied.

"Of what are you afraid?" I returned. "This seems one of the safest places on this very dangerous road."

"It makes a noise," he said, with a simplicity of awe that set my doubts at rest.

The lad was but a child in intellect; his mind was like his body, active and swift, but stunted in development; and I began from that time forth to regard him with a measure of pity, and to listen at first, with indulgence, and at last even with pleasure, to his disjointed babble.

By about four in the afternoon we had crossed the summit of the mountain line, said farewell to the western sunshine, and began to go down upon the other side, skirting the edge of many ravines and moving through the shadow of dusky woods. There rose upon all sides the voice of falling water, not condensed and formidable as in the gorge of the river, but scattered and sounding gaily and musically from glen to glen. Here, too, the spirits of my driver mended, and he began to sing aloud in a falsetto voice, and with a singular bluntness of musical perception, never true either to melody or key, but wandering at will, and yet somehow with an effect that was natural and pleasing, like that of the song of birds. As the dusk increased, I fell more and more under the spell of this artless warbling, listening and waiting for some articulate air, and still disappointed; and when at last I asked him what it was he sang—"O," cried he, "I am just singing!" Above all, I was taken with a trick he had of unweariedly repeating the same note at little intervals; it was not so monotonous as you would think, or, at least, not disagreeable; and it seemed to breathe a wonderful contentment with what is, such as we love to fancy in the attitude of trees, or the quiescence of a pool.

Night had fallen dark before we came out upon a plateau, and drew up a little after, before a certain lump of superior blackness which I could only conjecture to be the residencia. Here, my guide, getting down from the cart, hooted and whistled for a long time in vain; until at last an old peasant man came towards us from somewhere in the surrounding dark, carrying a candle in his hand. By the light of this I was able to perceive a great arched doorway of a Moorish character: it was closed by iron-studded gates, in one of the leaves of which Felipe opened a wicket. The peasant carried off the cart to some outbuilding; but my guide and I passed through the wicket, which was closed again behind us; and by the glimmer of the candle, passed through a court, up a stone stair, along a section of an open gallery, and up more stairs again, until we came at last to the door of a great and somewhat bare apartment. This room, which I understood was to be mine, was pierced by three windows, lined with some lustrous wood disposed in panels, and carpeted with the skins of many savage animals. A bright fire burned in the chimney, and shed abroad a changeable flicker; close up to the blaze there was drawn a table, laid for supper; and in the far end a bed stood ready. I was pleased by these preparations, and said so to Felipe; and he, with the same simplicity of disposition that I had already remarked in him, warmly re-echoed my praises. "A fine room," he said; "a very fine room. And fire, too; fire is good; it melts out the pleasure in your bones. And the bed," he continued, carrying over the candle in that direction—"see what fine sheets—how soft, how smooth, smooth;" and he passed his hand again and again over their texture, and then laid down his head and rubbed his cheeks among them with a grossness of content that somehow offended me. I took the candle from his hand (for I feared he would set the bed on fire) and walked back to the supper-table, where, perceiving a measure of wine, I poured out a cup and called to him to come and drink of it. He started to his feet at once and ran to me with a strong expression of hope; but when he saw the wine, he visibly shuddered.

"Oh, no," he said, "not that; that is for you. I hate it."

"Very well, Señor," said I; "then I will drink to your good health, and to the prosperity of your house and family. Speaking of which," I added, after I had drunk, "shall I not have the pleasure of laying my salutations in person at the feet of the Señora, your mother?"

But at these words all the childishness passed out of his face, and was succeeded by a look of indescribable cunning and secrecy. He backed away from me at the same time, as though I were an animal about to leap or some dangerous fellow with a weapon, and when he had got near the door, glowered at me sullenly with contracted pupils. "No," he said at last, and the next moment was gone noiselessly out of the room; and I heard his footing die away downstairs as light as rainfall, and silence closed over the house.

After I had supped I drew up the table nearer to the bed and began to prepare for rest; but in the new position of the light, I was struck by a picture on the wall. It represented a woman, still young. To judge by her costume and the mellow unity which reigned over the canvas, she had long been dead; to judge by the vivacity of the attitude, the eyes and the feature, I might have been beholding in a mirror the image of life. Her figure was very slim and strong, and of a just proportion; red tresses lay like a crown over her brow; her eyes, of a very golden brown, held mine with a look; and her face, which was perfectly shaped, was yet marred by a cruel, sullen, and sensual expression. Something in both face and figure, something exquisitely intangible, like the echo of an echo, suggested the features and bearing of my guide; and I stood awhile, unpleasantly attracted and wondering at the oddity of the resemblance. The common, carnal stock of that race, which had been originally designed for such high dames as the one now looking on me from the canvas, had fallen to baser uses, wearing country clothes, sitting on the shaft and holding the reins of a mule cart, to bring home a lodger. Perhaps an actual link subsisted; perhaps some scruple of the delicate flesh that was once clothed upon with the satin and brocade of the dead lady, now winced at the rude contact of Felipe's frieze.

The first light of the morning shone full upon the portrait, and, as I lay awake, my eyes continued to dwell upon it with growing complacency; its beauty crept about my heart insidiously, silencing my scruples one after another; and while I knew that to love such a woman were to sign and seal one's own sentence of degeneration, I still knew that, if she were alive, I should love her. Day after day the double knowledge of her wickedness and of my weakness grew clearer. She came to be the heroine of many day-dreams, in which her eyes led on to, and sufficiently rewarded, crimes. She cast a dark shadow on my fancy; and when I was out in the free air of heaven, taking vigorous exercise and healthily renewing the current of my blood, it was often a glad thought to me that my enchantress was safe in the grave, her wand of beauty broken, her lips closed in silence, her philtre spilt. And yet I had a half-lingering terror that she might not be dead after all, but re-arisen in the body of some descendant.

Felipe served my meals in my own apartment; and his resemblance to the portrait haunted me. At times it was not; at times, upon some change of attitude or flash of expression, it would leap out upon me like a ghost. It was above all in his ill tempers that the likeness triumphed. He certainly liked me; he was proud of my notice, which he sought to engage by many simple and childlike devices; he loved to sit close before my fire, talking his broken talk or singing his odd, endless, wordless songs, and sometimes drawing his hand over my clothes with an affectionate manner of caressing that never failed to cause in me an embarrassment of which I was ashamed. But for all that, he was capable of flashes of causeless anger and fits of sturdy sullenness. At a word of reproof, I have seen him upset the dish of which I was about to eat, and this not surreptitiously, but with defiance; and similarly at a hint of inquisition. I was not unnaturally curious, being in a strange place and surrounded by strange people, but at the shadow of a question, he shrank back, lowering and dangerous. Then it was that, for a fraction of a second, this rough lad might have been the brother of the lady in the frame. But these humours were swift to pass; and the resemblance died along with them.

In these first days I saw nothing of anyone but Felipe, unless the portrait is to be counted; and since the lad was plainly of weak mind, and had moments of passion, it may be wondered that I bore his dangerous neighbourhood with equanimity. As a matter of fact, it was for some time irksome; but it happened before long that I obtained over him so complete a mastery as set my disquietude at rest.

It fell in this way. He was by nature slothful, and much of a vagabond, and yet he kept by the house, and not only waited upon my wants, but laboured every day in the garden or small farm to the south of the residencia. Here he would be joined by the peasant whom I had seen on the night of my arrival, and who dwelt at the far end of the enclosure, about half a mile away, in a rude out-house; but it was plain to me that, of these two, it was Felipe who did most; and though I would sometimes see him throw down his spade and go to sleep among the very plants he had been digging, his constancy and energy were admirable in themselves, and still more so since I was well assured they were foreign to his disposition and the fruit of an ungrateful effort. But while I admired, I wondered what had called forth in a lad so shuttle-witted this enduring sense of duty. How was it sustained? I asked myself, and to what length did it prevail over his instincts? The priest was possibly his inspirer; but the priest came one day to the residencia. I saw him both come and go after an interval of close upon an hour, from a knoll where I was sketching, and all that time Felipe continued to labour undisturbed in the garden.

At last, in a very unworthy spirit, I determined to debauch the lad from his good resolutions, and, waylaying him at the gate, easily persuaded him to join me in a ramble. It was a fine day, and the woods to which I led him were green and pleasant and sweet-smelling and alive with the hum of insects. Here he discovered himself in a fresh character, mounting up to heights of gaiety that abashed me, and displaying an energy and grace of movement that delighted the eye. He leaped, he ran round me in mere glee; he would stop, and look and listen, and seemed to drink in the world like a cordial; and then he would suddenly spring into a tree with one bound, and hang and gambol there like one at home. Little as he said to me, and that of not much import, I have rarely enjoyed more stirring company; the sight of his delight was a continual feast; the speed and accuracy of his movements pleased me to the heart; and I might have been so thoughtlessly unkind as to make a habit of these walks, had not chance prepared a very rude conclusion to my pleasure. By some swiftness or dexterity the lad captured a squirrel in a treetop. He was then some way ahead of me, but I saw him drop to the ground and crouch there, crying aloud for pleasure like a child. The sound stirred my sympathies, it was so fresh and innocent; but as I bettered my pace to draw near, the cry of the squirrel knocked upon my heart. I have heard and seen much of the cruelty of lads, and above all of peasants; but what I now beheld struck me into a passion of anger. I thrust the fellow aside, plucked the poor brute out of his hands, and with swift mercy killed it. Then I turned upon the torturer, spoke to him long out of the heat of my indignation, calling him names at which he seemed to wither; and at length, pointing toward the residencia, bade him begone and leave me, for I chose to walk with men, not with vermin. He fell upon his knees, and, the words coming to him with more clearness than usual, poured out a stream of the most touching supplications, begging me in mercy to forgive him, to forget what he had done, to look to the future. "O, I try so hard," he said. "O, commandante, bear with Felipe this once; he will never be a brute again!" Thereupon, much more affected than I cared to show, I suffered myself to be persuaded, and at last shook hands with him and made it up. But the squirrel, by the way of penance, I made him bury; speaking of the poor thing's beauty, telling him what pains it had suffered, and how base a thing was the abuse of strength. "See, Felipe," said I, "you are strong indeed; but in my hands you are as helpless as that poor thing of the trees. Give me your hand in mine. You cannot remove it. Now suppose that I were cruel like you, and took a pleasure in pain. I only tighten my hold, and see how you suffer." He screamed aloud, his face stricken ashy and dotted with needle points of sweat; and when I set him free, he fell to the earth and nursed his hand and moaned over it like a baby. But he took the lesson in good part; and whether from that, or from what I had said to him, or the higher notion he now had of my bodily strength, his original affection was changed into a dog-like, adoring fidelity.

Meanwhile I gained rapidly in health. The residencia stood on the crown of a stony plateau; on every side the mountains hemmed it about; only from the roof, where was a bartizan, there might be seen between two peaks, a small segment of plain blue, with extreme distance. The air in these altitudes moved freely and largely; great clouds congregated there, and were broken up by the wind and left in tatters on the hilltops; a hoarse, and yet faint rumbling of torrents rose from all round; and one could there study all the ruder and more ancient characters of nature in something of their pristine force. I delighted from the first in the vigorous scenery and changeful weather; nor less in the antique and dilapidated mansion where I dwelt. This was a large oblong, flanked at two opposite corners by bastion-like projections, one of which commanded the door, while both were loopholed for musketry. The lower storey was, besides, naked of windows, so that the building, if garrisoned, could not be carried without artillery. It enclosed an open court planted with pomegranate trees. From this a broad flight of marble stairs ascended to an open gallery, running all round and resting, towards the court, on slender pillars. Thence again, several enclosed stairs led to the upper storeys of the house, which were thus broken up into distinct divisions. The windows, both within and without, were closely shuttered; some of the stonework in the upper parts had fallen; the roof, in one place, had been wrecked in one of the flurries of wind which were common in these mountains; and the whole house, in the strong, beating sunlight, and standing out above a grove of stunted cork-trees, thickly laden and discoloured with dust, looked like the sleeping palace of the legend. The court, in particular, seemed the very home of slumber. A hoarse cooing of doves haunted about the eaves; the winds were excluded, but when they blew outside, the mountain dust fell here as thick as rain, and veiled the red bloom of the pomegranates; shuttered windows and the closed doors of numerous cellars, and the vacant arches of the gallery, enclosed it; and all day long the sun made broken profiles on the four sides, and paraded the shadow of the pillars on the gallery floor. At the ground level there was, however, a certain pillared recess, which bore the marks of human habitation. Though it was open in front upon the court, it was yet provided with a chimney, where a wood fire would be always prettily blazing; and the tile floor was littered with the skins of animals.

It was in this place that I first saw my hostess. She had drawn one of the skins forward and sat in the sun, leaning against a pillar. It was her dress that struck me first of all, for it was rich and brightly coloured, and shone out in that dusty courtyard with something of the same relief as the flowers of the pomegranates. At a second look it was her beauty of person that took hold of me. As she sat back—watching me, I thought, though with invisible eyes—and wearing at the same time an expression of almost imbecile good-humour and contentment, she showed a perfectness of feature and a quiet nobility of attitude that were beyond a statue's. I took off my hat to her in passing, and her face puckered with suspicion as swiftly and lightly as a pool ruffles in the breeze; but she paid no heed to my courtesy. I went forth on my customary walk a trifle daunted, her idol-like impassivity haunting me; and when I returned, although she was still in much the same posture, I was half surprised to see that she had moved as far as the next pillar, following the sunshine. This time, however, she addressed me with some trivial salutation, civilly enough conceived, and uttered in the same deep-chested, and yet indistinct and lisping tones, that had already baffled the utmost niceness of my hearing from her son. I answered rather at a venture; for not only did I fail to take her meaning with precision, but the sudden disclosure of her eyes disturbed me. They were unusually large, the iris golden like Felipe's, but the pupil at that moment so distended that they seemed almost black; and what affected me was not so much their size as (what was perhaps its consequence) the singular insignificance of their regard. A look more blankly stupid I have never met. My eyes dropped before it even as I spoke, and I went on my way upstairs to my own room, at once baffled and embarrassed. Yet, when I came there and saw the face of the portrait, I was again reminded of the miracle of family descent. My hostess was, indeed, both older and fuller in person; her eyes were of a different colour; her face, besides, was not only free from the ill-significance that offended and attracted me in the painting; it was devoid of either good or bad—a moral blank expressing literally naught. And yet there was a likeness, not so much speaking as immanent, not so much in any particular feature as upon the whole. It should seem, I thought, as if when the master set his signature to that grave canvas, he had not only caught the image of one smiling and false-eyed woman, but stamped the essential quality of a race.

From that day forth, whether I came or went, I was sure to find the Señora seated in the sun against a pillar, or stretched on a rug before the fire; only at times she would shift her station to the top round of the stone staircase, where she lay with the same nonchalance right across my path. In all these days, I never knew her to display the least spark of energy beyond what she expended in brushing and re-brushing her copious coppercoloured hair, or in lisping out, in the rich and broken hoarseness of her voice, her customary idle salutations to myself. These, I think, were her two chief pleasures, beyond that of mere quiescence. She seemed always proud of her remarks, as though they had been witticisms: and, indeed, though they were empty enough, like the conversation of many respectable persons, and turned on a very narrow range of subjects, they were never meaningless or incoherent; nay, they had a certain beauty of their own, breathing, as they did, of her entire contentment. Now she would speak of the warmth in which (like her son) she greatly delighted; now of the flowers of the pomegranate trees, and now of the white doves and long-winged swallows that fanned the air of the court. The birds excited her. As they raked the eaves in their swift flight, or skimmed sidelong past her with a rush of wind, she would sometimes stir, and sit a little up, and seem to awaken from her doze of satisfaction. But for the rest of her days she lay luxuriously folded on herself and sunk in sloth and pleasure. Her invincible content at first annoyed me, but I came gradually to find repose in the spectacle, until at last it grew to be my habit to sit down beside her four times in the day, both coming and going, and to talk with her sleepily, I scarce knew of what. I had come to like her dull, almost animal neighbourhood; her beauty and her stupidity soothed and amused me. I began to find a kind of transcendental good sense in her remarks, and her unfathomable good nature moved me to admiration and envy. The liking was returned; she enjoyed my presence half-unconsciously, as a man in deep meditation may enjoy the babbling of a brook. I can scarce say she brightened when I came, for satisfaction was written on her face eternally, as on some foolish statue's; but I was made conscious of her pleasure by some more intimate communication than the sight. And one day, as I sat within reach of her on the marble step, she suddenly shot forth one of her hands and patted mine. The thing was done, and she was back in her accustomed attitude, before my mind had received intelligence of the caress; and when I turned to look her in the face I could perceive no answerable sentiment. It was plain she attached no moment to the act, and I blamed myself for my own more uneasy consciousness.

The sight and (if I may so call it) the acquaintance of the mother confirmed the view I had already taken of the son. The family blood had been impoverished, perhaps by long in-breeding, which I knew to be a common error among the proud and the exclusive. No decline, indeed, was to be traced in the body, which had been handed down unimpaired in shapeliness and strength; and the faces of to-day were struck as sharply from the mint as the face of two centuries ago that smiled upon me from the portrait. But the intelligence (that more precious heirloom) was degenerate; the treasure of ancestral memory ran low; and it had required the potent, plebeian crossing of a muleteer or mountain contrabandista to raise what approached hebetude in the mother into the active oddity of the son. Yet, of the two, it was the mother I preferred. Of Felipe, vengeful and placable, full of starts and shyings, inconstant as a hare, I could even conceive as a creature possibly noxious. Of the mother I had no thoughts but those of kindness. And, indeed, as spectators are apt ignorantly to take sides, I grew something of a partisan in the enmity which I perceived to smoulder between them. True, it seemed mostly on the mother's part. She would sometimes draw in her breath as he came near, and the pupils of her vacant eyes would contract with horror or fear. Her emotions, such as they were, were much upon the surface and readily shared; and this latent repulsion occupied my mind, and kept me wondering on what grounds it rested, and whether the son was certainly in fault.

I had been about ten days in the residencia, when there sprang up a high and harsh wind, carrying clouds of dust. It came out of malarious lowlands, and over several snowy sierras. The nerves of those on whom it blew were strung and jangled; their eyes smarted with the dust; their legs ached under the burthen of their body; and the touch of one hand upon another grew to be odious. The wind, besides, came down the gullies of the hills and stormed about the house with a great, hollow buzzing and whistling that was wearisome to the ear and dismally depressing to the mind. It did not so much blow in gusts as with the steady sweep of a waterfall, so that there was no remission of discomfort while it blew. But higher upon the mountain, it was probably of a more variable strength, with accesses of fury; for there came down at times a far-off wailing, infinitely grievous to hear; and at times, on one of the high shelves or terraces, there would start up, and then disperse, a tower of dust, like the smoke of an explosion.

I no sooner awoke in bed than I was conscious of the nervous tension and depression of the weather, and the effect grew stronger as the day proceeded. It was in vain that I resisted; in vain that I set forth upon my customary morning's walk; the irrational, unchanging fury of the storm had soon beat down my strength and wrecked my temper; and I returned to the residencia, glowing with dry heat, and foul and gritty with dust. The court had a forlorn appearance; now and then a glimmer of sun fled over it; now and then the wind swooped down upon the pomegranates, and scattered the blossoms, and set the window shutters clapping on the wall. In the recess the Señora was pacing to and fro with a flushed countenance and bright eyes; I thought, too, she was speaking to herself, like one in anger. But when I addressed her with my customary salutation, she only replied by a sharp gesture and continued her walk. The weather had distempered even this impassive creature; and as I went on upstairs I was the less ashamed of my own discomposure.

All day the wind continued; and I sat in my room and made a feint of reading, or walked up and down, and listened to the riot overhead. Night fell, and I had not so much as a candle. I began to long for some society, and stole down to the court. It was now plunged in the blue of the first darkness; but the recess was redly lighted by the fire. The wood had been piled high, and was crowned by a shock of flames, which the draught of the chimney brandished to and fro. In this strong and shaken brightness the Señora continued pacing from wall to wall with disconnected gestures, clasping her hands, stretching forth her arms, throwing back her head as in appeal to heaven. In these disordered movements the beauty and grace of the woman showed more clearly; but there was a light in her eye that struck on me unpleasantly; and when I had looked on awhile in silence, and seemingly unobserved, I turned tail as I had come, and groped my way back again to my own chamber.

By the time Felipe brought my supper and lights, my nerve was utterly gone; and, had the lad been such as I was used to seeing him, I should have kept him (even by force had that been necessary) to take off the edge from my distasteful solitude. But on Felipe, also, the wind had exercised its influence. He had been feverish all day; now that the night had come he was fallen into a low and tremulous humour that reacted on my own. The sight of his scared face, his starts and pallors and sudden harkenings, unstrung me; and when he dropped and broke a dish, I fairly leaped out of my seat.

"I think we are all mad to-day," said I, affecting to laugh.

"It is the black wind," he replied dolefully. "You feel as if you must do something, and you don't know what it is."

I noted the aptness of the description; but, indeed, Felipe had sometimes a strange felicity in rendering into words the sensations of the body. "And your mother, too," said I; "she seems to feel this weather much. Do you not fear she may be unwell?"

He stared at me a little, and then said, "No," almost defiantly; and the next moment, carrying his hand to his brow, cried out lamentably on the wind and the noise that made his head go round like a mill-wheel. "Who can be well?" he cried; and, indeed, I could only echo his question, for I was disturbed enough myself.

I went to bed early, wearied with day-long restlessness: but the poisonous nature of the wind, and its ungodly and unintermittent uproar, would not suffer me to sleep. I lay there and tossed, my nerves and senses on the stretch. At times I would doze, dream horribly, and wake again; and these snatches of oblivion confused me as to time. But it must have been late on in the night, when I was suddenly startled by an outbreak of pitiable and hateful cries. I leaped from my bed, supposing I had dreamed; but the cries still continued to fill the house, cries of pain, I thought, but certainly of rage also, and so savage and discordant that they shocked the heart. It was no illusion; some living thing, some lunatic or some wild animal, was being foully tortured. The thought of Felipe and the squirrel flashed into my mind, and I ran to the door, but it had been locked from the outside; and I might shake it as I pleased, I was a fast prisoner. Still the cries continued. Now they would dwindle down into a moaning that seemed to be articulate, and at these times I made sure they must be human; and again they would break forth and fill the house with ravings worthy of hell. I stood at the door and gave ear to them, till at last they died away. Long after that, I still lingered and still continued to hear them mingle in fancy with the storming of the wind; and when at last I crept to my bed, it was with a deadly sickness and a blackness of horror on my heart.

It was little wonder if I slept no more. Why had I been locked in? What had passed? Who was the author of these indescribable and shocking cries? A human being? It was inconceivable. A beast? The cries were scarce quite bestial; and what animal, short of a lion or a tiger, could thus shake the solid walls of the residencia? And while I was thus turning over the elements of the mystery, it came into my mind that I had not yet set eyes upon the daughter of the house. What was more probable than that the daughter of the Señora, and the sister of Felipe, should be herself insane? Or, what more likely than that these ignorant and half-witted people should seek to manage an afflicted kinswoman by violence? Here was a solution; and yet when I called to mind the cries (which I never did without a shuddering chill) it seemed altogether insufficient: not even cruelty could wring such cries from madness. But of one thing I was sure: I could not live in a house where such a thing was half conceivable, and not probe the matter home and, if necessary, interfere.

The next day came, the wind had blown itself out, and there was nothing to remind me of the business of the night. Felipe came to my bedside with obvious cheerfulness; as I passed through the court, the Señora was sunning herself with her accustomed immobility; and when I issued from the gateway, I found the whole face of nature austerely smiling, the heavens of a cold blue, and sown with great cloud islands, and the mountain-sides mapped forth into provinces of light and shadow. A short walk restored me to myself, and renewed within me the resolve to plumb this mystery; and when, from the vantage of my knoll, I had seen Felipe pass forth to his labours in the garden, I returned at once to the residencia to put my design in practice. The Señora appeared plunged in slumber; I stood awhile and marked her, but she did not stir; even if my design were indiscreet I had little to fear from such a guardian; and turning away, I mounted to the gallery and began my exploration of the house.

All morning I went from one door to another, and entered spacious and faded chambers, some rudely shuttered, some receiving their full charge of daylight, all empty and unhomely. It was a rich house, on which Time had breathed his tarnish and dust had scattered disillusion. The spider swung there; the bloated tarantula scampered on the cornices; ants had their crowded highways on the floor of halls of audience; the big and foul fly, that lives on carrion and is often the messenger of death, had set up his nest in the rotten woodwork, and buzzed heavily about the rooms. Here and there a stool or two, a couch, a bed, or a great carved chair remained behind, like islets on the bare floors, to testify of man's bygone habitation; and everywhere the walls were set with the portraits of the dead. I could judge, by these decaying effigies, in the house of what a great and what a handsome race I was then wandering. Many of the men wore orders on their breasts and had the port of noble offices; the women were all richly attired; the canvases most of them by famous hands. But it was not so much these evidences of greatness that took hold upon my mind, even contrasted, as they were, with the present depopulation and decay of that great house. It was rather the parable of family life that I read in this succession of fair faces and shapely bodies. Never before had I so realized the miracle of the continued race, the creation and recreation, the weaving and changing and handing down of fleshly elements. That a child should be born of its mother, that it should grow and clothe itself (we know not how) with humanity, and put on inherited looks, and turn its head with the manner of one ascendant, and offer its hand with the gesture of another, are wonders dulled for us by repetition. But in the singular unity of look, in the common features and common bearing, of all these painted generations on the walls of the residencia, the miracle started out and looked me in the face. And an ancient mirror falling opportunely in my way, I stood and read my own features a long while, tracing out on either hand the filaments of descent and the bonds that knit me with my family.

At last, in the course of these investigations, I opened the door of a chamber that bore the marks of habitation. It was of large proportions and faced to the north, where the mountains were most wildly figured. The embers of a fire smouldered and smoked upon the hearth, to which a chair had been drawn close. And yet the aspect of the chamber was ascetic to the degree of sternness; the chair was uncushioned; the floor and walls were naked; and beyond the books which lay here and there in some confusion, there was no instrument of either work or pleasure. The sight of books in the house of such a family exceedingly amazed me; and I began with a great hurry, and in momentary fear of interruption, to go from one to another and hastily inspect their character. They were of all sorts, devotional, historical, and scientific, but mostly of a great age and in the Latin tongue. Some I could see to bear the marks of constant study; others had been torn across and tossed aside as if in petulance or disapproval. Lastly, as I cruised about that empty chamber, I espied some papers written upon with pencil on a table near the window. An unthinking curiosity led me to take one up. It bore a copy of verses, very roughly metred in the original Spanish, and which I may render somewhat thus—

Pleasure approached with pain and shame,
Grief with a wreath of lilies came.
Pleasure showed the lovely sun;
Jesu dear, how sweet it shone!
Grief with her worn hand pointed on,
Jesu dear, to thee!

Shame and confusion at once fell on me; and, laying down the paper, I beat an immediate retreat from the apartment. Neither

Felipe nor his mother could have read the books nor written these rough but feeling verses. It was plain I had stumbled with sacrilegious feet into the room of the daughter of the house. God knows, my own heart most sharply punished me for my indiscretion. The thought that I had thus secretly pushed my way into the confidence of a girl so strangely situated, and the fear that she might somehow come to hear of it, oppressed me like guilt. I blamed myself besides for my suspicions of the night before; wondered that I should ever have attributed those shocking cries to one of whom I now conceived as of a saint, spectral of mien, wasted with maceration, bound up in the practices of a mechanical devotion, and dwelling in a great isolation of soul with her incongruous relatives; and as I leaned on the balustrade of the gallery and looked down into the bright close of pomegranates and at the gaily dressed and somnolent woman, who just then stretched herself and delicately licked her lips as in the very sensuality of sloth, my mind swiftly compared the scene with the cold chamber looking northward on the mountains, where the daughter dwelt.

That same afternoon, as I sat upon my knoll, I saw the Padre enter the gates of the residencia. The revelation of the daughter's character had struck home to my fancy, and almost blotted out the horrors of the night before; but at sight of this worthy man the memory revived. I descended, then, from the knoll, and making a circuit among the woods, posted myself by the wayside to await his passage. As soon as he appeared I stepped forth and introduced myself as the lodger of the residencia. He had a very strong, honest countenance, on which it was easy to read the mingled emotions with which he regarded me, as a foreigner, a heretic, and yet one who had been wounded for the good cause. Of the family at the residencia he spoke with reserve, and yet with respect. I mentioned that I had not yet seen the daughter, whereupon he remarked that that was as it should be, and looked at me a little askance. Lastly, I plucked up courage to refer to the cries that had disturbed me in the night. He heard me out in silence, and then stopped and partly turned about, as though to mark beyond doubt that he was dismissing me.

"Do you take tobacco powder?" said he, offering his snuff-box; and then, when I had refused, "I am an old man," he added, "and I may be allowed to remind you that you are a guest."

"I have, then, your authority," I returned, firmly enough, although I flushed at the implied reproof, "to let things take their course, and not to interfere?"

He said "yes," and with a somewhat uneasy salute turned and left me where I was. But he had done two things: he had set my conscience at rest, and he had awakened my delicacy. I made a great effort, once more dismissed the recollections of the night, and fell once more to brooding on my saintly poetess. At the same time, I could not quite forget that I had been locked in, and that night when Felipe brought me my supper I attacked him warily on both points of interest.

"I never see your sister," said I casually.

"Oh, no," said he; "she is a good, good girl," and his mind instantly veered to something else.

"Your sister is pious, I suppose," I asked in the next pause.

"Oh," he cried, joining his hands with extreme fervour, "a saint; it is she that keeps me up."

"You are very fortunate," said I, "for the most of us, I am afraid, and myself among the number, are better at going down."

"Señor," said Felipe earnestly, "I would not say that. You should not tempt your angel. If one goes down, where is he to stop?"

"Why, Felipe," said I, "I had no guess you were a preacher, and I may say a good one; but I suppose that is your sister's doing?"

He nodded at me with round eyes.

"Well, then," I continued, "she has doubtless reproved you for your sin of cruelty?"

"Twelve times!" he cried; for this was the phrase by which the odd creature expressed the sense of frequency. "And I told her you had done so—I remembered that," he added proudly—"and she was pleased."

"Then, Felipe," said I, "what were those cries that I heard last night? for surely they were cries of some creature in suffering."

"The wind," returned Felipe, looking in the fire.

I took his hand in mine, at which, thinking it to be a caress, he smiled with a brightness of pleasure that came near disarming my resolve. But I trod the weakness down. "The wind," I repeated; "and yet I think it was this hand," holding it up, "that had first locked me in." The lad shook visibly, but answered never a word. "Well," said I, "I am a stranger and a guest. It is not my part either to meddle or to judge in your affairs; in these you shall take your sister's counsel, which I cannot doubt to be excellent. But in so far as concerns my own I will be no man's prisoner, and I demand that key." Half an hour later my door was suddenly thrown open, and the key tossed ringing on the floor.

A day or two after I came in from a walk a little before the point of noon. The Señora was lying lapped in slumber on the threshold of the recess; the pigeons dozed below the eaves like snowdrifts; the house was under a deep spell of noontide quiet; and only a wandering and gentle wind from the mountain stole round the galleries, rustled among the pomegranates, and pleasantly stirred the shadows. Something in the stillness moved me to imitation, and I went very lightly across the court and up the marble staircase. My foot was on the topmost round, when a door opened, and I found myself face to face with Olalla. Surprise transfixed me; her liveliness struck to my heart; she glowed in the deep shadow of the gallery, a gem of colour; her eyes took hold upon mine and clung there, and bound us together like the joining of hands; and the moments we thus stood face to face, drinking each other in, were sacramental and the wedding of souls. I know not how long it was before I awoke out of a deep trance, and, hastily bowing, passed on into the upper stair. She did not move, but followed me with her great, thirsting eyes; and as I passed out of sight it seemed to me as if she paled and faded.

In my own room, I opened the window and looked out, and could not think what change had come upon that austere field of mountains that it should thus sing and shine under the lofty heaven. I had seen her—Olalla! And the stone crags answered, Olalla! and the dumb, unfathomable azure answered, Olalla! The pale saint of my dreams had vanished for ever; and in her place I beheld this maiden on whom God had lavished the richest colours and the most exuberant energies of life, whom he had made active as a deer, slender as a reed, and in whose great eyes he had lighted the torches of the soul. The thrill of her young life, strung like a wild animal's, had entered into me; the force of soul that had looked out from her eyes and conquered mine, mantled about my heart and sprang to my lips in singing. She passed through my veins: she was one with me.

I will not say that this enthusiasm declined; rather my soul held out in its ecstasy as in a strong castle, and was there besieged by cold and sorrowful considerations. I could not doubt but that I loved her at first sight, and already with a quivering ardour that was strange to my experience. What then was to follow? She was the child of an afflicted house, the Señora's daughter, the sister of Felipe; she bore it even in her beauty. She had the lightness and swiftness of the one, swift as an arrow, light as dew; like the other, she shone on the pale background of the world with the brilliancy of flowers. I could not call by the name of brother that half-witted lad, nor by the name of mother that immovable and lovely thing of flesh, whose silly eyes and perpetual simper now recurred to my mind like something hateful. And if I could not marry, what then? She was helplessly unprotected; her eyes, in that single and long glance which had been all our intercourse, had confessed a weakness equal to my own; but in my heart I knew her for the student of the cold northern chamber, and the writer of the sorrowful lines; and this was a knowledge to disarm a brute. To flee was more than I could find courage for; but I registered a vow of unsleeping circumspection.

As I turned from the window, my eyes alighted on the portrait. It had fallen dead, like a candle after sunrise; it followed me with eyes of paint. I knew it to be like, and marvelled at the tenacity of type in that declining race; but the likeness was swallowed up in difference. I remembered how it had seemed to me a thing unapproachable in the life, a creature rather of the painter's craft than of the modesty of nature, and I marvelled at the thought, and exulted in the image of Olalla. Beauty I had seen before, and not been charmed, and I had been often drawn to women, who were not beautiful except to me; but in Olalla all that I desired and had not dared to imagine was united.

I did not see her the next day, and my heart ached and my eyes longed for her, as men long for morning. But the day after, when I returned, about my usual hour, she was once more on the gallery, and our looks once more met and embraced. I would have spoken, I would have drawn near to her; but strongly as she plucked at my heart, drawing me like a magnet, something yet more imperious withheld me; and I could only bow and pass by; and she, leaving my salutation unanswered, only followed me with her noble eyes.

I had now her image by rote, and as I conned the traits in memory it seemed as if I read her very heart. She was dressed with something of her mother's coquetry, and love of positive colour. Her robe, which I knew she must have made with her own hands, clung about her with a cunning grace. After the fashion of that country, besides, her bodice stood open in the middle, in a long slit, and here, in spite of the poverty of the house, a gold coin, hanging by a ribbon, lay on her brown bosom. These were proofs, had any been needed, of her inborn delight in life and her own loveliness. On the other hand, in her eyes that hung upon mine, I could read depth beyond depth of passion and sadness, lights of poetry and hope, blacknesses of despair, and thoughts that were above the earth. It was a lovely body, but the inmate, the soul, was more than worthy of that lodging. Should I leave this incomparable flower to wither unseen on these rough mountains? Should I despise the great gift offered me in the eloquent silence of her eyes? Here was a soul immured; should I not burst its prison? All side considerations fell off from me; were she the child of Herod I swore I should make her mine; and that very evening I set myself, with a mingled sense of treachery and disgrace, to captivate the brother. Perhaps I read him with more favourable eyes, perhaps the thought of his sister always summoned up the better qualities of that imperfect soul; but he had never seemed to me so amiable, and his very likeness to Olalla, while it annoyed, yet softened me.

A third day passed in vain—an empty desert of hours. I would not lose a chance, and loitered all afternoon in the court where (to give myself a countenance) I spoke more than usual with the Señora. God knows it was with a most tender and sincere interest that I now studied her; and even as for Felipe, so now for the mother, I was conscious of a growing warmth of toleration. And yet I wondered. Even while I spoke with her, she would doze off into a little sleep, and presently awake again without embarrassment; and this composure staggered me. And again, as I marked her make infinitesimal changes in her posture, savouring and lingering on the bodily pleasure of the moment, I was driven to wonder at this depth of passive sensuality. She lived in her body; and her consciousness was all sunk into and disseminated through her members, where it luxuriously dwelt. Lastly, I could not grow accustomed to her eyes. Each time she turned on me these great beautiful and meaningless orbs, wide open to the day, but closed against human inquiry—each time I had occasion to observe the lively changes of her pupils which expanded and contracted in a breath—I know not what it was came over me, I can find no name for the mingled feeling of disappointment, annoyance, and distaste that jarred along my nerves. I tried her on a variety of subjects, equally in vain; and at last led the talk to her daughter. But even there she proved indifferent; said she was pretty, which (as with children) was her highest word of commendation, but was plainly incapable of any higher thought; and when I remarked that Olalla seemed silent, merely yawned in my face and replied that speech was of no great use when you had nothing to say. "People speak much, very much," she added, looking at me with expanded pupils; and then again yawned, and again showed me a mouth that was as dainty as a toy. This time I took the hint, and, leaving her to her repose, went up into my own chamber to sit by the open window, looking on the hills and not beholding them, sunk in lustrous and deep dreams, and hearkening in fancy to the note of a voice that I had never heard.

I awoke on the fifth morning with a brightness of anticipation that seemed to challenge fate. I was sure of myself, light of heart and foot, and resolved to put my love incontinently to the touch of knowledge. It should lie no longer under the bonds of silence, a dumb thing, living by the eye only, like the love of beasts; but should now put on the spirit, and enter upon the joys of the complete human intimacy. I thought of it with wild hopes, like a voyager to El Dorado; into that unknown and lovely country of her soul, I no longer trembled to adventure. Yet when I did indeed encounter her, the same force of passion descended on me and at once submerged my mind; speech seemed to drop away from me like a childish habit; and I but drew near to her as the giddy man draws near to the margin of a gulf. She drew back from me a little as I came; but her eyes did not waver from mine, and these lured me forward. At last, when I was already within reach of her, I stopped. Words were denied me; if I advanced I could but clasp her to my heart in silence; and all that was sane in me, all that was still unconquered, revolted against the thought of such an accost. So we stood for a second, all our life in our eyes, exchanging salvos of attraction and yet each resisting; and then, with a great effort of the will, and conscious at the same time of a sudden bitterness of disappointment, I turned and went away in the same silence.

What power lay upon me that I could not speak? And she, why was she also silent? Why did she draw away before me dumbly, with fascinated eyes? Was this love? or was it a mere brute attraction, mindless and inevitable, like that of the magnet for the steel? We had never spoken, we were wholly strangers; and yet an influence, strong as the grasp of a giant, swept us silently together. On my side, it filled me with impatience; and yet I was sure that she was worthy; I had seen her books, read her verses, and thus, in a sense, divined the soul of my mistress. But on her side, it struck me almost cold. Of me, she knew nothing but my bodily favour; she was drawn to me as stones fall to earth; the laws that rule the earth conducted her, unconsenting, to my arms; and I drew back at the thought of such a bridal, and began to be jealous for myself. It was not thus that I desired to be loved. And then I began to fall into a great pity for the girl herself. I thought how sharp must be her mortification, that she, the student, the recluse, Felipe's saintly monitress, should have thus confessed an overweening weakness for a man with whom she had never exchanged a word. And at the coming of pity, all other thoughts were swallowed up; and I longed only to find and console and reassure her; to tell her how wholly her love was returned on my side, and how her choice, even if blindly made, was not unworthy.

The next day it was glorious weather; depth upon depth of blue over-canopied the mountains; the sun shone wide; and the wind in the trees and the many falling torrents in the mountains filled the air with delicate and haunting music. Yet I was prostrated with sadness. My heart wept for the sight of Olalla, as a child weeps for its mother. I sat down on a boulder on the verge of the low cliffs that bound the plateau to the north. Thence I looked down into the wooded valley of a stream, where no foot came. In the mood I was in, it was even touching to behold the place untenanted; it lacked Olalla; and I thought of the delight and glory of a life passed wholly with her in that strong air, and among these rugged and lovely surroundings, at first with a whimpering sentiment, and then again with such a fiery joy that I seemed to grow in strength and stature, like a Samson.

And suddenly I was aware of Olalla drawing near. She appeared out of a grove of cork-trees, and came straight towards me; and I stood up and waited. She seemed in her walking a creature of such life and fire and lightness as amazed me; yet she came quietly and slowly. Her energy was in the slowness; but for inimitable strength, I felt she would have run, she would have flown to me. Still, as she approached, she kept her eyes lowered to the ground; and when she had drawn quite near, it was without one glance that she addressed me. At the first note of her voice I started. It was for this I had been waiting; this was the last test of my love. And lo, her enunciation was precise and clear, not lisping and incomplete like that of her family; and the voice, though deeper than usual with women, was still both youthful and womanly. She spoke in a rich chord; golden contralto strains mingled with hoarseness, as the red threads were mingled with the brown among her tresses. It was not only a voice that spoke to my heart directly; but it spoke to me of her. And yet her words immediately plunged me back upon despair.

"You will go away," she said, "to-day."

Her example broke the bonds of my speech; I felt as lightened of a weight, or as if a spell had been dissolved. I know not in what words I answered; but, standing before her on the cliffs, I poured out the whole ardour of my love, telling her that I loved upon the thought of her, slept only to dream of her loveliness, and would gladly forswear my country, my language, and my friends, to live for ever by her side. And then, strongly commanding myself, I changed the note; I reassured, I comforted her; I told her I had divined in her a pious and heroic spirit, with which I was worthy to sympathise, and which I longed to share and lighten. "Nature," I told her, "was the voice of God, which men disobey at peril; and if we were thus dumbly drawn together, ay, even as by a miracle of love, it must imply a divine fitness in our souls; we must be made," I said—"made for one another. We should be mad rebels," I cried out—"mad rebels against God, not to obey this instinct."

She shook her head. "You will go to-day," she repeated, and then with a gesture, and in a sudden, sharp note—"no, not to-day," she cried, "to-morrow."

But at this sign of relenting, power came in upon me in a tide. I stretched out my arms and called upon her name; and she leaped to me and clung to me. The hills rocked about us, the earth quailed; a shock as of a blow went through me and left me blind and dizzy. And the next moment she had thrust me back, broken rudely from my arms, and fled with the speed of a deer among the cork-trees.

I stood and shouted to the mountains; I turned and went back towards the residencia, walking upon air. She sent me away, and yet I had but to call upon her name and she came to me. These were but the weaknesses of girls, from which even she, the strangest of her sex, was not exempted. Go? Not I, Olalla—O, not I, Olalla, my Olalla! A bird sang near by; and in that season, birds were rare. It bade me be of good cheer. And once more the whole countenance of nature, from the ponderous and stable mountains down to the lightest leaf and the smallest darting fly in the shadow of the groves, began to stir before me and to put on the lineaments of life and wear a face of awful joy. The sunshine struck upon the hills, strong as a hammer on the anvil, and the hills shook; the earth, under that vigorous insolation, yielded up heady scents; the woods smouldered in the blaze. I felt the thrill of travail and delight run through the earth. Something elemental, something rude, violent, and savage, in the love that sang in my heart, was like a key to nature's secrets; and the very stones that rattled under my feet appeared alive and friendly. Olalla! Her touch had quickened, and renewed, and strung me up to the old pitch of concert with the rugged earth, to a swelling of the soul that men learn to forget in their polite assemblies. Love burned in me like rage; tenderness waxed fierce; I hated, I adored, I pitied, I revered her with ecstasy. She seemed the link that bound me in with dead things on the one hand, and with our pure and pitying God upon the other; a thing brutal and divine, and akin at once to the innocence and to the unbridled forces of the earth.

My head thus reeling, I came into the courtyard of the residencia, and the sight of the mother struck me like a revelation. She sat there, all sloth and contentment, blinking under the strong sunshine, branded with a passive enjoyment, a creature set quite apart, before whom my ardour fell away like a thing ashamed. I stopped a moment, and, commanding such shaken tones as I was able, said a word or two. She looked at me with her unfathomable kindness; her voice in reply sounded vaguely out of the realm of peace in which she slumbered, and there fell on my mind, for the first time, a sense of respect for one so uniformly innocent and happy, and I passed on in a kind of wonder at myself, that I should be so much disquieted.

On my table there lay a piece of the same yellow paper I had seen in the north room; it was written on with pencil in the same hand, Olalla's hand, and I picked it up with a sudden sinking of alarm, and read, "If you have any kindness for Olalla, if you have any chivalry for a creature sorely wrought, go from here to-day; in pity, in honour, for the sake of Him who died, I supplicate that you shall go." I looked at this awhile in mere stupidity, then I began to shake like a man in terror. The vacancy thus suddenly opened in my life unmanned me like a physical void. It was not my heart, it was not my happiness, it was life itself that was involved. I could not lose her. I said so, and stood repeating it. And then, like one in a dream, I moved to the window, put forth my hand to open the casement, and thrust it through the pane. The blood spurted from my wrist; and with an instantaneous quietude and command of myself, I pressed my thumb on the little leaping fountain, and reflected what to do. In that empty room there was nothing to my purpose; I felt, besides, that I required assistance. There shot into my mind a hope that Olalla herself might be my helper, and I turned and went downstairs, still keeping my thumb upon the wound.

There was no sign of either Olalla or Felipe, and I addressed myself to the recess, whither the Señora had now drawn quite back and sat dozing close before the fire, for no degree of heat appeared too much for her.

"Pardon me," said I, "if I disturb you, but I must apply to you for help."

She looked up sleepily and asked me what it was, and with the very words I thought she drew in her breath with a widening of the nostrils and seemed to come suddenly and fully alive.

"I have cut myself," I said, "and rather badly. See!" And I held out my two hands, from which the blood was oozing and dripping.

Her great eyes opened wide, the pupils shrank into points; a veil seemed to fall from her face, and leave it sharply expressive and yet inscrutable. And as I still stood, marvelling a little at her disturbance, she came swiftly up to me, and stooped and caught me by the hand; and the next moment my hand was at her mouth, and she had bitten me to the bone. The pang of the bite, the sudden spurting of blood, and the monstrous horror of the act, flashed through me all in one, and I beat her back; and she sprang at me again and again, with bestial cries, cries that I recognized, such cries as had awakened me on the night of the high wind. Her strength was like that of madness; mine was rapidly ebbing with the loss of blood; my mind besides was whirling with the abhorrent strangeness of the onslaught, and I was already forced against the wall, when Olalla ran betwixt us, and Felipe, following at a bound, pinned down his mother on the floor.

A trance-like weakness fell upon me; and I saw, heard, and felt, but I was incapable of movement. I heard the struggle roll to and fro upon the floor, the yells of the catamount ringing up to heaven as she strove to reach me. I felt Olalla clasp me in her arms, her hair falling on my face, and, with the strength of a man, raise and half drag, half carry me upstairs into my own room, where she cast me down upon the bed. Then I saw her hasten to the door and lock it, and stand an instant listening to the savage cries that shook the residencia. And then, swift and light as a thought, she was again beside me, binding up my hand, laying it in her bosom, moaning and mourning over it, with dove-like sounds. They were not words that came to her, they were sounds more beautiful than speech, infinitely touching, infinitely tender; and yet as I lay there, a thought stung to my heart, a thought wounded me like a sword, a thought, like a worm in a flower, profaned the holiness of my love. Yes, they were beautiful sounds, and they were inspired by human tenderness; but was their beauty human?

All day I lay there. For a long time the cries of that nameless female thing, as she struggled with her half-witted whelp, resounded through the house, and pierced me with despairing sorrow and disgust. They were the death-cry of my love; my love was murdered; it was not only dead, but an offence to me; and yet, think as I pleased, feel as I must, it still swelled within me like a storm of sweetness, and my heart melted at her looks and touch. This horror that had sprung out, this doubt upon Olalla, this savage and bestial strain that ran not only through the whole behaviour of her family, but found a place in the very foundations and story of our love—though it appalled, though it shocked and sickened me, was yet not of power to break the knot of my infatuation.

When the cries had ceased, there came the scraping at the door, by which I knew Felipe was without; and Olalla went and spoke to him—I know not what. With that exception, she stayed close beside me, now kneeling by my bed and fervently praying, now sitting with her eyes upon mine. So then, for these six hours I drank in her beauty, and silently perused the story in her face. I saw the golden coin hover on her breaths; I saw her eyes darken and brighten, and still speak no language but that of an unfathomable kindness; I saw the faultless face, and, through the robe, the lines of the faultless body. Night came at last, and in the growing darkness of the chamber, the sight of her slowly melted; but even then the touch of her smooth hand lingered in mine and talked with me. To lie thus in deadly weakness and drink in the traits of the beloved, is to reawake to love from whatever shock of disillusion. I reasoned with myself; and I shut my eyes on horrors, and again I was very bold to accept the worst. What mattered it, if that imperious sentiment survived; if her eyes still beckoned and attached me; if now, even as before, every fibre of my dull body yearned and turned to her? Late on in the night some strength revived in me, and I spoke:—

"Olalla," I said, "nothing matters; I ask nothing; I am content; I love you."

She knelt down awhile and prayed, and I devoutly respected her devotions. The moon had begun to shine in upon one side of each of the three windows, and make a misty clearness in the room, by which I saw her indistinctly. When she rearose she made the sign of the cross.

"It is for me to speak," she said, "and for you to listen. I know; you can but guess. I prayed, how I prayed for you to leave this place. I begged it of you, and I know you would have granted me even this; or if not, O let me think so!"

"I love you," I said.

"And yet you have lived in the world," she said; after a pause, "you are a man and wise; and I am but a child. Forgive me, if I seem to teach, who am as ignorant as the trees of the mountain; but those who learn much do but skim the face of knowledge; they seize the laws, they conceive the dignity of the design—the horror of the living fact fades from their memory. It is we who sit at home with evil who remember, I think, and are warned and pity. Go, rather, go now, and keep me in mind. So I shall have a life in the cherished places of your memory: a life as much my own, as that which I lead in this body."

"I love you," I said once more; and reaching out my weak hand, took hers, and carried it to my lips, and kissed it. Nor did she resist, but winced a little; and I could see her look upon me with a frown that was not unkindly, only sad and baffled. And then it seemed she made a call upon her resolution; plucked my hand towards her, herself at the same time leaning somewhat forward, and laid it on the beating of her heart. "There," she cried, "you feel the very footfall of my life. It only moves for you; it is yours. But is it even mine? It is mine indeed to offer you, as I might take the coin from my neck, as I might break a live branch from a tree, and give it you. And yet not mine! I dwell, or I think I dwell (if I exist at all), somewhere apart, an impotent prisoner, and carried about and deafened by a mob that I disown. This capsule, such as throbs against the sides of animals, knows you at a touch for its master; ay, it loves you! But my soul, does my soul? I think not; I know not, fearing to ask. Yet when you spoke to me your words were of the soul; it is of the soul that you ask—it is only from the soul that you would take me."

"Olalla," I said, "the soul and the body are one, and mostly so in love. What the body chooses, the soul loves; where the body clings, the soul cleaves; body for body, soul to soul they come together at God's signal; and the lower part (if we can call aught low) is only the footstool and foundation of the highest."

"Have you," she said, "seen the portraits in the house of my fathers? Have you looked at my mother or at Felipe? Have your eyes ever rested on that picture that hangs by your bed? She who sat for it died ages ago; and she did evil in her life. But look again: there is my hand to the least line, there are my eyes and my hair. What is mine, then, and what am I? If not a curve in this poor body of mine (which you love, and for the sake of which you dotingly dream that you love me) not a gesture that I can frame, not a tone of my voice, not any look from my eyes, no, not even now when I speak to him I love, but has belonged to others? Others, ages dead, have wooed other men with my eyes; other men have heard the pleading of the same voice that now sounds in your ears. The hands of the dead are in my bosom; they move me, they pluck me, they guide me; I am a puppet at their command; and I but reinform features and attributes that have long been laid aside from evil in the quiet of the grave. Is it me you love, friend? or the race that made me? The girl who does not know and cannot answer for the least portion of herself? or the stream of which she is a transitory eddy, the tree of which she is the passing fruit? The race exists; it is old, it is ever young, it carries its eternal destiny in its bosom; upon it, like waves upon the sea, individual succeeds to individual, mocked with a semblance of self-control, but they are nothing. We speak of the soul, but the soul is in the race."

"You fret against the common law," I said. "You rebel against the voice of God, which He has made so winning to convince, so imperious to command. Hear it, and how it speaks between us! Your hand clings to mine, your heart leaps at my touch, the unknown elements of which we are compounded awake and run together at a look; the clay of the earth remembers its independent life and yearns to join us; we are drawn together as the stars are turned about in space, or as the tides ebb and flow, by things older and greater than we ourselves."

"Alas!" she said, "what can I say to you? My fathers, eight hundred years ago, ruled all this province: they were wise, great, cunning, and cruel; they were a picked race of the Spanish; their flags led in war; the king called them his cousin; the people, when the rope was slung for them or when they returned and found their hovels smoking, blasphemed their name. Presently a change began. Man has risen; if he has sprung from the brutes, he can descend again to the same level. The breath of weariness blew on their humanity and the cords relaxed; they began to go down; their minds fell on sleep, their passions awoke in gusts, heady and senseless like the wind in the gutters of the mountains; beauty was still handed down, but no longer the guiding wit nor the human heart; the seed passed on, it was wrapped in flesh, the flesh covered the bones, but they were the bones and the flesh of brutes, and their mind was as the mind of flies. I speak to you as I dare; but you have seen for yourself how the wheel has gone backward with my doomed race. I stand, as it were, upon a little rising ground in this desperate descent, and see both before and behind, both what we have lost and to what we are condemned to go farther downward. And shall I—I that dwell apart in the house of the dead, my body, loathing its ways—shall I repeat the spell? Shall I bind another spirit, reluctant as my own, into this bewitched and tempest-broken tenement that I now suffer in? Shall I hand down this cursed vessel of humanity, charge it with fresh life as with fresh poison, and dash it, like a fire, in the faces of posterity? But my vow has been given; the race shall cease from off the earth. At this hour my brother is making ready; his foot will soon be on the stair; and you will go with him and pass out of my sight for ever. Think of me sometimes as one to whom the lesson of life was very harshly told, but who heard it with courage; as one who loved you indeed, but who hated herself so deeply that her love was hateful to her; as one who sent you away and yet would have longed to keep you for ever; who had no dearer hope than to forget you, and no greater fear than to be forgotten."

She had drawn towards the door as she spoke, her rich voice sounding softer and farther away; and with the last word she was gone, and I lay alone in the moonlit chamber. What I might have done had not I lain bound by my extreme weakness, I know not; but as it was there fell upon me a great and blank despair. It was not long before there shone in at the door the ruddy glimmer of a lantern, and Felipe coming, charged me without a word upon his shoulders, and carried me down to the great gate, where the cart was waiting. In the moonlight the hills stood out sharply, as if they were of cardboard; on the glimmering surface of the plateau, and from among the low trees which swung together and sparkled in the wind, the great black cube of the residencia stood out bulkily, its mass only broken by three dimly lighted windows in the northern front above the gate. They were Olalla's windows, and as the cart jolted onwards I kept my eyes fixed upon them till, where the road dipped into a valley, they were lost to my view for ever. Felipe walked in silence beside the shafts, but from time to time he would check the mule and seem to look back upon me; and at length drew quite near and laid his hand upon my head. There was such kindness in the touch, and such a simplicity, as of the brutes, that tears broke from me like the bursting of an artery.

"Felipe," I said, "take me where they will ask no questions."

He said never a word, but he turned his mule about, end for end, retraced some part of the way we had gone, and, striking into another path, led me to the mountain village, which was, as we say in Scotland, the kirkton of that thinly peopled district. Some broken memories dwell in my mind of the day breaking over the plain, of the cart stopping, of arms that helped me down, of a bare room into which I was carried, and of a swoon that fell upon me like sleep.

The next day and the days following, the old priest was often at my side with his snuff-box and prayer book, and after a while, when I began to pick up strength, he told me that I was now on a fair way to recovery, and must as soon as possible hurry my departure; whereupon, without naming any reason, he took snuff and looked at me sideways. I did not affect ignorance; I knew he must have seen Olalla. "Sir," said I, "you know that I do not ask in wantonness. What of that family?"

He said they were very unfortunate; that it seemed a declining race, and that they were poor and had been much neglected.

"But she has not," I said. "Thanks, doubtless, to yourself, she is instructed and wise beyond the use of women."

"Yes," he said; "the Señorita is well-informed. But the family has been neglected."

"The mother?" I queried.

"Yes, the mother too," said the Padre, taking snuff. "But Felipe is a well-intentioned lad."

"The mother is odd?" I asked.

"Very odd," replied the priest.

"My son," said the old gentleman, "I will be very frank with you on matters within my competence; on those of which I know nothing it does not require much discretion to be silent. I will not fence with you, I take your meaning perfectly; and what can I say, but that we are all in God's hands, and that His ways are not as our ways? I have even advised with my superiors in the church, but they, too, were dumb. It is a great mystery."

"Is she mad?" I asked.

"I will answer you according to my belief. She is not," returned the Padre, "or she was not. When she was young—God help me, I fear I neglected that wild lamb—she was surely sane; and yet, although it did not run to such heights, the same strain was already notable; it had been so before her in her father, ay, and before him, and this inclined me, perhaps, to think too lightly of it. But these things go on growing, not only in the individual but in the race."

"When she was young," I began, and my voice failed me for a moment, and it was only with a great effort that I was able to add, "was she like Olalla?"

"Now God forbid!" exclaimed the Padre. "God forbid that any man should think so slightingly of my favourite penitent. No, no; the Señorita (but for her beauty, which I wish most honestly she had less of) has not a hair's resemblance to what her mother was at the same age. I could not bear to have you think so; though, Heaven knows, it were, perhaps, better that you should."

At this, I raised myself in bed, and opened my heart to the old man; telling him of our love and of her decision, owning my own horrors, my own passing fancies, but telling him that these were at an end; and with something more than a purely formal submission, appealing to his judgment.

He heard me very patiently and without surprise; and when I had done, he sat for some time silent. Then he began: "The church," and instantly broke off again to apologize. "I had forgotten, my child, that you were not a Christian," said he. "And indeed, upon a point so highly unusual, even the church can scarce be said to have decided. But would you have my opinion? The Señorita is, in a matter of this kind, the best judge; I would accept her judgment."

On the back of that he went away, nor was he thenceforward so assiduous in his visits; indeed, even when I began to get about again, he plainly feared and deprecated my society, not as in distaste but much as a man might be disposed to flee from the riddling sphynx. The villagers, too, avoided me; they were unwilling to be my guides upon the mountain. I thought they looked at me askance, and I made sure that the more superstitious crossed themselves on my approach. At first I set this down to my heretical opinions; but it began at length to dawn upon me that if I was thus redoubted it was because I had stayed at the residencia. All men despise the savage notions of such peasantry; and yet I was conscious of a chill shadow that seemed to fall and dwell upon my love. It did not conquer, but I may not deny that it restrained my ardour.

Some miles westward of the village there was a gap in the sierra, from which the eye plunged direct upon the residencia; and thither it became my daily habit to repair. A wood crowned the summit; and just where the pathway issued from its fringes, it was overhung by a considerable shelf of rock, and that, in its turn, was surmounted by a crucifix of the size of life and more than usually painful in design. This was my perch; thence, day after day, I looked down upon the plateau, and the great old house, and could see Felipe, no bigger than a fly, going to and fro about the garden. Sometimes mists would draw across the view, and be broken up again by mountain winds; sometimes the plain slumbered below me in unbroken sunshine; it would sometimes be all blotted out by rain. This distant post, these interrupted sights of the place where my life had been so strangely changed suited the indecision of my humour. I passed whole days there, debating with myself the various elements of our position; now leaning to the suggestions of love, now giving an ear to prudence, and in the end halting irresolute between the two.

One day, as I was sitting on my rock, there came by that way a somewhat gaunt peasant wrapped in a mantle. He was a stranger, and plainly did not know me even by repute; for, instead of keeping the other side, he drew near and sat down beside me, and we had soon fallen in talk. Among other things he told me he had been a muleteer, and in former years had much frequented these mountains; later on, he had followed the army with his mules , had realized a competence, and was now living retired with his family.

"Do you know that house?" I inquired, at last, pointing to the residencia, for I readily wearied of any talk that kept me from the thought of Olalla.

He looked at me darkly and crossed himself.

"Too well," he said, "it was there that one of my comrades sold himself to Satan; the Virgin shield us from temptations! He has paid the price; he is now burning in the reddest place in Hell!"

A fear came upon me; I could answer nothing; and presently the man resumed, as if to himself. "Yes," he said, "O yes, I know it. I have passed its doors. There was snow upon the pass, the wind was driving it; sure enough there was death that night upon the mountains, but there was worse beside the hearth. I took him by the arm, Señor, and dragged him to the gate; I conjured him, by all he loved and respected, to go forth with me; I went on my knees before him in the snow; and I could see he was moved by my entreaty. And just then she came out on the gallery, and called him by his name; and he turned, and there was she standing with a lamp in her hand and smiling on him to come back. I cried out aloud to God, and threw my arms about him, but he put me by, and left me alone. He had made his choice; God help us. I would pray for him, but to what end? there are sins that not even the Pope can loose."

"And your friend," I asked, "what became of him?"

"Nay, God knows," said the muleteer; "If all be true that we hear, his end was like his sin, a thing to raise the hair."

"Do you mean that he was killed?" I asked.

"Sure enough, he was killed," returned the man. "But how? Ay, how? But these are things that it is sin to speak of."

"The people of that house . . . " I began.

But he interrupted me with a savage outburst.

"The people?" he cried. "What people? There are neither men nor women in that house of Satan's! What? have you lived here so long, and never heard?" And here he put his mouth to my ear and whispered, as if even the fowls of the mountain might have overheard and been striken with horror.

What he told me was not true, nor was it even original; being, indeed, but a new edition, vamped up again by village ignorance and superstition, of stories nearly as ancient as the race of man. It was rather the application that appalled me. In the old days, he said, the church would have burned out that nest of basilisks; but the arm of the church was now shortened; his friend Miguel had been unpunished by the hands by men, and left to the more awful judgment of an offended God. This was wrong; but it should be so no more. The Padre was sunk in age; he was even bewitched himself; but the eyes of his flock were now awake to their own danger; and some day—ay, and before long—the smoke of that house should go up to heaven.

He left me filled with horror and fear. Which way to turn I knew not; whether first to warn the Padre, or to carry my ill-news direct to the threatened inhabitants of the residencia. Fate was to decide for me; for, while I was still hesitating, I beheld the veiled figure of a woman drawing near to me up the pathway. No veil could deceive my penetration; by every line and every movement I recognized Olalla; and keeping hidden behind a corner of the rock, I suffered her to gain the summit. Then I came forward. She knew me and paused, but did not speak; I, too, remained silent; and we continued for some time to gaze upon each other with a passionate sadness.

"I thought you had gone," she said at length. "It is all that you can do for me—to go. It is all I ever asked of you. And you still stay. But do you know, that every day heaps up the peril of death, not only on your head, but on ours? A report has gone about the mountain; it is thought you love me, and the people will not suffer it."

I saw she was already informed of her danger, and I rejoiced at it. "Olalla," I said, "I am ready to go this day, this very hour, but not alone."

She stepped aside and knelt down before the crucifix to pray, and I stood by and looked now at her and now at the object of her adoration, now at the living figure of the penitent, and now at the ghastly, daubed countenance, the painted wounds, and the projected ribs of the image. The silence was only broken by the wailing of some large birds that circled sidelong, as if in surprise or alarm, about the summit of the hills. Presently Olalla rose again, turned towards me, raised her veil, and, still leaning with one hand on the shaft of the crucifix, looked upon me with a pale and sorrowful countenance.

"I have laid my hand upon the cross," she said. "The Padre says you are no Christian; but look up for a moment with my eyes, and behold the face of the Man of Sorrows. We are all such as He was—the inheritors of sin; we must all bear and expiate a past which was not ours; there is in all of us—ay, even in me—a sparkle of the divine. Like Him, we must endure for a little while, until morning returns bringing peace. Suffer me to pass on upon my way alone; it is thus that I shall be least lonely, counting for my friend Him who is the friend of all the distressed; it is thus that I shall be the most happy, having taken my farewell of earthly happiness, and willingly accepted sorrow for my portion."

I looked at the face of the crucifix, and, though I was no friend to images, and despised that imitative and grimacing art of which it was a rude example, some sense of what the thing implied was carried home to my intelligence. The face looked down upon me with a painful and deadly contraction; but the rays of a glory encircled it, and reminded me that the sacrifice was voluntary. It stood there, crowning the rock, as it still stands on so many highway sides, vainly preaching to passers-by, an emblem of sad and noble truths; that pleasure is not an end, but an accident; that pain is the choice of the magnanimous; that it is best to suffer all things and do well. I turned and went down the mountain in silence; and when I looked back for the last time before the wood closed about my path, I saw Olalla still leaning on the crucifix.

Leo Tolstoi
1828—1910

The author of War and Peace *and* Anna Karenina *also wrote short fiction throughout his career, though usually with an overtly moral earnestness foreign to the great masters of the short story then and since. Around 1880 the sophisticated and wealthy count seemingly committed to richly particularized portrayals of life in the aristocracy and upper middle class, and to the detailed and thoroughgoing psychological analysis that had become the accepted method for such depiction, underwent a religious conversion and thenceforth turned his immense energy toward preaching social reform. Always attracted to a sort of primitivism that exalted the peasantry's simple piety, animal vitality, and freedom from nerves into an idyl, but sympathetic with poverty and political helplessness, Tolstoi now assumed the role of champion and mentor of the masses—not just Russia's, but the world's. His conversion to "Christian communism" (a "Christianity" stripped of everything except its ethical teaching, and embracing communal living) did not bring him the personal serenity he had hoped for, but his immense influence in Russia did contribute to the political climate—sharp dissatisfaction with the present, repugnance to czardom and aristocracy, and radiant optimism about the future—that culminated in the upheaval of 1917.*

For his evangelical purpose, the short tale written in the least adorned style and carrying a minimum of localizing or particularizing detail was the logical choice: the peasantry had time for nothing longer, and the background for nothing more indirect or allusive. As precedent for conveying popular moral instruction by means of such simple narrative, Tolstoi had the illustrious figure of his new master, Christ himself.

Christ, however, did not pretend that his parables were literature. Tolstoi's problem was that of every literary supermoralist. Writers and other artists describe the creative process as being akin to the spirit of play: the time of creation is an open, receptive, exploratory, spontaneously imaginative, unselfconscious time. Self-conscious ideological purpose would seem to slam the door in the muse's face. When the paths are so few and the goal so fixed, how does the moral (or other) ideologist prevent his work from becoming imaginatively impoverished on the one hand and forced on the other?

Tolstoi often failed to solve the problem but did so in "God Sees the Truth but Waits." This story was actually written in 1872, well before the author's conversion, and both its moral vision and its method—concentration upon action in straightforward narrative in plain language and with a minimum of particulars—show that the later Tolstoi was by no means utterly different from the earlier. Other successes in this manner include "The Death of Ivan Ilyich" and "Master and Man."

God Sees the Truth but Waits

Leo Tolstoi

In the town of Vladimir lived a young merchant named Ivan Dmitritch Aksyonof. He had two shops and a house of his own.

Aksyonof was a handome, fair-haired, curly-headed fellow, full of fun, and very fond of singing. When quite a young man he had been given to drink, and was riotous when he had had too much; but after he married he gave up drinking, except now and then.

One summer Aksyonof was going to the Nijni Fair, and as he bade good-bye to his family his wife said to him, "Ivan Dmitritch, do not start today; I have had a bad dream about you."

Aksyonof laughed, and said, "You are afraid that when I get to the fair I shall go on a spree."

His wife replied: "I do not know what I am afraid of; all I know is that I had a bad dream. I dreamt you returned from the town, and when you took off your cap I saw that your hair was quite gray."

Aksyonof laughed. "That's a lucky sign," said he. "See if I don't sell out all my goods, and bring you some presents from the fair."

So he said good-bye to his family, and drove away.

When he had traveled half-way, he met a merchant whom he knew, and they put up at the same inn for the night. They had some tea together, and then went to bed in adjoining rooms.

It was not Aksyonof's habit to sleep late, and, wishing to travel while it was still cool, he aroused his driver before dawn, and told him to put in the horses.

Then he made his way across to the landlord of the inn (who lived in a cottage at the back), paid his bill, and continued his journey.

When he had gone about twenty-five miles, he stopped for the horses to be fed. Aksyonof rested awhile in the passage of the inn, then he stepped out into the porch, and ordering a samovar to be heated, got out his guitar, and began to play.

Suddenly a troika drove up with tinkling bells, and an official alighted, followed by two soldiers. He came to Aksyonof and began to question him, asking him who he was and whence he came. Aksyonof answered him fully, and said, "Won't you have some tea with me?" But the official went on cross-questioning him and asking him, "Where did you spend last night? Were you alone, or with a fellow-merchant? Did you see the other merchant this morning? Why did you leave the inn before dawn?"

Aksyonof wondered why he was asked all these questions, but he described all that had happened, and then added, "Why do you cross-question me as if I were a thief or a robber? I am traveling on business of my own, and there is no need to question me."

Then the official, calling the soldiers, said, "I am the police-officer of this district, and I question you because the merchant with whom you spent last night has been found with his throat cut. We must search your things."

They entered the house. The soldiers and the police-officer unstrapped Aksyonof's luggage and searched it. Suddenly the officer drew a knife out of a bag, crying, "Whose knife is this?"

Aksyonof looked, and seeing a blood-stained knife taken from his bag, he was frightened.

"How is it there is blood on this knife?"

Aksyonof tried to answer, but could hardly utter a word, and only stammered: "I—I don't know—not mine."

Then the police-officer said, "This morning the merchant was found in bed with his throat cut. You are the only person who could have done it. The house was locked from inside, and no one else was there. Here is this blood-stained knife in your bag, and your face and manner betray you! Tell me how you killed him, and how much money you stole?"

Aksyonof swore he had not done it; that he had not seen the merchant after they had had tea together; that he had no money except eight thousand rubles of his own, and that the knife was not his. But his voice was broken, his face pale, and he trembled with fear as though he were in truth guilty.

The police-officer ordered the soldiers to bind Aksyonof and to put him in the cart. As they tied his feet together and flung him into the cart, Aksyonof crossed himself and wept. His money and goods were taken from him, and he was sent to the nearest town and imprisoned there. Enquiries as to his character were made in Vladimir. The merchants and other inhabitants of that town said that in former days he used to drink and waste his time, but that he was a good man. Then the trial came on: he was charged with murdering a merchant from Ryazan, and robbing him of twenty thousand rubles.

His wife was in despair, and did not know what to believe. Her children were all quite small; one was a baby at her breast. Taking them all with her, she went to the town where her husband was in jail. At first she was not allowed to see him; but, after much begging, she obtained permission from the officials, and was taken to him. When she saw her husband in prison-dress and in chains, shut up with thieves and criminals, she fell down, and did not come to her senses for a long time. Then she drew her children to her, and sat down near him. She told him of things at home, and asked about what had happened to him. He told her all, and she asked, "What can we do now?"

"We must petition the Tsar not to let an innocent man perish."

His wife told him that she had sent a petition to the Tsar, but that it had not been accepted.

Aksyonof did not reply, but only looked downcast.

Then his wife said, "It was not for nothing I dreamt your hair had turned gray. You remember? You should not have started that day." And passing her fingers through his hair, she said: "Vanya dearest, tell your wife the truth; was it not you who did it?"

"So you, too, suspect me!" cried Aksyonof, and, hiding his face in his hands, he began to weep. Then a soldier came to say that the wife and children must go away; and Aksyonof said good-bye to his family for the last time.

When they were gone, Aksyonof recalled what had been said, and when he remembered that his wife also had suspected him, he said to himself, "It seems that only God can know the truth; it is to Him alone we must appeal, and from Him alone expect mercy."

And Aksyonof wrote no more petitions, gave up all hope, and only prayed to God.

Aksyonof was condemned to be flogged and sent to the mines. So he was flogged with a knout, and when the wounds made by the knout were healed, he was driven to Siberia with other convicts.

For twenty-six years Aksyonof lived as a convict in Siberia. His hair turned white as snow, and his beard grew long, thin, and gray. All his mirth went; he stooped; he walked slowly, spoke little, and never laughed, but he often prayed.

In prison Aksyonof learned to make boots, and earned a little money, with which he bought *The Lives of the Saints*. He read this book when there was light enough in the prison; and on Sundays in the prison-church he read the lessons and sang in the choir; for his voice was still good.

The prison authorities liked Aksyonof for his meekness, and his fellow-prisoners respected him: they called him "Grandfather," and "The Saint." When they wanted to petition the prison authorities about anything, they always made Aksyonof their spokesman, and when there were quarrels among the prisoners they came to him to put things right, and to judge the matter.

No news reached Aksyonof from his home, and he did not even know if his wife and children were still alive.

One day a fresh gang of convicts came to the prison. In the evening the old prisoners collected round the new ones and asked them what towns or villages they came from, and what they were sentenced for. Among the rest Aksyonof sat down near the newcomers, and listened with downcast air to what was said.

One of the new convicts, a tall, strong man of sixty, with a closely-cropped gray beard, was telling the others what he had been arrested for.

"Well, friends," he said, "I only took a horse that was tied to a sledge, and I was arrested and accused of stealing. I said I had only taken it to get home quicker, and had then let it go; besides, the driver was a personal friend of mine. So I said, 'It's all right.' 'No,' said they, 'you stole it.' But how or where I stole it they could not say. I once really did something wrong, and ought by rights to have come here long ago, but that time I was not found out. Now I have been sent here for nothing at all. . . . Eh, but it's lies I'm telling you; I've been to Siberia before, but I did not stay long."

"Where are you from?" asked someone.

"From Vladimir. My family are of that town. My name is Makar, and they also call me Semyonitch."

Aksyonof raised his head and said: "Tell me, Semyonitch, do you know anything of the merchants Aksyonof, of Vladimir? Are they still alive?"

"Know them? Of course I do. The Aksyonofs are rich, though their father is in Siberia: a sinner like ourselves, it seems! As for you, Gran'dad, how did you come here?"

Aksyonof did not like to speak of his misfortune. He only sighed, and said, "For my sins I have been in prison these twenty-six years."

"What sins?" asked Makar Semyonitch.

But Aksyonof only said, "Well, well—I must have deserved it!" He would have said no more, but his companions told the newcomer how Aksyonof came to be in Siberia: how someone had killed a merchant, and had put a knife among Aksyonof's things, and Aksyonof had been unjustly condemned.

When Makar Semyonitch heard this, he looked at Aksyonof, slapped his own knee, and exclaimed, "Well, this is wonderful! Really wonderful! But how old you've grown, Gran'dad!"

The others asked him why he was so surprised, and where he had seen Aksyonof before; but Makar Semyonitch did not reply. He only said: "It's wonderful that we should meet here, lads!"

These words made Aksyonof wonder whether this man knew who had killed the merchant; so he said, "Perhaps, Semyonitch, you have heard of that affair, or maybe you've seen me before?"

"How could I help hearing? The world's full of rumors. But it's long ago, and I've forgotten what I heard."

"Perhaps you heard who killed the merchant?" asked Aksyonof.

Makar Semyonitch laughed, and replied, "It must have been him in whose bag the knife was found! If someone else hid the knife there, 'He's not a thief till he's caught,' as the saying is. How could anyone put a knife into your bag while it was under your head? It would surely have woke you up?"

When Aksyonof heard these words, he felt sure this was the man who had killed the merchant. He rose and went away. All that night Aksyonof lay awake. He felt terribly unhappy, and all sorts of images rose in his mind. There was the image of his wife as she was when he parted from her to go to the fair. He saw her as if she were present; her face and her eyes rose before him; he heard her speak and laugh. Then he saw his children, quite little, as they were at that time: one with a little cloak on, another at his mother's breast. And then he remembered himself as he used to be—young and merry. He remembered how he sat playing the guitar in the porch of the inn where he was arrested, and how free from care he had been. He saw, in his mind, the place where he was flogged, the executioner, and the people standing around; the chains, the convicts, all the twenty-six years of his prison life, and his premature old age. The thought of it all made him so wretched that he was ready to kill himself.

"And it's all that villain's doing!" thought Aksyonof. And his anger was so great against Makar Semyonitch that he longed for vengeance, even if he himself should perish for it. He kept repeating prayers all night, but could get no peace. During the day he did not go near Makar Semyonitch, nor even look at him.

A fortnight passed in this way. Aksyonof could not sleep at nights, and was so miserable that he did not know what to do.

One night as he was walking about the prison he noticed some earth that came rolling out from under one of the shelves on which the prisoners slept. He stopped to see what it was. Suddenly Makar Semyonitch crept out from under the shelf, and looked up at Aksyonof with frightened face.

Aksyonof attempted to pass without looking at him, but Makar seized his hand and told him that he had dug a hole under the wall, getting rid of the earth by putting it into his high-boots, and emptying it out every day on the road when the prisoners were driven to their work.

"Just you keep quiet, old man, and you shall get out, too. If you blab they'll flog the life out of me, but I will kill you first."

Aksyonof trembled with anger as he looked at his enemy. He drew his hand away, saying, "I have no wish to escape, and you have no need to kill me; you killed me long ago! As to telling of you—I may do so or not, as God shall direct."

Next day, when the convicts were led out to work, the convoy soldiers noticed that one or other of the prisoners emptied some earth out of his boots. The prison was searched and the tunnel found. The Governor came and questioned all the prisoners to find out who had dug the hole. They all denied any knowledge of it. Those who knew would not betray Makar Semyonitch, knowing he would be flogged almost to death. At last the Governor turned to Aksyonof, whom he knew to be a just man, and said:

"You are a truthful man; tell me, before God, who dug the hole?"

Makar Semyonitch stood as if he were quite unconcerned, looking at the Governor and not so much as glancing at Aksyonof. Aksyonof's lips and hands trembled, and for a long time he could not utter a word. He thought, "Why should I screen him who ruined my life? Let him pay for what I have suffered. But if I tell, they will probably flog the life out of him, and maybe I suspect him wrongly. And, after all, what good would it be to me."

"Well, old man," repeated the Governor, "tell us the truth: who has been digging under the wall?"

Aksyonof glanced at Makar Semyonitch, and said, "I cannot say, your honor. It is not God's will that I should tell! Do what you like with me; I am in your hands."

However much the Governor tried, Aksyonof would say no more, and so the matter had to be left.

That night, when Aksyonof was lying on his bed and just beginning to doze, someone came quietly and sat down on his bed. He peered through the darkness and recognized Makar.

"What more do you want of me?" asked Aksyonof. "Why have you come here?"

Makar Semyonitch was silent. So Aksyonof sat up and said, "What do you want? Go away, or I will call the guard!"

Makar Semyonitch bent close over Aksyonof, and whispered, "Ivan Dmitritch, forgive me!"

"What for?" asked Aksyonof.

"It was I who killed the merchant and hid the knife among your things. I meant to kill you too, but I heard a noise outside; so I hid the knife in your bag and escaped out of the window."

Aksyonof was silent, and did not know what to say.

Makar Semyonitch slid off the bed-shelf and knelt upon the ground. "Ivan Dmitritch," said he, "forgive me! For the love of God, forgive me! I will confess that it was I who killed the merchant, and you will be released and can go to your home."

"It is easy for you to talk," said Aksyonof, "but I have suffered for you these twenty-six years. Where could I go now? . . . My wife is dead, and my children have forgotten me. I have nowhere to go. . . ."

Makar Semyonitch did not rise, but beat his head on the floor. "Ivan Dmitritch, forgive me!" he cried. "When they flogged me with the knout it was not so hard to bear as it is to see you now . . . yet you had pity on me, and did not tell. For Christ's sake forgive me, wretch that I am!" And he began to sob.

When Aksyonof heard him sobbing he, too, began to weep.

"God will forgive you!" said he. "Maybe I am a hundred times worse than you." And at these words his heart grew light, and the longing for home left him. He no longer had any desire to leave the prison, but only hoped for his last hour to come.

In spite of what Aksyonof had said, Makar Semyonitch confessed his guilt. But when the order for his release came, Aksyonof was already dead.

Nikolai Leskov

1831—1895

Critical recognition came far too late to brighten Leskov's days, but throughout his career as a writer ignored and disliked by the Russian intelligentsia (which consisted almost exclusively of liberals and revolutionaries) he maintained a self-confidence and an unrelenting will that Balzac would have admired. Leskov's antipathy to revolution and his humanistic refusal to countenance the subversion of truth for political ends permanently alienated the literary establishment. His readers were among the general public, and they existed in sufficient numbers to support his hope that the intellectuals would also, someday, concede his merit.

Deviation of a purely literary nature also stood in Leskov's way. In Russia as elsewhere, literary officialdom prescribed the lengthy, "well made," classically-phrased novel of character psychology as the recognizable path to greatness in fiction. But Leskov wrote as he pleased, without deference to amplitude, tight plotting, polished diction, or analytical characterization. He preferred shorter pieces anecdotal or episodic in technique and, in many cases, full of racy colloquialism.

Even today Leskov is not a familiar name in the New World, but in Europe he has very slowly acquired a stature that places him in the company of Dostoievski, Pushkin, and Turgenev. "The Sentry," based (as the prefatory remarks note) on an actual incident, is often considered the best of all his short stories. It tensely dramatizes a moral issue centering around a question of justice. Leskov's view of the situation is, as always, both sensible and humane. Laws and standards are needed, but there is also a need for moral compromise. As one commentator has put it, "natural human solidarity breaks through the terrifying structure of official rules and official inhumanity." But though the story implies a critique of despotic legalism and institutionalized inhumanity, it harbors no revolutionary intimations and makes no obeisance to sentimental or mindless humanism.

The Sentry

Nikolai Leskov

I

The events of the story which is now presented to the reader are so touching and terrible in their importance for the chief and heroic actor who took part in them, and the issue of the affair was so unique, that anything similar could scarcely have occurred in another country than Russia.

It forms in part a court anecdote, in part a historic event that characterizes fairly well the manners and the very strange tendencies of the uneventful period comprised in the third decade of this nineteenth century.

There is no invention in the following story.

II

During the winter of 1839, just before the Festival of the Epiphany, there was a great thaw in Petersburg. The weather was so warm, that it was almost like spring: the snow melted during the day, water dripped from the roofs, the ice on the rivers became blue, and open water appeared in many places. On the Neva, just in front of the Winter Palace, there was a large open space. A warm but very high wind blew from the west, the water was driven in from the gulf, and the signal guns were fired.

The guard at the Palace at that time was a company of the Ismailovsky regiment, commanded by a very brilliant well-educated officer named Nikolai Ivanovich Miller, a young man of the very best society (who subsequently rose to the rank of general and became the director of the Lyceum). He was a man of the so-called "humane tendencies," which had long since been noticed in him, and somewhat impaired his chances in the service, in the eyes of his superiors.

Miller was really an exact and trustworthy officer; the duty of the guard at the Palace was without any danger; the time was most uneventful and tranquil; the Palace sentries were only required to stand accurately at their posts. Nevertheless, just when Captain Miller was in command, a most extraordinary and very alarming event took place, which is probably scarcely remembered even by the few of his contemporaries who are now ending their days upon earth.

III

At first everything went well with the guard. The sentries were placed, the men were all at their posts and all was in the most perfect order. The Emperor Nikolai Pavlovich was well, he had been for a drive in the evening, returned home, and had gone to bed. The Palace slept, too. The night was most quiet. There was tranquillity in the guard-room. Captain Miller had pinned his white pocket handkerchief to the back of the officer's chair, with its traditionally greasy morocco high back and had settled down to while away the time by reading.

Captain Miller had always been a passionate reader, and therefore was never dull; he read and did not notice how the night passed away. When suddenly at about three o'clock he was alarmed by a terrible anxiety. The sergeant on duty, pale and trembling with fear, stood before him, and stammered hurriedly:

"A calamity, your honour, a calamity!"

"What has happened?"

"A terrible misfortune has occurred."

Captain Miller jumped up in indescribable agitation and with difficulty was able to ascertain what really was the nature of the "calamity" and the "terrible misfortune."

IV

The case was as follows: the sentry, a private of the Ismailovsky regiment named Postnikov, who was standing on guard at the outer door of the Palace, now called the "Jordan" entrance, heard that a man was drowning in the open spaces which had appeared in the ice just opposite the Palace, and was calling for help in his despair.

Private Postnikov, a domestic serf of some great family, was a very nervous and sensitive man. For a long time he listened to the distant cries and groans of the drowning man, and they seemed to benumb him with horror. He looked on all sides, but on the whole visible expanse of the quays and the Neva, as if on purpose, not a living soul could he see.

There was nobody who could give help to the drowning man, and he was sure to sink . . .

All this time the man struggled long and terribly.

It seemed as if there was but one thing left for him—to sink to the bottom without further struggle, but no! His cries of exhaustion were now broken and ceased, then were heard again, always nearer and nearer to the Palace quay. It was evident that the man had not lost his direction, but was making straight for the lights of the street lamps, but doubtless he would perish because just in his path, he would fall into the "Jordan" (a hole made in the ice of the river for the consecration of the water on the 6th of January.) There he would be drawn under the ice and it would be the end. Again he was quiet, but a minute later he began to splash through the water, and moan: "Save me, save me!" He was now so near that the splashing of the water could actually be heard as he waded along.

Private Postnikov began to realize that it would be quite easy to save this man. It was only necessary to run on to the ice, as the drowning man was sure to be there, throw him a rope, or stretch a pole or a gun towards him, and he would be saved. He was so near that he could take hold of it with his hand and save himself. But Postnikov remembered his service and his oath; he knew he was the sentry, and that the sentry dare not leave his sentry-box on any pretext or for any reason whatever.

On the other hand, Postnikov's heart was not at all submissive; it gnawed, it throbbed, it sank. He would have been glad to tear it out and throw it at his feet—he had become so uneasy at the sound of these groans and sobs. It was terrible to hear another man perishing and not to stretch out a hand to save him, when really it was quite possible to do so, because the sentry-box would not run away, and no other harm could happen. "Shall I run down? Will anybody see it? Oh, Lord, if it could only end! He's groaning again!"

For a whole half hour, while this was going on, Private Postnikov's heart tormented him so much that he began to feel doubts of his own reason. He was a clever and conscientious soldier with a clear judgment, and he knew perfectly well, that for a sentry to leave his post was a crime that would have to be tried by court-martial, and he would afterwards have to run the gauntlet between two lines of cat-o'-nine-tails and then have penal servitude, or perhaps even be shot—but from the direction of the swollen river again there rose, always nearer and nearer, groans, mumblings and desperate struggles.

"I am drowning! Save me, I am drowning!"

Soon he would come to the Jordan cutting and then—the end.

Postnikov looked round once or twice on all sides. Not a soul was to be seen, only the lamps rattled, shook and flickered in the wind, and on the wind were borne broken cries, perhaps the last cries . . . .

There was another splash, a single sob and a gurgling in the water.

The sentry could bear it no longer, and left his post.

V

Postnikov rushed to the steps, with his heart beating violently, ran on to the ice, then into the water that had risen above it. He soon saw where the drowning man was struggling for life and held out the stock of his gun to him. The drowning man caught hold of the butt-end and Postnikov, holding on to the bayonet, drew him to the bank.

Both the man who had been saved and his rescuer were completely wet; the man who had been saved was in a state of great exhaustion, shivered and fell; his rescuer Private Postnikov could not make up his mind to abandon him on the ice, but led him to the quay, and began looking about for somebody to whom he could confide him. While all this was happening, a sledge in which an officer was sitting had appeared on the quay. He was an officer of the Palace Invalid corps, a company which existed then, but has since been abolished.

This gentleman who arrived at such an inopportune moment for Postnikov was evidently a man of a very heedless character, and besides a very muddled-headed and impudent person. He jumped out of his sledge and inquired:

"What man is this? Who are these people?"

"He was nearly drowned—he was sinking," began Postnikov.

"How was he drowning? Who was drowning? Was it you? Why is he here?"

But he only spluttered and panted, and Postnikov was no longer there; he had shouldered his gun and had gone back to his sentry-box.

Possibly the officer understood what had happened, for he made no further inquiries, but at once took the man who had been rescued into his sledge and drove with him to the Admiralty Police station in the Morskaia Street.

Here the officer made a statement to the inspector, that the dripping man he had brought had nearly been drowned in one of the holes in the ice in front of the Palace, and that he, the officer, had saved him at the risk of his own life.

The man who had been saved was still quite wet, shivering and exhausted. From fright and owing to his terrible efforts he fell into a sort of unconsciousness, and it was quite indifferent to him who had saved him.

The sleepy police orderly bustled around him, while in the office a statement was drawn up from the officer's verbal deposition and, with the suspicion natural to members of the police, they were perplexed to understand how he had managed to come out of the water quite dry. The officer who was anxious to receive the life saving medal tried to explain this happy concurrence of circumstances, but his explanation was incoherent and improbable. They went to wake the police inspector, and sent to make inquiries.

Meantime in the Palace this occurrence was the cause of another rapid series of events.

VI

In the Palace guard-room all that had occurred since the officer took the half-drowned man into his sledge was unknown. There the Ismailovsky officer and the soldiers only knew that Postnikov, a private of their regiment, had left his sentry-box, and had hurried to save a man and, this being a great breach of military duty, Private Postnikov would certainly be tried by court-martial and have to undergo a thrashing, and all his superior officers, beginning from the commander of the company, would have to face terrible unpleasantness, to avert which they would have nothing to say, nor would they be able to defend themselves.

The wet and shivering soldier Postnikov, was of course at once relieved from his post, and when he was brought to the guard-room frankly related to Captain Miller all that we already know, with all the details to the moment when the officer of the Invalid Corps put the half-drowned man into his sledge, and ordered the coachman to drive to the Admiralty police station.

The danger grew greater and more unavoidable. It was certain the officer of the Invalid Corps would relate everything to the police inspector and the inspector would at once state all the facts to the chief of police, Kokoshkin, who in the morning would make his report to the Emperor, and then the trouble would begin.

There was no time for reflection; the advice of the superior officer must be obtained.

Nikolai Ivanovich Miller forthwith sent an alarming note to his immediate superior, the commander of his battalion, Lieutenant-Colonel Svinin, in which he begged him to come to the guard room as soon as he could to take every possible measure to help him out of the terrible misfortune that had occurred.

It was already about three o'clock, and Kokoshkin had to present his report to the Emperor fairly early in the morning, so that but little time remained for reflection and action.

VII

Lieutenant-Colonel Svinin did not possess that compassion and tenderness of heart for which Nikolai Ivanovich Miller had always been distinguished. Svinin was not a heartless man, but first and foremost a martinet (a type that is now remembered with regret). Svinin was known for his severity and he even liked to boast of his exacting discipline. He had no taste for evil, and never tried to cause anybody useless suffering, but when a man had violated any of the duties of the service, Svinin was inexorable. In the present case he considered it out of place to enter into the consideration of the causes that had guided the actions of the culprit, and held to the rule that every deviation from discipline was guilt. Therefore, in the company on guard all knew that Private Postnikov would have to suffer what he deserved for having left his post, and that Svinin would remain absolutely indifferent.

Such was the character by which the staff officer was known to his superiors, and also to his comrades, amongst whom there were men who did not sympathize with Svinin, because at that time "humaneness," and other similar delusions, had not entirely died out. Svinin was indifferent to whether he would be blamed or praised by the "humanitarians." To beg or entreat Svinin, or even to try to move him to pity was quite useless. To all this he was hardened with the well-tempered armour of the people of those times, who wanted to make their way in the world; but even he, like Achilles, had a weak spot.

Svinin's career in the service had commenced well, and he of course greatly valued it and was very careful that on it, as on a full dress uniform, not a grain of dust should settle, and now this unfortunate action of one of the men of the battalion entrusted to him would certainly throw a shadow on the discipline of the whole company. Those on whom Svinin's well started and carefully maintained military career depended would not stop to inquire if the commander of the battalion was guilty or not guilty of what one of his men had done, while moved by the most honourable feelings of sympathy, and many would gladly have put a spoke in his wheel, so as to make way for their relations or to push forward some fine young fellow with high patronage. If the Emperor, who would certainly be angry, said to the commander of the regiment that he had feeble officers, that their men were undisciplined: who was the cause of it? Svinin. So it would be repeated that Svinin was feeble, and the reproach of feebleness would remain a stain on his reputation that could not be washed out. Then he would never be in any way remarkable among his contemporaries, and he would not leave his portrait in the gallery of historical personages of the Russian Empire.

Although at that time but few cultivated the study of history, nevertheless they believed in it, and aspired, with special pleasure, to take part in its making.

VIII

At about three o'clock in the morning, as soon as Svinin received Captain Miller's disquieting letter, he at once jumped out of bed, put on his uniform, and swayed by fear and anger arrived at the guardroom of the Winter Palace. Here he forthwith examined Private Postnikov, and assured himself that the extraordinary event had really taken place. Private Postnikov again frankly confirmed to the commander of his battalion all that had occurred while he was on guard duty, and what he (Postnikov) had already related to the commander of his company, Captain Miller. The soldier said that he was guilty before God and the Emperor, and could not expect mercy; that he, standing on guard, hearing the groans of a man who was drowning in the open places of the ice, had suffered long, had struggled long between his sense of military duty and his feelings of compassion, and at last he had yielded to temptation and not being able to stand the struggle, had left his sentry-box, jumped on the ice and had drawn the drowning man to the bank, and there to his misfortune he met an officer of the Palace Invalid Corps.

Lieutenant-Colonel Svinin was in despair; he gave himself the only possible satisfaction by wreaking his anger on Postnikov, whom he at once sent under arrest to the regimental prison, and then said some biting words to Miller, reproaching him with "humanitarianism," which was of no use at all in military service; but all this was of no avail, nor would it improve the matter. It was impossible to find any excuse, still less justification, for a sentry who had left his post, and there remained only one way of getting out of the difficulty—to conceal the whole affair from the Emperor. . . .

But was it possible to conceal such an occurrence?

It was evident that this appeared to be impossible, as the rescue of the drowning man was known, not only to the whole of the guard, but also to that hateful officer of the Invalid Corps, who by now had certainly had time to report the whole matter to General Kokoshkin.

Which way was he to turn? To whom could he address himself? From whom could he obtain help and protection?

Svinin wanted to gallop off to the Grand Duke Michael Pavlovich and relate to him, quite frankly, all that had happened. Manoeuvres of this nature were then customary. The Grand Duke, who had a hot temper, would be angry and storm, but his humour and habits were such that the greater the harshness he showed at first, even when he grievously insulted the offender, the sooner he would forgive him and himself take up his defence. Similar cases were not infrequent, and they were even sometimes sought after. Words do not hurt: and Svinin was very anxious to bring the matter to a favourable conclusion; but was it possible at night to obtain entrance to the palace and disturb the Grand Duke? To wait for morning and appear before Michael Pavlovich, after Kokoshkin had made his report to the Emperor, would be too late.

While Svinin was agitated by these difficulties he became more subtle, and his mind began to see another issue, which till then had been hidden as in a mist.

IX

Among other well-known military tactics there is the following: at the moment when the greatest danger is threatened from the walls of a beleagured fortress, not to retire, but to advance straight under its walls. Svinin decided not to do any of the things that had at first occurred to him, but to go straight to Kokoshkin.

Many terrible things were related at that time in Petersburg about the chief of police Kokoshkin, and many absurd things too, but among others it was affirmed that he possessed such wonderful resource and tact, that with the assistance of this tact he was not only able to make a mountain out of a molehill but that he was able as easily to make a molehill out of a mountain.

Kokoshkin was really very stern and very terrible, and inspired great fear in all who came in contact with him, but he sometimes showed mercy to the gay young scamps among the officers, and such young scamps were not few in those days, and they had often found in him a merciful and zealous protector. In a word, he was able to do much, and knew how to do it, if he only chose. Both Svinin and Captain Miller knew this side of his character. Miller therefore encouraged his superior officer to risk going to Kokoshkin, and trust to the general's magnanimity and resource and tact, which would probably suggest to him the means of getting out of this unpleasant situation, without incurring the anger of the Emperor, which Kokoshkin, to his honour be it said, always made great efforts to avoid.

Svinin put on his overcoat, looked up to heaven, murmured several times, "Good Lord! Good Lord!" and drove off to Kokoshkin.

It was already past four o'clock in the morning.

X

The chief of police Kokoshkin was aroused, and the arrival of Svinin, who had come on important business that could not be postponed, was reported to him.

The general got up at once and, with an overcoat wrapped round him, wiping his forehead, yawning and stretching himself, came out to receive Svinin. Kokoshkin listened with great attention, but quite calmly, to all Svinin had to relate. During all these explanations and requests for indulgence he only said:

"The soldier left his sentry-box, and saved a man?"

"Yes, sir," answered Svinin.

"And the sentry-box?"

"Remained empty during that time."

"H'm! I knew that it remained empty. I'm very pleased that nobody stole it."

Hearing this Svinin felt certain that the general knew all about the case, and that he had already decided in what manner he would place the facts before the Emperor in his morning's report, and also that he would not alter this decision. Otherwise such an event as a soldier of the Palace Guard having left his post would without doubt have caused greater alarm to the energetic chief of police.

But Kokoshkin did not know anything about it. The police inspector to whom the officer of the Invalid Corps had conveyed the man saved from drowning did not consider it a matter of great importance. In his sight it was not at all a subject that required him to awaken the weary chief of police in the middle of the night, and besides the whole event appeared to the inspector somewhat suspicious, because the officer of the Invalids' was quite dry, which certainly could not have been the case if he had saved a man from drowning at the risk of his own life. The inspector looked upon the officer as an ambitious liar, who wanted to obtain another medal for his breast, and therefore detained him while the clerk on duty was taking down his statement, and tried to arrive at the truth by asking about all sorts of minute details.

It was disagreeable for the inspector that such an event should have occurred in his district, and that the man had been saved, not by a policeman but by an officer of the Palace Guard.

Kokoshkin's calmness could be explained very simply: first, by his terrible fatigue, after a day of anxiety and hard work, and by his having assisted in the night at the extinguishing of two fires, and secondly because the act of the sentry Postnikov did not concern him, as Chief of Police, at all.

Nevertheless, Kokoshkin at once gave the necessary instructions.

He sent to the Inspector of the Admiralty Quarter and ordered him to come at once and bring the officer of the Invalid Corps and the man who had been saved with him, and asked Svinin to remain in the small waiting room adjoining his office. Then Kokoshkin went into his study, without closing the door, sat down at the table, and began to sign various papers, but he soon rested his head on his hand and fell asleep in his arm-chair at the table.

XI

In those days there were neither municipal telegraphs nor telephones, and in order to transmit the commands of the chiefs the "forty thousand couriers" of whom Gogol has left a lasting memory in his comedy had to ride post haste in all directions.

This of course was not so quickly done as by telegraph or telephone, but lent considerable animation to the town and proved that the authorities were indefatigably vigilant.

Before the breathless inspector, the life-saving officer, and the man rescued from drowning had time to come from the Admiralty police station the nervous and energetic General Kokoshkin had had time to have a snooze and refresh himself. This was seen in the expression of his face, and by the revival of his mental faculties.

Kokoshkin ordered all who had arrived to come to his study and with them Svinin too.

"The official report?" the General demanded of the Inspector.

The latter silently handed a folded paper to the General and then whispered in a low voice:

"I must beg permission to communicate a few words to your Excellency in private."

"Very well."

Kokoshkin went towards the bay-window followed by the Inspector.

"What is it?"

The Inspector's indistinct whispers could be heard, and the General's loud interjections.

"H'm, yes! Well, what then? . . . . It is possible. . . . . They take care to come out dry. . . . . Anything more?"

"Nothing, sir."

The General came out of the bay-window, sat down at his desk, and began to read. He read the report in silence without showing any signs of uneasiness or suspicion, and then turning to the man who had been saved, asked in a loud voice:

"How comes it, my friend, that you got into the open places before the Palace?"

"Forgive me!"

"So! You were drunk?"

"Excuse me, I was not drunk, but only tipsy."

"Why did you get into the water?"

"I wanted to cut across the ice, lost my way, and got into the water."

"That means it was dark before your eyes."

"It was dark; it was dark all round, your Excellency."

"And you were not able to notice who pulled you out?"

"Pardon me, I could not notice anything. I think it was he"—he pointed to the officer and added: "I could not distinguish anything. I was so scared."

"That's what it comes to. You were loafing about when you ought to have been asleep. Now look at him well and remember who was your benefactor. An honourable man risked his life to save you."

"I shall never forget it."

"Your name, sir?"

The officer mentioned his name.

"Do you hear?"

"I hear, your Excellency."

"You are Orthodox?"

"I am Orthodox, your Excellency."

"In your prayers for health, remember this man's name."

"I will write it down, your Excellency."

"Pray to God for him, and go away. You are no longer wanted."

He bowed to the ground and cleared off immeasurably pleased that he was released.

Svinin stood there, and could not understand how by God's grace things were taking such a turn.

XII

Kokoshkin turned to the officer of the Invalid Corps.

"You saved this man, at the risk of your own life?"

"Yes, your Excellency."

"There were no witnesses to this occurrence, and owing to the late hour there could not have been any?"

"Yes, your Excellency, it was dark, and on the quay there was nobody except the sentry."

"There is no need to mention the sentry; the sentry has to stand at his post and has no right to occupy himself with anything else. I believe what is written in this report. Was it not taken down from your words?"

These words Kokoshkin pronounced with special emphasis, as if he were threatening or shouting.

The officer did not falter, but with staring eyes and expanded chest, standing at attention, answered:

"From my words and quite correctly, your Excellency."

"Your action deserves a reward."

The officer bowed gratefully.

"There is nothing to thank for," continued Kokoshkin. "I shall report your self-sacrificing act to His Majesty the Emperor, and your breast may be decorated with a medal even to-day. Now you may go home, have a warm drink, and don't leave the house, as perhaps you may be wanted."

The officer of the Invalid Corps beamed all over, bowed and retired.

Kokoshkin looking after him said:

"It is possible that the Emperor may wish to see him."

"I understand," answered the Inspector, with apprehension.

"I do not require you any more."

The Inspector left the room, closed the door, and in accordance with his religious habit crossed himself.

The officer of the Invalids' was waiting for the Inspector below, and they went away together much better friends than when they had come.

Only Svinin remained in the study of the Chief of Police. Kokoshkin looked at him long and attentively, and then asked:

"You have not been to the Grand Duke?"

At that time when the Grand Duke was mentioned everybody knew that it referred to the Grand Duke Michael.

"I came straight to you," answered Svinin.

"Who was the officer on guard?"

"Captain Miller."

Kokoshkin again looked at Svinin and said:

"I think you told me something different before."

Svinin did not understand to what this could refer, and remained silent, and Kokoshkin added:

"Well, it's all the same; good night."

The audience was over.

XIII

About one o'clock the officer of the Invalids was really sent for by Kokoshkin, who informed him most amiably the Emperor was very much pleased that among the officers of the Invalids' Corps of his palace there were to be found such vigilant and self-sacrificing men, and had honoured him with the medal for saving life. Then Kokoshkin decorated the hero with his own hands, and the officer went away to swagger about town with the medal on his breast.

This affair could therefore be considered as quite finished, but Lieutenant-Colonel Svinin felt it was not concluded and regarded himself as called upon to put the dots on the "i's."

He had been so much alarmed that he was ill for three days, and on the fourth drove to the Peter House, had a service of thanksgiving said for him before the icon of the Saviour, and returning home reassured in his soul, sent to ask Captain Miller to come to him.

"Well, thank God, Nikolai Ivanovich," he said to Miller, "the storm that was hanging over us has entirely passed away, and our unfortunate affair with the sentry has been quite settled. I think we can now breathe freely. All this we owe without doubt first to the mercy of God, and secondly to General Kokoshkin. Let people say he is not kind and heartless, but I am full of gratitude for his magnanimity and respect for his resourcefulness and tact. In what a masterly way he took advantage of that vainglorious Invalid swindler, who, in truth, for his impudence ought to have received not a medal but a good thrashing in the stable. There was nothing else for him to do; he had to take advantage of this to save many, and Kokoshkin manoeuvred the whole affair so cleverly that nobody had the slightest unpleasantness; on the contrary, all are very happy and contented. Between ourselves, I can tell you, I have been infomed by a reliable person that Kokoshkin is very satisfied with me. He was pleased I had not gone anywhere else, but came straight to him, and that I did not argue with this swindler, who received a medal. In a word, nobody has suffered, and all has been done with so much tact that there can be no fear for the future; but there is one thing wanting on our side. We must follow Kokoshkin's example and finish the affair with tact on our side, so as to guarantee ourselves from any future occurrences. There is still one person whose position is not regulated. I speak of Private Postnikov. He is still lying in prison under arrest, no doubt troubled with the thoughts of what will be done to him. We must put an end to his torments."

"Yes, it is time," said Miller, delighted.

"Well, certainly, and you are the best man to do it. Please go at once to the barracks, call your company together, lead Private Postnikov out of prison, and let him be punished with two hundred lashes before the whole company."

XIV

Miller was astonished, and made an attempt to persuade Svinin to complete the general happiness by showing mercy to Private Postnikov, and to pardon him as he had already suffered so much while lying in prison awaiting his fate, but Svinin only got angry and did not allow Miller to continue.

"No," he broke in, "none of that! I have only just talked to you about tact and you at once are tactless! None of that!"

Svinin changed his tone to a dryer, more official one, and added sternly:

"And as in this affair you too are not quite in the right, but really much to blame because your softness of heart is quite unsuitable for a military man, and this deficiency of your character is reflected in your subordinates, therefore you are to be present personally at the execution of my orders and to see that the flogging is done seriously—as severely as possible. For this purpose have the goodness to give orders that the young soldiers who have just arrived from the army shall do the whipping, because our old soldiers are all infected with the liberalism of the guards. They won't whip a comrade properly, but would only frighten the fleas away from his back. I myself will look in to see that they have done the guilty man properly."

To evade in any way instructions given by a superior officer was of course impossible, and kind-hearted Captain Miller was obliged to execute with exactitude the orders received from the commander of his battalion.

The company was drawn up in the court-yard of the Ismailovsky barracks; the rods were fetched in sufficient quantities from the stores, and Private Postnikov was brought out of his prison and "done properly" at the hands of the zealous comrades, who had just arrived from the army. These men, who had not as yet been tainted by the liberalism of the guards, put all the dots on the i's to the full, as ordered by the commander of the battalion. Then Postnikov, having received his punishment, was lifted up on the overcoat on which he had been whipped and carried to the hospital of the regiment.

XV

The commander of the battalion, Svinin, as soon as he heard that the punishment had been inflicted, went at once to visit Postnikov in the hospital in a most fatherly way, and to satisfy himself by a personal examination that his orders had been properly executed. Heart-sore and nervous, Postnikov had been "done properly." Svinin was satisfied and ordered that Postnikov should receive, on his behalf, a pound of sugar and a quarter of a pound of tea with which to regale himself while he was recovering. Postnikov from his bed heard this order about tea and said:

"I am very contented your honour. Thank you for your fatherly kindness."

And he really was contented, because while lying three days in prison he had expected something much worse. Two hundred lashes, according to the strict ideas of those days, was of very little consequence in comparison with the punishments that people suffered by order of the military courts; and that is the sort of punishment he would have had awarded him if, by good luck, all the bold and tactful evolutions, which are related above, had not taken place.

But the number of persons who were pleased at the events just described was not limited to these.

XVI

The story of the exploit of Private Postnikov was secretly whispered in various circles of society in the capital, which in those days, when the public Press had no voice, lived in a world of endless gossip. In these verbal transmissions the name of the real hero, Private Postnikov, was lost, but instead of that the episode became embellished and received a very interesting and romantic character.

It was related that an extraordinary swimmer had swum from the side of the Peter and Paul Fortress, and had been fired at and wounded by one of the sentries stationed before the Winter Palace and an officer of the Invalid Guard, who was passing at the time, threw himself into the water and saved him from drowning, for which the one had received the merited reward, and the other the punishment he deserved. These absurd reports even reached the Conventual House, inhabited at that time by His Eminence, a high ecclesiastic, who was cautious but not indifferent to worldly matters, and who was benevolently disposed towards and a well-wisher of the pious Moscow family Svinin.

The story of the shot seemed improbable to the astute ecclesiastic. What nocturnal swimmer could it be? If he was an escaped prisoner, why was the sentry punished, for he had only done his duty in shooting at him, when he saw him swimming across the Neva from the fortress. If he was not a prisoner, but another mysterious man, who had to be saved from the waves of the Neva, how could the sentry know anything about him? And then again, it could not have happened as it was whispered in frivolous society. In society much is accepted in a light-hearted and frivolous manner, but those who live in monasteries and conventual houses look upon all this much more seriously and are quite conversant with the real things of this world.

XVII

Once when Svinin happened to be at His Eminence's to receive his blessing the distinguished dignitary began: "By the by, about that shot?" Svinin related the whole truth, in which there was nothing whatever "about that shot."

The high ecclesiastic listened to the real story in silence, gently touching his white rosary and never taking his eyes off the narrator. When Svinin had finished His Eminence quietly murmured in rippling speech:

"From all this one is obliged to conclude that in this matter the statements made were neither wholly nor on every occasion strictly true."

Svinin stammered and then answered with the excuse that it was not he but General Kokoshkin who had made the report.

His Eminence passed his rosary through his waxen fingers in silence, and then murmured:

"One must make a distinction between a lie and what is not wholly true."

Again the rosary, again silence, and at last a soft ripple of speech:

"A half truth is not a lie, but the less said about it the better."

Svinin was encouraged and said:

"That is certainly true. What troubles me most is that I had to inflict a punishment upon the soldier, who, although he had neglected his duty . . . ."

The rosary and a soft rippling interruption:

"The duties of service must never be neglected."

"Yes, but it was done by him through magnanimity, through sympathy after such a struggle, and with danger. He understood that in saving the life of another man he was destroying himself. This is a high, a holy feeling . . . ."

"Holiness is known to God; corporal punishment is not destruction for a common man, nor is it contrary to the customs of the nations, nor to the spirit of the Scriptures. The rod is easier borne by the coarse body than delicate suffering by the soul. In this case your justice has not suffered in the slightest degree."

"But he was deprived of the reward for saving one who was perishing."

"To save those who are perishing is not a merit, but rather a duty. He who could save but did not save is liable to the punishment of the laws; but he who saves does his duty."

A pause, the rosary, and soft rippling speech:

"For a warrior to suffer degradation and wounds for his action is perhaps much more profitable than marks of distinction. But what is most important is to be careful in this case, and never to mention anywhere or on any occasion what anybody said about it."

It was evident His Eminence was also satisfied.

XVIII

If I had the temerity of the happy chosen of Heaven, who through their great faith are enabled to penetrate into the secrets of the Will of God, then I would perhaps dare to permit myself the supposition that probably God Himself was satisfied with the conduct of Postnikov's humble soul, which He had created. But my faith is small; it does not permit my mind to penetrate so high. I am of the earth, earthy. I think of those mortals who love goodness, simply because it is goodness and do not expect any reward for it, wherever it may be. I think these true and faithful people will also be entirely satisfied with this holy impulse of love, and not less holy endurance of the humble hero of my true and artless story.

Guy de Maupassant
1850—1893

In a life cut short by venereal disease, De Maupassant published, as well as much other work, about 300 short stories. They establish him as the greatest of all the masters of the form, and have even obscured somewhat his outstanding achievements in longer narratives such as Yvette *and* Une Vie. *(Tolstoi, generally hostile to De Maupassant, regarded the latter as one of the great novels of all time).*

The image of De Maupassant in the New World is essentially ignorant and distorted. He has served as a convenient whipping-boy for every moralist from Nordau to Saurat, and has been typecast as a "smart" and iconoclastic author who pioneered sexual realism and cynical portrayals of brutal episodes. His range, his intellectual knowledge, his understandings, and his sympathies are, in fact, immense, and his observation and retention of physical particulars is almost as dazzling as Balzac's. He emerges as more productive and more versatile than his great mentor Flaubert, and possessed of greater constructive ability, critical intelligence, and sense of restraint than any of the group of writers with whom he originally associated, including Daudet and Zola.

De Maupassant accepted Poe's notion that a short story should contain "no word written, of which the tendency, direct or indirect, is not to the one pre-established design." In lucidity and economy he outstripped Poe and just about everyone else. Even in his slighter contes *his style in itself compels interest, though not as a mannered or* précieux *display: it is at every point unforced simplicity, vigor, and crispness. The admiration it elicits usually prevents even the most pathetic or brutal portrayals from becoming depressing or deeply repugnant.*

Though his work is obviously that of a man strongly sexed, athletic rather than bookish, and averse to all puritanism and pointless convention and hypocrisy, it advocates neither primitivism nor libertinism. Until the onset of his madness, De Maupassant's private life was far from wild. With women he was often the pursued rather than the pursuer. He managed his business affairs astutely. The homage he paid to law extended even to litigiousness. And like many other titled country gentlemen—a class he was content to belong to—he was an apolitical conservative.

Too much has been made of De Maupassant the "realist." He liked neither the word nor the concept. Tough-minded analyst of human weaknesses and follies, expert painter of unfortunates, of physical ugliness and moral deformity, he is. But seldom is he unnecessarily graphic, and he never offers Zola's confusion of art with pseudo-science, of selection and symbolization with pseudo-scientific roll-calls of minutiae. In certain respects De Maupassant belongs to romanticism. Somewhat like the romantic realist Balzac, he inspirits the reader by conveying his own intellectual delight in the feat of intensely succinct artistic portraiture. He repudiates prescription-bound French classicism and adopts the romantics' insistence on the writer's liberty to reject preconceived or customary rules and forms. He shares the romantics' fascination with woman and with the evocative power of water. The realists à la Zola *emphasized content; De Maupassant gave sovereignty to style and originality. The lyricism, tenderness, and good-natured humor in his work are all the more effective for being uneffusive. He would have endorsed Chekhov's advice to a fellow writer: "Try to be somewhat colder . . . . you have to be cold when you write touching stories . . . . The more objective you are, the stronger will be the impression you make."*

Though it sounds like egotism, De Maupassant's own assessment of his contribution is entirely accurate: "It was I who restored a pronounced taste for the short story and the novelette in France."

Mademoiselle Fifi

Guy de Maupassant

The Major Graf von Farlsberg, the Prussian commandant, was reading his newspaper, lying back in a great armchair, with his booted feet on the beautiful marble fireplace, where his spurs had made two holes which grew deeper every day during the three months that he had been in the château of Urville.

A cup of coffee was smoking on a small inlaid table which was stained with liqueurs, burnt by cigars, notched by the penknife of the victorious officer who occasionally would stop while sharpening a pencil to jot down figures or to make a drawing on it, just as it took his fancy.

When he had read his letters and the German newspapers which his baggagemaster had brought him he got up, and after throwing three or four enormous pieces of green wood onto the fire—for these gentlemen were gradually cutting down the park in order to keep themselves warm—he went to the window. The rain was descending in torrents, a regular Normandy rain, which looked as if it were being poured out by some furious hand, a slanting rain, which was as thick as a curtain and which formed a kind of wall with oblique stripes and which deluged everything, a regular rain, such as one frequently experiences in the neighborhood of Rouën, which is the watering pot of France.

For a long time the officer looked at the sodden turf and at the swollen Andelle beyond it, which was overflowing its banks, and he was drumming a waltz from the Rhine on the windowpanes with his fingers, when a noise made him turn round; it was his second in command, Captain Baron von Kelweinstein.

The major was a giant with broad shoulders and a long, fair beard, which hung like a cloth onto his chest. His whole solemn person suggested the idea of a military peacock, a peacock who was carrying his tail spread out onto his breast. He had cold, gentle blue eyes and the scar from a sword cut which he had received in the war with Austria; he was said to be an honorable man as well as a brave officer.

The captain, a short, red-faced man who was tightly girthed in at the waist, had his red hair cropped quite close to his head and in certain lights almost looked as if he had been rubbed over with phosphorus. He had lost two front teeth one night, though he could not quite remember how. This defect made him speak so that he could not always be understood, and he had a bald patch on the top of his head, which made him look rather like a monk with a fringe of curly, bright golden hair round the circle of bare skin.

The commandant shook hands with him and drank his cup of coffee (the sixth that morning) at a draught, while he listened to his subordinate's report of what had occurred; and then they both went to the window and declared that it was a very unpleasant outlook. The major, who was a quiet man with a wife at home, could accommodate himself to everything, but the captain, who was rather fast, being in the habit of frequenting low resorts and much given to women, was mad at having been shut up for three months in the compulsory chastity of that wretched hole.

There was a knock at the door, and when the commandant said, "Come in," one of their automatic soldiers appeared and by his mere presence announced that breakfast was ready. In the dining room they met three other officers of lower rank: a lieutenant, Otto von Grossling, and two sublieutenants, Fritz Scheunebarg and Count von Eyrick, a very short, fair-haired man, who was proud and brutal toward men, harsh toward prisoners and very violent.

Since he had been in France his comrades had called him nothing but "Mademoiselle Fifi." They had given him that nickname on account of his dandified style and small waist, which looked as if he wore stays, from his pale face, on which his budding mustache scarcely showed, and on account of the habit he had acquired of employing the French expression, *fi, fi donc*, which he pronounced with a slight whistle when he wished to express his sovereign contempt for persons or things.

The dining room of the château was a magnificent long room whose fine old mirrors, now cracked by pistol bullets, and Flemish tapestry, now cut to ribbons and hanging in rags in places from sword cuts, told too well what Mademoiselle Fifi's occupation was during his spare time.

There were three family portraits on the walls: a steel-clad knight, a cardinal and a judge, who were all smoking long porcelain pipes which had been inserted into holes in the canvas, while a lady in a long pointed waist proudly exhibited an enormous pair of mustaches drawn with a piece of charcoal.

The officers ate their breakfast almost in silence in that mutilated room which looked dull in the rain and melancholy under its vanquished appearance, although its old oak floor had become as solid as the stone floor of a public house.

When they had finished eating and were smoking and drinking, they began, as usual, to talk about the dull life they were leading. The bottle of brandy and of liqueurs passed from hand to hand, and all sat back in their chairs, taking repeated sips from their glasses and scarcely removing the long bent stems, which terminated in china bowls painted in a manner to delight a Hottentot, from their mouths.

As soon as their glasses were empty they filled them again with a gesture of resigned weariness, but Mademoiselle Fifi emptied his every minute, and a soldier immediately gave him another. They were enveloped in a cloud of strong tobacco smoke; they seemed to be sunk in a state of drowsy, stupid intoxication, in that dull state of drunkenness of men who have nothing to do, when suddenly the baron sat up and said: "By heavens! This cannot go on; we must think of something to do." And on hearing this, Lieutenant Otto and Sublieutenant Fritz, who pre-eminently possessed the grave, heavy German countenance, said: "What, Captain?"

He thought for a few moments and then replied: "What? Well, we must get up some entertainment if the commandant will allow us."

"What sort of an entertainment, Captain?" the major asked, taking his pipe out of his mouth.

"I will arrange all that, Commandant," the baron said. "I will send *Le Devoir* to Rouën, who will bring us some ladies. I know where they can be found. We will have supper here, as all the materials are at hand, and at least we shall have a jolly evening."

Graf von Farlsberg shrugged his shoulders with a smile: "You must surely be mad, my friend."

But all the other officers got up, surrounded their chief and said: "Let Captain have his own way, Commandant; it is terribly dull here."

And the major ended by yielding. "Very well," he replied, and the baron immediately sent for *Le Devoir*.

The latter was an old corporal who had never been seen to smile, but who carried out all orders of his superiors to the letter, no matter what they might be. He stood there with an impassive face while he received the baron's instructions and then went out; five minutes later a large wagon belonging to the military train, covered with a miller's tilt, galloped off as fast as four horses could take it under the pouring rain, and the officers all seemed to awaken from their lethargy; their looks brightened, and they began to talk.

Although it was raining as hard as ever, the major declared that it was not so dull, and Lieutenant von Grossling said with conviction that the sky was clearing up, while Mademoiselle Fifi did not seem to be able to keep in his place. He got up and sat down again, and his bright eyes seemed to be looking for something to destroy. Suddenly, looking at the lady with the mustaches, the young fellow pulled out his revolver and said: "You shall not see it." And without leaving his seat he aimed and with two successive bullets cut out both the eyes of the portrait.

"Let us make a mine!" he then exclaimed, and the conversation was suddenly interrupted, as if they had found some fresh and powerful subject of interest. The mine was his invention, his method of destruction and his favorite amusement.

When he left the château the lawful owner, Count Fernand d'Amoys d'Urville, had not had time to carry away or to hide anything except the plate, which had been stowed away in a hole made in one of the walls so that, as he was very rich and had good taste, the large drawing room, which opened into the dining room, had looked like the gallery in a museum before his precipitate flight.

Expensive oil paintings, water colors and drawings hung upon the walls, while on the tables, on the hanging shelves and in elegant glass cupboards there were a thousand knickknacks: small vases, statuettes, groups in Dresden china, grotesque Chinese figures, old ivory and Venetian glass, which filled the large room with their precious and fantastical array.

Scarcely anything was left now; not that the things had been stolen, for the major would not have allowed that, but Mademoiselle Fifi *would have a mine*, and on that occasion all the officers thoroughly enjoyed themselves for five minutes. The little marquis went into the drawing room to get what he wanted, and he brought back a small, delicate china teapot, which he filled with gunpowder, and carefully introduced a piece of German tinder into it, through the spout. Then he lighted it and took this infernal machine into the next room, but he came back immediately and shut the door. The Germans all stood expectantly, their faces full of childish, smiling curiosity, and as soon as the explosion had shaken the château they all rushed in at once.

Mademoiselle Fifi, who got in first, clapped his hands in delight at the sight of a terra-cotta Venus, whose head had been blown off, and each picked up pieces of porcelain and wondered at the strange shape of the fragments, while the major was looking with a paternal eye at the large drawing room which had been wrecked in such a Neronic fashion and which was strewn with the fragments of works of art. He went out first and said, with a smile: "He managed that very well!"

But there was such a cloud of smoke in the dining room mingled with the tobacco smoke that they could not breathe, so the commandant opened the window, and all the officers, who had gone into the room for a glass of cognac, went up to it.

The moist air blew into the room and brought a sort of spray with it which powdered their beards. They looked at the tall trees which were dripping with the rain, at the broad valley which was covered with mist and at the church spire in the distance which rose up like a gray point in the beating rain.

The bells had not rung since their arrival. That was the only resistance which the invaders had met with in the neighborhood. The parish priest had not refused to take in and to feed the Prussian soldiers; he had several times even drunk a bottle of beer or claret with the hostile commandant, who often employed him as a benevolent intermediary, but it was no use to ask him for a single stroke of the bells; he would sooner have allowed himself to be shot. That was his way of protesting against the invasion, a peaceful and silent protest, the only one, he said, which was suitable to a priest who was a man of mildness and not of blood; and everyone for twenty-five miles round praised Abbé Chantavoine's firmness and heroism in venturing to proclaim the public mourning by the obstinate silence of his church bells.

The whole village grew enthusiastic over his resistance and was ready to back up their pastor and to risk anything, as they looked upon that silent protest as the safeguard of the national honor. It seemed to the peasants that thus they had deserved better of their country than Belfort and Strassburg, that they had set an equally valuable example and that the name of their little village would become immortalized by that, but with that exception, they refused their Prussian conquerors nothing.

The commandant and his officers laughed among themselves at that inoffensive courage, and as the people in the whole country round showed themselves obliging and compliant toward them, they willingly tolerated their silent patriotism. Only little Count Wilhelm would have liked to have forced them to ring the bells. He was very angry at his superior's politic compliance with the priest's scruples, and every day he begged the commandant to allow him to sound "dingdong, dingdong" just once, only just once, just by way of a joke. And he asked it like a wheedling woman, in the tender voice of some mistress who wishes to obtain something, but the commandant would not yield, and to console *herself* Mademoiselle Fifi made a *mine* in the château.

The five men stood there together for some minutes, inhaling the moist air, and at last Subliertenant Fritz said with a laugh: "The ladies will certainly not have fine weather for their drive." Then they separated, each to his own duties, while the captain had plenty to do in seeing about the dinner.

When they met again as it was growing dark, they began to laugh at seeing each other as dandified and smart as on the day of a grand review. The commandant's hair did not look as gray as it did in the morning, and the captain had shaved—had only kept his mustache on, which made him look as if he had a streak of fire under his nose.

In spite of the rain they left the window open, and one of them went to listen from time to time. At a quarter past six the baron said he heard a rumbling in the distance. They all rushed down, and soon the wagon drove up at a gallop with its four horses, splashed up to their backs, steaming and panting. Five women got out at the bottom of the steps, five handsome girls whom a comrade of the captain, to whom *Le Devoir* had taken his card, had selected with care.

They had not required much pressing, as they were sure of being well treated, for they had got to know the Prussians in the three months during which they had had to do with them. So they resigned themselves to the men as they did to the state of affairs. "It is part of our business, so it must be done," they said as they drove along, no doubt to allay some slight, secret scruples of conscience.

They went into the dining room immediately, which looked still more dismal in its dilapidated state when it was lighted up, while the table, covered with choice dishes, the beautiful china and glass and the plate, which had been found in the hole in the wall, where its owner had hidden it, gave to the place the look of a bandits' resort, where they were supping after committing a robbery. The captain was radiant; he took hold of the women as if he were familiar with them, appraising them, kissing them, valuing them for what they were worth as *ladies of pleasure*, and when the three young men wanted to appropriate one each he opposed them authoritatively, reserving to himself the right to apportion them justly, according to their several ranks, so as not to wound the hierarchy. Therefore, so as to avoid all discussion, jarring and suspicion of partiality, he placed them all in a line according to height and addressing the tallest, he said in a voice of command:

"What is your name?"

"Pamela," she replied, raising her voice.

Then he said: "Number one, called Pamela, is adjudged to the commandant."

Then, having kissed Blondina, the second, as a sign of proprietorship, he proffered stout Amanda to Lieutenant Otto, Eva, "the Tomato," to Sublieutenant Fritz, and Rachel, the shortest of them all, a very young, dark girl, with eyes as black as ink, a Jewess, whose snub nose confirmed by exception the rule which allots hooked noses to all her race, to the youngest officer, frail Count Wilhelm von Eyrick.

They were all pretty and plump, without any distinctive features, and all were very much alike in look and person from their daily dissipation and the life common to houses of public accommodation.

The three younger men wished to carry off their women immediately, under the pretext of finding them brushes and soap, but the captain wisely opposed this, for he said they were quite fit to sit down to dinner and that those who went up would wish for a change when they came down, and so would disturb the other couples, and his experience in such matters carried the day. There were only many kisses, expectant kisses.

Suddenly Rachel choked and began to cough until the tears came into her eyes, while smoke came through her nostrils. Under pretense of kissing her the count had blown a whiff of tobacco into her mouth. She did not fly into a rage and did not say a word, but she looked at her possessor with latent hatred in her dark eyes.

They sat down to dinner. The commandant seemed delighted; he made Pamela sit on his right and Blondina on his left and said as he unfolded his table napkin: "That was a delightful idea of yours, Captain."

Lieutenants Otto and Fritz, who were as polite as if they had been with fashionable ladies, rather intimidated their neighbors, but Baron von Kelweinstein gave the reins to all his vicious propensities, beamed, made doubtful remarks and seemed on fire with his crown of red hair. He paid them compliments in French from the other side of the Rhine and sputtered out gallant remarks, only fit for a low pothouse, from between his two broken teeth.

They did not understand him, however, and their intelligence did not seem to be awakened until he uttered nasty words and broad expressions which were mangled by his accent. Then all began to laugh at once, like mad women, and fell against each other, repeating the words which the baron then began to say all wrong, in order that he might have the pleasure of hearing them say doubtful things. They gave him as much of that stuff as he wanted, for they were drunk after the first bottle of wine and, becoming themselves once more and opening the door to their usual habits, they kissed the mustaches on the right and left of them, pinched their arms, uttered furious cries, drank out of every glass and sang French couplets and bits of German songs which they had picked up in their daily intercourse with the enemy.

Soon the men themselves, intoxicated by that which was displayed to their sight and touch, grew very amorous, shouted and broke the plates and dishes, while the soldiers behind them waited on them stolidly. The commandant was the only one who put any restraint upon himself.

Mademoiselle Fifi had taken Rachel onto his knees and, getting excited, at one moment kissed the little black curls on her neck, inhaling the pleasant warmth of her body and all the savor of her person through the slight space there was between her dress and her skin, and at another pinched her furiously through the material and made her scream, for he was seized with a species of ferocity and tormented by his desire to hurt her. He often held her close to him, as if to make her part of himself, and put his lips in a long kiss on the Jewess's rosy mouth until she lost her breath, and at last he bit her until a stream of blood ran down her chin and onto her bodice.

For the second time she looked him full in the face, and as she bathed the wound she said: "You will have to pay for that!"

But he merely laughed a hard laugh and said: "I will pay."

At dessert champagne was served, and the commandant rose, and in the same voice in which he would have drunk to the health of the Empress Augusta he drank: "To our ladies!" Then a series of toasts began, toasts worthy of the lowest soldiers and of drunkards, mingled with filthy jokes which were made still more brutal by their ignorance of the language. They got up, one after the other, trying to say something witty, forcing themselves to be funny, and the women, who were so drunk that they almost fell off their chairs, with vacant looks and clammy tongues applauded madly each time.

The captain, who no doubt wished to impart an appearance of gallantry to the orgy, raised his glass again and said: "To our victories over hearts!" Thereupon Lieutenant Otto, who was a species of bear from the Black Forest, jumped up, inflamed and saturated with drink and seized by an access of alcoholic patriotism, cried: "To our victories over France!"

Drunk as they were, the women were silent, and Rachel turned round with a shudder and said: "Look here, I know some Frenchmen in whose presence you would not dare to say that." But the little count, still holding her on his knees, began to laugh, for the wine had made him very merry, and said: "Ha! ha! ha! I have never met any of them myself. As soon as we show ourselves they run away!"

The girl, who was in a terrible rage, shouted into his face: "You are lying, you dirty scoundrel!"

For a moment he looked at her steadily, with his bright eyes upon her, as he had looked at the portrait before he destroyed it with revolver bullets, and then he began to laugh: "Ah yes, talk about them, my dear! Should we be here now if they were brave?" Then, getting excited, he exclaimed: "We are the masters! France belongs to us!" She jumped off his knees with a bound and threw herself into her chair, while he rose, held out his glass over the table and repeated: "France and the French, the woods, the fields and the houses of France belong to us!"

The others, who were quite drunk and who were suddenly seized by military enthusiasm, the enthusiasm of brutes, seized their glasses and, shouting, "Long live Prussia!" emptied them at a draught.

The girls did not protest, for they were reduced to silence and were afraid. Even Rachel did not say a word, as she had no reply to make, and then the little count put his champagne glass, which had just been refilled, onto the head of the Jewess and exclaimed: "All the women in France belong to us also!"

At that she got up so quickly that the glass upset, spilling the amber-colored wine onto her black hair, as if to baptize her, and broke into a hundred fragments as it fell onto the floor. With trembling lips she defied the looks of the officer, who was still laughing, and she stammered out in a voice choked with rage: "That—that—that—is not true—for you shall certainly not have any French women."

He sat down again, so as to laugh at his ease and, trying effectually to speak in the Parisian accent, he said: "That is good, very good! Then what did you come here for, my dear?"

She was thunderstruck and made no reply for a moment, for in her agitation she did not understand him at first, but as soon as she grasped his meaning she said to him indignantly and vehemently: "I! I am not a woman; I am only a strumpet, and that is all that Prussians want."

Almost before she had finished he slapped her full in her face, but as he was raising his hand again, as if he would strike her, she, almost mad with passion, took up a small dessert knife from the table and stabbed him right in the neck, just above the breastbone. Something that he was going to say was cut short in his throat, and he sat there with his mouth half open and a terrible look in his eyes.

All the officers shouted in horror and leaped up tumultuously, but, throwing her chair between Lieutenant Otto's legs, who fell down at full length, she ran to the window, opened it before they could seize her and jumped out into the night and pouring rain.

In two minutes Mademoiselle Fifi was dead. Fritz and Otto drew their swords and wanted to kill the women, who threw themselves at their feet and clung to their knees. With some difficulty the major stopped the slaughter and had the four terrified girls locked up in a room under the care of two soldiers. Then he organized the pursuit of the fugitive as carefully as if he were about to engage in a skirmish, feeling quite sure that she would be caught.

The table, which had been cleared immediately, now served as a bed on which to lay Fifi out, and the four officers made for the window, rigid and sobered, with the stern faces of soldiers on duty, and tried to pierce through the darkness of the night, amid the steady torrent of rain. Suddenly a shot was heard and then another a long way off, and for four hours they heard from time to time near or distant reports and rallying cries, strange words uttered as a call in guttural voices.

In the morning they all returned. Two soldiers had been killed and three others wounded by their comrades in the ardor of that chase and in the confusion of such a nocturnal pursuit, but they had not caught Rachel.

Then the inhabitants of the district were terrorized; the houses were turned topsy-turvy; the country was scoured and beaten up over and over again, but the Jewess did not seem to have left a single trace of her passage behind her.

When the general was told of it he gave orders to hush up the affair so as not to set a bad example to the army, but he severely censured the commandant, who in turn punished his inferiors. The general had said: "One does not go to war in order to amuse oneself and to caress prostitutes." And Graf von Farlsberg, in his exasperation, made up his mind to have his revenge on the district, but as he required a pretext for showing severity, he sent for the priest and ordered him to have the bell tolled at the funeral of Count von Eyrick.

Contrary to all expectation, the priest showed himself humble and most respectful, and when Mademoiselle Fifi's body left the Château d'Urville on its way to the cemetery, carried by soldiers, preceded, surrounded and followed by soldiers, who marched with loaded rifles, for the first time the bell sounded its funereal knell in a lively manner, as if a friendly hand were caressing it. At night it sounded again, and the next day and every day; it rang as much as anyone could desire. Sometimes even it would start at night and sound gently through the darkness, seized by strange joy, awakened; one could not tell why. All the peasants in the neighborhood declared that it was bewitched, and nobody except the priest and the sacristan would now go near the church tower, and they went because a poor girl was living there in grief and solitude, secretly nourished by those two men.

She remained there until the German troops departed, and then one evening the priest borrowed the baker's cart and himself drove his prisoner to Rouën. When they got there he embraced her, and she quickly went back on foot to the establishment from which she had come, where the proprietress, who thought that she was dead, was very glad to see her.

A short time afterward a patriot who had no prejudices, who liked her because of her bold deed and who afterward loved her for herself, married her and made a lady of her.

Moonlight

Guy de Maupassant

The Abbé Marignan bore his fighting title well. He was a tall, thin priest, always in a state of mental exaltation, and without guile. All his beliefs were fixed, with never a wavering. He honestly believed that he knew his God, that he could fathom His desires, His will, His purposes.

When he strode along the path of his little country rectory, a question sometimes arose in his mind, "Why did God do thus?" And he persistently sought the reason, mentally assuming God's place; and he almost always found it. He would not have murmured, in an outburst of pious humility, "O Lord, Thy designs are past finding out!" He said to himself, "I am God's servant; it is my duty to know the reasons for His actions, and to divine them if I know them not."

Everything in Nature seemed to him to be created with absolute and marvellous logicality. The "why" and the "because" always balanced. The dawn was made that our waking might be cheerful, the day to ripen the crops, the rain to water them, the evenings to prepare for slumber, and the dark nights to sleep.

The four seasons provided perfectly for all the necessities of agriculture; and the priest was utterly unable to harbour such a thought as that Nature acts without design, and that all living things are subjected to the stern necessities of time, of climate, and of matter.

But he hated woman; he hated her unconscionably, and instinctively despised her. He often repeated the words of Christ, "Woman, what have I to do with thee?" And he would add, "One would think that God Himself was displeased with that work of His hands." Woman was to him the "child twelve times unclean" of whom the poet sings. She was the tempter who had led the first man astray, and who ever continued her work of damnation; a weak, dangerous, mysteriously disquieting creature. And even more bitterly than her body of perdition, he hated her loving heart.

He had often been conscious that women had fixed their affections upon him; but, although he knew that he was impervious to attack, he was enraged by that craving for love with which they were always aquiver.

In his opinion God created woman only to tempt man and to put him to the test. One should not approach her without defensive precautions, and the same fear that one has of traps. In truth, she closely resembled a trap, with her lips open and her arms outstretched towards man.

He had no indulgence save for nuns, whom their vows rendered harmless; but he treated them harshly none the less, because he felt that, even in the depths of their fettered and humbled hearts, there still lived that everlasting affection, which went out to him, priest though he was.

He felt it in their glances, which were more melting with pious fervour than those of the monks; in those ecstatic transports in which their sex was wont to indulge; in their outbursts of love towards the Christ, which angered him because it was woman's love, carnal love; he was conscious of that accursed tenderness in their very docility, in the softness of their voices when they spoke to him, in their downcast eyes, and in their submissive tears when he reproved them roughly.

And he would shake his cassock when he went out of the door of the convent, and would stride swiftly away as if he were flying from some danger.

He had a niece who lived with her mother in a small house near by. He strove earnestly to make her a Sister of Charity.

She was a pretty creature, giddy and bantering. When the abbé preached at her, she laughed; and when he lost his temper with her, she would embrace him passionately, pressing him to her heart, while he instinctively tried to extricate himself from that embrace, which nevertheless caused him a delicious thrill of pleasure, arousing in the depths of his being that instinct of fatherhood which slumbers in every man.

He often spoke to her of God, of his God, as he walked by her side along the country roads. She hardly listened to him, but gazed at the sky, the grass, and the flowers, with a joy in living that could be read in her eyes. Sometimes she would dart away to catch some flying thing, and would exclaim as she brought it back, "See how pretty it is, uncle; I would like to kiss it." And that longing to kiss insects or lilac flowers disturbed, irritated, and disgusted the priest, who recognised therein that ineradicable tenderness which is always budding in a woman's heart.

And behold one day the sacristan's wife, who did Abbé Marignan's housework, informed him cautiously that his niece had a lover.

He was terribly shocked, and stood gasping for breath, with his face covered with lather, for he was shaving.

When he was once more in condition to think and to speak, he cried:

"That is not true; you are lying, Mélanie!"

But the peasant woman placed her hand over her heart:

"May our Lord judge me if I am lying, Monsieur le Curé. I tell you that she goes out every night as soon as your sister's gone to bed. They meet down by the river. All you need to do is just go there, and see for yourself, between ten o'clock and midnight."

He ceased to scrape his chin, and began to pace the floor excitedly, as he always did when he was engaged in serious meditation. When he concluded to return to his shaving, he cut himself three times, from nose to ear.

All day long he said not a word, bursting with indignation and wrath. His priestly rage, in face of love unconquerable, was intensified by the moral exasperation of a father, a guardian, entrusted with the keeping of a soul, who has been deceived, robbed, tricked by a mere child; the selfish, suffocating wrath of parents to whom their daughter declares that she has chosen a husband, without their help and in spite of them.

After dinner he tried to read a little, but he could not do it; and he became more and more indignant. When the clock struck ten he seized his cane, a formidable oaken staff which he always used in his walks at night when he went out to visit some sick person. And he glanced with a smile at the huge cudgel as he twirled it threateningly in his muscular countryman's fist. Then, of a sudden, he sprang to his feet, and, grinding his teeth, brought it down upon a chair, the back of which fell shattered to the floor.

He opened his door to go out; but paused in the doorway, surprised by such a splendour of moonlight as one seldom sees.

And as he was blessed with an exalted imagination, of the sort that the Fathers of the Church, those poetic dreamers, must have had, he suddenly became distraught, profoundly moved by the grand yet tranquil beauty of the pallid night.

In his little garden, bathed with soft light, his fruit-trees, set in rows, cast the shadow of their slender limbs, scarce clothed with verdure, on the gravelled paths; while the giant honeysuckle clinging to the wall of his house exhaled a fragrant, as it were a sweetened breath, so that a sort of perfumed soul seemed to hover about in the warm, clear evening.

He began to breathe deep, drinking the air as drunkards drink their wine, and he walked slowly, enchanted, wonder-struck, his niece almost forgotten.

When he had gained the open country, he stopped to gaze upon the broad expanse, all inundated by that caressing radiance, drowned in the soft and languorous charm of a cloudless night. The frogs at every instant threw into space their short, metallic notes, and the distant nightingales added their rippling music, which induces dreams without thought—that airy, vibrating melody, made to serve as an accompaniment to kisses, to moonlight seduction.

The abbé walked on, with a sinking at his heart which he could not understand. He felt as it were enfeebled, suddenly exhausted; he longed to sit down, and to remain there, in contemplation, marvelling at God in all His work.

Farther on, following the curving of the little stream, wound a row of white poplars. A fine haze, a white vapour through which the moon's rays shone, turning it to glistening silver, hung about and above the banks, enveloping the whole winding course of the stream with a sort of light, transparent down.

Again the priest halted, stirred to the depths of his soul by an increasing, irresistible emotion. And a doubt, a vague disquietude stole over him; he felt the birth within him of one of those problems which he sometimes propounded to himself.

Why had God done this? As the night was intended for sleep, for oblivion, for rest, why make it lovelier than the day, softer than the dawn and the sunsets; and why did that stately, seductive star, more poetic than the sun, and to all seeming (so discreet it is) destined to shine upon things too delicate, too mysterious for the broad light of day—why was it come to brighten all the shades?

Why did not the most talented of singing birds rest like the others, instead of performing in the disquieting darkness?

Why was this half-veil cast over the world? Why this fluttering of the heart, this emotion of the soul, this languor of the flesh?

Why this display of charms which men never see, because they are in their beds? For whom was this sublime spectacle intended, that profusion of poetic beauty cast from heaven upon earth?

The abbé did not understand.

But behold, at the end of the field, beneath the arched trees wet with glistening mist, two shadows appeared, walking side by side.

The man was the taller and had his arm about his sweetheart's neck; and from time to time he kissed her on the forehead. They animated suddenly the lifeless landscape, which enveloped them like a divine frame fashioned for them. They seemed a single being, the being for whom that tranquil and silent night was made; and they walked towards the priest, like a living answer, his Master's answer, to his question.

He stood there, overwhelmed, his heart beating fast; and he fancied that he had before him some biblical scene, like the loves of Ruth and Boaz—the accomplishment of the Lord's will in one of those magnificent settings spoken of in Holy Writ. The verses of the Song of Songs began to hum in his ears—the ardent cries, the cravings of the body, all the glowing poetry of that poem aflame with love.

And he said to himself, "Perhaps God has made such nights, in order to throw a veil of idealism over the loves of men."

He withdrew before this couple who went ever arm in arm. It was his niece, to be sure; but he asked himself if he had not been on the point of disobeying God. And must it not be that love is lawful in God's sight, since He visibly encompasses it with such splendour?

And he fled, bewildered, almost ashamed, as if he had penetrated into a temple where he had not the right to go.

Love

Guy de Maupassant

I have just read among the general news in one of the papers a drama of passion. He killed her and then he killed himself, so he must have loved her. What matters He or She? Their love alone matters to me, and it does not interest me because it moves me or astonishes me or because it softens me or makes me think, but because it recalls to my mind a remembrance of youth, a strange recollection of a hunting adventure where Love appeared to me, as the Cross appeared to the early Christians, in the midst of the heavens.

I was born with all the instincts and the senses of primitive man, tempered by the arguments and the restraints of a civilized being. I am passionately fond of shooting, yet the sight of the wounded animal, of the blood on its feathers and on my hands, affects my heart so as almost to make it stop.

That year the cold weather set in suddenly toward the end of autumn, and I was invited by one of my cousins, Karl de Rauville, to go with him and shoot ducks on the marshes at daybreak.

My cousin was a jolly fellow of forty with red hair, very stout and bearded, a country gentleman, an amiable semibrute of a happy disposition and endowed with that Gallic wit which makes even mediocrity agreeable. He lived in a house, half farmhouse, half château, situated in a broad valley through which a river ran. The hills right and left were covered with woods, old manorial woods where magnificent trees still remained and where the rarest feathered game in that part of France was to be found. Eagles were shot there occasionally, and birds of passage, such as rarely venture into our overpopulated part of the country, invariably lighted amid these giant oaks as if they knew or recognized some little corner of a primeval forest which had remained there to serve them as a shelter during their short nocturnal halt.

In the valley there were large meadows watered by trenches and separated by hedges; then, further on, the river, which up to that point had been kept between banks, expanded into a vast marsh. That marsh was the best shooting ground I ever saw. It was my cousin's chief care, and he kept it as a preserve. Through the rushes that covered it, and made it rustling and rough, narrow passages had been cut, through which flat-bottomed boats, impelled and steered by poles, passed along silently over dead water, brushing up against the reeds and making the swift fish take refuge in the weeds and the wild fowl, with their pointed black heads, dive suddenly.

I am passionately fond of the water; of the sea, though it is too vast, too full of movement, impossible to hold; of the rivers which are so beautiful but which pass on and flee away; and above all of the marshes, where the whole unknown existence of aquatic animals palpitates. The marsh is an entire world in itself on the world of earth—a different world which has its own life, its settled inhabitants, and its passing travelers, its voices, its noises and above all its mystery. Nothing is more impressive, nothing more disquieting, more terrifying occasionally, than a fen. Why should a vague terror hang over these low plains covered with water? Is it the low rustling of the rushes, the strange will-o'-the-wisp lights, the silence which prevails on calm nights, the still mists which hang over the surface like a shroud; or is it the almost inaudible splashing, so slight and so gentle, yet some times more terrifying than the cannons of men or the thunders of the skies, which make these marshes resemble countries one has dreamed of, terrible countries holding an unknown and dangerous secret?

No, something else belongs to it—another mystery, perhaps the mystery of the creation itself! For was it not in stagnant and muddy water, amid the heavy humidity of moist land under the heat of the sun, that the first germ of life pulsated and expanded to the day?

I arrived at my cousin's in the evening. It was freezing hard enough to split the stones.

During dinner, in the large room whose sideboards, walls and ceiling were covered with stuffed birds with wings extended or perched on branches to which they were nailed—hawks, herons, owls, nightjars, buzzards, tercels, vultures, falcons—my cousin, who, dressed in a sealskin jacket, himself resembled some strange animal from a cold country, told me what preparations he had made for that same night.

We were to start at half-past three in the morning so as to arrive at the place he had chosen for our watching place at about half-past four. On that spot a hut had been built of lumps of ice so as to shelter us somewhat from the trying wind which precedes daybreak, a wind so cold as to tear the flesh like a saw, cut it like the blade of a knife, prick it like a poisoned sting, twist it like a pair of pincers and burn it like fire.

My cousin rubbed his hands. "I have never known such a frost," he said; "it is already twelve degrees below zero at six o'clock in the evening."

I threw myself onto my bed immediately after we had finished our meal and went to sleep by the light of a bright fire burning in the grate.

At three o'clock he woke me. In my turn I put on a sheepskin and found my cousin Karl covered with a bearskin. After having each swallowed two cups of scalding coffee, followed by glasses of liqueur brandy, we started, accompanied by a gamekeeper and our dogs, Plongeon and Pierrot.

From the first moment that I got outside I felt chilled to the very marrow. It was one of those nights on which the earth seems dead with cold. The frozen air becomes resisting and palpable, such pain does it cause; no breath of wind moves it, it is fixed and motionless; it bites you, pierces through you, dries you, kills the trees, the plants, the insects, the small birds themselves, who fall from the branches onto the hard ground and become stiff themselves under the grip of the cold.

The moon, which was in her last quarter and was inclining all to one side, seemed fainting in the midst of space, so weak that she was unable to wane, forced to stay up yonder, seized and paralyzed by the severity of the weather. She shed a cold mournful light over the world, that dying and wan light which she gives us every month at the end of her period.

Karl and I walked side by side, our backs bent, our hands in our pockets and our guns under our arms. Our boots, which were wrapped in wool so that we might be able to walk without slipping on the frozen river, made no sound, and I looked at the white vapor which our dogs' breath made.

We were soon on the edge of the marsh and entered one of the lanes of dry rushes which ran through the low forest.

Our elbows, which touched the long ribbonlike leaves, left a slight noise behind us, and I was seized, as I had never been before, by the powerful and singular emotion which marshes cause in me. This one was dead, dead from cold, since we were walking on it in the middle of its population of dried rushes.

Suddenly, at the turn of one of the lanes, I perceived the ice hut which had been constructed to shelter us. I went in, and as we had nearly an hour to wait before the wandering birds would awake I rolled myself up in my rug in order to try and get warm. Then, lying on my back, I began to look at the misshapen moon, which had four horns through the vaguely transparent walls of this polar house. But the frost of the frozen marshes, the cold of these walls, the cold from the firmament penetrated me so terribly that I began to cough. My cousin Karl became uneasy.

"No matter if we do not kill much today," he said. "I do not want you to catch cold; we will light a fire." And he told the gamekeeper to cut some rushes.

We made a pile in the middle of our hut, which had a hole in the middle of the roof to let out the smoke, and when the red flames rose up to the clear crystal blocks they began to melt, gently, imperceptibly, as if they were sweating. Karl, who had remained outside, called out to me: "Come and look here!" I went out of the hut and remained struck with astonishment. Our hut, in the shape of a cone, looked like an enormous diamond with a heart of fire which had been suddenly planted there in the midst of the frozen water of the marsh. And inside we saw fantastic forms, those of our dogs, who were warming themselves at the fire.

But a peculiar cry, a lost, a wandering cry, passed over our heads, and the light from our hearth showed us the wild birds. Nothing moves one so much as the first clamor of a life which one does not see, which passes through the somber air so quickly and so far off, just before the first streak of a winter's day appears on the horizon. It seems to me, at this glacial hour of dawn, as if that passing cry which is carried away by the wings of a bird is the sigh of a soul from the world!

"Put out the fire," said Karl; "It is getting daylight."

The sky was, in fact, beginning to grow pale, and the flights of ducks made long rapid streaks which were soon obliterated on the sky.

A stream of light burst out into the night; Karl had fired, and the two dogs ran forward.

And then nearly every minute now he, now I, aimed rapidly as soon as the shadow of a flying flock appeared above the rushes. And Pierrot and Plongeon, out of breath but happy, retrieved the bleeding birds whose eyes still, occasionally, looked at us.

The sun had risen, and it was a bright day with a blue sky, and we were thinking of taking our departure, when two birds with extended necks and outstretched wings glided rapidly over our heads. I fired, and one of them fell almost at my feet. It was a teal with a silver breast, and then, in the blue space above me, I heard a voice, the voice of a bird. It was a short, repeated, heart-rending lament; and the bird, the little animal that had been spared, began to turn round in the blue sky over our heads, looking at its dead companion which I was holding in my hand.

Karl was on his knees, his gun to his shoulder, watching it eagerly until it should be within shot. "You have killed the duck," he said, "and the drake will not fly away."

He certainly did not fly away; he circled over our heads continually and continued his cries. Never have any groans of suffering pained me so much as that desolate appeal, as that lamentable reproach of this poor bird which was lost in space.

Occasionally he took flight under the menace of the gun which followed his movements and seemed ready to continue his flight alone, but as he could not make up his mind to this he returned to find his mate.

"Leave her on the ground," Karl said to me; "he will come within shot by and by," And he did indeed come near us, careless of danger, infatuated by his animal love, by his affection for his mate which I had just killed.

Karl fired, and it was as if somebody had cut the string which held the bird suspended. I saw something black descend, and I heard the noise of a fall among the rushes. And Pierrot brought it to me.

I put them—they were already cold—into the same gamebag, and I returned to Paris the same evening.

Emile Pouvillon
1840—1906

Pouvillon's modest but abiding ambition was to render authentic portraits of the people and places of his native Garonne, a rural and sparsely populated area bordering on Spain. He admired the realism of Zola and titled his first book—a collection of short stories— Nouvelles Réalistes *(1878). But he was too strongly attracted to the health and poetry of the outdoors to feel inclined to follow Zola's lead in reportorial accounts of urban depravities. His masterpiece in pastoral realism is* Césette: the History of a Peasant Girl *(1881), a novel acclaimed by the French Academy. But the critical success of that book brought the author neither fame nor many readers.*

Throughout the 1880s Pouvillon produced several other novels; in the 1890s he wrote a number of plays. His latest collections of short stories were Le Cheval bleu *(1888) and* Petites gens *(1905). All were written in a style plain but not naïve, yet they availed no more than* Césette *to widen his reputation or readership. To this day Pouvillon remains one of the most neglected talents in French letters, and very little of his work has been translated.*

Pouvillon dedicated his novel L'Innocent *(1884) to Pierre Loti, prose-poet of the local color of exotic places. The affinity for the master stylist and romancer Loti—in every way the antithesis of Zola—to whom Pouvillon apologizes for using five words native to*

Garonne but not to classical French, again shows the author's concern for expression, his essential modesty and independence of literary and ideological schools.

"Duck Shooting," a story worthy of De Maupassant at his best, is also reminiscent of De Maupassant in its efficiency and strength, effects achieved largely by fusing, rather than separating, descriptive detail and action, so that all is forward movement, dramatic thrust. The story's never-belabored parallel between the animal and human worlds rises into poetry and into one of the most impressive endings in the history of narration.

Duck Shooting

Emile Pouvillon

"And when is the wedding?" I asked my friend, Vidian Sorède.

We had not seen each other for years, and he was telling me of his approaching marriage, while the carriage, which had come to fetch me on the arrival of the night train, took us, all booted and rigged out from head to foot, to the meeting-place at Saint Nazaire, where the famous wild-duck shooting, praised on every occasion by my friend, was about to take place.

"My marriage?" replied Vidian; "it was settled to take place just before Lent, the contract drawn up, the wedding presents ordered at Toulouse. And now everything is put off to Easter, or to Trinity Sunday, perhaps. A whim of my future sister-in-law! I do not know what has come over her. Very bright, very charming and friendly with me when she came from the convent school. Then all of a sudden a complete change; a face of woe. She is upset at any talk about the marriage. Swears she will die of grief if she is separated from her sister."

"Jealous of you?"

"No doubt. Unless it is some religious mania working in her. She has her own ideas about marriage. Men horrify her, and she is scarcely fifteen. She wants a good whipping."

"A spoilt child! Unless . . . You do not think . . . It cannot be that . . ."

An explanation had struck me, but the matter was so delicate I hesitated to speak of it. Useless to trouble this simple-hearted Vidian, and put him perhaps on a false trail.

Besides, our chat was over: we had arrived. Beneath the pale radiance of the stars, the house of the Rudelles, the future parents by marriage of my friend Sorède, loomed before us, big and lonely, between the lake, the mountain, and the sea. The approach of the duck shooting filled it that night with a joyful tumult. In a very large dining-room, used for long country meals and yearly feasts, the lady of the house and her two daughters were looking after the guests, while our host, a patriarch in marsh boots, a sailor's oil-skin over his shoulder, went from one to the other shaking hands and exchanging forecasts of the weather.

A little on one side, in the bay of a window, Vidian was talking gaily to his sweetheart, Estelle, a lovely girl, a flower of twenty years, with a splendid figure. Thérèse, the younger girl, watched them from afar, with evil glances showing beneath her eyelashes, sudden flashes that lighted up for the moment her long pale form, pale with almost the greenish tinge of growing youth. Jealous certainly. But of whom? of Vidian, or of Estelle?

Our host, however, signed to us to depart. Not a moment to lose if we wished to surprise the velvet ducks, and surround them in their nocturnal haunts.

Outside the day was breaking. Behind us, westward, above the black mass of the houses of Saint Nazaire, the Canigou shot aloft, a white phantom alongside the pale-blue chaos of the Albères. Opposite, between a terrace of vineyards and the thin line of an isthmus of sand that separated it from the sea, the widespread sheet of a lake twinkled behind a curtain of wandering haze.

Boats were waiting for us a few steps from the house: a score of black-bottomed wherries, with prows rising in a crosier shape, like the ships of the ancient Greeks. Primitive also, in keeping with his boat, was the silent chewer of quids, a pensioned sailor, who helped us with our boxes of cartridges and our spare oars.

At the order of Rudelle, supreme head and organiser of the shoot, the flotilla got under way and set out to conquer the lake. Upright in the bows, we scanned the sky-line in search of the famous velvet ducks. Nothing yet. Not a sign of life on the vast plain just beginning to be wrinkled by the early morning breeze. Then, as the wind grew in strength, the mists lifted. On our left, then, close to the shore, a movement was seen.

Sometimes bright, sometimes obscure, according as they turned their backs or bellies to the light, flocks of sea-birds arose, oscillating between the land and the lake. Ducks! In long, in slow movements, like a swarm of anxious ghosts on the banks of Styx, they floated, frightened, hesitating between the noises of the land and the line of boats that cut off their retreat from the side of the lake. But soon, as under orders, the different individuals fell into their places and the wild whirl was organised. Two flocks with their leaders and their rearguard drew off in a spiral climb, and when they were out of reach of our guns, passed slowly over our heads and disappeared like travelling clouds towards the high seas.

"Good-bye to the common ducks, and welcome to the velvet ducks! Can you see them over there?" said Vidian to me. "The dance is about to begin. Attention!"

The boats now were deploying in a semicircle towards the shore. At the same time some black points were stirring on the water: the heavy wings arose, fell back again, and restless heads appeared between two dives. The velvet-backs were there. A gunshot made them resolved to flee. But instead of the skilful and well-ordered retreat of the ordinary ducks, this was the wild chance scurry of a stampede. In twos and threes the birds rose up and tried to pass over the wall of boats. Taken between two fires and half massacred, they stopped in full flight and fell back in heaps on the water. And after them came others—a fusillade of fifteen minutes' sheer slaughter.

Vidian never stopped firing and recharging. He thought no more about his marriage, Vidian. Love was far away, and the smile of his dark-haired lady-love and the hostile glance of the little sister were forgotten. He was given over entirely to the passion of the hunter, the joy of murder. And the faces of the other shooters, in view on the neighbouring boats, had all the same expression of triumphant brutality. The elemental feelings of the race, the privateers and the fierce mountain fighters of old, came fully out in the cries and the gestures of these civilized men, plunged for the moment back into the barbarity of their ancestors. The spectacle of the victims, the dead bodies heaped up in the bottom of our boat, aggravated the repugnance, the nausea with which this festival of blood and death filled me. And the carnage, finishing here, began again farther off. The flotilla, dispersed for the moment in search of the wounded and the dead, reformed and dashed in pursuit of the unhappy creatures escaped from the slaughter. My gorge rose. I pretended I was tired by my long journey and sickened by the motion of the boat dancing on the waves. I landed.

Stretched out on the warm sands of the dune, I watched the flotilla lessen in size as it went far away over the lake. I heard the sound of the firing move away and thin out. Then, suddenly, all around me the sweetness of silence and the boon of solitude were felt. Some chickens were pecking on the threshold of the fisherman's hut, a hut of reeds that evoked the stillness of the desert, plundering the first frail flowers of spring, and through a break in the dunes the surf of the sea reached me with a vision of a sail, of a fringe of foam twinkling suddenly on the crest of a wave, abruptly, with a bewildered beat of wings, the velvetbacks alighted two steps from the shore. Ignorant of danger, forgetful of the others, of the unhappy creatures who fell over there under the guns, they will soon begin to play, to pitch over, to dig in the mud in search of food. . . . The arrival of Vidian and his boat interrupted my reflections. Vidian was exalted—three double shots, and I don't know how many single ones, a score and a half of coots, and as many velvetbacks—a triumph!

My want of interest extinguished his enthusiasm. Our return was a dull affair. As though the last shot fired in the air by the hunters had wounded the sun, daylight faded very quickly. On high, towards the sunset, the snows of the Canigou took on mournful tints and livid, ghastly colours. The lake grew pale. The agonies of dying birds, palpitating in the hollow of the waves, trails of feathers floated here and there, funereal flotsam. In silence we let ourselves sway to the rhythm of the slow melody—an old song in Catalanian—that the old rower sang to the knocking of his oars against the rowlocks.

Madame Rudelle and her daughters were waiting for us at the landing-stage, cries of joy welcomed the hunters, and Vidian was hailed as the king of the battle. But Thérèse was upset at the sight of the blood remaining on the hand of the hero.

"You are wounded!" she exclaimed, in an outburst that revealed the secret of her heart, of her little sorrowful heart that did not know its own feelings.

"Little silly!" laughed Estelle. "Don't you see it is only the blood of the birds!"

The boats were beached, the kill was counted and taken into the house. As soon as they entered the hunters sat down and gathered round the table. It was the bestiality of eating after the brutality of carnage, and jokes, hunting stories, boasts of wonderful kills, suggested by the day's shooting and deep draughts of wine.

I watched Thérèse, silent before an empty plate. Sulking over the dinner as she had over the shooting, the sad child spied on Vidian and Estelle who were sitting opposite her, and, isolated amid the laughing and chatter, pursuing their loving conversation.

At dessert, one of the guests proposed the health of the lovers. Glasses were raised in their honour, but Thérèse's glass slipped from her fingers and broke as it fell on the table. The act had been beyond her strength! She had fainted. They carried her away, pale as a corpse. Estelle and Vidian accompanied the bearers as far as the bedroom. The meal ended, the guests departed, before the sick girl appeared again.

"Good news!" said Vidian to me a little later, as we in turn left Saint Nazaire. "Thérèse has recovered, and I shall be married in a month. She knew well what she was doing, the little sly thing. Thanks to her attack of nerves, she has got what she was asking for. Her parents have given up trying to tame her, and are sending her back to the convent. Let her stay there and leave us alone, especially as she now wants to become a nun."

We climbed up the hill above the village. Below, the lake slept under the moon. The straw huts of the fishermen by the shore, the farmsteads in the vineyards, with their hedges of cypress and thuyas, slumbered, wrapped in the stillness of night. But my nerves, still vibrating from the double drama of the day, were bent on evoking in my mind, across the peace and silence of the present hour, the images of murder and sorrow that had shaken them since the morning. I thought of the velvet-backs, I thought of Thérèse. I had before me now the scared flight, with necks stretched out to the sea, of the poor innocent birds reeling under the gun-fire, now the pale figure of the little passionate child, struck down in a moment by the storms of this world, and who escaped, with beating wings, towards heaven.

Honoré de Balzac

1799—1850

Educated for the law, and displaying no precocious talent for imaginative writing, Balzac quite unpredictably became the creator of the modern realistic novel and the author of what remains the most impressive body of fiction in modern letters: The Human Comedy. *Before his death he had fitted ninety novels (as well as some shorter works), many of them intricately inter-related, into this thousand-character panorama of French society between 1789 and 1850.*

A lover of pre-republican France, and politically a passionate but also clear-sighted ultra-royalist, Balzac was one of the earliest acute critics of both the new bourgeois-capitalist order arising out of the French Revolution and the still newer socialist alternatives. His historical and political portraiture and interpretation are almost invariably accurate and fair as well as vivid. In fact, he constitutes a striking exception to the widely and uncritically accepted principle that one cannot be both passionate and objective. His work offers a refreshing alternative to modern history books, most of which are consciously or unconsciously biased in favor of the progressivist version of history. But Balzac's historical orientation is seldom self-consciously or pedantically contrived. He simply sets his native genius tracking the universal in distinctly historical settings. One reads him for the literature; the history picked up along the way is a side-benefit.

In vibrancy and memorableness, many of his purely fictional characters rank with the creations of Shakespeare. Vautrin has become a byword for unscrupulous criminal machination, Eugénie Grandet for tortured purity of heart, Old Goriot for the pater familias ruined by indulgence of his children. Balzac is one of the great creators of female characters who are at once individualized and representative of perennial types. He is no sentimentalist over the sex—witness the spidery Cousin Bette and the niggardly and venal Mme. Vauquer—but he has an unusually well developed intuitive understanding of the special difficulties entailed in being a woman—difficulties heightened, rather than lessened, he thought, by the advent of modernity. In his personal life he unfailingly honored all the women he knew and saw. His marriage to Mme. Hanska, however, was not a lucky one; the only good fortune in it was that it happened in his very last year.

Balzac was a batteur de pavement. Among writers, perhaps only Francis Thompson was as much of a walker. And he walked not idly, though also not in the self-conscious, pseudo-scientific notetaking manner of Zola. On his walks he learned, down to the tiniest details, the atmospheric, architectural, and social textures of Paris; and he forgot or misremembered almost nothing. A fairly detailed map of Paris could be constructed on the basis of the Comédie humaine alone. His walking was not unrelated to his passion for bric-a-brac. Filling his shelves with trinkets was simply one more aspect of the zestful homage he paid to the diversity and intricacy of God's and man's creation. All Paris comes into his collector's view. The details and images with which he crams his stories strike us very often as being pieces of his great collection: in other hands they could bore, as they would later in Zola's, but Balzac holds them up to the light in the spirit of discovery and joy.

Balzac has been described as a romantic realist. Certainly his sensibility is of that rare order which reconciles poetic vision, innocence, with worldly sophistication, and imaginative, almost mystical intensity with a penchant for the minutely realistic details that, skilfully and spiritedly handled, help literary work create an impression of density and diversity not unlike that of experience itself.

Most writers, even among the giants, who have been as profoundly intellectual and searching as Balzac show far less ability to "transport the audience out of itself," as Longinus puts it, with poetry and passion. At his best—and he is very often at his best—he creates a *literary form that, in its dramatic encounters, incisive dialogue, and living phrase, seems like theatre but at the same time has the intellectuality and imaginative freedom not possible on the stage (incidentally, Balzac is the author of one highly successful drama,* Mercadet, *still sometimes staged).*

Enormously inventive, analytical, personally interested in every sort of thing, and well stocked with details and facts crying out to be utilized, Balzac naturally required a large canvas. With extremely few exceptions—"A Passion in the Desert" is among the noblest of them—he achieves greatness in short fiction only when it is not particularly short. Such "short" masterpieces as The Girl with the Golden Eyes, At the Sign of the Cat and Racket, *and* A Commission in Lunacy *run to fifty or sixty pages each. In any event, many millions of readers over several generations have begun collecting books by Balzac because they liked what they found in the story of the soldier and the panther.*

A Passion in the Desert

Honoré de Balzac

"The whole show is dreadful," she cried, coming out of the menagerie of M. Martin. She had just been looking at that daring speculator "working with his hyena"—to speak in the style of the program.

"By what means," she continued, "can we have tamed these animals to such a point as to be certain of their affection for—."

"What seems to you a problem," said I, interrupting, "is really quite natural."

"Oh!" she cried, letting an incredulous smile wander over her lips.

"You think that beasts are wholly without passions?" I asked her. "-"Quite the reverse; we can communicate to them all the vices arising in our own state of civilization."

She looked at me with an air of astonishment.

"Nevertheless," I continued, "the first time I saw M. Martin, I admit, like you, I did give vent to an exclamation of surprise. I found myself next to an old soldier with the right leg amputated, who had come in with me. His face had struck me. He had one of those intrepid heads, stamped with the seal of warfare, and on which the battles of Napoleon are written. Besides, he had that frank good-humored expression which always impresses me favorably. He was without doubt one of those troopers who are surprised at nothing, who find matter for laughter in the contortions of a dying comrade, who bury or plunder him quite light-heartedly, who stand intrepidly in the way of bullets; in fact, one of those men who waste no time in deliberation, and would not hesitate to make friends with the devil himself. After looking very attentively at the proprietor of the menagerie getting out of his box, my companion pursed up his lips with an air of mockery and contempt, with that peculiar and expressive twist which superior people assume to show they are not taken in. Then when I was expatiating on the courage of M. Martin, he smiled, shook his head knowingly, and said, 'Well known.'

"How 'well known'?" I said. "If you would only explain to me the mystery I should be vastly obliged.

"After a few minutes, during which we made acquaintance, we went to dine at the first *restaurateur's* whose shop caught our eye. At dessert a bottle of champagne completely refreshed and brightened up the memories of this odd old soldier. He told me his story and I said he had every reason to exclaim, 'Well known.' "

When she got home, she teased me to that extent and made so many promises, that I consented to communicate to her the old soldier's confidences. Next day she received the following episode of an epic which one might call "The Frenchman in Egypt."

During the expedition in Upper Egypt under General Desaix, a Provençal soldier fell into the hands of the Maugrabins, and was taken by these Arabs into the deserts beyond the falls of the Nile.

In order to place a sufficient distance between themselves and the French army, the Maugrabins made forced marches, and only rested during the night. They camped round a well over-shadowed by palm trees under which they had previously concealed a store of provisions. Not surmising that the notion of flight would occur to their prisoner, they contented themselves with binding his hands, and after eating a few dates, and giving provender to their horses, went to sleep.

When the brave Provençal saw that his enemies were no longer watching him, he made use of his teeth to steal a scimitar, fixed the blade between his knees, and cut the cords which prevented using his hands; in a moment he was free. He at once seized a rifle and dagger, then taking the precaution to provide himself with a sack of dried dates, oats, and powder and shot, and to fasten a scimitar to his waist he leaped onto a horse, and spurred on vigorously in the direction where he thought to find the French army. So impatient was he to see a bivouac again that he pressed on the already tired courser at such speed that its flanks were lacerated with his spurs, and at last the poor animal died, leaving the Frenchman alone in the desert. After walking some time in the sand with all the courage of an escaped convict, the soldier was obliged to stop, as the day had already ended. In spite of the beauty of an oriental sky at night, he felt he had not strength enough to go on. Fortunately he had been able to find a small hill, on the summit of which a few palm trees shot up into the air; it was their verdure seen from afar which had brought hope and consolation to his heart. His fatigue was so great that he lay down upon a rock of granite, capriciously cut out like a camp-bed; there he fell asleep without taking any precaution to defend himself while he slept. He had made the sacrifice of his life. His last thought was one of regret. He repented having left the Maugrabins, whose nomad life seemed to smile on him now that he was afar from them and without help. He was awakened by the sun, whose pitiless rays fell with all their force on the granite and produced an intolerable heat—for he had had the stupidity to place himself inversely to the shadow thrown by the verdant majestic heads of the palm trees. He looked at the solitary trees and shuddered—they reminded him of the graceful shafts crowned with foliage which characterize the Saracen columns in the cathedral of Aries.

But when, after counting the palm trees, he cast his eye around him, the most horrible despair was infused into his soul. Before him stretched an ocean without limit. The dark sand of the desert spread farther than sight could reach in every direction, and glittered like steel struck with a bright light. It might have been a sea of looking-glass, or lakes melted together in a mirror. A fiery vapor carried up in streaks made a perpetual whirlwind over the quivering land. The sky was lit with an oriental splendor of insupportable purity, leaving naught for the imagination to desire. Heaven and earth were on fire.

The silence was awful in its wild and terrible majesty. Infinity, immensity, closed in upon the soul from every side. Not a cloud in the sky, not a breath in the air, not a flaw on the bosom of the sand, ever moving in diminutive waves; the horizon ended as at sea on a clear day, with one line of light, definite as the cut of a sword.

The Provençal threw his arms around the trunk of one of the palm trees, as though it were the body of a friend, and then in the shelter of the thin straight shadow that the palm cast upon the granite, he wept. Then sitting down he remained as he was, contemplating with profound sadness the implacable scene, which was all he had to look upon. He cried aloud, to measure the solitude. His voice, lost in the hollows of the hill, sounded faintly, and aroused no echo—the echo was in in his own heart. The Provençal was twenty-two years old;—he loaded his carbine.

"There'll be time enough," he said to himself, laying on the ground the weapon which alone could bring him deliverance.

Looking by turns at the black expanse and the blue expanse, the soldier dreamed of France—he smelt with delight the gutters of Paris—he remembered the towns through which he had passed, the faces of his fellow-soldiers, the most minute details of his life. His southern fancy soon showed him the stones of his beloved Provence, in the play of the heat which waved over the spread sheet of the desert. Fearing the danger of this cruel mirage, he went down the opposite side of the hill to that by which he had come up the day before. The remains of a rug showed that this place of refuge had at one time been inhabited; at a short distance he saw some palm trees full of dates. Then the instinct which binds us to life awoke again in his heart. He hoped to live long enough to await the passing of some Arabs, or perhaps he might hear the sound of cannon; for at this time Bonaparte was traversing Egypt.

This thought gave him new life. The palm tree seemed to bend with the weight of the ripe fruit. He shook some of it down. When he tasted this unhoped-for manna, he felt sure that the palms had been cultivated by a former inhabitant—the savory, fresh meat of the dates was proof of the care of his predecessor. He passed suddenly from dark despair to an almost insane joy. He went up again to the top of the hill, and spent the rest of the day in cutting down one of the sterile palm trees, which the night before had served him for shelter. A vague memory made him think of the animals of the desert; and in case they might come to drink at the spring, visible from the base of the rocks but lost farther down, he resolved to guard himself from their visits by placing a barrier at the entrance of his hermitage.

In spite of his diligence, and the strength which the fear of being devoured asleep gave him, he was unable to cut the palm in pieces, though he succeeded in cutting it down. At eventide the king of the desert fell; the sound of its fall resounded far and wide, like a sign in the solitude; the soldier shuddered as though he had heard some voice predicting woe.

But like an heir who does not long bewail a deceased parent, he tore off from this beautiful tree the tall broad green leaves which are its poetic adornment, and used them to mend the mat on which he was to sleep.

Fatigued by the heat and his work, he fell asleep under the red curtains of his wet cave.

In the middle of the night his sleep was troubled by an extraordinary noise; he sat up, and the deep silence around him allowed him to distinguish the alternative accents of a respiration whose savage energy could not belong to a human creature.

A profound terror, increased still further by the darkness, the silence, and his waking images, froze his heart within him. He almost felt his hair stand on end, when by straining his eyes to their utmost he perceived through the shadows two faint yellow lights. At first he attributed these lights to the reflection of his own pupils, but soon the vivid brilliance of the night aided him gradually to distinguish the objects around him in the cave, and he beheld a huge animal lying but two steps from him. Was it a lion, a tiger, or a crocodile?

The Provençal was not educated enough to know under what species his enemy ought to be classed; but his fright was all the greater, as his ignorance led him to imagine all terrors at once; he endured a cruel torture, noting every variation of the breathing close to him without daring to make the slightest movement. An odor, pungent like that of a fox, but more penetrating, profounder—so to speak—filled the cave, and when the Provençal became sensible of this, his terror reached its height, for he could no longer doubt the proximity of a terrible companion, whose royal dwelling served him for shelter.

Presently the reflection of the moon, descending on the horizon, lit up the den, rendering gradually visible and resplendent the spotted skin of a panther.

The lion of Egypt slept, curled up like a bit dog, the peaceful possessor of a sumptuous niche at the gate of a hotel; its eyes opened for a moment and closed again; its face was turned toward the man. A thousand confused thoughts passed through the Frenchman's mind; first he thought of killing it with a bullet from his gun, but he saw there was not enough distance between them for him to take proper aim—the shot would miss the mark. And if it were to wake!—the thought made his limbs rigid. He listened to his own heart beating in the midst of the silence, and cursed the too violent pulsations which the flow of blood brought on, fearing to disturb that sleep which allowed him time to think of some means of escape.

Twice he placed his hand on his scimitar, intending to cut off the head of his enemy; but the difficulty of cutting the stiff, short hair compelled him to abandon this daring project. To miss would be to die for *certain,* he thought; he preferred the chances of fair fight, and made up his mind to wait till morning; the morning did not leave him long to wait.

He could now examine the panther at ease; its muzzle was smeared with blood.

"She's had a good dinner," he thought, without troubling himself as to whether her feast might have been on human flesh. "She won't be hungry when she gets up."

It was a female. The fur on her belly and flanks was glistening white; many small marks like velvet formed beautiful bracelets round her feet; her sinuous tail was also white, ending with black rings; the overpart of her dress, yellow like unburnished gold, very lissom and soft, had the characteristic blotches in the form of rosettes, which distinguish the panther from every other feline species.

This tranquil and formidable hostess snored in an attitude as graceful as that of a cat lying on a cushion. Her blood-stained paws, nervous and well-armed, were stretched out before her face, which rested upon them and from which radiated her straight, slender whiskers, like threads of silver.

If she had been like that in a cage, the Provencal would doubtless have admired the grace of the animal, and the vigorous contrasts of vivid color which gave her robe an imperial splendor; but just then his sight was troubled by her sinister appearance.

The presence of the panther, even asleep, could not fail to produce the effect which the magnetic eyes of the serpent are said to have on the nightingale.

For a moment the courage of the soldier began to fail before this danger, though no doubt it would have risen at the mouth of a cannon charged with shell. Nevertheless, a bold thought brought daylight to his soul and sealed up the source of the cold sweat which sprang forth on his brow. Like men driven to bay who defy death and offer their body to the smiter, so he, seeing in this merely a tragic episode, resolved to play his part with honor to the last.

"The day before yesterday the Arabs would have killed me perhaps," he said; so considering himself as good as dead already, he waited bravely, with excited curiosity, his enemy's awakening.

When the sun appeared, the panther suddenly opened her eyes; then she put out her paws with energy, as if to stretch them and get rid of cramp. At last she yawned, showing the formidable apparatus of her teeth and pointed tongue, rough as a file.

"A regular *petite maitresse*," thought the Frenchman, seeing her roll herself about so softly and coquettishly. She licked off the blood which stained her paws and muzzle, and scratched her head with reiterated gestures full of prettiness. "All right, make a little toilet," the Frenchman said to himself, beginning to recover his gaiety with his courage; "we'll say good morning to each other presently," and he seized the small, short dagger which he had taken from the Mangrabins. At this moment the panther turned her head toward the man and looked at him fixedly without moving.

The rigidity of her metallic eyes and their insupportable luster made him shudder, especially when the animal walked toward him. But he looked at her caressingly, staring into her eyes in order to magnetize her, and let her come quite close to him; then with a movement both gentle and amorous, as though he were caressing the most beautiful of women, he passed his hand over her whole body, from the head to the tail, scratching the flexible vertebrae which divided the panther's yellow back. The animal waved her tail voluptuously, and her eyes grew gentle; and when for the third time the Frenchman accomplished this interesting flattery, she gave forth one of those purrings by which our cats express their pleasure; but this murmur issued from a throat so powerful and so deep, that it resounded through the cave like the last vibrations of an organ in a church. The man, understanding the importance of his caresses, redoubled them in such a way as to surprise and stupefy his imperious courtesan. When he felt sure of having extinguished the ferocity of his capricious companion, whose hunger had so fortunately been satisfied the day before, he got up to go out of the cave; the panther let him go out, but when he had reached the summit of the hill she sprang with the lightness of a sparrow hopping from twig to twig, and rubbed herself against his legs, putting up her back after the manner of all the race of cats. Then regarding her guest with eyes whose glare had softened a little, she gave vent to that wild cry which naturalists compare to the grating of a saw.

"She is exacting," said the Frenchman, smilingly.

He was bold enough to play with her ears; he caressed her belly and scratched her head as hard as he could.

When he saw that he was successful, he tickled her skull with the point of his dagger, watching for the right moment to kill her, but the hardness of her bones made him tremble for his success.

The sultana of the desert showed herself gracious to her slave; she lifted her head, stretched out her neck, and manifested her delight by the tranquility of her attitude. It suddenly occurred to the soldier that to kill this savage princess with one blow he must poignard her in the throat.

He raised the blade, when the panther, satisfied no doubt, laid herself gracefully at his feet, and cast up at him glances in which, in spite of their natural fierceness, was mingled confusedly a kind of good-will. The poor Provençal ate his dates, leaning against one of the palm trees, and casting his eyes alternately on the desert in quest of some liberator and on his terrible companion to watch her uncertain clemency.

The panther looked at the place where the date stones fell, and every time that he threw one down her eyes expressed an incredible mistrust.

She examined the man with an almost commercial prudence. However, this examination was favorable to him, for when he had finished his meager meal she licked his boots with her powerful rough tongue, brushing off with marvellous skill the dust gathered in the creases.

"Ah, but when she's really hungry!" thought the Frenchman. In spite of the shudder this thought caused him, the soldier began to measure curiously the proportions of the panther, certainly one of the most splendid specimens of its race. She was three feet high and four feet long without counting her tail; this powerful weapon, rounded like a cudgel, was nearly three feet long. The head, large as that of a lioness, was distinguished by a rare expression of refinement. The cold cruelty of a tiger was dominant, it was true, but there was also a vague resemblance to the face of a sensual woman. Indeed, the face of this solitary queen had something of the gaiety of a drunken Nero: she had satiated herself with blood, and she wanted to play.

The soldier tried if he might walk up and down, and the panther left him free, contenting herself with following him with her eyes, less like a faithful dog than a big Angora cat, observing everything and every movement of her master.

When he looked around, he saw, by the spring, the remains of his horse; the panther had dragged the carcass all that way; about two-thirds of it had been devoured already. The sight reassured him.

It was easy to explain the panther's absence, and the respect she had had for him while he slept. The first piece of good luck emboldened him to tempt the future, and he conceived the wild hope of continuing on good terms with the panther during the entire day, neglecting no means of taming her, and remaining in her good graces.

He returned to her, and had the unspeakable joy of seeing her wag her tail with an almost imperceptible movement at his approach. He sat down then, without fear, by her side, and they began to play together; he took her paws and muzzle, pulled her ears, rolled her over on her back, stroked her warm, delicate flanks. She let him do whatever he liked, and when he began to stroke the hair on her feet she drew her claws in carefully.

The man, keeping the dagger in one hand, thought to plunge it into the belly of the too-confiding panther, but he was afraid that he would be immediately strangled in her last conclusive struggle; besides, he felt in his heart a sort of remorse which bid him respect a creature that had done him no harm. He seemed to have found a friend, in a boundless desert; half unconsciously he thought of his first sweetheart, whom he had nicknamed "Mignonne" by way of contrast, because she was so atrociously jealous that all the time of their love he was in fear of the knife with which she had always threatened him.

This memory of his early days suggested to him the idea of making the young panther answer to this name, now that he began to admire with less terror her swiftness, suppleness, and softness. Toward the end of the day he had familiarized himself with his perilous position; he now almost liked the painfulness of it. At last his companion had got into the habit of looking up at him whenever he cried in a falsetto voice, "Mignonne."

At the setting of the sun Mignonne gave, several times running, a profound melancholy cry. "She's been well brought up," said the light-hearted soldier; "she says her prayers." But this mental joke only occurred to him when he noticed what a pacific attitude his companion remained in. "Come, *ma petite blonde*, I'll let you go to bed first," he said to her, counting on the activity of his own legs to run away as quickly as possible, directly she was asleep, and seek another shelter for the night.

The soldier waited with impatience the hour of his flight, and when it had arrived he walked vigorously in the direction of the Nile; but hardly had he made a quarter of a league in the sand when he heard the panther bounding after him, crying with that saw-like cry more dreadful even than the sound of her leaping.

"Ah!" he said, "then she's taken a fancy to me; she has never met any one before, and it is really quite flattering to have her first love." That instant the man fell into one of those movable quicksands so terrible to travellers and from which it is impossible to save oneself. Feeling himself caught, he gave a shriek of alarm; the panther seized him with her teeth by the collar, and, springing vigorously backward, drew him as if by magic out of the whirling sand.

"Ah, Mignonne!" cried the soldier, caressing her enthusiastically; "we're bound together for life and death—but no jokes, mind!" and he retraced his steps.

From that time the desert seemed inhabited. It contained a being to whom the man could talk, and whose ferocity was rendered gentle by him, though he could not explain to himself the reason for their strange friendship. Great as was the soldier's desire to stay upon guard, he slept.

On awakening he could not find Mignonne; he mounted the hill, and in the distance saw her springing toward him after the habit of these animals, who cannot run on account of the extreme flexibility of the vertebral column. Mignonne arrived, her jaws covered with blood; she received the wonted caress of her companion, showing with much purring how happy it made her. Her eyes, full of languor, turned still more gently than the day before toward the Provençal who talked to her as one would to a tame animal.

"Ah! Mademoiselle, you are a nice girl, aren't you? Just look at that! so we like to be made much of, don't we? Aren't you ashamed of yourself? So you have been eating some Arab or other, have you? that doesn't matter. They're animals just the same as you are; but don't you take to eating Frenchmen, or I shan't like you any longer."

She played like a dog with its master, letting herself be rolled over, knocked about, and stroked, alternately; sometimes she herself would provoke the soldier, putting up her paw with a soliciting gesture.

Some days passed in this manner. This companionship permitted the Provençal to appreciate the sublime beauty of the desert; now that he had a living thing to think about, alternations of fear and quiet, and plenty to eat, his mind became filled with contrast and his life began to be diversified.

Solitude revealed to him all her secrets, and enveloped him in her delights. He discovered in the rising and setting of the sun sights unknown to the world. He knew what it was to tremble when he heard over his head the hiss of a bird's wing, so rarely did they pass, or when he saw the clouds, changing and many-colored travellers, melt one into another. He studied in the night time the effect of the moon upon the ocean of sand, where the simoom made waves swift of movement and rapid in their change. He lived the life of the Eastern day, marvelling at its wonderful pomp; then, after having revelled in the sight of a hurricane over the plain where the whirling sands made red, dry mists and death-bearing clouds, he would welcome the night with joy, for then fell the healthful freshness of the stars, and he listened to imaginary music in the skies. Then solitude taught him to unroll the treasures of dreams. He passed whole hours in remembering mere nothings, and comparing his present life with his past.

At last he grew passionately fond of the panther; for some sort of affection was a necessity.

Whether it was that his will powerfully projected had modified the character of his companion, or whether, because she found abundant food in her predatory excursions in the desert, she respected the man's life, he began to fear for it no longer, seeing her so well tamed.

He devoted the greater part of his time to sleep, but he was obliged to watch like a spider in its web that the moment of his deliverance might not escape him, if any one should pass the line marked by the horizon. He had sacrificed his shirt to make a flag with, which he hung at the top of a palm tree, whose foliage he had torn off. Taught by necessity, he found the means of keeping it spread out, by fastening it with little sticks; for the wind might not be blowing at the moment when the passing traveller was looking through the desert.

It was during the long hours, when he had abandoned hope, that he amused himself with the panther. He had come to learn the different inflections of her voice, the expressions of her eyes; he had studied the capricious patterns of all the rosettes which marked the gold of her robe. Mignonne was not even angry when he took hold of the tuft at the end of her tail to count her rings, those graceful ornaments which glittered in the sun like jewelry. It gave him pleasure to contemplate the supple, fine outlines of her form, the whiteness of her belly, the graceful pose of her head. But it was especially when she was playing that he felt most pleasure in looking at her; the agility and youthful lightness of her movements were a continual surprise to him; he wondered at the supple way in which she jumped and climbed, washed herself and arranged her fur, crouched down and prepared to spring. However rapid her spring might be, however slippery the stone she was on, she would always stop short at the word "Mignonne."

One day, in a bright mid-day sun, an enormous bird coursed through the air. The man left his panther to look at this new guest; but after waiting a moment the deserted sultana growled deeply.

"My goodness! I do believe she's jealous," he cried, seeing her eyes become hard again; "the soul of Virginie has passed into her body; that's certain."

The eagle disappeared into the air, while the soldier admired the curved contour of the panther.

But there was such youth and grace in her form! she was beautiful as a woman! the blond fur of her robe mingled well with the delicate tints of faint white which marked her flanks.

The profuse light cast down by the sun made this living gold, these russet markings, to burn in a way to give them an indefinable attraction.

The man and the panther looked at one another with a look full of meaning; the coquette quivered when she felt her friend stroke her head; her eyes flashed like lightning—then she shut them tightly.

"She has a soul," he said, looking at the stillness of this queen of the sands, golden like them, white like them, solitary and burning like them.

"Well," she said, "I have read your plea in favor of beasts; but how did two so well adapted to understand each other end?"

"Ah, well! you see, they ended as all great passions do end—by a misunderstanding. For some reason *one* suspects the other of treason; they don't come to an explanation through pride, and quarrel and part from sheer obstinacy."

"Yet sometimes at the best moments a single word or a look is enough—but anyhow go on with your story."

"It's horribly difficult, but you will understand, after what the old villain told me over his champagne.

"He said—'I don't know if I hurt her, but she turned round, as if enraged, and with her sharp teeth caught hold of my leg—gently, I dare-say; but I, thinking she would devour me, plunged my dagger into her throat. She rolled over, giving a cry that froze my heart; and I saw her dying, still looking at me without anger. I would have given all the world—my cross even, which I had not got then—to have brought her to life again. It was as though I had murdered a real person; and the soldiers who had seen my flag, and were come to my assistance, found me in tears.'

" 'Well sir,' he said, after a moment of silence, 'since then I have been in war in Germany, in Spain, in Russia, in France; I've certainly carried my carcass about a good deal, but never have I seen anything like the desert. Ah! yes, it is very beautiful!'

" 'What did you feel there?' I asked him.

" 'Oh! that can't be described, young man. Besides, I am not always regretting my palm trees and my panther. I should have to be very melancholy for that. In the desert, you see, there is everything, and nothing.'

" 'Yes, but explain—'

" 'Well,' he said, with an impatient gesture, 'it is God without mankind.' "

The Red Inn

Honoré de Balzac

To Monsieur le Marquis de Custine.

Once upon a time (I forget the exact year) a Parisian banker, who had very extensive business relations with Germany, gave a dinner party in honor of one of the friends that merchants make in this place and that by correspondence, a sort of friendship that subsists for a long while between men who have never met. The friend, the senior partner of some considerable firm in Nuremberg, was a stout, good-natured German, a man of learning and of taste, more particularly in the matter of tobacco pipes. He was a typical Nuremberger, with a pleasant, broad countenance and a massive, square forehead, with a few stray fair hairs here and there; a typical German, a son of the stainless and noble Fatherland, so fertile in honorable characters, preserving its manners uncorrupted even after seven invasions. The stranger laughed simply, listened attentively, and drank with marked enjoyment, seeming to like champagne perhaps as well as the pale red wines of the Johannisberg. Like nearly every German in nearly every book, he was named Hermann; and in the quality of a man who does nothing with levity, he was comfortably seated at the banker's table, eating his way through the dinner with the Teutonic appetite renowned all over Europe, and thorough indeed was his manner of bidding adieu to all the works of the great Carême.

The master of the house had invited several intimate friends to do honor to his guest. These were for the most part financiers or merchants, interspersed with a few pretty and agreeable women, whose light, graceful talk and frank manner harmonized with German open-heartedness. And, indeed, if you could have seen, as I had the pleasure of seeing, this blithe gathering of folk who had sheathed the active claws employed in raking in wealth, that they might make the best of an opportunity of enjoying the pleasures of life, you would scarcely have found it in your heart to grudge high rates of interest or to revile defaulters. A man cannot always be in mischief. Even in the society of pirates, for instance, there must surely be a pleasant hour now and then when you may feel at your ease beneath the black flag.

"Oh, I do hope that before M. Hermann goes he will tell us another dreadful, thrilling German story!"

The words were uttered over the dessert by a pale, fair-haired young lady, who had doubtless been reading Hoffmann's tales and Sir Walter Scott's novels. She was the banker's only daughter, an irresistibly charming girl, whose education was being finished at the Gymnase; she was wild about the plays given there. The dinner party had just reached the period of lazy contentment and serene disinclination to talk that succeeds an excellent dinner in the course of which somewhat heavy demands have been made upon the digestion; when the guests lean back in their chairs and play idly with the gilded knife-blades, while their wrists repose lightly on the table edge; the period of decline when some torment apple pips, or knead a crumb of bread between thumb and finger, when the sentimental write illegible initials among the *débris* of the dessert, and the penurious count the stones on their plates, and arrange them round the edge, as a playwright marshals the supernumeraries at the back of the stage. These are minor gastronomical pleasures which Brillat-Savarin has passed over unnoticed, exhaustively as he has treated his subject in other respects.

The servants had disappeared. The dessert, like a squadron after an action, was quite disorganized, disarrayed, forlorn. In spite of persistent efforts on the part of the mistress of the house, the various dishes strayed about the table. People fixed their eyes on the Swiss views that adorned the gray walls of the dining-room. No one felt it tedious. The man has yet to be found who can mope while he digests a good dinner. At that time we like to sit steeped in an indescribable calm, a sort of golden mean between the two extremes of the thinker's musings and the sleek content of the ruminating brute, which should be termed the physical melancholy of gastronomy.

So the party turned spontaneously towards the worthy German, all of them delighted to listen to a tale, even if it should be a dull one. During this beatific pause, the mere sound of the voice of the one who tells the story is soothing to our languid senses; it is one more aid to passive enjoyment. As an amateur of pictures, I watched the faces, bright with smiles, lit up by the light of the tapers and flushed with good cheer; the different expressions produced piquant effects among the sconces, the porcelain baskets of fruit, and the crystal glasses.

One face, exactly opposite, particularly struck my imagination. It belonged to a middle-sized man, tolerably stout and jovial-looking; who from his manner and appearance seemed to be a stockbroker, and, so far as one could see, gifted with no extraordinary amount of brains. Hitherto I had not noticed him, but at that moment his face, obscured, to be sure, by a bad light, seemed to me to undergo a total change; it took a cadaverous hue, veined with purple streaks. You might have taken it for the ghastly countenance of a man in the death agony. Impassive as a painted figure in a diorama, he was staring stupidly at the facets of a crystal decanter-stopper, but he certainly took no heed of them; he seemed to be deep in some visionary contemplation of the future or of the past. A long scrutiny of this dubious-looking face made me think.

"Is he ill?" I asked myself. "Has he taken too much wine? Is he ruined by the fall of the funds? Is he thinking how to cheat his creditors?—Look!" I said to the lady who sat next to me, calling her attention to the stranger's face, "that is a budding bankruptcy, is it not?"

"Oh!" she answered, "if it were, he would be in better spirits." Then, with a graceful toss of her head, she added: "If that individual ever ruins himself, I will take the news to Pekin myself. He is a rather eccentric old gentleman worth a million in real estate; he used to be a contractor to the Imperial armies. He married again, as a business speculation, but he makes his wife very happy for all that. He has a pretty daughter, whom for a very long time he would not recognize; but when his son died by a sad accident in a duel, he was obliged to take her home, for he was not likely to have any more children. So all at once the poor girl became one of the richest heiresses in Paris. The loss of his only son threw the poor dear man into great grief, and he still shows signs of it at times."

As she spoke the army contractor looked up, and our eyes met; his expression made me shudder, it was so gloomy and so sad. Assuredly a whole life was summed up in that glance. Then in a moment he looked cheerful. He took up the glass stopper, put in unthinkingly into the mouth of the water decanter that stood on the table in front of him, and turned smilingly towards M. Hermann. The man was positively beaming with full-fed content, and had, no doubt, not two ideas in his head; he had been thinking of nothing! I was in some sort ashamed to have thrown away my powers of divination *in animâ vili*, to have taken this thick-skulled financier as a subject. But while I was making my phrenological observations in pure waste, the good-natured German had flicked a few grains of snuff off his face and begun his story.

It would be a passably difficult matter to give it in the same words, with his not infrequent interruptions and wordy digressions; so I have written it after my own fashion, omitting these defects of the Nuremberger's narrative, and helping myself to such elements of poetry and interest as it may possess, emulating the modesty of other writers who omit the formula *translated from the German* from their title-pages.

I.

THE IDEA AND THE DEED

"Towards the end of Vendémiaire, in the year VII of the Republican era (a date that corresponds to the 20th of October, present style), two young men were making their way towards Andernach, a little town on the left bank of the Rhine, a few leagues from Coblentz. The travelers had set out from Bonn that morning, and now the day was drawing to a close. At that particular time a French army under command of General Augereau was keeping in check the Austrians on the right bank of the river. The headquarters of the Republican division were at Coblentz, and one of the demi-brigades belonging to Augereau's corps was quartered in Andernach.

"The two wayfarers were Frenchmen. At first sight of their blue and white uniforms, with red velvet facings, their sabres, and, above all, their caps covered with green oilcloth and adorned with a tricolor cockade, the German peasants themselves might have known them for a pair of army surgeons, men of science and of sterling worth, popular for the most part not only in the army, but also in the countries occupied by French troops. At that time many young men of good family, torn from their medical studies by General Jourdan's conscription law, not unnaturally preferred to continue their studies on the battlefield to compulsory service in the ranks, a life ill suited to their antecedents and unwarlike ambitions. Men of this stamp, studious, serviceable, peaceably inclined, did some good among so many evils, and found congenial spirits among the learned of the various countries invaded by the ruthless affranchisement of the Republic.

"These two, provided with a map of the road, and with assistant-surgeons' commissions signed by La Coste and Bernadotte, were on their way to join the demi-brigade to which they were attached. Both belonged to well-to-do middle-class families in Beauvais, the traditions of gentle breeding and of provincial integrity had been a part of their inheritance. A curiosity quite natural in youth had brought them to the seat of war before the time fixed for entrance on active service, and they had come by the *diligence* as far as Strasbourg. Maternal prudence had suffered them to leave home with a very scanty supply of money, but they felt rich in the possession of a few louis; and, indeed, at a time when assignats had reached the lowest point of depreciation, those few louis meant wealth, for gold was at a high premium.

"The two assistant-surgeons, aged twenty years at most, gave themselves up to the romance of their situation with all the enthusiasm of youth. They had traversed the Palatinate from Strasbourg to Bonn in the quality of artists, philosophers, and observers. When we have a scientific career before us, there are, in truth, at that age many natures within us; and even while making love or traveling about, an assistant-surgeon should be laying the foundations of his future fame and fortune. Accordingly, the pair had been carried away by the profound admiration that every well-read man must feel at the sight of the scenery of Swabia and the banks of the Rhine between Mayence and Cologne. They saw a vigorous and fertile country, an undulating green landscape full of strong contrasts and of memories of feudal times, and everywhere scarred by fire and sword. Louis XIV and Turenne once before laid that fair land in ashes; heaps of ruins bear witness to the pride, or, it may be, to the prudence of the monarch of Versailles, who razed the wonderful castles which once were the glory of this part of Germany. You arrive at some conception of the German mind; you understand its dreaminess and its mysticism from this wonderful forestland of theirs, full of remains of the Middle Ages, picturesque, albeit in ruins.

"The two friends had made some stay in Bonn with two objects in view—scientific knowledge and pleasure. The grand hospital of the Gallo-Batavian army and of Augereau's division had been established in the Electoral palace itself, and thither the two novices had gone to see their comrades, to deliver letters of recommendation to their chiefs, and to make their first acquaintance with the life of army surgeons. But with the new impressions, there as elsewhere, they parted with some of their national prejudices, and discovered that France had no monopoly of beautiful public buildings and landscapes. The marble columns that adorn the Electoral palace took them by surprise; they admired the magnificence of German architecture and found fresh treasures of ancient and modern art at every step.

"Now and again in the course of their wanderings toward Andernach their way led them over some higher peak among the granite hills. Through a clear space in the forest, or a chasm in the rocks, they caught a glimpse of the Rhine, a picture framed in the gray stone, or in some setting of luxuriant trails of green leaves. Every valley, fieldpath, and forest was filled with autumn scents that conduce to musings and with signs of the aging of the year; the tree-tops were turning golden, taking warmer hues and shades of brown; the leaves were falling, but the sky was blue and cloudless overhead; the roads were dry, and shone like threads of gold across the country in the late afternoon sunlight.

"Half a league from Andernach the country through which the two friends were traveling lay in a silence as deep as if there were no war laying waste the beautiful land. They were following a goat track among the steep crags of bluish granite that rise like walls above the eddying Rhine, and before very long were descending the sloping sides of the ravine above the little town, nestling coyly at its foot on the river bank, its picturesque quay for the Rhine boatmen.

" 'Germany is a very beautiful country!' cried one of the two, Prosper Magnan by name, as he caught sight of the painted houses of Andernach lying close together like eggs in a basket, among the trees and flower-gardens.

"For a few minutes they looked at the high-pitched roofs with their projecting beams, at the balconies and wooden staircases of all those peaceful dwellings, and at the boats swaying in the current by the quay."

When M. Hermann mentioned the name of Prosper Magnan, my opposite neighbor, the army contractor, snatched up the decanter, poured himself out a glass of water, and drank it down at a gulp. This proceeding recalled my attention to him; I thought I saw a slight quiver in his hands and a trace of perspiration on his forehead.

"What is the army contractor's name?" I inquired of my gracious neighbor.

"His name is Taillefer," said she.

"Are you feeling unwell?" I exclaimed, as this unaccountable being turned pale.

"Not at all, not at all," he said, with a courteous gesture of acknowledgment. "I am listening," he said, with a nod to the rest of the party, for all eyes were turned at once upon him.

"I forget the other young man's name," said M. Hermann. "But, at any rate, from Prosper Magnan's confidences I learned that his friend was dark, lively, and rather thin. If you have no objection, I will call him Wilhelm for the sake of clearness in the story." And the good German took up his tale again, after baptizing a French assistant-surgeon with a German name, totally regardless of local color and of the demands of Romanticism.

"So by the time these two young fellows reached Andernach night had fallen; and they, fancying that it was too late to report themselves to their chiefs, make themselves known and obtain billets in a place already full of soldiers, made up their minds to spend their last night of freedom in an inn, about a hundred paces outside the town. They had seen it from the crags above, and had admired the warm colors of the house, heightened by the glow of the sunset. The whole building was painted red, and produced a piquant effect in the landscape, whether it was seen against the crowd of houses in the town, or as a mass of bright color against a background of forest trees, or a patch of scarlet by the gray water's edge. Doubtless the inn owed its external decoration, and consequently its name, to the whim of the builder in some forgotten time. The color had come to be literally a matter of custom to successive owners, for the inn had a name among the Rhine boatmen who frequented it. The sound of horses' hoofs brought the landlord of the Red Inn to the threshold.

" '*Pardieu!* gentlemen,' cried he, 'a little later you would have had to sleep out of doors like most of your countrymen bivouacking yonder at the other end of Andernach. The house is full. If you positively must have a bed to sleep in, I have only my own room to offer you. As for the horses, I can lay down some litter in a corner of the yard for them; my stables are full of christened men this day.—The gentlemen will be from France?" he went on after a brief pause.

" 'From Bonn,' cried Prosper, 'and we have had nothing to eat since morning.'

" 'Oh! as to victuals,' said the landlord, jerking his head, 'people come to the Red Inn for ten leagues round for wedding feasts. You shall have a banquet fit for a prince, fish from the Rhine! That tells you everything.'

"When they had given over their tired beasts into the host's care, they left him to shout in vain for the stable folk, and went into the public room of the inn. It was so full of dense white clouds blown from the pipes of a room full of smokers, that at first they could not make out what kind of company they had fallen among; but after they had sat for a while at a table, and put in practice the patience of traveled philosophers who know when it is useless to make a fuss, they gradually made out the inevitable accessories of a German inn. The stove, the clock, the tables, pots of beer and long pipes, loomed out through the tobacco smoke; so did the faces of the motley crew, Jews, Germans, and what not, with one or two rough boatmen thrown in.

"The epaulettes of a few French officers shone through the thick mist, and spurs and sabres clanked incessantly upon the flagstones. Some were playing at cards, the rest quarreled among themselves, or were silent, ate, or drank, and came or went. A stout little woman, who wore the black velvet cap, blue stomacher embroidered with silver, the pincushion, bunch of keys, silver clasps, and plaited hair of the typical German landlady (a costume made so familiar in all its details by a host of prints that it is too well known to need description), came to the two friends and soothed their impatience, while she stimulated their interest in their supper with very remarkable skill.

"Gradually the noise diminished, the travelers went off one by one, the clouds of tobacco smoke cleared away. By the time that the table was set for the assistant-surgeons, and the classic carp from the Rhine appeared, it was eleven o'clock, and the room was empty. Through the stillness of the night it was possible to hear faint noises of horses stamping or crunching their provender, the ripple of the Rhine, the vague indefinable sounds in an inn full of people when everyone has retired to rest. Doors and windows opened or shut; there was an inarticulate murmur of voices, or a name was called out in some room overhead. During this time of silence and of commotion, while the two Frenchmen were eating their supper and the landlord engaged in extolling Andernach, the meal, his Rhine wine, his wife, and the Republican army, for the benefit of his guests, the three heard, with a certain degree of interest, the hoarse shouts of boatmen and the rattling sound of a boat being moored alongside the quay. The innkeeper, doubtless accustomed to be hailed by the guttural cries of the boatmen, hurried out, and soon came in again with a short, stout man, a couple of the boat's crew following them with a heavy valise and several packages. As soon as the baggage was deposited in the room, the short man picked up his valise and seated himself without ceremony at the table opposite the two surgeons.

" 'You can sleep on board,' said he to the boatmen, 'as the inn is full. All things considered, that will be the best way.'

" 'All the provisions I have in the house are here before you, sir,' said the landlord, and he indicated the Frenchmen's supper. 'I have not a crust of bread, and not so much as a bone——'

" 'And no sauerkraut?'

" 'Not so much as would fill my wife's thimble! As I had the honor of telling you just now, you can have no bed but the chair you are sitting on, and this is the only unoccupied room.'

"At these words the short personage glanced at the landlord, at the room, and at the two Frenchmen, caution and alarm equally visible in the expression of his countenance.

"At this point," said M. Hermann, interrupting himself, "I should tell you that we never knew this stranger's real name, nor his history; we found out from his papers that he came from Aix-la-Chapelle, that he had assumed the name of Walhenfer, and owned a rather large pin factory somewhere near Neuwied—that was all.

"He wore, like other manufacturers in that part of the world, an ordinary cloth overcoat, waistcoat and breeches of dark-green velvet, high boots, and a broad leather belt. His face was perfectly round, his manners frank and hearty, and during the evening he found it very difficult to disguise some inward apprehensions, or, it may be, cruel anxieties. The innkeeper always said that the German merchant was fleeing the country, and I learned later on that his factory had been burned down through one of the unlucky accidents so frequent in time of war. But in spite of the uneasy look that his face generally wore, its natural expression denoted good-humor and good-nature. He had good features, and a particularly noticeable personal trait was a thick neck, so white in contrast with a black cravat, that Wilhelm jokingly pointed it out to Prosper——"

Here M. Taillefer drank another glass of water.

"Prosper courteously invited the merchant to share their supper, and Walhenfer fell to without more ado, like a man who is conscious that he can repay a piece of civility. He set down his valise on the floor, put his feet upon it, took off his hat, drew his chair to the table, and laid down his gloves beside him, together with a pair of pistols, which he carried in his belt. The landlord quickly set a place for him, and the three began to satisy their hunger silently enough.

"The room was so close and the flies so troublesome, that Prosper requested the landlord to open the window that looked out upon the quay to let in fresh air. This window was fastened by an iron bar that dropped into a socket on either side of the window frame, and for greater security, a nut fastened to each of the shutters received a bolt. It so happened that Prosper watched the landlord unfasten the window.

"But since I am going into these particulars," Mr. Hermann remarked, "I ought to describe the internal arrangements of the house; for the whole interest of the story depends on an accurate knowledge of the place.

"There were two entrance doors in the room where these three persons were sitting. One opened on to the road that followed the river bank to Andernach, and, as might be expected, just opposite the inn, there was a little jetty where the boat which the merchant had hired for his voyage was moored at that moment. The other door gave admittance to the inn-yard, a court shut in by very high walls, and at the moment full of horses and cattle, for human beings occupied the stables.

"The house door had been so carefully bolted and barred that, to save time, the landlord had opened the street door of the sitting-room to admit the merchant and the boatmen, and now, when he had opened the window at Prosper Magnan's instance, he set to work to shut this door, slipping the bolts and screwing the nuts.

"The landlord's bedroom, where the friends were to sleep, was next to the public room of the inn, and only separated from the kitchen, where the host and hostess were probably to pass the night, by a sufficiently thin partition wall. The maid-servant had just gone out to find a nook in some manger, or in the corner of a hay loft somewhere or other. It will be readily understood that the public room, the landlord's bedroom, and the kitchen were in a manner apart from the rest of the inn. The deep barking of two great dogs in the yard indicated that the house had vigilant and wakeful guardians.

" 'How quiet it is, and what a glorious night!' said Wilhelm, looking out at the sky when the landlord had bolted the door. There was not a sound to be heard at the moment save the rippling of the water.

" 'Gentlemen,' said the merchant, addressing the Frenchmen, 'allow me to offer you a bottle or two of wine to wash down your carp. A glass will refresh us after a tiring day. By the look of you and the condition of your clothes, I can see that, like myself, you have come a good way.'

"The two friends accepted the proposal, and the landlord went out through the kitchen to the cellar, doubtless situated beneath that part of the establishment. About the time that five venerable bottles appeared upon the table, the landlord's wife had finished serving the supper. She gave a housewife's glance over the dishes and round the room, assured herself that the travelers had everything they were likely to want, and went back to the kitchen. The four boon companions, for the host was asked to join the party, did not hear her go off to bed; but before long, in the pauses of the chat over the wine, there came an occasional very distinct sound of snoring from the loft above the kitchen where she was sleeping, a sound rendered still more resonant by reason of the thin plank floor. This made the guests smile, and the landlord smiled still more.

"Towards midnight, when there was nothing left on the table but cheese and biscuits, dried fruit, and good wine, the whole party, and the young Frenchmen more particularly, grew communicative. They talked about their country, their studies, and the war. After a while the conversation grew lively. Prosper Magnan drew tears to the merchant's eyes when, with a Picard's frankness and the simplicity of a kindly and affectionate nature, he began to imagine what his mother would be doing while he, her son, was here on the bank of the Rhine.

" 'It is just as if I can see her,' he said; 'she is reading the evening paper, the last thing at night! She will not forget me, I know; she is sure to say, "Where is my poor Prosper, I wonder?" Then if she has won a few sous at cards—of *your* mother perhaps,' he added, jogging Wilhelm's elbow—'she will be putting them in the big red jar, where she keeps the money she is saving up to buy those thirty acres that lie within her own little bit of land at Lescheville. The thirty acres will be worth something like sixty thousand francs. Good meadow land it is! Ah! if I were to have it some day, I would live all the rest of my life at Lescheville, and want nothing better! How often my father wanted those thirty acres and the nice little stream that winds along through the fields! And, after all, he died and could not buy the land. . . . I have played there many and many a time!'

" 'M. Walhenfer, haven't you also your *hoc erat in votis*?' asked Wilhelm.

" 'Yes, sir, yes! But it all came to me as it was, and now . . . .' the good man stopped short and said no more.

" 'For my own part,' said the landlord, whose countenance was slightly flushed, 'I bought a bit of meadow last year that I had set my mind on these ten years past.'

"So they chatted on, as folk will talk when wine has unloosed their tongues, and struck up one of those travelers' friendships that we are a little chary of making on a journey, in such a sort that when they rose to go to their room Wilhelm offered his bed to the merchant.

" 'You can take the offer without hesitation,' he said, 'for Prosper and I can sleep together. It will not be the first time nor the last either, I expect. You are the oldest among us, and we ought to honor old age.'

" 'Pooh!' said the landlord, 'there are several mattresses on our bed, one can be laid on the floor for you,' and he went to shut the window with the usual clatter caused by this precaution.

" 'I accept your offer,' said the merchant, addressing Wilhelm. 'I confess,' he added, lowering his voice, and looking at the friends, 'that I wanted you to make it. I feel that I cannot trust my boatmen; and I am not sorry to find myself in the company of two decent young fellows, two French military men, moreover, for the night. I have a hundred thousand francs in gold and diamonds in that valise.'

"The two younger men received this incautious communication with a discreet friendliness that reassured the worthy German. The landlord helped his guests to shift one of the mattresses, and, when things had been arranged as comfortably as possible, wished them a good-night and went off to bed. The merchant and the surgeons joked each other about their pillows. Prosper put Wilhelm's case of surgical instruments, as well as his own, under the mattress, to raise the end and supply the place of a bolster, just as Walhenfer, in an access of extreme caution, bestowed his valise under his bolster.

" 'We are both going to sleep on our fortunes—you on your money, and I on my case of instruments! It remains to be seen whether my case will bring me in as much money as you have made.'

" 'You may hope so,' said the merchant. 'Honest work will accomplish most things, but you must have patience.'

"Before very long Walhenfer and Wilhelm fell asleep. But whether it was because his bed was too hard, or he himself was over-tired and wakeful, or through some unlucky mood of mind, Prosper Magnan lay broad awake. Imperceptibly his thoughts took an ill turn. He could think of nothing but that hundred thousand francs beneath the merchant's pillow. For him a hundred thousand francs was a vast fortune ready made. He began by laying out the money in endless ways, building castles in the air, as we are all apt to do with so much enjoyment just before we drop off to sleep, when indistinct and hazy ideas arise in our minds, and not seldom night and silence give a magical vividness to our thoughts.

"In these visions Prosper Magnan overtopped his mother's ambitions; he bought the thirty acres of meadow, and married a young lady in Beauvais, to whole hand he could not aspire at present owing to inequality of fortune. With this wealth he planned out a whole pleasant lifetime, saw himself the prosperous father of a family, rich, looked up to in the neighborhood, possibly even Mayor of Beauvais. The Picard head was on fire; he cast about for the means of realizing these dreams of his. With extraordinary warmth of imagination he set himself to plan out a crime, and gold and diamonds were the most vivid and distinct portion of a vision of the merchant's death; the glitter dazzled him. His heart beat fast. He had committed a crime, no doubt, by harboring such thoughts as these. The spell of the gold was upon him; his moral nature was intoxicated by insidious reasonings. He asked himself whether there was any reason why the poor German should live, and imagined how it would have been if he had never existed. To put it briefly, he plotted out a way to do the deed with complete impunity.

"The Austrians held the other bank of the Rhine; a boat lay there under the windows; there were boatmen there; he could cut the man's throat, fling him into the Rhine, escape with the valise through a casement, bribe the boatmen, and go over to the Austrian side. He even went so far as to count upon his surgeon's dexterity with the knife; he knew of a way of decapitating his victim before the sleeper could utter a single shriek . . . ."

M. Taillefer wiped his forehead at this point, and again he drank a little water.

"Then Prosper Magnan rose—slowly and noiselessly. He assured himself that he had awakened nobody, dressed and went into the public room. Then, with the fatal lucidity of mind that suddenly comes at certain crises, with the heightened power of intuition and strength of will that is never lacking to criminals, or to prisoners in the execution of their designs, he unscrewed the iron bars, and drew them from their sockets, and set them against the wall without the slightest sound, hanging with all his weight on to the shutters lest they should creak as they turned on their hinges. In the pale moonlight he could dimly see the objects in the room where Wilhelm and Walhenfer were sleeping.

"Then, he told me, he stopped short for a moment. His heart beat so hard and so heavily, that the sound seemed to ring through the room, and he stood like one dismayed as he heard it. He began to fear for his coolness; his hands shook, he felt as if he were standing on burning coals. But so fair a prospect depended upon the execution of his design, that he saw something like a providence in this dispensation of fate that had brought the merchant thither. He opened the window, went back to his room, took up his case, and looked through it for an instrument best adapted to his purpose.

" 'And when I stood by the bed' (he told me this), 'I asked God for His protection, unthinkingly.'

"He had just raised his arm, and was summoning all his strength for the blow, when something like a voice cried within him, and he thought he saw a light. He flung down the surgical instrument on his bed, fled into the next room, and stood at the window. A profound horror of himself came over him, and feeling how little he could trust himself, fearing to yield to the fascination that held him, he sprang quickly out of the window and walked along by the Rhine, acting as sentinel, as it were, before the inn. Again and again he walked restlessly to and from Andernach, often also his wanderings led him to the slope of the ravine which they had descended that afternoon to reach the inn; but so deep was the silence of the night, and so strong his dread of arousing the watch-dogs, that he kept away from the Red Inn, and lost sight altogether more than once of the window that he had left open. He tried to weary himself out, and so to induce sleep. Yet, as he walked to and fro under the cloudless sky, watching the brilliant stars, it may be that the pure night air and the melancholy lapping of the water wrought upon him, and restored him by degrees to moral sanity. Sober reason completed the work and dispelled that short-lived madness. His education, the precepts of religion, and, above all things (so he told me), visions of the homely life that he had led beneath his father's roof, got the better of his evil thoughts. He thought and pondered for long, his elbow resting on a boulder by the side of the Rhine; and when he turned to go in again, he could not only have slept, so he said, but have watched over millions of gold.

"When his honesty emerged strengthened and triumphant from that ordeal, he knelt in joy and ecstasy to thank God; he felt as happy, light-hearted, and content as on the day when he took the sacrament for the first time, and felt not unworthy of the angels because he had spent the day without sin in word, or thought, or deed.

"He went back again to the inn, shut the window without care to move noiselessly, and went to bed at once. Mind and body were utterly exhausted, and sleep overcame him. He had scarcely laid his head on the mattress before the dreamy drowsiness that precedes sound slumber crept over him; when the senses grow torpid, conscious life ebbs away, thought grows fragmentary, and the last communications of sense to the brain are like the impressions of a dream.

" 'How close the air is!' said Prosper to himself. 'It is just as if I were breathing a damp mist . . . .'

"Dimly he sought to account for this state of things by attributing it to the difference between the outside temperature in the pure country air and the closed room; but before long he heard a constantly recurring sound, very much like the slow drip of water from a leaking tap. On an impulse of panic terror, he thought of rising and calling the landlord, or the merchant, or Wilhelm; but, for his misfortune, he bethought himself of the wooden clock in the next room, fancied that the sound was the beat of the pendulum, and dropped off to sleep with this dim and confused idea in his head."

"Do you want some water, M. Taillefer?" asked the master of the house, seeing the banker take up the empty decanter mechanically.

M. Hermann went on with his story after the slight interruption of the banker's reply.

"The next morning," he went on, "Prosper Magnan was awakened by a great noise. It seemed to him that he had heard shrill cries, and he felt that violent nervous tremor which we experience when we wake to a painful sensation that began during slumber. The thing that takes place in us when we 'wake with a start,' to use the common expression, has been insufficiently investigated, though it presents interesting problems to physiological science. The terrible shock, caused it may be by the too sudden reunion of the two natures in us that are almost always apart while we sleep, is usually momentary, but it was not so for the unlucky young surgeon. The horror grew, and his hair bristled hideously all at once, when he saw a pool of blood between his own mattress and Walhenfer's bedstead. The unfortunate German's head was lying on the floor, the body was still on the bed, all this blood had drained from the neck. Prosper Magnan saw Walhenfer's eyes unclosed and staring, saw red on the sheets that he had slept in, and even on his own hands, saw his own surgeon's knife on the bed, and fainted away on the blood-stained floor.

" 'I was punished already for my thoughts,' he said to me afterwards.

"When he came to himself again, he was sitting in a chair in the public room of the inn, a group of French soldiers round about him, and an inquisitive and interested crowd. He stared in dull bewilderment at a Republican officer who was busy taking down the depositions of several witnesses and drawing up an official report; he recognized the landlord and his wife, the two boatmen, and the maid-servant. The surgical instrument used by the murderer——"

Here M. Taillefer coughed, drew out his pocket-handkerchief, and wiped his forehead. His movements were so natural, that I alone noticed them; indeed, all eyes were fixed on M. Hermann with a kind of greedy interest. The army-contractor leaned his elbow on the table, propped his head on his right hand, and looked fixedly at Hermann. From that time forward I saw no involuntary signs of agitation nor of interest in the tale, but his face was grave and corpse-like; he looked just as he had done while he was playing with the decanter-stopper.

"The surgical instrument used by the murderer lay on the table, beside the case with Prosper's pocket-book and papers. The crowd looked by turns at the young surgeon and at these convincing proofs of his guilt; he himself appeared to be dying; his dull eyes seemed to have no power of sight in them. A confused murmur outside made it evident that a crowd had gathered about the inn, attracted by the news of the murder, and perhaps by a wish to catch a sight of the criminal. The tramp of the sentries posted under the windows and the clanking of their weapons rose over the whispered talk of the populace. The inn itself was shut up, the courtyard was silent and deserted.

"The gaze of the officer who has drawing up the report was intolerable; Prosper Magnan felt some one grasp his hand; looked up to see who it was that stood by him among that unfriendly crowd, and recognized, by the uniform that he wore, the senior surgeon of the demi-brigade quartered in Andernach. So keen and merciless were those eyes, that the poor young fellow shuddered, and his head dropped on to the back of the chair. One of the men held vinegar for him to inhale, and Prosper regained consciousness at once; but his haggard eyes were so destitute of life and intelligence, that the senior surgeon felt his pulse, and spoke to the officer.

" 'Captain,' he said, 'it is impossible to examine the man just now—'

" 'Very well. Take him away,' returned the captain, cutting the surgeon short, and speaking to a corporal who stood behind the junior's chair.

" 'Confounded scoundrel!' the man muttered; 'try at least to hold up your head before these German beggars, to save the honor of the Republic.'

"Thus adjured, Prosper Magnan came to his senses, rose, and went forward a few paces; but when the door opened, when he felt the outer air, and saw the people crowding up, all his strength failed him, his knees bent under him, he tottered.

" 'The confounded sawbones deserves to be put an end to twice over!—March, can't you!' said the two men on either side of him, on whom he leaned.

" 'Oh, the coward! the coward! Here he comes! here he comes! . . . There he is!'

"The words were uttered as by one voice, the clamorous voice of the mob who hemmed him in, insulting and reviling him at every step. During the time that it took to go from the inn to the prison, the trampling feet of the crowd and the soldiers who guarded him, the muttered talk of those about him, the sky above, the morning air, the streets of Andernach, the rippling murmur of the current of the Rhine, all reached him as dull, vague impressions, confused and dim, like all his experiences since his awakening. At times he thought that he had ceased to exist, so he told me afterwards.

"I myself was in prison just then," said M. Hermann, interrupting himself. "We are all enthusiasts at twenty. I was on fire to defend my country, and commanded a volunteer troop raised in and about

Andernach. A short time previously, I managed to fall in one night with a French detachment of eight hundred men. There were two hundred of us at the most; my scouts had betrayed me. I was thrown into the prison at Andernach while they debated whether or not to have me shot by way of a warning to the country. The French, moreover, talked of reprisals, but the murder for which they had a mind to avenge themselves on me turned out to have been committed outside the Electorate. My father had obtained a reprieve of three days, to make application for my pardon to General Augereau, who granted it.

"So I saw Prosper Magnan as soon as he came into the prison at Andernach, and the first sight of him filled me with the deepest pity for him. Haggard, exhausted, and blood-stained though he was, there was a certain frankness in his face that convinced me of his innocence, and made a deep impression upon me. It was as if Germany stood there visibly before me—the prisoner with the long, fair hair and blue eyes, was for my imagination the very personification of the prostrate Fatherland,—this was no murderer, but a victim. As he went past my window, a sad, bitter smile lit up his face for a moment, as if a transitory gleam of sanity crossed a disordered brain. Such a smile would surely not be seen on a murderer's lips. When I next saw the turnkey, I asked him about his new prisoner.

" 'He hasn't said a word since he went into his cell. He sits there with his head on his hands, and sleeps or thinks about his trouble. From what I hear the Frenchmen saying, they will settle his case to-morrow, and he will be shot within twenty-four hours.'

"That evening I lingered a little under his windows during the short time allowed for exercise in the prison yard. We talked together, and he told me very simply the story of his ill-luck, giving sufficiently straightforward answers to my different questions. After that conversation I no longer doubted his innocence. I asked and obtained the favor of spending a few hours in his company, and saw him in this way several times. The poor boy let me into the secret of his thoughts without reserve. In his own opinion, he was at once innocent and guilty. He remembered the hideous temptation which he had found strength to resist, and was afraid that he had committed the murder planned while he was awake in an access of somnambulism.

" 'But how about your companion?' said I.

" 'Oh, Wilhelm is incapable!——' he cried vehemently. He did not even finish the sentence. I grasped his hand at the warm-hearted outburst, so fraught with youth and virtue.

" 'I expect he was frightened when he woke,' he said; 'he must have lost his presence of mind and fled——'

" 'Without waking you?' I asked. 'Why, in that case your defence is soon made, for Walhenfer's valise will not have been stolen.'

"All at once he burst into tears.

" 'Oh, yes, yes!' he cried; 'I am not guilty. I cannot have killed him. I remember the dreams I had. I was at school, playing at prisoners-base. I could not have cut his throat while I was dreaming of running about.'

"But in spite of the gleams of hope that quieted his mind somewhat at times, he still felt crushed by the weight of remorse. There was no blinking the fact he had raised his arm to strike the blow. He condemned himself, and considered that he was morally guilty after committing the crime in imagination.

" 'And yet, I am not a bad fellow.' he cried. 'Oh, poor mother! Perhaps just now she is happily playing at cards with her friends in the little tapestried room at home. If she knew that I had so much as raised my hand to take another man's life—Oh! it would kill her! And I am in prison, and accused of murder! If I did not kill the man, I shall certainly be the death of my mother!'

"He shed no tears as he spoke. In a wild fit of frenzy, not uncommon among Picards, he sprang up, and if I had not forcibly restrained him, would have dashed his head against the wall.

" 'Wait until you have been tried,' I said. 'You will be acquitted; you are innocent. And your mother——'

" 'My mother,' he cried wildly; 'my mother will hear that I have been accused of murder, that is the main point. You always hear things like that in little places, and my poor mother will die of grief. Besides, I am not innocent. Do you care to know the whole truth! I feel that I have lost the virginity of my conscience.'

"With those terrible words, he sat down, folded his arms across his chest, bowed his head, and fixed his eyes gloomily on the floor. Just then the turnkey came to bid me return to my cell; but loath to leave my companion when his discouragement seemed at its blackest, I clasped him in a friendly embrace. 'Be patient,' I said, 'perhaps it will all come right. If an honest man's opinion can silence your doubts, I tell you this—that I esteem you and love you. Accept my friendship, and repose on my heart, if you cannot feel at peace with your own.'

"On the following day, about nine o'clock, a corporal and four fusiliers came for the assistant surgeon. I heard the sound of the soldiers' footsteps, and went to the window; our eyes met as he crossed the court. Never shall I forget the glance fraught with so many thoughts and forebodings, nor the resignation and indescribably sad and melancholy sweetness in his expression. In that dumb swift transference of thought, my friend conveyed his testament to me; he left his lost life to the one friend who was beside him at the last.

"That night must have been very hard to live through, a very lonely night for him; but perhaps the pallor that overspread his face was a sign of newly acquired stoicism, based on a new view of himself. Perhaps he felt purified by remorse, and thought to expiate his sin in this anguish and shame. He walked with a firm step; and I noticed that he had removed the accidental stains of blood that soiled his clothing the night before.

" 'Unluckily I stained my hands while I was asleep; I always was an uneasy sleeper,' he had said, a dreadful despair in the tones of his voice.

"I was told that he was about to be tried by a court-martial. The division was to go forward in two days' time, and the commandant of the demi-brigade meant to try the criminal on the spot before leaving Andernach.

"While that court-martial was sitting, I was in an agony of suspense. It was noon before they brought Prosper Magnan back to prison. I was taking my prescribed exercise when he came; he saw me, and rushed into my arms.

" 'I am lost!' he said. 'Lost beyond hope! Every one here must look on me as a murderer——'

"Then he raised his head proudly. 'This injustice has completely given me back my innocence,' he said. 'If I had lived, my life must always have been troubled, but my death shall be without reproach. But is there anything beyond?'

"The whole eighteenth century spoke in that sudden questioning. He was absorbed in thought.

" 'But what did you tell them? What did they ask you?' I cried. 'Did you not tell them the simple truth as you told it to me?'

"He gazed at me for a minute, then after the brief, dreadful pause, he answered with a feverish readiness of speech:

" 'First of all they asked me: "Did you go out of the inn during the night?"—"Yes," I told them.—"How did you get out?"—I turned red, and answered, "Through the window."—"Then you must have opened it?"—"Yes," I said.—"You set about it very cautiously; the landlord heard nothing!"—I was like one stupefied all the time. The boatmen swore that they had seen me walking, sometimes towards Andernach, sometimes towards the forest. I went to and fro many times, they said. I had buried the gold and diamonds. As a matter of fact the valise has not been found. Then, the whole time, I myself was struggling against remorse. Whenever I opened my mouth to speak, a merciless voice seemed to cry, "*You meant to do it!*" Everything was against me, even myself! . . . They wanted to know about my comrade, and I completely exonerated *him*. Then they said, "One of you four must be guilty—you or your comrade, the innkeeper or his wife. All the doors and windows were shut fast this morning!" When they said that,' he went on, 'I had no voice, no strength, no spirit left in me. I was more sure of my friend than of myself; I saw very well that they thought us both equally guilty of the murder, and I was the clumsier one of the two. I tried to explain the thing by somnambulism; I tried to clear my friend; then I got muddled, and it was all over with me. I read my sentence in the judges' eyes. Incredulous smiles stole across their faces. That is all. The suspense is over. I am to be shot to-morrow—— I do not think of myself now,' he said, 'but of my poor mother.'

"He stopped short and looked up to heaven. He shed no tears; his eyes were dry and contracted with pain.

"Frédéric! . . .

"Ah! I remember now! The other one was called Frédéric . . . Frédéric! Yes, I am sure that was the name," M. Hermann exclaimed triumphantly.

I felt the pressure of my fair neighbor's foot; she made a sign to me, and looked across at M. Taillefer. The sometime army-contractor's hand drooped carelessly over his eyes, but through the fingers we thought we saw a smouldering blaze in them.

"Eh?" she said in my ear, "and now suppose that his name is Frédéric?"

I gave the lady a side glance of entreaty to be silent. Hermann went on with his tale.

" 'It is cowardly of Frédéric to leave me to my fate. He must have been afraid. Perhaps he is hiding in the inn, for both our horses were there in the yard that morning.—What an inexplicable mystery it is!' he added, after a pause. 'Somnambulism, somnambulism! I never walked in my sleep but once in my life, and then I was not six years old. And I am to go out of this,' he went on, striking his foot against the earth, 'and take with me all the friendship that there is in the world.

Must I die twice over, doubting the friendship that began when we were five years old, and lasted through our school life and our student days! Where is Frédéric?'

"The tears filled his eyes. We cling more closely to a sentiment than to our life, it seems!

" 'Let us go in again,' he said; 'I would rather be in my cell. I don't mean them to see me crying. I shall go bravely to my death, but I cannot play the hero in season and out of season, and I confess that I am sorry to leave my life, my fair life, and my youth. I did not sleep last night; I remembered places about my home when I was a child; I saw myself running about in the meadows, perhaps it was the memories of those fields that led to my ruin.—I had a future before me' (he interrupted himself). 'A dozen men, a sub-lieutenant who will cry, "Ready! present! fire!" a roll of drums, and disgrace! that is my future now! Ah! there is a God, there is a God, or all this would be too nonsensical.'

"Then he grasped my arm, put his arms about me, and held me tightly to him.

" 'Ah! you are the last human soul to whom I can pour out my soul. *You* will be free again! You will see your mother! I do not know whether you are rich or poor, but no matter for that, you are all the world for me. . . . They cannot keep the fighting up for ever. Well and good then, when they make peace, go to Beauvais. If my mother survives the disastrous news of my death, you will find her out and tell her "He was innocent," to comfort her. She will believe you,' he went on. 'I shall write to her as well, but you will carry my last look to her; you shall tell her how that you were the last friend whom I embraced before I died. Ah! how she will love you, my poor mother, you who have stood my friend at the last!' He was silent for a moment or two, the burden of his memories seemed too heavy for him to bear. 'Here they are all strangers to me,' he said, 'the other surgeons and the men, and they all shrink from me in horror. But for you, my innocence must remain a secret between me and heaven.'

"I vowed to fulfill his last wishes as a sacred charge. He felt that my heart went out to him, and was touched by my words. A little later the soldiers came back to take him before the court-martial again. He was doomed.

"I know nothing of the formalities or circumstances that attend a sentence of this kind; I do not know whether there is any appeal, nor whether the young surgeon's defence was made according to rule and precedent, but he prepared to go to his death early on the morrow, and spent that night in writing to his mother.

" 'We shall both be set free to-day,' he said, smiling, when I went the next day to see him. 'The general his signed your pardon, I hear.'

"I said nothing, and gazed at him to engrave his features on my memory.

"A look of loathing crossed his face, and he said, 'I have been a miserable coward! All night long I have been praying the very walls for mercy,' and he looked round his cell. 'Yes, yes,' he went on, 'I howled with despair, I rebelled against this, I have been through the most fearful inward conflict. . . . I was alone! . . . Now I am thinking of what others will say of me—Courage is like a garment that we put on. I must go decently to my death. . . . And so . . . .' "

II

A DOUBLE RETRIBUTION

"Oh! do not tell us any more!" cried the girl who had asked for the story, cutting short the Nuremberger. "I want to live in suspense, and to believe that he was saved. If I were to know to-night that they shot him, I should not sleep. You must tell me the rest to-morrow."

We rose. M. Hermann offered his arm to my fair neighbor, who asked as she took it, "They shot him, did they not?"

"Yes. I was there."

"What, monsieur, you could——"

"He wished it, madame. It is something very ghastly to attend the funeral of a living man, your own friend who is not guilty of the crime laid to his charge. The poor young fellow never took his eyes off me. He seemed to have no life but mine left. 'He wished,' he said, 'that I should bear his last sigh to his mother.' "

"Well, and did you see her?"

"After the Peace of Amiens I went to France to take the glad tidings 'He was innocent!' That pilgrimage was like a sacred duty laid upon me. But Mme. Magnan was dead, I found; she had died of consumption. I burned the letter I had brought for her, not without deep emotion. Perhaps you will laugh at my German high-flown sentimentality; but for me there was a tragedy most sublimely sad in the eternal silence which was about to swallow up those farewells uttered in vain from one grave to another grave, and heard by none, like the cry of some traveler in the desert surprised by a beast of prey."

Here I broke in with a "How if some one were to bring you face to face with one of the men in this drawing-room, and say, 'There is the murderer!' would not that be another tragedy? And what would you do?"

M. Hermann took up his hat and left.

"You are acting like a young man, and very thoughtlessly," said the lady. "Just look at Taillefer; there he sits in a low chair by the fire, Mademoiselle Fanny is handing him a cup of coffee; he is smiling. How could a murderer display such quiet self-possession as that, after a story that must have been torture to him. He looks quite patriarchal, does he not?"

"Yes; but just ask him if he has been with the army in Germany!" I exclaimed.

"Why not?" and with the audacity rarely lacking in womankind when occasion tempts, or curiosity gets the better of her, my fair neighbor went across to the army-contractor.

"Have you been in Germany, M. Taillefer?" she asked.

Taillefer all but dropped his saucer.

"I, madame?—No, never."

"Why, what is that you are saying, Taillefer?" protested the banker, chiming in. "You were in the Wagram campaign, were you not—on the victualing establishment?"

"Oh yes!" answered Taillefer; "I was there, that once."

"You are wrong about him; he is a good sort of man," decided the lady when she came back to me.

"Very well," said I to myself, "before this evening is over I will drive the murderer out of the mire in which he is hiding."

There is a phenomenon of consciousness that takes place daily beneath our eyes, so commonplace that no one notices it, and yet there are astounding depths beneath it. Two men meet in a drawing-room who have some cause to disdain or to hate each other; perhaps one of them knows something which is not to the credit of the other; perhaps it is a condition of things that is kept a secret; perhaps one of them is meditating a revenge; but both of them are conscious of the gulf that divides them, or that ought to divide them. Before they know it, they are watching each other and absorbed in each other; some subtle emanation of their thought seems to distil from every look and gesture; they have a magnetic influence. Nor can I tell which has the more power of attraction—revenge or crime, hatred or contempt. Like some priest who cannot consecrate the house where an evil spirit abides, the two are ill at ease and suspicious; one of them, it is hard to say which, is polite, and the other sullen; one of them turns pale or red, and the other trembles, and it often happens that the avenger is quite as cowardly as the victim. For very few of us have the nerve to cause pain, even if it is necessary pain, and many a man passes over a matter or forgives from sheer hatred of fuss or dread of making a tragical scene.

With this inter-susceptibility of minds, and apprehensiveness of thought and feeling, there began a mysterious truggle between the army-contractor and me. Ever since my interruption of M. Hermann's story he had shunned my eyes. Perhaps in like manner he looked none of the party in the face. He was chatting now with the inexperienced Fanny, the banker's daughter; probably, like all criminals, he felt a longing to take shelter with innocence, as if the mere proximity of innocence might bring him peace for a little. But though I stood on the other side of the room, I still listened to all that he said; my direct gaze fascinated him. When he thought he could glance at me in turn, unnoticed, our eyes met, and his eyelids fell directly. Taillefer found this torture intolerable, and hastened to put a stop to it by moving to a card-table. I backed his opponent, hoping to lose my money. It fell out as I had wished. The other player left the table, I cut in, and the guilty man and I were now face to face.

"Monsieur," I said, as he dealt the cards, "will you be so good as to begin a fresh score?" He swept his counters from right to left somewhat hastily. The lady, my neighbor at dinner, passed by; I gave her a significant glance.

"M. Frédéric Taillefer," I asked, addressing my opponent, "are you related to a family in Beauvais with whom I am well acquainted?"

"Yes, sir." He let the cards fall, turned pale, hid his face in his hands, begged one of his backers to finish the game for him, and rose.

"It is too warm here," he gasped; "I am afraid . . . ."

He did not finish his sentence. An expression of horrible anguish suddenly crossed his face, and he hurried out of the room; the master of the house followed him with what appeared to be keen anxiety. My neighbor and I looked at each other, but her face was overcast by indescribable sadness; there was a tinge of bitterness in it.

"Is your behavior very merciful?" she asked, as I rose from the card-table, where I had been playing and losing. She drew me into the embrasure of the window as she spoke. "Would you be willing to accept the power of reading all hearts if you could have it? Why interfere with man's justice or God's? We may escape the one; we shall never escape the other. Is the prerogative of a President of a Court of Assize so enviable? And you have all but done the executioner's office as well—"

"After sharing and stimulating my curiosity," I said, "you are lecturing me!"

"You have made me think," she answered.

"So it is to be peace to scoundrels, and woe to the unfortunate, is it? Let us down on our knees and worship gold! But shall we change the subject?" I said with a laugh. "Please look at the young lady who is just coming into the room."

"Well?"

"I met her three days ago at a ball at the Neapolitan embassy, and fell desperately in love. For pity's sake, tell me who she is. No one could tell me——"

"That is Mlle. Victorine Taillefer!"

Everything swam before my eyes; I could scarcely hear the tones of the speaker's voice.

"Her stepmother brought her home only a while ago from the convent where she has been finishing her education somewhat late. . . . For a long time her father would not recognize her. She comes here today for the first time. She is very handsome—and very rich!"

A sardonic smile went with the words. Just as she spoke, we heard loud cries that seemed to come from an adjoining room; stifled though they were, they echoed faintly through the garden.

"Is not that M. Taillefer's voice?" I asked. We both listened intently to the sounds, and fearful groans reached our ears. Just then our hostess hurried towards us and closed the window.

"Let us avoid scenes," she said to us. "If Mlle. Taillefer were to hear her father, it would be quite enough to send her into a fit of hysterics."

The banker came back to the drawing-room, looked for Victorine, and spoke a few low words in her ear. The girl sprang at once towards the door with an exclamation, and vanished. This produced a great sensation. The card-parties broke up; every one asked his neighbor what had happened. The buzz of talk grew louder, and groups were formed.

"Has M. Taillefer——?" I began.

"Killed himself?" put in my sarcastic friend. "You would wear mourning for him with a light heart, I can see."

"But what can have happened to him?"

"Poor man!" (it was the lady of the house who spoke) "he suffers from a complaint—I cannot recollect the name of it, though M. Brousson has told me about it often enough—and he has just had a seizure."

"What kind of complaint is it?" asked an examining magistrate suddenly.

"Oh, it is something dreadful," she answered; "and the doctors can do nothing for him. The agony must be terrible. Taillefer had a seizure, I remember, once, poor man, when he was staying with us in the country: I was obliged to go to a neighbor's house so as not to hear him; his shrieks are fearful; he tries to kill himself; his daughter had to have him put into a strait jacket and tied down to his bed. Poor man! he says there are live creatures in his head gnawing his brain; it is a horrible, sawing, shooting pain that throbs through every nerve. He suffers so fearfully with his head that he did not feel the blisters that they used to apply at one time to draw the inflammation; but M. Brousson, his present doctor, forbade this; he says that it is nervous inflammation, and put leeches on the throat, and applies laudanum to the head; and, indeed, since they began this treatment the attacks have been less frequent; he seldom has them oftener than once a year, in the late autumn. When he gets over one of these seizures, Taillefer always says that he would rather be broken on the wheel than endure such agony again."

"That looks as if he suffered considerably!" said a stockbroker, the wit of the party.

"Oh! last year he very nearly died," the lady went on. "He went alone to his country-house on some urgent business; there was no one at hand perhaps, for he lay stiff and stark, like one dead, for twenty-two hours. They only saved his life by a scalding hot bath."

"Then is it some kind of tetanus?" asked the stockbroker.

"I do not know," returned she. "He has had the complaint nearly thirty years; it began while he was with the army. He says that he had a fall on a boat, and a splinter got into his head, but Brousson hopes to cure him. People say that in England they have found out a way of treating it with prussic acid, and that you run no risks——"

A shrill cry, louder than any of the preceding ones, rang through the house. The blood ran cold in our veins.

"There!" the banker's wife went on, "that is just what I was expecting every moment. It makes me start in my chair and creep through every nerve. But—it is an extraordinary thing!—poor Taillefer, suffering such unspeakable pain as he does, never runs any risk of his life! He eats and drinks as usual whenever he has a little respite from that ghastly torture. . . . Nature has such strange freaks. Some German doctor once told him that it was a kind of gout in the head; and Brousson's opinion was pretty much the same."

I left the little group about our hostess and went out with Mlle. Taillefer. A servant had come for her. She was crying.

"*Oh, mon Dieu, mon Dieu!*" she sobbed; "how can my father have offended heaven to deserve such suffering as this? . . . So kind as he is."

I went downstairs with her, and saw her into the carriage; her father was lying doubled up inside it. Mlle. Taillefer tried to smother the sound of her father's moaning by covering his mouth with a handkerchief. Unluckily, he saw me, and his drawn face seemed further distorted, a scream of agony rent the air, he gave me a dreadful look, and the carriage started.

That dinner party and the evening that followed it was to exercise a painful influence on my life and on my views. Honor and my own scruples forbade me to connect myself with a murderer, no matter how good a husband and father he might be, and so I must needs fall in love with Mlle. Taillefer. It was well-nigh incredible how often chance drew me to visit at houses where I knew I might meet Victorine. Again and again, when I had pledged myself to renounce her society, the evening would find me hovering about her. The pleasures of this life were immense. It gave the color of an illicit passion to this unforbidden love, and a chimerical remorse filled up the measure of my bliss. I scorned myself when I greeted Taillefer, if by accident he was with his daughter; but, after all, I bowed to him.

Unluckily, in fact, Victorine, being something more than a pretty girl, was well read, charming, and gifted in no small degree, without being in the least a blue stocking, without the slightest taint of affectation. There is a certain reserve in her light talk, and a pensive graciousness about her that no one could resist. She liked me, or, at any rate, she allowed me to think so; there was a certain smile that she kept for me; for me the tones of her voice grew sweeter still. Oh! she cared about me, but she worshipped her father; she would praise his kindness to me, his gentleness, his various perfections, and all her praises were like so many daggers thrust into my heart.

At length I all but became an accessory after the fact, an accomplice in the crime which had laid the foundation of the wealth of the Taillefers. I was fain to ask for Victorine's hand. I fled. I traveled abroad. I went to Germany and to Andernach. But I came back again, and Victorine was looking thinner and paler than her wont. If she had been well and in good spirits, I should have been safe; but now the old feeling for her was rekindled with extraordinary violence.

Fearing lest my scruples were degenerating into monomania, I resolved to convene a Sanhedrin of consciences that should not have been tampered with, and so to obtain some light on this problem of the higher morality and philosophy. The question had only become more complex since my return.

So the day before yesterday I assembled those among my friends whom I looked upon as notably honest, scrupulous, and honorable. I asked two Englishmen, a Secretary to the Embassy and a Puritan; a retired Minister, in the character of matured worldly wisdom; a few young men still under the illusions of inexperience; a priest, an elderly man; my old guardian, a simple-hearted being, who gave me the best account of his management of my property that ever trustee has been known to give in the annals of the Palais; an advocate, a notary, and a judge,—in short, all social opinions were represented, and all practical wisdom. We had begun by a good dinner, good talk, and a deal of mirth; and over the dessert I told my story plainly and simply (suppressing the name of my lady-love), and asked for sound counsel.

"Give me your advice," I said to my friends as I came to an end. "Go thoroughly into the question as if it were a point of law. I will have an urn and billiard-balls brought round, and you shall vote for or against my marriage, the secrecy of the ballot shall be scrupulously observed."

Deep silence prevailed all at once. Then the notary declined to act.

"There is a contract to draw up," he alleged.

Wine had had a quieting effect on my guardian; indeed, it clearly behoved me to find a guardian for *him* if he was to reach his home in safety.

"I see how it is!" I said to myself. "A man who does not give me an opinion is telling me pretty forcibly what I ought to do."

There was a general movement round the table. A landowner, who had subscribed to a fund for putting a headstone to General Foy's grave and providing for his family, exclaimed:

" 'Even, as virtue, crime hath its degrees.' "

"The babbler," said the Minister in a low voice, as he nudged my elbow.

"Where is the difficulty?" asked a duke, whose property consisted of lands confiscated from Protestants after the Revocation of the Edict of Nantes.

The advocate rose to his feet.

"In law," opined the mouthpiece of Justice, "the case before us presents no difficulty whatever. Monsieur le Duc is right! Is there not a statute of limitations? Begin to inquire into the origins of a fortune, and where should we all of us be? This is matter of conscience, and not of law. If you must drag the case before some tribunal, the confessional is the proper place in which to hear it."

And the Code incarnate, having said his say, sat down and drank a glass of champagne. The man intrusted with the interpretation of the Gospel, the good priest, spoke next.

"God has made us weak," he said with decision. "If you love the criminal's heiress, marry her; but content yourself with her mother's property, and give her father's money to the poor."

"Why, in all likelihood the father only made a great match because he had made money first," cried one of the pitiless quibblers that you meet with everywhere. "And it is just the same with every little bit of good fortune—it all came of his crime!"

"The fact that the matter can be discussed is enough to decide it! There are some things which a man cannot weigh and ponder," cried my guardian, thinking to enlighten the assembly by this piece of drunken gravity.

"True!" said the Secretary to the Embassy.

"True!" exclaimed the priest, each meaning quite differently.

A doctrinaire, who escaped being elected by a bare hundred and fifty votes out of a hundred and fifty-five, rose next.

"Gentlemen," said he, "this phenomenal manifestation of the intellectual nature is one of the most strongly marked instances of an exception to the normal condition of things, the rules which society obeys. The decision, therefore, on an abnormal case should be an extemporaneous effort of the conscience, a sudden conception, a delicate discrimination of the inner consciousness, not unlike the flashes of insight that constitute perception in matters of taste. . . . Let us put it to the vote."

"Yes, let us put it to the vote," cried the rest of the party.

Each was provided with two billiard-balls—one white, the other red.

White, the color of virginity, was to proscribe marriage; red to count in favor of it. My scruples prevented me from voting. My friends being seventeen in number, nine made a decisive majority. We grew excited and curious as each dropped his ball into the narrow-mouthed wicker basket, which holds the numbered balls when players draw for their places at pool, for there was a certain novelty in this process of voting by ballot on a nice point of conduct. When the basket was turned out there were nine white balls. To me this did not come as a surprise; but it occurred to me to count up the young men of my own age among this Court of Appeal. There were exactly nine of these casuists; one thought had been in all their minds.

"Aha!" I said to myself, "there was a unanimous feeling against the marriage in their minds, and a no less unanimous verdict in favor of it among the rest! Here is a fix, and how am I to get out of it?"

"Where does the father-in-law live?" one of my school-fellows, less crafty than the rest, asked carelessly.

"There is no longer a father-in-law in the case!" I exclaimed. "A while ago my conscience spoke sufficiently plainly to make your verdict superfluous. And if it speaks more uncertainly to-day, here are the inducements that led me to waver. Here is the tempter—this letter that I received two months ago;" and I drew a card from my pocket-book and held it up.

> *"You are requested to be present,"* so it ran, *"at the funeral and burial service of*
>
> M. JEAN-FREDERIC TAILLEFER
>
> *of the firm of Taillefer and Company, sometime contractor of provisions to the Army, late Chevalier of the Legion of Honor and of the Order of the Golden Spur, Captain of the First Company of Grenadiers of the National Guard, Paris: who died on May 1st, at his house in the Rue Joubert. The interment will take place,"* and so forth, and so forth.
>
> *"On behalf of,"* and so forth.

"What am I to do now?" I continued. "I will just put the question roughly before you. There is unquestionably a pool of blood on Mlle. Taillefer's estates. Her father's property is one vast *Aceldama*. . . . Granted! But, then, Prosper Magnan has no representatives, and I could not find any traces of the family of the pin-maker who was murdered that night at Andernach. To whom should the fortune be returned? And ought it all to be returned? Have I any right to betray a secret discovered by accident, to add a severed human head to an innocent girl's marriage portion, to give her ugly dreams, to destroy her pleasant illusions, to kill the father she loved a second time, by telling her that there is a dark stain on all her wealth?

"I have borrowed a *Dictionary of Cases of Conscience* from an old ecclesiastic, and found therein no solution whatever of my doubts. Can you make a religious foundation for the souls of Prosper Magnan and Walhenfer and Taillefer now midway through this nineteenth century of ours? And as for endowing a charitable institution or awarding periodic prizes to virtue—most of our charitable institutions appear to me to be harboring scoundrels, and the prize of virtue would fall to the greatest rogues.

"And not only so. Would these investments, more or less gratifying to vanity, be any reparation? And is it my place to make any? Then I am in love, passionately in love. My love has come to be my life. If, without any apparent reason, I propose that a young girl, accustomed to splendor and elegance, and a life abundant in all the luxuries art can devise, a girl who indolently enjoys Rossini's music at the Bouffons,—if to her I should propose that she should rob herself of fifteen hundred thousand francs for the benefit of aged imbeciles and problematical scrofula patients, she would laugh and turn her back upon me, or her confidante would take me for a wag who makes jokes in poor taste. If in an ecstasy of love I extol the charms of humble life in a cottage by the Loire, if I ask her to give up, for my sake, her life in Paris, it would be a virtuous life to begin with, and probably would end in a sad experience for me, for I should lose the girl's heart; she is passionately fond of dancing and of pretty dresses, and, for the time being, of me. Enter some smart stripling of an officer with a nicely curled moustache, who shall play the piano, rave about Byron, and mount a horse gracefully, and I shall be supplanted. What is to be done? Gentlemen, advise me, for pity's sake?"

Then one of the party, who hitherto had not breathed a word, the Englishman with a Puritanical cast of face, not unlike the father of Jeanie Deans, shrugged his shoulders.

"Idiot that you were," he said. "What made you ask him if he came from Beauvais?"

Ivan Bunin

1870—1953

Bunin, a Nobel Prize winner in 1933, was born to a noble family established at Vorenzh, a city on the Don, halfway between Moscow and Rostov. After 1917 he never saw his homeland again: finding Communism abhorrent, he went into permanent exile, moving freely about Europe and finally settling in Paris. Both the man and the work suffered from being uprooted, and though Bunin continued fairly productive, most of his very best work was achieved before his self-exile.

In his early years he was interested mainly in poetry and was honored both for his own work and for his translations from French, English, and American poets (Pushkin Prize, 1903; Russian Academy membership, 1909). Devotion to poetry implies a belief in the importance of style. Bunin took up prose fiction in the spirit of that belief; there is no break in the continuity of development, no aesthetic crisis.

The fiction of his middle years brought him international fame. His novel The Village *(1910-1911), blending realism, satire, and compassion, is an authentic portrayal of both peasants and gentry in the still-feudal patriarchy that was soon to disappear and that was already ridden by the sense of obsolescence and extinction. Neither in* The Village, *still regarded as his masterpiece, nor elsewhere did Bunin follow Tolstoi and Turgenev in romanticizing the peasantry.*

Bunin does, however, belong to the literary tradition that reached its zenith in Turgenev and the Tolstoi of War and Peace *and* Anna

Karenina. *He continues their psychological realism and cosmopolitanism, and forges a style fully as clear and classical and generally so restrained that he often seems, as one commentator remarks, not a Slav but "a Gaul who has chosen impeccable Russian as his medium." As "Sunstroke" demonstrates, he also shares his predecessors' ability to describe topography and weather in a way that is at once realistic and evocative of the archetypal and cosmic. He is more drawn to irony than either and is more hard-bitten. His social-political outlook is far more conservative even than that of the early Tolstoi. In fact, Bunin is one of the few major Russian writers who holds to a self-examined and self-consistent aristocratic reaction distinct from and largely unsympathetic to the mystic slavophile reaction exemplified by writers like Dostoievski and Soloviev.*

Again and again Bunin returns to the problem of irony in human experience. His interest is not in the external circumstances productive of ironic situation but in the shock, agony, or spiritual struggle of the individual caught in the situation. In other words, he does not utilize irony chiefly as a means of producing a clever or superficially wry effect, but treats it as a pervasive and inescapable aspect of the pathetic and the tragic. Ironic in this sense is "The Gentleman from San Francisco" (1915), one of the most famous stories of the modern era. Like Tolstoi's "The Death of Ivan Ilyich" it evokes powerfully the ironic sense of wasted human potential and the spiritual meaninglessness of modern materialasm.

Interestingly, and fittingly, D. H. Lawrence, arch-enemy of modernity's "foul mechanicalness," had a hand in producing the first English translation of The Gentleman from San Francisco and Other Stories *(1922).*

*Equally characteristic of Bunin is preoccupation with the contingency and transitoriness of individual existence, the motif enunciated in "Dark Avenues": "Everything passes . . . . Love, youth—everything." But Bunin's pessimism is, like Thomas Hardy's, poetic and compassionate. Somerset Maugham is to be credited with bringing "Sunstroke" to a wide audience (*Tellers of Tales, *1939). In English the story first appeared in Bunin's collection* Grammar of Love *(1935).* Dark Avenues *(trans. 1949) collects the stories Bunin wrote between 1938 and 1944.*

Sunstroke

Ivan Bunin

Leaving the hot, brightly lighted dining saloon after dinner, they went on deck and stood near the rail. She closed her eyes, leant her cheek on the back of her hand, and laughed—a clear, charming laugh—everything about this little woman was charming.

"I am quite drunk," she said. "In fact I have gone mad. Where did you come from? Three hours ago I did not know of your existence. I don't even know where you got on the boat. Was it Samara? But it doesn't matter, you're a dear. Am I dizzy, or is the boat really turning round?"

In front of them lay darkness and the light of lamps. A soft wind blew strongly against their faces and carried the light to one side. With the smartness characteristic of the Volga boats, the steamer was making a wide curve towards the small wharf.

The lieutenant took her hand and raised it to his lips. The firm little fragrant hand was tanned. His heart became faint with fear and ecstasy as he thought how strong and bronzed must be the body under the light linen dress after having basked in the Southern sun on the hot beach for a whole month. (She had told him that she was on her way from Anapi.)

"Let's get off," he murmured.

"Where?" she asked in surprise.

"At this wharf."

"What for?"

He was silent. She raised her hand to her hot cheek again.

"You are mad."

"Let's get off," he repeated stubbornly. "I implore you—"

"Oh, do as you like," she said, turning from him.

With its final impetus, the steamer bumped gently against the dimly lit wharf, and they nearly fell over each other. The end of a rope flew over their heads, the boat heaved back, there was a foam of churning waters, the gangways clattered. The lieutenant rushed away to collect their things.

A moment later they passed through the sleepy ticket office into the ankle-deep sand of the road, and silently got into a dusty open cab. The soft, sandy road sloping gradually uphill, lit by crooked lamp-posts at long intervals on either side, seemed unending, but they reached its top and clattered along a high-road until they came to a sort of square with municipal buildings and a watch-tower. It was all full of warmth and the smells peculiar to a hot night in a small provincial town. The cab drew up at a lighted portico, behind the door of which a steep old wooden stairway was visible, and an old unshaven waiter, in a pink shirt and black coat, reluctantly took their luggage, and led the way in his down-at-heel slippers. They entered a large room stuffy from the hot sun which had beaten on it all day, its white curtains drawn. On the toilet table were two unlit candles.

The instant the door closed on the waiter, the lieutenant sprang towards her with such impetuosity, and they were carried away by a breathless kiss of such passion, that they remembered it for many, many years. Neither of them had ever before experienced anything like it.

At ten o'clock next morning the little, nameless woman left. She never told him her name, and referred to herself jokingly as "the fair stranger." It was a hot, sunny morning. Church bells were ringing, and a market was in full swing in the square in front of the hotel. There were scents of hay and tar and all the odours characteristic of a Russian provincial town.

They had not slept much, but when she emerged from behind the screen, where she had washed and dressed in five minutes, she was as fresh as a girl of seventeen. Was she embarrassed? Very little, if at all. She was as simple and gay as before, and—already rational. "No, no, dear," she said in reply to his request that they should continue the journey together. "No, you must wait for the next boat. If we go together, it will spoil it all. It would be very unpleasant for me. I give you my word of honour that I am not in the least what you may think I am. Nothing at all like this has ever happened to me before or will ever happen again. I seem to have been under a spell. Or, rather, we both seem to have had something like sunstroke."

The lieutenant readily agreed with her. In a bright, happy mood he drove her to the wharf—just before the pink steamer of the Samolet

Line started. He kissed her openly on the deck, and had barely time to get ashore before the gangway was lowered. He returned to the hotel in the same care-free, easy mood. But something had changed. The room without her seemed quite different from what it had been with her. He was still full of her; he did not mind, but it was strange. The room still held the scent of her excellent English lavender water, her unfinished cup of tea still stood on the tray, but she was gone . . . . The lieutenant's heart was suddenly filled with such a rush of tenderness that he hurriedly lit a cigarette and began to pace the room, switching his top-boots with his cane.

"A strange adventure," he said aloud, laughing and feeling tears well up in his eyes. " 'I give you my word of honour that I am not in the least what you think I am,' and she's gone. Absurd woman!"

The screen had been moved—the bed had not been made. He felt that he had not the strength to look at that bed. He put the screen in front of it, closed the window to shut out the creaking of the wheels and the noisy chatter of the market, drew the white billowing curtains, and sat down on the sofa. Yes, the roadside adventure was over. She was gone, and now, far away, she was probably sitting in the windowed saloon, or on deck, gazing at the enormous river glittering in the sun, at the barges drifting down-stream, at the yellow shoals, at the shining horizon of sky and water, at the immeasurable sweep of the Volga. And it was good-bye for ever and ever. For where could they possibly meet again? "For," he thought, "I can hardly appear on the scene without any excuse, in the town where she lives her everyday life with her husband, her three-year-old daughter and all her family."

The town seemed to him a special, a forbidden town. He was aggravated and stunned by the thought that she would live her lonely life there, often perhaps remembering him, recalling their brief encounter, that he would never see her again. No, it was impossible. It would be too mad, too unnatural, too fantastic. He suffered and was overwhelmed by horror and despair in feeling that without her his whole life would be futile. "Damn it all!" he thought, as he got up and began to pace the room again, trying not to look at the bed behind the screen. "What in the world's the matter with me? It's not the first time, is it? And yet—Was there anything very special about her, or did anything very special happen? It really is like sunstroke. And how on earth am I to spend a whole day in this hole without her?"

He still remembered all of her, down to the minutest detail: her sunburn, her linen frock, her strong body, her unaffected, bright, gay voice . . . . The sense of ecstatic joy which her feminine charm had given him was still extraordinarily strong, but now a second feeling rose uppermost in his mind—a new, strange, incomprehensible feeling, which had not been there while they had been together, and of which he would not, the day before, have believed himself capable when he had started what he had thought to be the amusement of a passing acquaintance. And now there was no one, no one, whom he could tell. "And the point is," he thought, "that I never shall be able to tell anyone! And how am I go get through this endless day with these memories, this inexplicable agony, in this god-forsaken town on the banks of that same Volga along which the steamer is carrying her away?" He must do something to save himself, something to distract him, he must go somewhere. He put on his hat with an air of determination, took his stick and walked along the corridor with his spurs jingling, ran down the stairs and out onto the porch. But where should he go? A cab was drawn up in front of the hotel. A young, smartly-dressed driver sat on the box calmly smoking a cigar. He was obviously waiting for someone. The lieutenant stared at him, bewildered and astonished: How could anyone sit calmly on a box and smoke and in general be unmoved and indifferent? "I suppose that in the whole town there is no one so miserably uphappy as I am," he thought, as he went towards the market.

It was already breaking up. For some unknown reason he found himself making his way over fresh droppings, among carts, loads of cucumbers, stacks of pots and pans, and women seated on the ground who outdid each other in their efforts to attract his attention. They lifted basins and tapped them that he might hear how sound they were, while the men deafened him with cries of "First-class cucumbers, your honour." It was all so stupid, so riciculous that he fled from the square. He went into the cathedral, where the choir was singing loudly, resolutely, as though conscious of fulfilling a duty; then he strolled aimlessly about a small, hot, unkempt garden on the edge of a cliff overhanging the silvery steel breadth of the river.

The epaulettes and buttons of his linen uniform were unbearably hot to the touch. The inside of his hat was wet, his face was burning. He returned to the hotel and was delighted to get into the large, empty, cool dining-room, delighted to take off his hat and seat himself at a small table near the open window. The heat penetrated from outside, but it was airy. He ordered iced soup.

Everything was all right in this unknown town, happiness and joy emanated from everything, from the heat and the market smells. Even this old provincial hotel seemed full of gladness, and yet his heart was being torn to pieces. He drank several glasses of vodka and ate a salted cucumber with parsley. He felt that he would unhesitatingly die to-morrow if, by some miracle, he could achieve her return and spend to-day, only this one day, with her, solely, solely in order that he might tell her and prove to her and convince her somehow of his agonising and exalted love for her. "Why prove? Why convince?" He did not know why, but it was more essential than life.

"My nerves have all gone to pieces," he said, pouring out his fifth glass of vodka. He drank the entire contents of the small decanter, hoping to stupefy, to benumb himself, hoping to get rid at last of this agonising and exalted feeling. But, instead, it increased. He pushed away the soup, ordered black coffee, and began to smoke and to think with intensity. What was he to do now, how was he to free himself from this sudden and unexpected love? To free himself—but he felt only too clearly that that was impossible. He rose abruptly, quickly, took his hat and his stick, asked the way to the post office and hurried off, the text of the telegram already composed in his mind: "Henceforth all my life, for all time till death, is yours, in your power." But on reaching the thick-walled old building which housed the post and telegraph, he stopped in dismay. He knew the name of her town, he knew that she had a husband and a child of three, but he knew neither her first name nor her surname. Last night, while they were dining at the hotel, he had asked her several times, and each time she had answered with a laugh: "Why do you want to know who I am? I am Marie Marevna, the mysterious princess of the fairy story; or the fair stranger; isn't that enough for you?"

At the corner of the street, near the post office, was a photographer's window. He stared for a long time at the portrait of an officer in braided epaulettes, with protruding eyes, a low forehead, unusually luxuriant whiskers, and a very broad chest entirely covered with orders. How mad, how ridiculous, how terrifyingly ordinary, everyday things appear when the heart is struck—yes, *struck*, he understood it now, by the "sunstroke" of a love too great, a joy too immense. He looked at the picture of a bridal couple—a young man in a frock-coat and white tie, with closely-cropped hair, very erect, arm-in-arm with a girl in white tulle. His gaze wandered to a pretty, piquant girl wearing a student's cap on the back of her head.

Then, filled with envy of all these unknown people who were not suffering, he stared fixedly down the street. "Where shall I go? What shall I do?" The difficult, unanswerable questions occupied both mind and soul.

The street was completely empty. All the houses were alike middle-class, two-storied white houses with large gardens, but they were lifeless; the pavement was covered with thick white dust; it was all blinding, all bathed in hot, flaming, joyful sun which now somehow seemed futile. In the distance the street rose, humped and ran into the clear, cloudless, grey-mauve horizon. There was something southern about it; it reminded one of Sebastopol, Kertch—Anapi. This was more than he could bear. With eyes half closed and head bowed from the light, staring intently at the pavement, staggering, stumbling, catching one spur in the other, the lieutenant retraced his steps.

He returned to the hotel worn out with fatigue, as though he had done a long day's march in Turkestan or the Sahara. With a final effort he got to his large empty room. It had been "done." The last traces of her were gone except for one hairpin forgotten by her on the table. He took off his coat and looked at himself in the mirror. He saw reflected, skin bronzed and moustache bleached by the sun, the bluish whites of the eyes looking so much whiter on account of the tan, an ordinary enough officer's face, but now wild and excited. And about the whole figure standing there in the thin white shirt and stiff collar was something pathetically young and terribly unhappy. He lay down on the bed, on his back, rested his dusty boots on the footrail. The windows were open, the blinds were lowered. From time to time a slight wind billowed them out, letting in the heat, the smell of hot roofs and of all the radiant, but now empty, silent, deserted Volga country-side. He lay there, his hands under his head, and stared into space. In his mind he had a vague picture of the far-away south: sun and sea, Anapi. Then arose something fantastic, a town unlike any other town—the town in which she lived, which she had probably already reached. The thought of suicide stubbornly persisted. He closed his eyes and felt hot, smarting tears well up under his eyelids. Then at last he fell asleep, and when he woke he could see by the reddish-yellow light of the sun that it was evening. The wind had died down, the room was as hot and dry as an oven. Yesterday and this morning both seemed ten years ago. Unhurriedly he rose, unhurriedly he washed, drew up the blinds and rang for a samovar and his bill, and for a long time sat there drinking tea with lemon. Then he ordered a cab to be called and his things to be carried down. As he got into the cab with its faded red seat, he gave the waiter five roubles. "I believe I brought you here last night, your honour," said the driver gaily as he gathered up the reins.

By the time they reached the wharf, the Volga was roofed by the blue of the summer night. Multitudes of many-tinted lights were dotted along the river, and bright lamps shone from the masts of the ships.

"I got you here in the nick of time," said the cabdriver ingratiatingly.

The lieutenant gave five roubles to him also, took his ticket and went to the landing-place. Just as it had done yesterday, the boat bumped gently as it touched the wharf, there was the same slight dizziness from the unsteadiness underfoot, the end of a rope was thrown, there was a sound of foaming and rushing water under the paddles as the steamer backed a little . . . .

The brightly lighted, crowded steamer, smelling of food, seemed unusually friendly and agreeable, and in a few minutes it was speeding forward up the river, whither in the morning she had been carried.

The last glimmer of summer twilight gradually faded on the far horizon: capriciously, lazily reflecting their varied hues in the river, making here and there bright patches on the rippling surface under the dim dome of blue, the gleaming lights everywhere sprinkled in the darkness seemed to be swimming, swimming back.

Under an awning on deck sat the lieutenant. He felt older by ten years.

Theodor Storm

1817—1888

Storm's semi-autobiographical "Immensee" (1849-50) was one of the most popular stories of the latter half of the nineteenth century, both in Europe and America. Equally masterful but never as well known are "Beneath the Flood" ("Aquis submersus," 1876) and "The Rider on the White Horse," 1888), a story Storm lived to complete only because of the confidence he regained when a doctor told him (with benevolent deceit) that his illness was not terminal. An early story, "Immensee" is written in much the same spirit as the songlike lyrics that had earned the youthful Storm a place among the masters of German musical poetry; it has been somewhat neglected in recent decades only because of the taboo on tenderness decreed by literary modernism.

By choice, Storm lived most of his life in or near his birthplace, Husum, a Schleswig city of grey houses and buildings on the North Sea. Spiritual conservatism and melancholy sensitivity to time's inexorable claims against the visions of childhood and the glories of youth made continuity with his roots the deepest need of his nature. His art profited: setting nearly all his stories in the North Sea dyke country he knew so thoroughly, he could write with great authenticity and confidence, and without self-consciousness. Yet his intellectual power and his preoccupation with motifs of universal significance—time and its changes, the poignancy of memory, idealistic love—assured that he would be more than a local colorist.

The seeming uneventfulness of his life as an attorney and judge in an unimportant town is deceptive. It was leavened by one of the rarities of human experience: a love triangle (Storm, his wife Konstanze Esmarch, and his lady love Dorothea Jensen) fruitful for all three parties, and of long duration. There was also the excitement of Germany's mid-century quarrel with Denmark over the disputed duchy of Schleswig, and of Storm's friendship, correspondence, and editorial collaboration with leading scholars of the day, including Theodor Mommsen and Gottfried Keller.

All but a very few of Storm's stories are longish; yet he wrote no novels. He was not strongly interested in that which gives the modern novel its characteristic form and length: detailed analysis of the psychology and development of character and manners. A poet first and last, his narrative, even in his later and more realistic tales, remains centered around the response of sensibility to love and to the lyrical and awesome aspects of nature—in other words, to incidents and attitudes that tend not to require hundreds of pages. On the other hand, his romantic inclination to linger over pastoral detail and his preoccupation with memory—which forces him to bring both past and present into the story—predicate a certain lengthiness.

Storm's best translator, Geoffrey Skelton, notes that this writer's techniques are "more typical of English than of German literature . . . he depicts people and their problems directly and in quick-moving scenes of action and leaves the deeper meanings to the reader's own imagination."

Immensee

Theodor Storm

THE OLD MAN

One afternoon in the late autumn a well-dressed old man was walking slowly down the street. He appeared to be returning home from a walk, for his buckle-shoes, which followed a fashion long since out of date, were covered with dust.

Immensee

Under his arm he carried a long, gold-headed cane; his dark eyes, in which the whole of his long-lost youth seemed to have centered, and which contrasted strangely with his snow-white hair, gazed calmly on the sights around him or peered into the town below as it lay before him, bathed in the haze of sunset.

He appeared to be almost a stranger, for of the passers-by only a few greeted him, although many a one involuntarily was compelled to gaze into those grave eyes.

At last he halted before a high, gabled house, cast one more glance out toward the town, and then passed into the hall. At the sound of the door-bell some one in the room within drew aside the green curtain from a small window that looked out on to the hall, and the face of an old woman was seen behind it. The man made a sign to her with his cane.

"No light yet!" he said in a slightly southern accent, and the housekeeper let the curtain fall again.

The old man now passed through the broad hall, through an inner hall, wherein against the walls stood huge oaken chests bearing porcelain vases; then through the door opposite he entered a small lobby, from which a narrow staircase led to the upper rooms at the back of the house. He climbed the stairs slowly, unlocked a door at the top, and landed in a rooom of medium size.

It was a comfortable, quiet retreat. One of the walls was lined with cupboards and bookcases; on the other hung pictures of men and places; on a table with a green cover lay a number of open books, and before the table stood a massive armchair with a red velvet cushion.

After the old man had placed his hat and stick in a corner, he sat down in the armchair and, folding his hands, seemed to be taking his rest after his walk. While he sat thus, it was growing gradually darker; and before long a moonbeam came streaming through the window-panes and upon the pictures on the wall; and as the bright band of light passed slowly onward the old man followed it involuntarily with his eyes.

Now it reached a little picture in a simple black frame. "Elisabeth!" said the old man softly; and as he uttered the word, time had changed: *he was young again.*

THE CHILDREN

Before very long the dainty form of a little maiden advanced toward him. Her name was Elisabeth, and she might have been five years old. He himself was twice that age. Round her neck she wore a red silk kerchief which was very becoming to her brown eyes.

"Reinhard!" she cried, "we have a holiday, a holiday! No school the whole day and none to-morrow either!"

Reinhard was carrying his slate under his arm, but he flung it behind the front door, and then both the children ran through the house into the garden and through the garden gate out into the meadow. The unexpected holiday came to them at a most happily opportune moment.

It was in the meadow that Reinhard, with Elisabeth's help, had built a house out of sods of grass. They meant to live in it during the summer evenings; but it still wanted a bench. He set to work at once; nails, hammer, and the necessary boards were already to hand.

While he was thus engaged, Elisabeth went along the dyke, gathering the ring-shaped seeds of the wild mallow in her apron, with the object of making herself chains and necklaces out of them; so that when Reinhard had at last finished his bench in spite of many a crookedly hammered nail, and came out into the sunlight again, she was already wandering far away at the other end of the meadow.

"Elisabeth!" he called, "Elisabeth!" and then she came, her hair streaming behind her.

"Come here," he said; "our house is finished now. Why, you have got quite hot! Come in, and let us sit on the new bench. I will tell you a story."

So they both went in and sat down on the new bench. Elisabeth took the little seed-rings out of her apron and strung them on long threads. Reinhard began his tale: "There were once upon a time three spinning-women . . ."

"Oh!" said Elisabeth, "I know that off by heart; you really must not always tell me the same story."

Accordingly Reinhard had to give up the story of the three spinning-women and tell instead the story of the poor man who was cast into the den of lions.

"It was now night," he said, "black night, you know, and the lions were asleep. But every now and then they would yawn in their sleep and shoot out their red tongues. And then the man would shudder and think it was morning. All at once a bright light fell all about him, and when he looked up an angel was standing before him. The angel beckoned to him with his hand and then went straight into the rocks.

Elisabeth had been listening attentively. "An angel?" she said. "Had he wings, then?"

"It is only a story," answered Reinhard; "there are no angels, you know."

"Oh, fie! Reinhard!" she said, staring him straight in the face.

He looked at her with a frown, and she asked him hesitatingly: "Well, why do they always say there are? Mother, and Aunt, and at school as well?"

"I don't know," he answered.

"But tell me," said Elisabeth, "are there no lions either?"

"Lions? Are there lions? In India, yes. The heathen priests harness them to their carriages, and drive about the desert with them. When I'm big, I mean to go out there myself. It is thousands of times more beautiful in that country than it is here at home; there's no winter at all there. And you must come with me. Will you?"

"Yes," said Elisabeth; "but Mother must come with us, and your mother as well."

"No," said Reinhard, "they will be too old then, and cannot come with us."

"But I mayn't go by myself."

"Oh but you may right enough; you will then really be my wife, and the others will have no say in the matter."

"But Mother will cry!"

"We shall come back again, of course," said Reinhard impetuously.

"Now just tell me straight out, will you go with me? If not, I will go all alone, and then I shall never come back again."

The little girl came very near to crying. "Please don't look so angry," said she; "I will go to India with you."

Reinhard siezed both her hands with frantic glee, and rushed out with her into the meadow.

"To India, to India!" he sang, and swung her round and round, so that her little red kerchief was whirled from off her neck. Then he suddenly let her go and said solemnly:

"Nothing will come of it, I'm sure; you haven't the pluck."

"Elisabeth! Reinhard!" some one was now calling from the garden gate. "Here we are!" the children answered, and raced home hand in hand.

IN THE WOODS

So the children lived together. She was often too quiet for him, and he was often too headstrong for her, but for all that they stuck to one another. They spent nearly all their leisure hours together: in winter in their mothers' tiny rooms, during the summer in wood and field.

Once when Elisabeth was scolded by the teacher in Reinhard's hearing, he angrily banged his slate upon the table in order to turn upon himself the master's wrath. This failed to attract attention.

But Reinhard paid no further attention to the geography lessons, and instead he composed a long poem, in which he compared himself to a young eagle, the schoolmaster to a gray crow, and Elisabeth to a white dove; the eagle vowed vengeance on the gray crow, as soon as his wings had grown.

Tears stood in the young poet's eyes: he felt very proud of himself. When he reached home he contrived to get hold of a little parchment-bound volume with a lot of blank pages in it; and on the first pages he elaborately wrote out his first poem.

Soon after this he went to another school. Here he made many new friendships among boys of his own age, but this did not interrupt his comings and goings with Elisabeth. Of the stories which he had formerly told her over and over again he now began to write down the ones which she had liked best, and in doing so the fancy often took him to weave in something of his own thoughts; yet, for some reason he could not understand, he could never manage it.

So he wrote them down exactly as he had heard them himself. Then he handed them over to Elisabeth, who kept them carefully in a drawer of her writing-desk, and now and again of an evening when he was present it afforded him agreeable satisfaction to hear her reading aloud to her mother these little tales out of the notebooks in which he had written them.

Seven years had gone by. Reinhard was to leave the town in order to proceed to his higher education. Elisabeth could not bring herself to think that there would now be a time to be passed entirely without Reinhard. She was delighted when he told her one day that he would continue to write out stories for her as before; he would send them to her in the letters to his mother, and then she would have to write back to him and tell him how she liked them.

The day of departure was approaching, but ere it came a good deal more poetry found its way into the parchment-bound volume. This was the one secret he kept from Elisabeth, although she herself had inspired the whole book and most of the songs which gradually had filled up almost half of the blank pages.

It was the month of June, and Reinhard was to start on the following day. It was proposed to spend one more festive day together, and therefore a picnic was arranged for a rather large party of friends in an adjacent forest.

It was an hour's drive along the road to the edge of the wood, and there the company took down the provision baskets from the carriages and walked the rest of the way. The road lay first of all through a pine grove, where it was cool and darksome, and the ground was all strewed with pine needles.

After half an hour's walk they passed out of the gloom of the pine trees into a bright fresh beech wood. Here everything was light and green; every here and there a sunbeam burst through the leafy branches, and high above their heads a squirrel was leaping from branch to branch.

The party came to a halt at a certain spot, over which the topmost branches of ancient beech trees interwove a transparent canopy of leaves. Elisabeth's mother opened one of the baskets, and an old gentleman constituted himself quartermaster.

"Round me, all of you young people," he cried, "and attend carefully to what I have to say to you. For lunch each one of you will now get two dry rolls; the butter has been left behind at home. The extras every one must find for himself. There are plenty of strawberries in the wood—that is, for any one who knows where to find them. Unless you are sharp, you'll have to eat dry bread; that's the way of the world all over. Do you understand what I say?"

"Yes, yes," cried the young folks.

"Yes, but look here," said the old gentleman, "I have not done yet. We old folks have done enough roaming about in our time, and therefore we will stay at home now, here, I mean, under these wide-spreading trees, and we'll peel the potatoes and make a fire and lay the table, and by twelve o'clock the eggs shall be boiled.

"In return for all this you will be owing us half of your strawberries, so that we may also be able to serve some dessert. So off you go now, east and west, and mind be honest."

The young folks cast many a roguish glance at one another.

"Wait," cried the old gentleman once again. "I suppose I need not tell you this, that whoever finds none need not produce any; but take particular note of this, that he will get nothing out of us old folks either. Now you have had enough good advice for to-day; and if you gather strawberries to match you will get on very well for the present at any rate."

The young people were of the same opinion, and pairing off in couples set out on their quest.

"Come along, Elisabeth," said Reinhard. "I know where there is a clump of strawberry bushes; you shan't eat dry bread."

Elisabeth tied the green ribbons of her straw hat together and hung it on her arm. "Come on, then," she said, "the basket is ready."

Off into the wood they went, on and on; on through moist shady glens, where everything was so peaceful, except for the cry of the falcon flying unseen in the heavens far above their heads; on again through the thick brushwood, so thick that Reinhard must needs go on ahead to make a track, here snapping off a branch, there bending aside a trailing vine. But ere long he heard Elisabeth behind him calling out his name. He turned round.

"Reinhard!" she called, "do wait for me! Reinhard!"

He could not see her, but at length he caught sight of her some way off struggling with the undergrowth, her dainty head just peeping out over the tops of the ferns. So back he went once more and brought her out from the tangled mass of briar and brake into an open space where blue butterflies fluttered among the solitary wood blossoms.

Reinhard brushed the damp hair away from her heated face, and would have tied the straw hat upon her head, but she refused; yet at his earnest request she consented after all.

"But where are your strawberries?" she asked at length, standing still and drawing a deep breath.

"They were here," he said, "but the toads have got here before us, or the martens, or perhaps the fairies."

"Yes," said Elisabeth, "the leaves are still here; but not a word about fairies in this place. Come along, I'm not a bit tired yet; let us look farther on."

In front of them ran a little brook, and on the far side the wood began again. Reinhard raised Elisabeth in his arms and carried her over. After a while they emerged from the shady foliage and stood in a wide clearing.

"There must be strawberries here," said the girl, "it all smells so sweet."

They searched about the sunny spot, but they found none. "No," said Reinhard, "it is only the smell of the heather."

Everywhere was a confusion of raspberry-bushes and holly, and the air was filled with a strong smell of heather, patches of which alternated with the short grass over these open spaces.

"How lonely it is here!" said Elisabeth: "I wonder where the others are?"

Reinhard had never thought of getting back.

"Wait a bit," he said, holding his hand aloft; "where is the wind coming from?" But wind there was none.

"Listen!" said Elisabeth; "I think I heard them talking. Just give a call in that direction."

Reinhard hollowed his hand and shouted: "Come here!"

"Here!" was echoed back.

"They answered," cried Elisabeth, clapping her hands.

"No, that was nothing; it was only the echo."

Elisabeth seized Reinhard's hand. "I'm frightened!" she said.

"Oh! no, you must not be frightened. It is lovely here. Sit down there in the shade among the long grass. Let us rest awhile: we'll find the others soon enough."

Elisabeth sat down under the overhanging branch of a beech and listened intently in every direction. Reinhard sat a few paces off on a tree stump, and gazed over at her in silence.

The sun was just above their heads, shining with the full glare of mid-day heat. Tiny, gold-flecked, steel-blue flies poised in the air with vibrating wings. Their ears caught a gentle humming and buzzing all round them, and far away in the wood were heard now and again the tap-tap of the wood-pecker and the screech of other birds.

"Listen," said Elisabeth, "I hear a bell."

"Where?" asked Reinhard.

"Behind us. Do you hear it? It is striking twelve o'clock."

"Then the town lies behind us, and if we go straight through in this direction we are bound to fall in with the others."

So they started on their homeward way; they had given up looking for strawberries, for Elisabeth had become tired. And at last there rang out from among the trees the laughing voices of the picnic party; then they saw too a white cloth spread gleaming on the ground; it was the luncheon-table and on it were strawberries enough and to spare.

The old gentleman had a table-napkin tucked in his button-hole and was continuing his moral sermon to the young folks and vigorously carving a joint of roast meat.

"Here come the stragglers," cried the young people when they saw Reinhard and Elisabeth advancing among the trees.

"This way," shouted the old gentleman. "Empty your handkerchiefs, upside down with your hats! Now show us what you have found."

"Only hunger and thirst," said Reinhard.

"If that's all," replied the old man, lifting up and showing them the bowl full of fruit, "you must keep what you've got. You remember the agreement: nothing here for lazybones to eat."

But in the end he was prevailed on to relent; the banquet proceeded, and a thrush in a juniper bush provided the music.

So the day passed. But Reinhard had, after all, found something, and though it was not strawberries yet it was something that had grown in the wood. When he got home this is what he wrote in his old parchment-bound volume:

Out on the hillside yonder
The wind to rest is laid;
Under the drooping branches
There sits the little maid.

She sits among the wild thyme,
She sits in the fragrant air;
The blue flies hum around her,
Bright wings flash everywhere.

And through the silent woodland
She peers with watchful eyen,
While on her hazel ringlets
Sparkles the glad sunshine.

And afar, far off the cuckoo
Laughs out his song, I ween
Hers are the bright, the golden
Eyes of the woodland queen.

So she was not only his little sweetheart, but was also the expression of all that was lovely and wonderful in his opening life.

BY THE ROADSIDE THE CHILD STOOD

The time is Christmas Eve. Before the close of the afternoon Reinhard and some other students were sitting together at an old oak table in the Ratskeller. The lamps on the wall were lighted, for down here in the basement it was already growing dark; but there was only a thin sprinkling of customers present, and the waiters were leaning idly up against the pillars let into the walls.

In a corner of the vaulted room sat a fiddler and a fine-featured gypsy-girl with a zither; their instruments lay in their laps, and they seemed to be looking about them with an air of indifference.

A champagne cork popped off the table occupied by the students. "Drink, my gypsy darling!" cried a young man of aristocratic appearance, holding out to the girl a glass full of wine.

"I don't care about it," she said, without altering her position.

"Well, then, give us a song," cried the young nobleman, and threw a silver coin into her lap. The girl slowly ran her fingers through her black hair while the fiddler whispered in her ear. But she threw back her head, and rested her chin on her zither.

"For him," she said, "I'm not going to play."

Reinhard leapt up with his glass in his hand and stood in front of her.

"What do you want?" she asked defiantly.

"To have a look at your eyes."

"What have my eyes to do with you?"

Reinhard's glance flashed down on her.

"I *know* they are false."

She laid her cheek in the palm of her hand and gave him a searching look. Reinhard raised his glass to his mouth.

"Here's to your beautiful, wicked eyes!" he said, and drank.

She laughed and tossed her head.

"Give it here," she said, and fastening her black eyes on his, she slowly drank what was left in the glass. Then she struck a chord and sang in a deep, passionate voice:

To-day, to-day thou think'st me
Fairest maid of all;
To-morrow, ah! then beauty
Fadeth past recall.
While the hour remaineth,
Thou art yet mine own;
Then when death shall claim me,
I must die alone.

While the fiddler struck up an allegro finale, a new arrival joined the group.

"I went to call for you, Reinhard, " he said. "You had already gone out, but Santa Claus had paid you a visit."

"Santa Claus?" said Reinhard. "Santa Claus never comes to me now."

"Oh, yes, he does! The whole of your room smelt of Christmas tree and ginger cakes."

Reinhard dropped the glass out of his hand and seized his cap.

"Well, what are you going to do now?" asked the girl.

"I'll be back in a minute."

She frowned. "Stay," she said gently, casting an amorous glance at him.

Reinhard hesitated. "I can't," he said.

She laughingly gave him a tap with the toe of her shoe and said: "Go away, then, you good-for-nothing; you are one as bad as the other, all good-for-nothings." And as she turned away from him, Reinhard went slowly up the steps of the Ratskeller.

Outside in the street deep twilight had set in; he felt the cool winter air blowing on his heated brow. From some window every here and there fell the bright gleam of a Christmas tree all lighted up, now and then was heard from within some room the sound of little pipes and tin trumpets mingled with the merry din of children's voices.

Crowds of beggar children were going from house to house or climbing up on to the railings of the front steps, trying to catch a glimpse through the window of a splendor that was denied to them. Sometimes too a door would suddenly be flung open, and scolding voices would drive a whole swarm of these little visitors away out into the dark street. In the vestibule of yet another house they were singing an old Christmas carol, and little girls' clear voices were heard among the rest.

But Reinhard heard not; he passed quickly by them all, out of one street into another. When he reached his lodging it had grown almost quite dark; he stumbled up the stairs and so gained his apartment.

A sweet fragrance greeted him: it reminded him of home; it was the smell of the parlor in his mother's house at Christmas time. With trembling hand he lit his lamp; and there lay a mighty parcel on the table. When he opened it, out fell the familiar ginger cakes. On some of them were the initial letters of his name written in sprinkles of sugar; no one but Elisabeth could have done that.

Next came to view a little parcel containing neatly embroidered linen, handkerchiefs and cuffs; and finally letters from his mother and Elisabeth. Reinhard opened Elisabeth's letter first, and this is what she wrote:

"The pretty sugared letters will no doubt tell you who helped with the cakes. The same person also embroidered the cuffs for you. We shall have a very quiet time at home this Christmas Eve. Mother always puts her spinning-wheel away in the corner as early as half-past nine. It is so very lonesome this winter now that you are not here.

"And now, too, the linnet you made me a present of died last Sunday. It made me cry a good deal, though I am sure I looked after it well.

"It always used to sing of an afternoon when the sun shone on its cage. You remember how often mother would hang a piece of cloth over the cage in order to keep it quiet when it sang so lustily.

"Thus our room is now quieter than ever, except that your old friend Eric now drops in to see us occasionally. You told us once that he was just like his brown top-coat. I can't help thinking of it every time he comes in at the door, and it is really too funny; but don't tell mother, it might easily make her angry.

"Guess what I am giving your mother for a Christmas present! You can't guess! Well, it is myself! Eric is making a drawing of me in black chalk; I have had to give him three sittings, each time for a whole hour.

"I simply loathed the idea of a stranger getting to know my face so well. Nor did I wish it, but mother pressed me, and said it would very much please dear Frau Werner.

"But you are not keeping your word, Reinhard. You haven't sent me any stories. I have often complained to your mother about it, but she always says you now have more to do than to attend to such childish things. But I don't believe it; there's something else perhaps."

After this Reinhard read his mother's letter, and when he had read them both and slowly folded them up again and put them away, he was overcome with an irresistible feeling of homesickness. For a long while he walked up and down his room, talking softly to himself, and then, under his breath, he murmured:

I have err'd from the straight path,
Bewildered I roam;
By the roadside the child stands
And beckons me home.

Then he went to his desk, and stepped down into the street again. During all this while it had become quieter out there; the lights on the Christmas trees had burnt out, the processions of children had come to an end. The wind was sweeping through the deserted streets; old and young alike were sitting together at home in family parties; the second period of Christmas Eve celebrations had begun.

As Reinhard drew near the Ratskeller he heard from below the scraping of the fiddle and the singing of the zither girl. The restaurant door bell tinkled and a dark form staggered up the broad dimly-lighted stair.

Reinhard drew aside into the shadow of the houses and then passed swiftly by. After a while he reached the well-lighted shop of a jeweler, and after buying a little cross studded with red corals, he returned by the same way he had come.

Not far from his lodgings he caught sight of a little girl, dressed in miserable rags, standing before a tall door, in a vain attempt to open it.

"Shall I help you?" he said.

The child gave no answer, but let go the massive door-handle. Reinhard had soon opened the door.

"No," he said; "they might drive you out again. Come along with me, and I'll give you some Christmas cake."

He then closed the door again and gave his hand to the little girl, who walked along with him in silence to his lodgings.

On going out he had left the light burning.

"Here are some cakes for you," he said, pouring half of his whole stock into her apron, though he gave none that bore the sugar letters.

"Now, off you go home, and give your mother some of them too."

The child cast a shy look up at him; she seemed unaccustomed to such kindness and unable to say anything in reply. Reinhard opened the door, and lighted her way, and then the little thing like a bird flew downstairs with her cakes and out of the house.

Reinhard poked the fire in the stove, set the dusty ink-stand on the table, and then sat down and wrote and wrote letters the whole night long to his mother and Elisabeth.

The remainder of the Christmas cakes lay untouched by his side, but he had buttoned on Elisabeth's cuffs, and odd they looked on his shaggy coat of undyed wool. And there he was still sitting when the winter sun cast its light on the frosted window-panes, and showed him a pale, grave face reflected in the looking-glass.

HOME

When the Easter vacation came Reinhard journeyed home. On the morning after his arrival he went to see Elisabeth.

"How tall you've grown!" he said, as the pretty, slender girl advanced with a smile to meet him. She blushed, but made no reply; he had taken her hand in his own in greeting, and she tried to draw it gently away. He looked at her doubtingly, for never had she done that before; but now it was as if some strange thing was coming between them.

The same feeling remained, too, after he had been at home for sometime and came to see her constantly day after day. When they sat alone together there ensued pauses in the conversation which distressed him, and which he anxiously did his best to avoid. In order to have a definite occupation during the holidays, he began to give Elisabeth some instruction in botany, in which he himself had been keenly interested during the early months of his university career.

Elisabeth, who was wont to follow him in all things and was, moreover, very quick to learn, willingly entered into the proposal. So now several times in the week they made excursions into the fields or the moors, and if by midday they brought home their green field-box full of plants and flowers, Reinhard would come again later in the day and share with Elisabeth what they had collected in common.

With this same object in view, he entered the room one afternoon while Elisabeth was standing by the window and sticking some fresh chickweed in a gilded birdcage which he had not seen in the place before. In the cage was a canary, which was flapping its wings and shrilly chirruping as it pecked at Elisabeth's fingers. Previously to this Reinhard's bird had hung in that spot.

"Has my poor linnet changed into a goldfinch after its death?" he asked jovially.

"Linnets are not accustomed to do any such thing," said Elisabeth's mother, who sat spinning in her armchair. "Your friend Eric sent it this noon from his estate as a present for Elisabeth."

"What estate?"

"Why, don't you know?"

"Know what?"

"That a month ago Eric took over his father's second estate by the Immensee."

"But you have never said a word to me about it."

"Well," said the mother, "you haven't yet made a single word of inquiry after your friend. He is a very nice, sensible young man."

The mother went out of the room to make the coffee. Elisabeth had her back turned to Reinhard, and was still busy with the making of her little chickweed bower.

"Please, just a little longer," she said. "I'll be done in a minute."

As Reinhard did not answer, contrary to his wont, she turned round and faced him. In his eyes there was a sudden expression of trouble which she had never observed before in them.

"What is the matter with you, Reinhard?" she said, drawing nearer to him.

"With me?" he said, his thoughts far away and his eyes resting dreamily on hers.

"You look so sad."

"Elisabeth," he said, "I cannot bear that yellow bird."

She looked at him in astonishment, without understanding his meaning. "You are so strange," she said.

He took both her hands in his, and she let him keep them there. Her mother came back into the room shortly after; and after they had drunk their coffee she sat down at her spinning-wheel, while Reinhard and Elisabeth went off into the next room to arrange their plants.

Stamens were counted, leaves and blossoms carefully opened out, and two specimens of each sort were laid to dry between the pages of a large folio volume.

All was calm and still this sunny afternoon; the only sounds to be heard were the hum of the mother's spinning-wheel in the next room, and now and then the subdued voice of Reinhard, as he named the orders of the families of the plants, and corrected Elisabeth's awkward pronunciation of the Latin names.

"I am still short of that lily of the valley which I didn't get last time," said she, after the whole collection had been classified and arranged.

Reinhard pulled a little white vellum volume from his pocket. "Here is a spray of the lily of the valley for you," he said, taking out a half-pressed bloom.

When Elisabeth saw the pages all covered with writing, she asked: "Have you been writing stories again?"

"These aren't stories," he answered, handing her the book.

The contents were all poems, and the majority of them at most filled one page. Elisabeth turned over the leaves one after another; she appeared to be reading the titles only. "When she was scolded by the teacher." "When they lost their way in the woods." "An Easter story." "On her writing to me for the first time." Thus ran most of the titles.

Reinhard fixed his eyes on her with a searching look, and as she kept turning over the leaves he saw that a gentle blush arose and gradually mantled over the whole of her sweet face. He would fain have looked into her eyes, but Elisabeth did not look up, and finally laid the book down before him without a word.

"Don't give it back like that," he said.

She took a brown spray out of the tin case. "I will put your favorite flower inside," she said, giving back the book into his hands.

At length came the last day of the vacation and the morning of his departure. At her own request Elisabeth received permission from her mother to accompany her friend to the stage-coach, which had its station a few streets from their house.

When they passed out of the front door Reinhard gave her his arm, and thus he walked in silence side by side with the slender maiden. The nearer they came to their destination the more he felt as if he had something he must say to her before he bade her a long farewell, something on which all that was worthy and all that was sweet in his future life depended, and yet he could not formulate the saving word. In his anguish, he walked slower and slower.

"You'll be too late," she said; "it has already struck ten by St. Mary's clock."

But he did not quicken his pace for all that. At last he stammered out:

"Elisabeth, you will not see me again for two whole years. Shall I be as dear to you as ever when I come back?"

She nodded, and looked affectionately into his face.

"I stood up for you," she said, after a pause.

"Me? And against whom had you to stand up for me?"

"Against my mother. We were talking about you a long time yesterday evening after you left. She thought you were not so nice now as you once were."

Reinhard held his peace for a moment: then he took her hand in his, and looking gravely into her childish eyes, he said:

"I am still just as nice as I ever was; I would have you firmly believe that. Do you believe it, Elisabeth?"

"Yes," she said.

He freed her hand and quickly walked with her through the last street. The nearer he felt the time of parting approach, the happier became the look on his face; he went almost too quickly for her.

"What is the matter with you, Reinhard?" she asked.

"I have a secret, a beautiful secret," said Reinhard, looking at her with a light in his eyes. "When I come back again in two years' time, then you shall know it."

Meanwhile they had reached the stage-coach; they were only just in time. Once more Reinhard took her hand. "Farewell!" he said, "farewell, Elisabeth! Do not forget!"

She shook her head. "Farewell," she said. Reinhard climbed up into the coach and the horses started. As the coach rumbled round the corner of the street he saw her dear form once more as she slowly wended her way home.

A LETTER

Nearly two years later Reinhard was sitting by lamplight with his books and papers around him, expecting a friend with whom he used to study in common. Some one came upstairs. "Come in." It was the landlady. "A letter for you, Herr Werner," and she went away.

Reinhard had never written to Elisabeth since his visit home, and he had received no letter from her. Nor was this one from her; it was in his mother's handwriting.

Reinhard broke the seal and read, and ere long he came to this paragraph:

"At your time of life, my dear boy, nearly every year still brings its own peculiar experience; for youth is apt to turn everything to the best account. At home, too, things have changed very much, and all this will, I fear, cause you much pain at first, if my understanding of you is at all correct.

"Yesterday Eric was at last accepted by Elisabeth, after having twice proposed in vain during the last three months. She had never been able to make up her mind to it, but now in the end she has done so. To my mind she is still far too young. The wedding is to take place soon, and her mother means to go away with them."

IMMENSE

Again years have passed. One warm afternoon in spring a young man, whose sunburnt face was the picture of health, was walking along a shady road through the wood leading down to the valley below.

His grave dark eyes looked intently into the distance, as though he was expecting to find every moment some change in the monotony of the road, a change, however, which seemed reluctant to come about. At length he saw a cart slowly coming up from below.

"Hullo! my friend," shouted the traveler to the farmer, who was walking by the side of the cart, "is this the right road to Immensee?"

"Yes, straight on," answered the man, touching his slouch hat.

"Is it still far off?"

"You are close to the place, sir. In less time than it takes to smoke half a pipe of tobacco you'll be at the lake side, and the manor is hard by."

The farmer passed on, while the other quickened his pace as he went along under the trees. After a quarter of an hour's walk the shade to the left of him suddenly came came to an end; the road led along a steep slope from which the ancient oaks growing below hardly reared their topmost branches.

Away over their crests opened out a broad, sunny landscape. Far below lay the peaceful, dark-blue lake, almost entirely surrounded by green sun-lit woods, save where on one spot they divided and afforded an extensive view until it closed in the distant blue mountains.

Straight opposite, in the middle of all this forest verdure, there lay a patch of white, like driven snow. This was an expanse of blossoming fruit-trees, and out of them, up on the high lake shore, rose the manor-house, shining white with tiles of red. A stork flew up from the chimney, and circled slowly above the waters.

"Immensee!" exclaimed the traveler.

It almost seemed as if he had now reached the end of his journey, for he stood motionless, looking out over the tops of the trees at his feet, and gazing at the farther shore, where the reflection of the manor-house floated, rocking gently, on the bosom of the water. Then he suddenly started on his way again.

His road now led almost steeply down the mountainside, so that the trees that had once stood below him again gave him their shade, but at the same time cut off from him the view of the lake, which only now and then peeped out between the gaps in the branches.

Soon the way went gently upwards again, and to left and right the woods disappeared, yielding place to vine-clad hills stretching along the pathway; while on either side stood fruit-trees in blossom, filled with the hum of the bees as they busily pried into the blossoms. A tall man wearing a brown overcoat advanced to meet the traveler. When he had almost come up to him, he waved his cap and cried out in a loud voice:

"Welcome, welcome, brother Reinhard! Welcome to my Immensee estate!"

"God's greeting to you, Eric, and thank you for your welcome," replied the other.

By this time they had come up close to one another, and clasped hands.

"And is it really you?" said Eric, when he at last got a near sight of the grave face of his old school-fellow.

"It is I right enough, Eric, and I recognize you too; only you almost look cheerier than you ever did before."

At these words a glad smile made Eric's plain features all the more cheerful.

"Yes, brother Reinhard," he said, as he once more held out his hand to him, "but since those days, you see, I have won the great prize; but you know that well enough."

Then he rubbed his hands and cried cheerily, "This *will* be a surprise! You are the last person she expects to see."

"A surprise?" asked Reinhard. "For whom, pray?"

"Why, for Elisabeth."

"Elisabeth! You haven't told her a word about my visit?"

"Not a word, brother Reinhard; she has no thought of you, nor her mother either. I invited you entirely on the quiet, in order that the pleasure might be all the greater. You know I always had little quiet schemes of my own."

Reinhard turned thoughtful; he seemed to breathe more heavily the nearer they approached the house.

On the left side of the road the vineyards came to an end, and gave place to an extensive kitchen-garden, which reached almost as far as the lake-shore. The stork had meanwhile come to earth and was striding solemnly between the vegetable beds.

"Hullo!" cried Eric, clapping his hands together, "if that long-legged Egyptian isn't stealing my short pea-sticks again!"

The bird slowly rose and flew on to the roof of a new building, which ran along the end of the kitchen-garden, and whose walls were covered with the branches of the peach and apricot trees that were trained over them.

"That's the distillery," said Eric. "I built it only two years ago. My late father had the farm buildings rebuilt; the dwelling-house was built as far back as my grandfather's time. So we go ever forward a little bit at a time."

Talking thus they came to a wide, open space, enclosed at the sides by farm-buildings, and in the rear by the manor-house, the two wings of which were connected by a high garden wall. Behind this wall ran dark hedges of yew trees, while here and there syringa trees trailed their blossoming branches over into the courtyard.

Men with faces scorched by the sun and heated with toil were walking over the open space and gave a greeting to the two friends, while Eric called out to one or another of them some order or question about their day's work.

By this time they had reached the house. They entered a high, cool vestibule, at the far end of which they turned to the left into a somewhat darker passage.

Here Eric opened a door and they passed into a spacious room that opened into a garden. The heavy mass of leafage that covered the opposite windows filled this room at either end with a green twilight, while between the windows two lofty wide-open folding-doors let in the full glow of spring sunshine, and afforded a view into a garden, laid out with circular flower-beds and steep hedgerows and divided by a straight, broad path, along which the eye roamed out on to the lake and away over the woods growing on the opposite shore.

As the two friends entered, a breath of wind bore in upon them a perfect stream of fragrance.

On a terrace in front of the door leading to the garden sat a girlish figure dressed in white. She rose and came to meet the two friends as they entered, but half-way she stood stock-still as if rooted to the spot and stared at the stranger. With a smile he held out his hand to her.

"Reinhard!" she cried. "Reinhard! Oh! is it you? It is such a long time since we have seen each other."

"Yes, a long time," he said, and not a word more could he utter; for on hearing her voice he felt a keen, physical pain at his heart, and as he looked up to her, there she stood before him, the same slight, graceful figure to whom he had said farewell years ago in the town where he was born.

Eric had stood back by the door, with joy beaming from his eyes.

"Now, then, Elisabeth," he said, "isn't he really the very last person in the world you would have expected to see?"

Elisabeth looked at him with the eyes of a sister. "You are so kind, Eric," she said.

He took her slender hand carressingly in his. "And now that we have him," he said, "we shall not be in a hurry to let him go. He has been so long away abroad, we will try to make him feel at home again. Just see how foreign-looking he has become, and what a distinguished appearance he has!"

Elisabeth shyly scanned Reinhard's face. "The time that we have been separated is enough to account for that," she said.

At this moment in at the door came her mother, key basket on arm.

"Herr Werner!" she cried, when she caught sight of Reinhard; "ah! you are as dearly welcome as you are unexpected."

And so the conversation went smoothly on with questions and answers. The ladies sat over their work, and while Reinhard enjoyed the refreshment that had been prepared for him, Eric had lighted his huge meerschaum pipe and sat smoking and conversing by his side.

Next day Reinhard had to go out with him to see the fields, the vineyards, the hop-garden, the distillery. It was all well appointed; the people who were working on the land or at the vats all had a healthy and contented look.

For dinner the family assembled in the room that opened into the garden, and the day was spent more or less in company just according to the leisure of the host and hostess. Only during the hours preceding the evening meal, as also during the early hours of the forenoon, did Reinhard stay working in his own room.

For some years past, whenever he could come across them, he had been collecting the rhymes and songs that form part of the life of the people, and now set about arranging his treasure, and wherever possible increasing it by means of fresh records from the immediate neighborhood.

Elisabeth was at all times gentle and kind. Eric's constant attentions she received with an almost humble gratitude, and Reinhard thought at times that the gay, cheerful child of bygone days had given promise of a somewhat less sedate womanhood.

Ever since the second day of his visit he had been wont of an evening to take a walk along the shore of the lake. The road led along close under the garden. At the end of the latter, on a projecting mound, there was a bench under some tall birch trees. Elisabeth's mother had christened it the Evening Bench, because the spot faced westward, and was mostly used at that time of the day in order to enjoy a view of the sunset.

One evening Reinhard was returning from his walk along this road when he was overtaken by the rain. He sought shelter under one of the linden trees that grew by the waterside, but the heavy drops were soon pelting through the leaves. Wet through as he was he resigned himself to his fate and slowly continued his homeward way.

It was almost dark; the rain fell faster and faster. As he drew near to the Evening Bench he fancied he could make out the figure of a woman dressed in white standing among the gleaming birch tree trunks. She stood motionless, and, as far as he could make out on approaching nearer, with her face turned in his direction, as if she was expecting some one.

He thought it was Elisabeth. But when he quickened his pace in order that he might catch up to her and then return together with her through the garden into the house, she turned slowly away and disappeared among the dark sidepaths.

He could not understand it; he was almost angry with Elisabeth, and yet he doubted whether it had really been she. He was, however, shy of questioning her about it—nay, he even avoided going into the garden-room on his return to the house for fear he should happen to see Elisabeth enter through the garden-door.

BY MY MOTHER'S HARD DECREE

Some days later, as evening was already closing in, the family was, as usual at this time of the day, sitting all together in their garden-room, The doors stood wide open, and the sun had already sunk behind the woods on the far side of the lake.

Reinhard was invited to read some folk-songs which had been sent to him that afternoon by a friend who lived away in the country. He went up to his room and soon returned with a roll of papers which seemed to consist of detached neatly written pages.

So they all sat down to the table, Elisabeth beside Reinhard. "We shall read them at random," said the latter, "I have not yet looked through them myself."

Elisabeth unrolled the manuscript. "Here's some music," she said, "you must sing it, Reinhard."

To begin with he read some Tyrolese ditties, and as he read on he would now and then hum one or other of the lively melodies. A general feeling of cheeriness pervaded the little party. "And who, pray, made all these pretty songs?" asked Elisabeth.

"Oh," said Eric, "you can tell that by listening to the rubbishy things—tailors' apprentices and barbers and such-like merry folk."

Reinhard said: "They are not made; they grow, they drop from the clouds, they float over the land like gossamer, hither and thither, and are sung in a thousand places at the same time. We discover in these songs our very inmost activities and sufferings: it is as if we all had helped to write them."

He took up another sheet: "I stood on the mountain height . . ."

"I know that one," cried Elisabeth; "begin it, do, Reinhard, and I will help you out."

So they sang that famous melody, which is so mysterious that one can hardly believe that it was ever conceived by the heart of man, Elisabeth with her slightly clouded contralto taking the second part to the young man's tenor.

The mother meanwhile sat busy with her needlework, while Eric listened attentively, with one hand clasped in the other. The song finished, Reinhard laid the sheet on one side in silence. Up from the lake-shore came through the evening calm the tinkle of the cattle bells; they were all listening without knowing why, and presently they heard a boy's clear voice singing:

I stood on the mountain height
And viewed the deep valley beneath . . .

Reinhard smiled. "Do you hear that now? So it passes from mouth to mouth."

"It is often sung in these parts," said Elisabeth.

"Yes," said Eric, "it is Casper the herdsman; he is driving the heifers home."

They listened a while longer until the tinkle of the bells died away behind the farm buildings. "These melodies are as old as the world," said Reinhard; "they slumber in the depths of the forest; God knows who discovered them."

He drew forth a fresh sheet.

It had now grown darker; a crimson evening glow lay like foam over the woods in the farther side of the lake. Reinhard unrolled the sheet, Elisabeth caught one side of it in her hand, and they both examined it together. Then Reinhard read:

By my Mother's hard decree
Another's wife I needs must be;
Him on whom my heart was set,
Him, alas! I must forget;
My heart protesting, but not free.

Bitterly did I complain
That my mother brought me pain.
What mine honor might have been,
That is turned to deadly sin.
Can I ever Hope again?

For my pride what can I show,
And my joy, save grief and woe?
Ah! could I undo what's done,
O'er the moor scorched by the sun
Beggarwise I'd gladly go.

During the reading of this Reinhard had felt an imperceptible quivering of the paper; and when he came to an end Elisabeth gently pushed her chair back and passed silently out into the garden. Her mother followed her with a look. Eric made as if to go after, but the mother said: "Elisabeth has one or two little things to do outside," so he remained where he was.

But out of doors the evening brooded darker and darker over garden and lake. Moths whirred past the open doors through which the fragrance of flower and bush floated in increasingly; up from the water came the croak of the frogs, under the windows a nightingale commenced his song answered by another from within the depths of the garden; the moon appeared over the tree-tops.

Reinhard looked for a little while longer at the spot where Elisabeth's sweet form had been lost to sight in the thick-foliaged garden paths, and then he rolled up his manuscript, bade his friends good-night and passed through the house down to the water.

The woods stood silent and cast their dark shadow far out over the lake, while the center was bathed in the haze of a pale moonlight. Now and then a gentle rustle trembled through the trees, though wind there was none: it was but the breath of summer night.

Reinhard continued along the shore. A stone's throw from the land he perceived a white water-lily. All at once he was seized with the desire to see it quite close, so he threw off his clothes and entered the water. It was quite shallow; sharp stones and water plants cut his feet, and yet he could not reach water deep enough for him to swim in.

Then suddenly he stepped out of his depth: the waters swirled above him, and it was some time before he rose to the surface again. He struck out with hands and feet and swam about in a circle until he had made quite sure from what point he had entered the water. And soon too he saw the lily again floating lonely among the large, gleaming leaves.

He swam slowly out, lifting every now and then his arms out of the water so that the drops trickled down and sparkled in the moonlight. Yet the distance between him and the flower showed no signs of diminishing, while the shore, as he glanced back at it, showed behind him in a hazy mist that ever deepened. But he refused to give up the venture and vigorously continued swimming in the same direction.

At length he had come so near the flower that he was able clearly to distinguish the silvery leaves in the moonlight; but at the same time he felt himself entangled in a net formed by the smooth stems of the water plants which swayed up from the bottom and wound themselves round his naked limbs.

The unfamiliar water was black all round about him, and behind him he heard the sound of a fish leaping. Suddenly such an uncanny feeling overpowered him in the midst of this strange element that with might and main he tore asunder the network of plants and swam back to land in breathless haste. And when from the shore he looked back upon the lake, there floated the lily on the bosom of the darkling water as far away and as lonely as before.

He dressed and slowly wended his way home. As he passed out of the garden into the room he discovered Eric and the mother busied with preparations for a short journey which had to be undertaken for business purposes on the morrow.

"Wherever have you been so late in the dark?" the mother called out to him.

"I?" he answered; "oh, I wanted to pay a call on the water-lily, but I failed."

"That's beyond the comprehension of any man," said Eric. "What on earth had you to do with the water-lily?"

"Oh, I used to be friends with the lily once," said Reinhard; "but that was long ago."

ELISABETH

The following afternoon Reinhard and Elisabeth went for a walk on the farther side of the lake, strolling at times through the woodland, at other times along the shore where it jutted out into the water. Elisabeth had received injunctions from Eric, during the absence of himself and her mother, to show Reinhard the prettiest views in the immediate neighborhood, particularly the view toward the farm itself from the other side of the lake. So now they proceeded from one point to another.

At last Elisabeth got tired and sat down in the shade of some overhanging branches. Reinhard stood opposite to her, leaning against a tree trunk; and as he heard the cuckoo calling farther back in the woods, it suddenly struck him that all this had happened once before. He looked at her and with an odd smile asked:

"Shall we look for strawberries?"

"It isn't strawberry time," she said.

"No, but it will soon be here."

Elisabeth shook her head in silence; then she rose and the two strolled on together. And as they wandered side by side, his eyes ever and again were bent toward her; for she walked gracefully and her step was light. He often unconsciously fell back a pace in order that he might feast his eyes on a full view of her.

So they came to an open space overgrown with heather where the view extended far over the country-side. Reinhard bent down and plucked a bloom from one of the little plants that grew at his feet.

When he looked up again there was an expression of deep pain on his face.

"Do you know this flower?" he asked.

She gave him a questioning look. "It is an erica. I have often gathered them in the woods."

"I have an old book at home," he said; "I once used to write in it all sorts of songs and rhymes, but that is all over and done with long since. Between its leaves also there is an erica, but it is only a faded one. Do you know who gave it me?"

She nodded without saying a word; but she cast down her eyes and fixed them on the bloom which he held in his hand. For a long time they stood thus. When she raised her eyes on him again he saw that they were brimming over with tears.

"Elisabeth," he said, "beyond yonder blue hills lies our youth. What has become of it?"

Nothing more was spoken. They walked dumbly by each other's side down to the lake. The air was sultry; to westward dark clouds were rising. "There's going to be a storm," said Elisabeth, hastening her steps. Reinhard nodded in silence, and together they rapidly sped along the shore till they reached their boat.

On the way across Elisabeth rested her hand on the gunwale of the boat. As he rowed Reinhard glanced along at her, but she gazed past him into the distance. And so his glance fell downward and rested on her hand, and the white hand betrayed to him what her lips had failed to reveal.

It revealed those fine traces of secret pain that so readily mark a woman's fair hands, when they lie at nights folded across an aching heart. And as Elisabeth felt his glance resting on her hand she let it slip gently over the gunwale into the water.

On arriving at the farm they fell in with a scissors grinder's cart standing in front of the manor-house. A man with black, loosely-flowing hair was busily plying his wheel and humming a gypsy melody between his teeth, while a dog that was harnessed to the cart lay panting hard by. On the threshold stood a girl dressed in rags, with features of faded beauty, and with outstretched hand she asked alms of Elisabeth.

Reinhard thrust his hand into his pocket, but Elisabeth was before him, and hastily emptied the entire contents of her purse into the beggar's open palm. Then she turned quickly away, and Reinhard heard her go sobbing up the stairs.

He would fain have detained her, but he changed his mind and remained at the foot of the stairs. The beggar girl was still standing at the doorway, motionless, and holding in her hand the money she had received.

"What more do you want?" asked Reinhard.

She gave a sudden start: "I want nothing more," she said; then, turning her head toward him and staring at him with wild eyes, she passed slowly out of the door. He uttered a name, but she heard him not; with drooping head, with arms folded over her breast, she walked down across the farmyard:

Then when death shall claim me,
I must die alone.

An old song surged in Reinhard's ears, he gasped for breath; a little while only, and then he turned away and went up to his chamber.

He sat down to work, but his thoughts were far afield. After an hour's vain attempt he descended to the parlor. Nobody was in it, only cool, green twilight; on Elisabeth's work-table lay a red ribbon which she had worn round her neck during the afternoon. He took it up in his hand, but it hurt him, and he laid it down again.

He could find no rest. He walked down to the lake and untied the boat. He rowed over the water and trod once again all the paths which he and Elisabeth had paced together but a short hour ago. When he got back home it was dark. At the farm he met the coachman, who was about to turn the carriage horses out into the pasture; the travelers had just returned.

As he came into the entrance hall he heard Eric pacing up and down the garden-room. He did not go in to him; he stood still for a moment, and then softly climbed the stairs and so to his own room. Here he sat in the armchair by the window. He made himself believe that he was listening to the nightingale's throbbing music in the garden hedges below, but what he heard was the throbbing of his own heart. Downstairs in the house every one went to bed, the night-hours passed, but he paid no heed.

For hours he sat thus, till at last he rose and leaned out of the open window. The dew was dripping among the leaves, the nightingale had ceased to trill. By degrees the deep blue of the darksome sky was chased away by a faint yellow gleam that came from the east; a fresh wind rose and brushed Reinhard's heated brow; the early lark soared triumphant up into the sky.

Reinhard suddenly turned and stepped up to the table. He groped about for a pencil and when he had found one he sat down and wrote a few lines on a sheet of white paper. Having finished his writing he took up hat and stick, and leaving the paper behind him, carefully opened the door and descended to the vestibule.

The morning twilight yet brooded in every corner; the big house-cat stretched its limbs on the straw mat and arched its back against Reinhard's hand, which he unthinkingly held out to it. Outside in the garden the sparrows were already chirping their patter from among the branches, and giving notice to all that the night was now past.

Then within the house he heard a door open on the upper floor; some one came downstairs, and on looking up he saw Elisabeth standing before him. She laid her hand upon his arm, her lips moved, but not a word did he hear.

Presently she said: "You will never come back. I know it; do not deny it; you will never come back."

"No, never," he said.

She let her hand fall from his arm and said no more. He crossed the hall to the door, then turned once more. She was standing motionless on the same spot and looking at him with lifeless eyes. He advanced one step and opened his arms toward her; then, with a violent effort, he turned away and so passed out of the door.

Outside the world lay bathed in morning light, the drops of pearly dew caught on the spiders' webs glistened in the first rays of the rising sun. He never looked back; he walked rapidly onward; behind him the peaceful farmstead gradually disappeared from view as out in front of him rose the great wide world.

THE OLD MAN

The moon had ceased to shine in through the windowpanes, and it had grown quite dark; but the old man still sat is his armchair with folded hands and gazed before him into the emptiness of the room.

Gradually the murky darkness around him dissolved away before his eyes and changed into a broad dark lake; one black wave after another went rolling on farther and farther, and on the last one, so far away as to be almost beyond the reach of the old man's vision, floated lonely among its broad leaves a white water-lily.

The door opened, and a bright glare of light filled the room.

"I am glad that you have come, Bridget," said the old man. "Set the lamp upon the table."

Then he drew his chair up to the table, took one of the open books and buried himself in studies to which he had once applied all the strength of his youth.

Sidonie Gabrielle Colette

1873—1954

The girl who was to become the most famous woman writer of twentieth-century France was born in a small town in Burgundy (Saint-Sauveur-en-Puisaye) that would often provide the setting and characters of her stories. Her father was an officer at the army academy (St. Cyr); her mother was a wise and loving person Colette never tired of commemorating. The mother seems to have passed along to her daughter the artistic talent evident in her own forebears. Colette received no education beyond the village school. She adds one more illustrious instance to the venerable principle that the finest writers come from out-of-the-way places and are not holders of advanced degrees.

It is difficult, in any event, to see what advantage any higher education could have brought Colette. Her taste, her gift is wholly for the personal and particular, which she observes or intuits and then records with a brilliant Gallic precision that delights in itself. Ideology held no interest for her; she felt no temptation to set up as savant *about the economic, social, or political problems of the modern age. The problems the individual encounters in working out relationships with other individuals—or, in some cases, with animals—consumed all her attention. The progressive invasion of artistic culture by political activism is responsible for a certain underestimation of Collette's achievements in the traditional domains of literature but has not been able to bring about general devaluation.*

At twenty Colette married Henri Gauthier-Villars, a writer who forced her to produce fiction (the Claudine *series, 1900-1903) which he then published under his own pseudonym, "Willy." The marriage broke up in 1906, and Colette then took her talents to the music-hall, acting and writing skits. In 1912 Henri de Jouvenel, owner and editor of* Le Matin, *became her second husband and she became a drama critic and miscellaneous writer for his periodical. Her reviews of plays and commentary on theatre run to four volumes. In 1924 this marriage too ended in divorce. In 1935 she married the writer Maurice Goudeket, and the third time held the charm of permanence.*

Hampered by arthritis as she grew older, Colette nevertheless continued productive into the post-war era. Her favorite form continued to be short fiction—the short story and short novel, where her gift for narrative condensation and verbal conciseness could work to best advantage. Among her more famous novels are Chéri *(1920),* La Chatte *(1933), and* Gigi *(1944); the latter was turned into an immensely successful movie.*

Colette is fond of exploring romantic relationships that feature a notable disparity in age between the man and woman; she is particularly successful in portraits of young girls who are about equally receptive to men and mistrustful of them. Treatment of disillusionment or disappointment in love characteristically draws what lies deepest in her. What is most original, though, manifests itself when she deals with animals. Her unsentimentalized empathy with them is, in its own way, as intense and ambient as that of D. H. Lawrence—who prefers, of course, the undomesticated animal. A Colette story like "The Fox," for example, stands at the evolutionary apex of the long development of the French animal fabliau; all the old comic sparkle and surprise and all the newer urban sophistication and psychological nuance are there.

A peculiarity of Colette's style is her counterbalancing of simple diction and rather ornate sentences. The orginality and aptness of her figures of speech will match what one finds in the best poetry.

The Bracelet

Colette

" . . . Twenty-seven, twenty-eight, twenty-nine. . . . There really are twenty-nine. . . ."

In mechanical fashion Madame Angelier counted and re-counted the little rows of diamonds. Twenty-nine brilliant, square diamonds, set in a bracelet, sliding coldly like a thin, supple snake between her fingers. Very white, not very big, admirably well matched—a real connoisseur's piece. She fastened it round her wrist and made it sparkle under the electric candles; a hundred tiny rainbows, ablaze with colour, danced on the white tablecloth. But Madame Angelier looked more closely at the other bracelet, three finely engraved wrinkles which encircled her wrist above the brilliant snake.

"Poor François. . . . If we're both still here, what will he give me next year?"

François Angelier was a businessman travelling in Algeria at the time but, present or absent, his gift marked the end of the year and the anniversary of their wedding. Twenty-eight pieces of green jade, last year, the year before, twenty-seven plaques of old enamel mounted on a belt. . . .

"And the twenty-six little Dresden plates. . . . And the twenty-five metres of old Alençon lace. . . ." With a slight effort of memory Madame Angelier could have gone as far back as the four modest sets of knives and forks, the three pairs of silk stockings. . . .

"We weren't rich, just then. . . . Poor François, how he has always spoiled me. . . ." She called him, within her secret self, "poor François," because she felt guilty about not loving him enough, failing to appreciate the power of affectionate habit and enduring fidelity.

Madame Angelier raised her hand, crooked her little finger upwards, extended her wrist in order to erase the bracelet of wrinkles, and repeated with concentration, "How pretty it is. . . . How clear the diamonds are. . . . How pleased I am. . . ." Then she let fall her hand and admitted that she was already tired of the brand-new piece of jewellery.

"But I'm not ungrateful," she sighed naively. Her bored glance wandered from the flowered table-cloth to the sparkling window. The smell of Calville apples in a silver basket made her feel slightly sick and she left the dining-room.

In her boudoir she opened the steel case which contained her jewellery and decked out her left hand in honour of the new bracelet. The ring finger had a ring of black onyx, a brilliant tinged with blue; over the little finger, which was delicate, pale and slightly wrinkled, Madame Angelier slipped a hoop of dark sapphires. Her prematurely white hair, which she did not dye, looked whiter when she fixed into its light curls a narrow little band sprinkled with a dust of diamonds, but she removed the ornament at once.

"I don't know what's the matter with me. I'm not in form. It's tedious being fifty, in fact. . . ."

She felt uneasy, greedy, but not hungry, like a convalescent whose appetite has not yet been restored by the fresh air.

"Actually, is a diamond as pretty as all that?"

Madame Angelier yearned for visual pleasure combined with the pleasure of taste; the unexpected sight of a lemon, the unbearable squeak of the knife which cuts it in two, makes one's mouth water with desire. . . .

"I don't want a lemon. But the nameless pleasure which escapes me, it exists, I know it, I remember it! So, the blue glass bracelet. . . ."

A shudder contracted Madame Angelier's relaxed cheeks. A miracle, the duration of which she could not measure, allowed her, for the second time, the moment she had lived through forty years earlier, the incomparable moment when she looked in rapture at the light of day, the rainbow-coloured and misshapen image of objects through a piece of blue glass, bent into a circle, which had just been given to her. That piece of glass, which might have come from the East and was broken a few hours later, had contained a new universe, shapes that dreaming did not invent, slow, serpentine animals which moved in pairs, lamps, rays congealed in an atmosphere of indescribable blue. . .

The miracle ended and Madame Angelier, feeling bruised, was thrown back into the present and the real.

But from the next day she went from antique dealers to bargain basements, from bargain basements to glassware shops, looking for a glass bracelet of a certain blue. She did so with the passion of a collector, the care and dissimulation of a crank. She ventured into what she called "impossible districts," left her car at the corner of strange streets and in the end, for a few centimes, found a hoop of blue glass that she recognized in the darkness, bought mutteringly and took away. . . .

By the suitably adjusted shade of her favourite lamp, on the dark background of old velvet, she put down the bracelet, bent over it, awaited the shock. . . . But she saw only a circle of bluish glass, an ornament for a child or a savage, moulded hastily, full of bubbles; an object whose colour and material she recalled; but the powerful and sensuous genie who creates and feeds the visions of childhood, who dies mysteriously within us, progressively disappearing, did not stir.

With resignation Madame Angelier realized in this way her true age and measured the infinite plain over which there moved a being forever detached from herself, inaccessible, foreign, turning away from her, free and rebellious even to the command of memory: a little girl of ten wearing round her wrist a bracelet of blue glass.

Dawn

Colette

The surgical suddenness of their break left him stupefied. Alone in the house where the two of them had lived together in near-conjugal fashion for some twenty years he could not succeed, after a week, in finding grief. He struggled comically against the disappearance of ordinary objects and trounced his valet in childish fashion: "Those collars can't really have been eaten! And don't tell me I haven't any more sticks of shaving-soap, there were two in the bathroom cupboard! You won't make me believe that I haven't any more shaving-soap because Madame isn't here!"

He was terrified by the feeling that he was no longer being organized, he forgot meal-times, came home for no reason, went out in order to escape, mumbled in a half-choked voice into the telephone, which was no longer handed to him in imperious fashion by a woman. He called his friends to witness, embarrassed them and shocked them, whether they were unfaithful or enslaved. "My dear chap, it's incredible! Cleverer men than me wouldn't understand it. . . . Aline's gone. She's gone, there it is. And not alone, you understand. She's gone. I could say it a hundred times and find nothing more to add. Apparently these things happen every day to lots of husbands. What can I say? I can't get over it. No, I can't get over it."

His eyes would grow round, he would spread out his arms, then let them drop again. He looked neither tragic nor humiliated and his friends despised him slightly: "He's going downhill. . . . At his age it's been a blow to him." They talked about him as though he were old, secretly pleased that they could at last belittle this handsome man whose hair was turning slightly grey and who had never had any disappointments in love.

"His beautiful Aline . . . . He found it quite natural that at forty-five she suddenly went blonde, with a complexion like an artificial flower, and that she changed her dressmaker and her shoemaker. He wasn't suspicious. . . ."

One day he took the train; his valet had asked him for a week's leave: "Since there's less work because Madame's not here, I thought . . . ." And also because he was losing more and more sleep, dozing off at dawn after staying awake like a huntsman on the lookout, motionless in the dark, his jaws clenched and his ears twitching. He left one evening, avoiding the house in the country he had bought fifteen years earlier and furnished for Aline. He took a ticket for a large provincial town where he remembered having acted as spokesman for *L'Extension économique* and banqueted at their expense.

"A good hotel," he told himself, "a restaurant with old-style French cooking, that's what I need. I don't want this thing to kill me, do I? All right, let's go away. Travel, good food . . . ."

During the journey the railway-compartment mirror reflected the figure that was still upright and the grey moustache concealing the relaxed mouth. "Not bad, not bad. Good heavens, it won't kill me! The minx!" This was the only word he used to insult the unfaithful woman, the moderate, old-fashioned word still used by elderly people to praise the rashness of youth.

At the hotel he asked for the same room he had had the previous year. "A bay window, you know, with a nice view over the square"; he supped off cold meat and beer and went to bed when the evening was almost over. His exhaustion led him to believe that his flight would be rewarded by prompt sleep. Lying on his back he relished the coolness of the damp sheets, and worked out in the dark the forgotten location of the big bay window, starting from two tall shafts of bluish light between the drawn curtains. In fact he sank quietly to sleep for a few seconds and then woke up for good: he had unconsciously moved his legs back to leave room for her who was now absent day and night but returned faithfully when he slept. He woke up and bravely uttered the conspiratorial words: "Come now, it'll soon be daylight, be patient." The two blue shafts of light were turning pink, and from the square he heard the cheerful, rasping din of the iron-hooped wooden buckets and the plonk of the horses' big patient hoaves. "The same sound as the stables at Fontainebleau, exactly what we heard at that villa we'd rented near the hotel. . . . When dawn broke we used to listen . . . ." He shuddered, turned over and once more sought sleep. The horses and the buckets were quiet now. Other sounds, more discreet, came up through the open window. He distinguished the solid, muffled sound of flower-pots being unloaded from a van, a sound like light rain as the plants were watered, and the gentle thud as large armfuls of leaves were thrown down on to the ground.

"A flower-market," said the sleepless man to himself. "Oh, I can't be mistaken about it. In Strasbourg during that trip we made, the early morning revealed a delightful flower-market beneath our windows, and she said she had never seen such blue cinerarias as . . . ." He sat up, in order to combat more effectively a mood of despair whose tide flowed in regular waves, a new kind of despair, quite different, unknown. Beneath the nearby bridge, oars struck the sleeping river and the flight of the first swallows whistled through the air: "It's early morning at Como, the swallows behind the gardener's boat, the smell of fruit and vegetables came through our windows at the Villa d'Este . . . . God be merciful . . . ." He still had the strength to blush as he started a prayer, although the pain of loneliness and memory left him hunched up on his bed like a man with tuberculosis. Twenty years . . . all the dawns of twenty years poured over the companion, sleeping or wakeful at his side, their faint or brilliant ray of light, their bird-call, their pearly raindrops, twenty years . . . .

"I don't want it to kill me, damn it. Twenty years, it's a long time. But before her I knew other dawns . . . . So let's see, when I was a very young man . . . ."

But he could resurrect only the half-light known to poor students, the grey mornings at the law school warmed by skimmed milk or alcohol, mornings in furnished rooms with narrow wash-basins or zinc buckets. He turned away from them, invoked the aid of his adolescence and the dawns of that time, but they came to him cringing and bitter, rising from a rickety iron bed, prisoners of a wretched time, marked on the cheek by a violent blow, dragging shoes with rotten soles . . . . The abandoned man realized that there was no escape for him and that he would struggle in vain against the returning light, that the cruel and familiar harmony of the first hour of the day would sing one name only, reopen one wound only, each time recent and renewed; then he went down into bed again and obediently burst into tears.

The Little Bouilloux Girl

Colette

The little Bouilloux girl was so lovely that even we children noticed it. It is unusual for small girls to recognize beauty in one of themselves and pay homage to it. But there could be no disputing such undeniable loveliness as hers. Whenever my mother met the little Bouilloux girl in the street, she would stop her and bend over her as she was wont to bend over her yellow tea-rose, her red flowering cactus or her Azure Blue butterfly trustfully asleep on the scaly bark of the pine tree. She would stroke her curly hair, golden as a half-ripe chestnut, and her delicately tinted cheeks, and watch the incredible lashes flutter over her great dark eyes. She would observe the glimmer of the perfect teeth in her peerless mouth, and when, at last, she let the child go on her way, she would look after her, murmuring, "It's prodigious!"

Several years passed, bringing yet further graces to the little Bouilloux girl. There were certain occasions recorded by our admiration: a prize-giving at which, shyly murmuring an unintelligible recitation, she glowed through her tears like a peach under a summer shower. The little Bouilloux girl's first communion caused a scandal: the same evening, after vespers, she was seen drinking a half pint at the *Café du Commerce,* with her father, the sawyer, and that night she danced, already feminine and flirtatious, a little unsteady in her white slippers, at the public ball.

With an arrogance to which she had accustomed us, she informed us later, at school, that she was to be apprenticed.

"Oh! Who to?"

"To Madame Adolphe."

"Oh! And are you to get wages at once?"

"No. I'm only thirteen, I shall start earning next year."

She left us without emotion, and coldly we let her go. Already her beauty isolated her and she had no friends at school, where she learned very little. Her Sundays and her Thursdays brought no intimacy with us; they were spent with a family that was considered "unsuitable," with girl cousins of eighteen well known for their brazen behavior, and with brothers, cartwright apprentices, who sported ties at fourteen and smoked when they escorted their sister to the Parisian shooting-gallery at the fair or to the cheerful bar that the widow Pimolle had made so popular.

The very next morning on my way to school I met the little Bouilloux girl setting out for the dressmaker's workrooms, and I remained motionless, thunderstruck with jealous admiration, at the corner of the Rue des Soeurs, watching Nana Bouilloux's retreating form. She had exchanged her black pinafore and short childish frock for a long skirt and a pleated blouse of pink sateen. She wore a black alpaca apron and her exuberant locks, disciplined and twisted into a "figure of eight," lay close as a helmet about the charming new shape of a round imperious head that retained nothing childish except its freshness and the not yet calculated impudence of a little village adventuress.

That morning the upper forms hummed like a hive.

"I've seen Nana Bouilloux! In a long dress, my dear, would you believe it? And her hair in a chignon! She had a pair of scissors hanging from her belt too!"

At noon I flew home to announce breathlessly:

"Mother! I met Nana Bouilloux on the street! She was passing our door. And she had a long dress! Mother, just imagine, a long dress! And her hair in a chignon! And she had high heels and a pair of . . ."

"Eat, Minet-Chéri, eat, your cutlet will be cold."

"And an apron, mother, such a lovely alpaca apron that looked like silk! Couldn't I possibly . . ."

"No, Minet-Chéri, you certainly couldn't."

"But if Nana Bouilloux can . . ."

"Yes, Nana Bouilloux, at thirteen, can, in fact she should, wear a chignon, a short apron and a long skirt—it's the uniform of all little Bouilloux girls throughout the world, at thirteen—more's the pity."

"But . . ."

"Yes, I know you would like to wear the complete uniform of a little Bouilloux girl. It includes all that you've seen, and a bit more besides: a letter safely hidden in the apron pocket, an admirer sho smells of wine and of cheap cigars; two admirers, three admirers and a little later on plenty of tears . . . and a sickly child hidden away, a child that has lain for months crushed by constricting stays. There it is, Minet-Chéri, the entire uniform of the little Bouilloux girls. Do you still want it?"

"Of course not, mother. I only wanted to see if a chignon . . ."

But my mother shook her head, mocking but serious.

"No, no! You can't have the chignon without the apron, the apron without the letter, the letter without the high-heeled slippers, or the slippers without . . . all the rest of it! It's just a matter of choice!"

My envy was soon exhausted. The resplendent little Bouilloux girl became no more than a daily passer-by whom I scarcely noticed. Bareheaded in winter and summer, her gaily colored blouses varied from week to week, and in very cold weather she swathed her elegant shoulders in a useless little scarf. Erect, radiant as a thorny rose, her eyelashes sweeping her cheeks or half revealing her dark and dewy eyes, she grew daily more worthy of queening it over crowds, of being gazed at, adorned and bedecked with jewels. The severely smoothed crinkliness of her chestnut hair could still be discerned in little waves that caught the light in the golden mist at the nape of her neck and round her ears. She always looked vaguely offended with her small, velvety nostrils reminding one of a doe.

She was fifteen or sixteen now—and so was I. Except that she laughed too freely on Sundays, in order to show her white teeth, as she hung on the arms of her brothers or her girl cousins, Nana Bouilloux was behaving fairly well.

"For a little Bouilloux girl, very well indeed!" was the public verdict.

She was seventeen, then eighteen; her complexion was like a peach on a south wall, no eyes could meet the challenge of hers and she had the bearing of a goddess. She began to take the floor at fêtes and fairs, to dance with abandon, to stay out very late at night, wandering in the lanes with a man's arm round her waist. Always unkind, but full of laughter, provoking boldness in those who would have been content merely to love her.

Then came a St. John's Eve when she appeared on the dance floor that was laid down on the Place du Grand-Jeu under the melancholy light of malodorous oil lamps. Hobnailed boots kicked up the dust between the planks of the "floor." All the young men, as was customary, kept their hats on while dancing. Blonde girls became claret-colored in their tight bodices, while the dark ones, sunburned from their work in the fields, looked black. But there, among a band of haughty workgirls, Nana Bouilloux, in a summer dress sprigged with little flowers, was drinking lemonade laced with red wine when the Parisians arrived on the scene.

They were two Parisians such as one sees in the country in summer, friends of a neighboring landowner, and supremely bored; Parisians in tussore and white serge, come for a moment to mock at a village mid-summer fête. They stopped laughing when they saw Nana Bouilloux and sat down near the bar in order to see her better. In low voices they exchanged comments which she pretended not to hear, since her pride as a beautiful creature would not let her turn her eyes in their direction and giggle like her companions. She heard the words, "A swan among geese! A Greuze! A crime to let such a wonder bury herself here . . . ." When the young man in the white suit asked the little Bouilloux girl for a waltz she got up without surprise and danced with him gravely, in silence. From time to time her eyelashes, more beautiful than a glance, brushed against her partner's fair mustache.

After the waltz the two Parisians went away, and Nana Bouilloux sat down by the bar fanning herself. There she was soon approached by young Leriche, by Houette, even by Honce the chemist, and even by Possy the cabinet-maker, who was ageing, but none the less a good dancer. To all of them she replied, "Thank you, but I'm tired," and she left the ball at half-past ten o'clock.

And after that, nothing more ever happened to the little Bouilloux girl. The Parisians did not return, neither they, nor others like them. Houette, Honce, young Leriche, the commercial travelers with their gold watch-chains, soldiers on leave and sheriff's clerks vainly climbed our steep street at the hours when the beautifully coiffed seamstress, on her way down it, passed them by stiffly with a distant nod. They looked out for her at dances, where she sat drinking lemonade with an air of distinction and answered their importunities with, "Thank you very much, but I'm not dancing, I'm tired." Taking offense, they soon began to snigger: "Tired! Her kind of tiredness lasts for thirty-six weeks!" and they kept a sharp watch on her figure. But nothing happened to the little Bouilloux girl, neither that nor anything else. She was simply waiting, possessed by an arrogant faith, conscious of the debt owed by the hazard that had armed her too well. She was awaiting . . . not the return of the Parisian in white serge, but a stranger, a ravisher. Her proud anticipation kept her silent and pure; with a little smile of surprise, she rejected Honce, who would have raised her to the rank of chemist's lawful wife, and she would have nothing to say to the sheriff's chief clerk. With never another lapse, taking back, once and for all, the smiles, the glances, the glowing bloom of her cheeks, the red young lips, the shadowy blue cleft of her breasts which she had so prodigally lavished on mere rustics, she awaited her kingdom and the prince without a name.

Years later, when I passed through my native village, I could not find the shade of her who had so lovingly refused me what she called "The uniform of little Bouilloux girls." But as the car bore me slowly, though not slowly enough—never slowly enough—up a street where I have now no reason to stop, a woman drew back to avoid the wheel. A slender woman, her hair well dressed in a bygone fashion, dressmaker's scissors hanging from a steel "châtelaine" on her black apron. Large, vindictive eyes, a tight mouth sealed by long silence, the sallow cheeks and temples of those who work by lamplight; a woman of forty-five or . . . Not at all; a woman of thirty-eight, a woman of my own age, of exactly my age, there was no room for doubt. As soon as the car allowed her room to pass, "the little Bouilloux girl" went on her way down the street, erect and indifferent, after one anxious, bitter glance had told her that the car did not contain the long-awaited ravisher.

Alphonse Daudet
1840—1897

Like Charles Dickens, Daudet delighted in the robust comedy of spirited personality and right away found a style that conveyed his own vivacity as well as that of his characters and situations. And like Dickens he was unselfconsciously compassionate for the neglected or abused of the world, and in general went out of his way—arriving, sometimes, at sentimentality—to discover admirable traits in common folk. Daudet was generous, amiable, a patron of younger writers (e.g., Marcel Proust), and a good father to his three children, Edmée, Lucien, and Léon (Léon inherited his father's elan, channeled much of it into politics, and became a redoubtable publicist for the French Right). Again like Dickens, Daudet began as an exuberant humorist working mostly in sketches and short tales and gradually developed a taste for a more restrained manner, a larger canvas, and an interest in characters caught up in morally and psychologically difficult situations.

In nearly all Daudet's work one finds the Mediterranean clarity and sensibleness so much admired by Santayana and Valéry. A child of lively, sunny Provence, Daudet had to move to Lyons when he was nine, but in his early twenties he renewed his spiritual commitment to the south and captured its charm in much of his best and best-known fiction, including "L'Arlèsienne," "The Pope's Mule," "Father Gaucher's Elixir," and Tartarin of Tarascon. *He was equally adept in short fiction and full-length novels. The semi-autobiographical* Sapho *(1884), based on Daudet's youthful and ill-fated liaison with the model Marie Rieu, is a novel that has not dated.*

Most of Daudet's short stories are collected in Letters from My Mill *(1869) and* Monday Tales *(1872-73). In his later work Daudet shows the influence of the naturalists, mainly in the abundance of detail drawn from actual observation and faithfully recorded. But, wanting to be a "merchant of happiness," he objected to most of the naturalist programme: to its pessimism, its obsession with the ugly or morbid subject, its scientific and clinical pretensions, and its characteristic antipathy to traditional religion and government. Daudet's rapport with the passionate traditionalism of the Catholic peasantry of Provence, his friendship with the tradition-loving Frédéric Mistral, and his service to the conservative duc de Morny confirmed his feeling for church and crown.*

The Last Class

Alphonse Daudet

I started for school very late that morning and was in great dread of a scolding, especially because M. Hamel had said that he would question us on participles, and I did not know the first word about them. For a moment I thought of running away and spending the day out of doors. It was so warm, so bright! The birds were chirping at the edge of the woods; and in the open field back of the sawmill the Prussian soldiers were drilling. It was all much more tempting than the rule for participles, but I had the strength to resist, and hurried off to school.

When I passed the town hall there was a crowd in front of the bulletin board. For the last two years all our bad news had come from there—the lost battles, the draft, the orders of the commanding officer—and I thought to myself, without stopping:

"What can be the matter now?"

Then, as I hurried by as fast as I could go, the blacksmith, Wachter, who was there, with his apprentice, reading the bulletin, called after me:

"Don't go so fast, bud; you'll get to your school in plenty of time!"

I thought he was making fun of me, and reached M. Hamel's little garden all out of breath.

Usually, when school began, there was a great bustle, which could be heard out in the street, the opening and closing of desks, lessons repeated in unison, very loud, with our hands over our ears to understand better, and the teacher's great ruler rapping on the table. But now it was all so still! I had counted on the commotion to get to my desk without being seen; but, of course, that day everything had to be as quiet as Sunday morning. Through the window I saw my classmates, already in their places, and M. Hamel walking up and down with his terrible iron ruler under his arm. I had to open the door and go in before everybody. You can imagine how I blushed and how frightened I was.

But nothing happened. M. Hamel saw me and said very kindly:

"Go to your place quickly, little Franz. We were beginning without you."

I jumped over the bench and sat down at my desk. Not till then, when I had got a little over my fright, did I see that our teacher had on his beautiful green coat, his frilled shirt, and the little black silk cap, all embroidered, that he never wore except on inspection and prize days. Besides, the whole school seemed so strange and solemn. But the thing that surprised me most was to see, on the back benches that were always empty, the village people sitting quietly like ourselves; old Hauser, with his three-cornered hat, the former mayor, the former postmaster, and several others besides. Everybody looked sad; and Hauser had brought an old primer, thumbed at the edges, and he held it open on his knees with his great spectacles lying across the pages.

While I was wondering about it all, M. Hamel mounted his chair, and, in the same grave and gentle tone which he had used to me, he said:

"My children, this is the last lesson I shall give you. The order has come from Berlin to teach only German in the schools of Alsace and Lorraine. The new master comes to-morrow. This is your last French lesson. I want you to be very attentive."

What a thunder-clap these words were to me!

Oh, the wretches; that was what they had put up at the town hall!

My last French lesson! Why, I hardly knew how to write! I should never learn any more! I must stop there, then! Oh, how sorry I was for not learning my lessons, for seeking birds' eggs, or going sliding on the Soar! My books, that had seemed such a nuisance a while ago, so heavy to carry, my grammar, and my history of the saints, were old friends now that I couldn't give up. And M. Hamel, too; the idea that he was going away, that I should never see him again, made me forget all about his ruler and how cranky he was.

Poor man! It was in honor of this last lesson that he had put on his fine Sunday-clothes, and now I understood why the old men of the village were sitting there in the back of the room. It was because they were sorry, too, that they had not gone to school more. It was their way of thanking our master for his forty years of faithful service and of showing their respect for the country that was theirs no more.

While I was thinking of all this, I heard my name called. It was my turn to recite. What would I not have given to be able to say that dreadful rule for the participle all through, very loud and clear, and without one mistake? But I got mixed up on the first words and stood there, holding on to my desk, my heart beating, and not daring to look up. I heard M. Hamel say to me:

"I won't scold you, little Franz; you must feel bad enough. See how it is! Every day we have said to ourselves: 'Bah! I've plenty of time. I'll learn it to-morrow.' And now you see where we've come out. Ah, that's the great trouble with Alsace; she puts off learning till to-morrow. Now those fellows out there will have the right to say to you: 'How is it; you pretend to be Frenchmen, and yet you can neither speak nor write your own language?' But you are not the worst, poor little Franz. We've all a great deal to reproach ourselves with.

"Your parents were not anxious enough to have you learn. They preferred to put you to work on a farm or at the mills, so as to have a little more money. And I? I've been to blame also. Have I not often sent you to water my flowers instead of learning your lessons? And when I wanted to go fishing, did I not just give you a holiday?"

Then, from one thing to another, M. Hamel went on to talk of the French language, saying that it was the most beautiful language in the world—the clearest, the most logical; that we must guard it among us and never forget it, because when a people are enslaved, as long as they hold fast to their language it is as if they had the key to their prison. Then he opened a grammar and read us our lesson. I was amazed to see how well I understood it. All he said seemed so easy, so easy! I think, too, that I had never listened so carefully, and that he had never explained everything with so much patience. It seemed almost as if the poor man wanted to give us all he knew before going away, and to put it all into our heads at one stroke.

After the grammar, we had a lesson in writing. That day M. Hamel had new copies for us, written in a beautiful round hand: France, Alsace, France, Alsace. They looked like little flags floating everywhere in the school-room, hung from the rod at the top of our desks. You ought to have seen how every one set to work, and how quiet it was! The only sound was the scratching of the pens over the paper. Once some beetles flew in; but nobody paid any attention to them, not even the littlest ones, who worked right on tracing their fish-hooks, as if that was French, too. On the roof the pigeons cooed very low, and I thought to myself:

"Will they make them sing in German, even the pigeons?"

Whenever I looked up from my writing I saw M. Hamel sitting motionless in his chair and gazing first at one thing, then at another, as if he wanted to fix in his mind just how everything looked in that little school-room. Fancy! For forty years he had been there in the same place, with his garden outside the window and his class in front of him, just like that. Only the desks and benches had been worn smooth; the walnut-trees in the garden were taller, and the hop-vine that he had planted himself twined about the windows to the roof. How it must have broken his heart to leave it all, poor man; to hear his sister moving about in the room above, packing their trunks! For they must leave the country next day.

But he had the courage to hear every lesson to the very last. After the writing, we had a lesson in history, and then the babies chanted their ba, be, bi, bo, bu. Down there at the back of the room old Hauser had put on his spectacles and, holding his primer in both hands, spelled the letters with them. You could see that he, too, was crying; his voice trembled with emotion, and it was so funny to hear him that we all wanted to laugh and cry. Ah, how well I remember it, that last lesson!

All at once the church-clock struck twelve. Then the Angelus. At the same moment the trumpets of the Prussians, returning from drill, sounded under our windows. M. Hamel stood up, very pale, in his chair. I never saw him look so tall.

"My friends," said he, "I—I—" But something choked him. He

could not go on.

Then he turned to the blackboard, took a piece of chalk, and, bearing on with all his might, he wrote as large as he could:

"VIVE LA FRANCE!"

Then he stopped and leaned his head against the wall, and without a word, he made a gesture to us with his hand:

"School is dismissed—you may go."

Elizabeth Bowen

1899—1973

"Man does, woman is," said Robert Graves. Isak Dinesen (Karen Blixen) put the case less gnomically: "A man's center of gravity, the substance of his being, consists in what he has executed and performed in life; the woman's, in what she is." Apparently, however, over the past few centuries it has become increasingly difficult for women to fulfill their innate genius for being. *Modernity—as would be expected of any commercial-industrial civilization, is built around the concept of* having*: things, money, career, security. Whatever is quintessentially feminine in woman does not adapt without cost to the technological consumption-production world created, under the aegis of rationalism, by the male obsession with analysis and material achievement. Elizabeth Bowen regarded woman as the emotionally more sensitive, hence more vulnerable sex; and the child or young woman as the most vulnerable of all.*

In any case, the unhappiness and suffering of young people in general and young women in particular is the recurring subject of her fiction. Her stories show the characters not so much victims of "sexism" as of money materialism and the general modern flight from the spiritual claim, the claim of being. A good career "at equal pay" would solve none of the problems of Bowen's heroines. Characteristically dealing with figures from upper middle-class society, her work reminds us that it is not only the "underdogs" who suffer.

She started with the short story. Encounters *(1923) was the first of several collections that gave her a place among the masters of the genre. Other collections include* The Cat Jumps *(1934),* The Heat of the Day *(1949), and* Look at All Those Roses *(1941), the volume in which "Tears, Idle Tears" appeared. Her* Collected Stories *appeared in 1981. She is at least equally well known as a novelist.* The Death of the Heart *(1938) probably remains her best-known book.*

Brave and full of good sense, Bowen articulates her cultural pessimism without despair or shrillness and without proffering chimeric or eccentric panaceas. She defends property and rootedness not because of unexamined hearthside prejudices but because she felt *their contribution to sanity, personal equilibrium, and high culture. Taking a long look at history, she concluded that "We have everything to dread from the dispossessed." She loved her eighteenth-century ancestral mansion (Bowen's Court, in Ireland) but was too poor to keep it up after the death of her husband, Alan Cameron; it was sold in 1959 and razed shortly after. It inspired* Bowen's Court *(1942, revised 1964), which ranks among the greatest tributes ever rendered to a family home.*

Like nearly all of the many brilliant writers born into the Anglo-Irish gentry or associated with it, Bowen commanded an admirable style and yet worked constantly to make it even more supple. She would have agreed with her countryman W. B. Yeats that style is the "salt" of literature—that which preserves a piece of writing.

Tears, Idle Tears

Elizabeth Bowen

Frederick burst into tears in the middle of Regent's Park. His mother, seeing what was about to happen, had cried: "Frederick, you *can't*—in the middle of Regent's Park!" Really, this was a corner, one of those lively corners just inside a big gate, where two walks meet and a bridge starts across the pretty winding lake. People were passing quickly; the bridge rang with feet. Poplars stood up like delicate green brooms; diaphanous willows whose weeping was not shocking quivered over the lake. May sun spattered gold through the breezy trees; the tulips though falling open were still gay; three girls in a long boat shot under the bridge. Frederick, knees trembling, butted towards his mother a crimson convulsed face, as though he had the idea of burying himself in her. She whipped out a handkerchief and dabbed at him with it under his grey felt hat, exclaiming meanwhile in fearful mortification: "You really haven't got to be such a *baby*!" Her tone attracted the notice of several people, who might otherwise have thought he was having something taken out of his eye.

He was too big to cry: the whole scene was disgraceful. He wore a grey flannel knickerbocker suit and looked like a schoolboy; though in fact he was seven, still doing lessons at home. His mother said to him almost every week: "I don't know what they will think when you go to school!" His tears were a shame of which she could speak to no one; no offensive weakness of body could have upset her more. Once she had got so far as taking her pen up to write to the Mother's Advice Column of a helpful woman's weekly about them. She began: "I am a widow; young, good tempered, and my friends all tell me that I have great control. But my little boy—" She intended to sign herself "Mrs. D., Surrey." But then she had stopped and thought no, no: after all, he is Toppy's son . . . . She was a gallant-looking, correct woman, wearing to-day in London a coat and skirt, a silver fox, white gloves and a dark-blue toque put on exactly right—not the sort of woman you ought to see in a Park with a great blubbering boy belonging to her. She looked a mother of sons, but not of a son of this kind, and should more properly, really, have been walking a dog. "Come on!" she said, as though the bridge, the poplars, the people staring were to be borne no longer. She began to walk on quickly, along the edge of the lake, parallel with the park's girdle of trees and the dark, haughty windows of Cornwall Terrace looking at her over the red may. They had meant to go to the Zoo, but now she had changed her mind: Frederick did not deserve the Zoo.

Frederick stumbled along beside her, too miserable to notice. His mother seldom openly punished him, but often revenged herself on him in small ways. He could feel how just this was. His own incontinence in the matter of tears was as shocking to him, as bowing-down, as annulling, as it could be to her. He never knew what happened—a cold black pit with no bottom opened inside himself; a red-hot bellwire jagged up through him from the pit of his frozen belly to the caves of his eyes. Then the hot gummy rush of tears, the convulsion of his features, the terrible square grin he felt his mouth take all made him his own shameful and squalid enemy. Despair howled round his inside like a wind, and through his streaming eyes he saw everything quake. Anyone's being there—and most of all his mother—drove this catastrophe on him. He never cried like this when he was alone.

Crying made him so abject, so outcast from other people that he went on crying out of despair. His crying was not just reflex, like a baby's; it dragged up all unseemliness into view. No wonder everyone was repelled. There is something about an abject person that rouses cruelty in the kindest breast. The plate-glass windows of the lordly houses looked at him through the may-trees with judges' eyes. Girls with their knees crossed, reading on the park benches, looked up with unkind smiles. His apathetic stumbling, his not seeing or caring that they had given up their trip to the Zoo, became more than Mrs.

Dickinson, his mother, could bear. She pointed out, in a voice tense with dislike: "I'm not taking you to the Zoo."

"Mmmph-mmph-mmph," sobbed Frederick.

"You know, I so often wonder what your father would think."

"Mmmph-mmph-mmph."

"He used to be so proud of you. He and I used to look forward to what you'd be like when you were a big boy. One of the last things he ever said was: 'Frederick will take care of you.' You almost make me glad he's not here now."

"Ough-ough."

"What do you say?"

"I'm t-t-trying to stop."

"Everybody's looking at you, you know."

She was one of those women who have an unfailing sense of what not to say, and say it: despair, perversity or stubborn virtue must actuate them. She had a horror, also, of the abnormal and had to hit out at it before it could hit at her. Her husband, an R.A.F. pilot who had died two days after a ghastly crash, after two or three harrowing spaces of consciousness, had never made her ashamed or puzzled her. Their intimacies, then even his death, had had a bold naturalness.

"Listen, I shall walk on ahead," said Frederick's mother, lifting her chin with that noble, decided movement so many people liked. "You stay here and look at that duck till you've stopped that noise. Don't catch me up till you have. No, I'm really ashamed of you."

She walked on. He had *not* been making, really, so very much noise. Drawing choppy breaths, he stood still and looked at the duck that sat folded into a sleek white cypher on the green grassy margin of the lake. When it rolled one eye open over a curve, something unseeing in its expression calmed him. His mother walked away under the gay tree-shadows; her step quickened lightly, the tip of her fox fur swung. She thought of the lunch she had had with Major and Mrs. Williams, the party she would be going to at five. First, she must leave Frederick at Aunt Mary's, and what would Aunt Mary say to his bloated face? She walked fast; the gap between her and Frederick widened: she was a charming woman walking by herself.

Everybody had noticed how much courage she had; they said: "How plucky Mrs. Dickinson is." It was five years since her tragedy and she had not remarried, so that her gallantness kept on coming into play. She helped a friend with a little hat shop called *Isobel* near where they lived in Surrey, bred puppies for sale and gave the rest of her time to making a man of Frederick. She smiled nicely and carried her head high. Those two days while Toppy had lain dying she had hardly turned a hair, for his sake: no one knew when he might come conscious again. When she was not by his bed she was waiting about the hospital. The chaplain hanging about her and the doctor had given thanks that there were women like this; another officer's wife who had been her friend had said she was braver than could be good for anyone. When Toppy finally died the other woman had put the unflinching widow into a taxi and driven back with her to the Dickinsons' bungalow. She kept saying: "Cry, dear, cry: you'd feel better." She made tea and clattered about, repeating: "Don't mind me, darling: just have a big cry." The strain became so great that tears streamed down her own face. Mrs. Dickinson looked past her palely, with a polite smile. The empty-feeling bungalow with its rustling curtains still smelt of Toppy's pipe; his slippers were under a chair. Then Mrs. Dickinson's friend, almost tittering with despair, thought of a poem of Tennyson's she had learnt as a child. She said: "Where's Frederick? He's quiet. Do you think he's asleep?" The widow, rising, perfectly automatic, led her into the room where Frederick lay in his cot. A nursemaid rose from beside him, gave them one morbid look and scurried away. The two-year-old baby, flushed, and drawing up his upper lip in his sleep as his father used to do, lay curved under his blue blanket, clenching one fist on nothing. Something suddenly seemed to strike his mother, who, slumping down by the cot, ground her face and forehead into the fluffy blanket, then began winding the blanket round her two fists. Her convulsions, though proper, were fearful: the cot shook. The friend crept away into the kitchen, where she stayed an half-hour, muttering to the maid. They made more tea and waited for Mrs. Dickinson to give full birth to her grief. Then extreme silence drew them back to the cot. Mrs. Dickinson knelt asleep, her profile pressed to the blanket, one arm crooked over the baby's form. Under his mother's arm, as still as an image, Frederick lay wide awake, not making a sound. In conjunction with a certain look in his eyes, the baby's silence gave the two women the horrors. The servant said to the friend: "You would think he knew."

Mrs. Dickinson's making so few demands on pity soon rather alienated her women friends, but men liked her better for it: several of them found in her straight look an involuntary appeal to themselves alone, more exciting than coquetry, deeply, nobly exciting: several wanted to marry her. But courage had given her a new intractable kind of virgin pride: she loved it too much; she could never surrender it. "No, don't ask me that," she would say, lifting her chin and with that calm, gallant smile. "Don't spoil things. You've been splendid to me: such a support. But you see, there's Frederick. He's the man in my life now. I'm bound to put him first. That wouldn't be fair, would it?" After that, she would simply go on shaking her head. She became the perfect friend for men who wished to wish to marry but were just as glad not to, and for married men who liked just a little pathos without being upset.

Frederick had stopped crying. This left him perfectly blank, so that he stared at the duck with abstract intensity, perceiving its moulded feathers and porcelain-smooth neck. The burning, swirling film had cleared away from his eyes, and his diaphragm felt relief, as when retching has stopped. He forgot his focus of grief and forgot his mother, but saw with joy a quivering bough of willow that, drooping into his gaze under his swollen eyelids, looked as pure and strong as something after the Flood. His thought clutched at the willow, weak and wrecked but happy. He knew he was now qualified to walk after his mother, but without feeling either guilty or recalcitrant did not wish to do so. He stepped over the rail—no park keeper being at hand to stop him—and, tenderly and respectfully, attempted to touch the white duck's tail. Without a blink, with automatic uncoyness, the duck slid away from Frederick into the lake. Its lovely white china body balanced on the green glass water as it propelled itself gently round the curve of the bank. Frederick saw with a passion of observation its shadowy webbed feet lazily striking out.

"The keeper'll eat you," said a voice behind him.

Frederick looked cautiously round with his bunged-up eyes. The *individual* who had spoken sat on a park bench; it was a girl with a despatch case beside her. Her big bony knee-joints stuck out through her thin crepe-de-chine dress; she was hatless and her hair made a frizzy, pretty outline, but she wore spectacles, her skin had burnt dull red: her smile and the cock of her head had about them something pungent and energetic, not like a girl's at all. "Whatcher mean, eat me?"

"You're on his grass. And putting salt on his duck's tail."

Frederick stepped back carefully over the low rail. "I haven't got any salt." He looked up and down the walk: his mother was out of sight but from the direction of the bridge a keeper was approaching, still distant but with an awesome gait. "My goodness," the girl said, "what's been biting *you*?" Frederick was at a loss. "Here," she said, "have an apple." She opened her case, which was full of folded grease-paper that must have held sandwiches, and rummaged out an apple with a waxy, bright skin. Frederick came up, tentative as a pony, and finally took the apple. His breath was still hitching and catching; he did not wish to speak.

"Go on," she said, "swallow: it'll settle your chest. Where's your mother gone off to? What's all the noise about?" Frederick only opened his jaws as wide as they would go, then bit slowly, deeply into the apple. The girl re-crossed her legs and tucked her thin crepe-de-chine skirt round the other knee. "What had you done—cheeked her?"

Frederick swept the mouthful of apple into one cheek. "No," he said shortly. "Cried."

"I should say you did. Bellowed. I watched you all down the path." There was something ruminative in the girl's tone that made her remark really not at all offensive; in fact, she looked at Frederick as though she were meeting an artist who had just done a turn. He had been standing about, licking and biting the apple, but now he came and sat down at the other end of the bench. "How do you do it?" she said.

Frederick only turned away: his ears began burning again.

"What gets at you?" she said.

"Don't know."

"Someone coming it over you? I know another boy who cries like you, but he's older. He knots himself up and bellows."

"What's his name?"

"George."

"Does he go to school?"

"Oh, lord, no; he's a boy at the place where I used to work." She raised one arm, leaned back, and watched four celluloid bangles, each of a different colour, slide down it to her elbow joint, where they stuck. "He doesn't know why he does it," she said, "but he's got to. It's as though he saw something. You can't ask him. Some people take him that way: girls do. I never did. It's as if he knew about something he'd better not. I said once, well, what just *is* it, and he said if he *could* tell me he wouldn't do it. I said, well, what's the *reason*, and he said, well, what's the reason not to? I knew him well at one time."

Frederick spat out two pips, looked round cautiously for the keeper, then dropped the apple-core down the back of the seat. "Whered's George live?"

"I don't know now," she said, "I often wonder. I got sacked from that place where I used to work, and he went right off and I never saw him again. You snap out of that, if you can, before you are George's age. It does you no good. It's all in the way you see things. Look, there's your mother back. Better move, or there'll be *more* trouble." She held out her hand to Frederick, and when he put his in it shook hands so cheerfully, with such tough decision, that the four celluloid bangles danced on her wrist. "You and George," she said. "Funny to meet two of you. Well, good-bye, Henry: cheer up."

"I'm Frederick."

"Well, cheer up, Freddie."

As Frederick walked away, she smoothed down the sandwich papers inside her despatch case and snapped the case shut again. Then she put a finger under hair at each side, to tuck her spectacles firmly down on her ears. Her mouth, an unreddened line across her harshly-burnt face, still wore the same truculent, homely smile. She crossed her arms under the flat chest, across her stomach, and sat there holding her elbows idly, wagging one foot in its fawn sandal, looking fixedly at the lake through her spectacles wondering about George. She had the afternoon, as she had no work. She saw George's face lifted abjectly from his arms on a table, blotchy over his clerk's collar. The eyes of George and Frederick seemed to her to be wounds in the world's surface, through which its inner, terrible, unassuageable, necessary sorrow constantly bled away and as constantly welled up.

Mrs. Dickinson came down the walk under the band of trees, carefully unanxious, looking lightly at objects to see if Frederick were near them: he had been a long time. Then she saw Frederick shaking hands with a sort of girl on a bench and starting to come her way. So she quickly turned her frank, friendly glance on the lake, down which, as though to greet her, a swan came swimming. She touched her fox fur lightly, sliding it up her shoulder. What a lovely mother to have. "Well, Frederick," she said, as he came into earshot, "coming?" Wind sent a puff of red mayflowers through the air. She stood still and waited for Frederick to come up. She could not think what to do now: they had an hour to put in before they were due at Aunt Mary's. But this only made her manner calmer and more decisive.

Frederick gave a great skip, opened his mouth wide, shouted: "Oo, I say, mother, I nearly caught a duck!"

"Frederick, dear, how silly you are: you couldn't."

"Oo, yes, I could, I could. If I'd had salt for its tail!" Years later, Frederick could still remember, with ease, pleasure and with a sense of lonely shame being gone, that calm white duck swimming off round the bank. But George's friend with the bangles, and George's trouble, fell through a cleft in his memory and were forgotten soon.

Prosper Mérimée
1803—1870

A friend and disciple of Stendhal, Mérimée continued the master's penchant for the stuff of melodrama treated in a style of classical realism so severe that it implies a hatred of all magniloquence and effusiveness. Mérimée regarded verbal and emotional floridity—the manner of Hugo, for example—as the product of a contemptible vulgarity and mindlessness. Mind, Mérimée was determined to cultivate, and its cultivation led, as with Stehdhal, to a personality governed by intellectual hedonism and a desire for the only thing that could assure its satisfaction: a secure niche in cultivated society. Well born of society painters, he was appointed Inspector General of Historical Monuments in 1835; in 1853, through his friendship with Mme. de Montijo, whose daughter became the Empress of Louis Napoleon, he was made a senator and handled diplomatic assignments astutely. Few writers have walked through life on such an easy path.

Mérimée's one concession to Romanticism was his predilection for the passionate, even violent subject in an exotic setting. Otherwise he lived through the Romantic era as a typically skeptical Enlightenment dandy and aesthete whose style of living was ultimately more important than artistic openness and productivity. Writing was never an end in itself to be achieved at any sacrifice, but an adornment of high society, an ornament that must be made conformable to the tastes and values of an élite devoted to the critical intelligence and the spirit of exclusiveness.

In short, Mérimée's aesthetic was ultra-conservative, not at all open-minded about the virtues that might be discoverable in the motley and hurly-burly of life, and allowing no legitimate place in literature for any element of social criticism or reformist ideal. Traditionalism is often salutary for the writer; ultra-conservatism summons the spectre of sterility. Arthur Symons pointedly suggests that Mérimée showed "a certain drying up of the sources of emotion as the man of the world came to accept almost the point of view of society, reading his stories to a little circle of court ladies, when, once in a while, he permitted himself to write a story." Given his temper and circumstances, it is not surprising that Mérimée wrote only a small body of fiction, nearly all of it before he was forty-five, and then turned almost exclusively to historical and archaeological writing and research.

On the other hand Mérimée illustrates the point that the creation of durable art does not necessarily depend upon a constant willingness to sacrifice everything to the muses. When he did write it was almost always within his strength. He chose only what was temperamentally congenial and known to him through personal experience or observation. His love of the facts and of absolute precision provided richness and authenticity. The violence and piquancy of the subjects nicely counterbalanced the intellectualism of style and technique; and the austerity of the manner created an understatement that reflected admirable self-control and generated the maximum of power from powerful but potentially melodramatic situations. Hence the best of Mérimée's fiction survives his own interest in producing more of it. "Mateo Falcone" and the longer Carmen *have remained the chief favorites.*

Mateo Falcone

Prosper Mérimée

Coming out of Porto-Vecchio, and turning northwest towards the centre of the island, you find that the ground rises very rapidly; and after three hours' walk by tortuous paths, blocked by large boulders of rocks, and sometimes cut by ravines, the traveller finds himself on the edge of a very broad *maquis*, or open plateau. These plateaus are the home of the Corsican shepherds, and the resort of those who have come in conflict with the law. The Corsican peasant sets fire to a certain stretch of forest to spare himself the trouble of manuring his lands: if the flames spread further than is needed, so much the worse. Whatever happens, he is sure to have a good harvest by sowing upon this ground, fertilized by the ashes of the trees which grew on it. When the grain is gathered, they leave the straw because it is too much trouble to gather. The roots, which remain in the earth without being consumed, sprout, in the following spring, into very thick shoots, which, in a few years, reach to a height of seven or eight feet. It is this kind of underwood which is called *maquis*. It is composed of different kinds of trees and shrubs mixed up and entangled as in a wild state of nature. Only with hatchet in hand can man open a way through, and there are *maquis* so dense and so thick that not even the wild sheep can penetrate them.

If you have killed a man, go into the *maquis* of Porto-Vecchio, with a good gun and powder and shot, and you will live there in safety. Do not forget to take a brown cloak, furnished with a hood, which will serve as a coverlet and mattress. The shepherds will give you milk, cheese, and chestnuts, and you will have nothing to fear from the hand of the law, nor from the relatives of the dead, except when you go down into the town to renew your stock of ammunition.

When I was in Corsica in 18—, Mateo Falcone's house was half a league from this *maquis*. He was a comparatively rich man for that country, living handsomely—that is to say, without doing anything—

from the produce of his herds, which the shepherds, a sort of nomadic people, led to pasture here and there over the mountains. When I saw him, two years after the event that I am about to tell, he seemed about fifty years of age at the most. Imagine a small but robust man, with jet-black, curly hair, an aquiline nose, thin lips, large and piercing eyes, and a deeply tanned complexion. His skill in shooting passed for extraordinary, even in his country, where there are so many crack shots. For example, Mateo would never fire on a wild sheep with buckshot, but, at one hundred and twenty paces, he would strike it with a bullet in its head or shoulders as he chose. He could use his gun at night as easily as by day, and I was told the following example of his adroitness, which will seem almost incredible to those who have not travelled in Corsica. A lighted candle was placed behind a transparent piece of paper, as large as a plate, at eighty paces off. He put himself into position, then the candle was extinguished, and in a minute's time, in complete darkness, he shot and pierced the paper three times out of four.

With this conspicuous talent Mateo Falcone had earned a great reputation. He was said to be a loyal friend, but a dangerous enemy; in other respects he was obliging and gave alms, and he lived at peace with everybody in the district of Porto-Vecchio. But it is told of him that when at Corte, where he had found his wife, he had very quickly freed himself of a rival reputed to be equally formidable in love as in war; at any rate, people attributed to Mateo a certain gun-shot which surprised his rival while in the act of shaving before a small mirror hung in his window.

After the affair had been hushed up, Mateo married. His wife Giuseppa at first presented him with three daughters, which enraged him, but finally a son came whom he named Fortunato; he was the hope of the family, the inheritor of its name. The girls were well married; their father could reckon in case of need upon the daggers and rifles of his sons-in-law. The son was only ten years old, but he had already shown signs of a promising disposition.

One autumn day Mateo and his wife set out early to visit one of their flocks in a clearing of the *maquis*. Little Fortunato wanted to go with them, but the clearing was too far off; besides, it was necessary that someone should stay and mind the house; so his father refused. We shall soon see that he had occasion to repent of this.

He had been gone several hours and little Fortunato was quietly lying out in the sunshine, looking at the blue mountains, and thinking that on the following Sunday he would be going to town to dine with his uncle the *caporal*, when his meditations were suddenly interrupted by the firing of a gun. He got up and turned towards that side of the plain from which the sound had proceeded. Other shots followed, fired at irregular intervals, and each time they came nearer and nearer until he saw a man on the path which led from the plain to Mateo's house. He wore a pointed cap like a mountaineer, he was bearded, and clothed in rags, and he dragged himself along with difficulty, leaning on his gun. He had just received a gunshot in the thigh.

This man was a bandit (in Corsica one who is proscribed) who, having set out at night to get some powder from the town, had fallen on the way into an ambush of Corsican police-soldiers. After a vigorous defence he had succeeded in escaping, but they gave chase hotly, firing at him from rock to rock. He was only a little in advance of the soldiers, and his wound made it out of the question for him to reach the *maquis* before being overtaken.

He came up to Fortunato and said:

"Are you the son of Mateo Falcone?"

"Yes."

"I am Gianetto Sanpiero. I am pursued by the yellow-collars. Hide me, for I cannot go any further."

"But what will my father say if I hide you without his permission?"

"He will say that you did right."

"How do you know?"

"Hide me quickly; they're coming."

"Wait till my father comes back."

"Damnation! how can I wait? They'll be here in five minutes. Come, hide me or I'll kill you."

Fortunato replied with the utmost coolness:

"You gun is unloaded, and there are no more cartridges in your belt."

"I have my stiletto."

"But could you run as fast as I can?"

With a bound he put himself out of reach.

"You are no son of Mateo Falcone! Will you let me be taken in front of his house?"

The child seemed moved.

"What will you give me if I hide you?" he said, drawing nearer.

The bandit felt in the leather pocket that hung from his side and took out a five-franc piece, which he had put aside, no doubt, for powder. Fortunato smiled at the sight of the piece of silver, and, seizing hold of it, he said to Gianetto:

"Don't be afraid."

He quickly made a large hole in a haystack which stood close by the house. Gianetto crouched down in it, and the child covered him up so as to leave a little breathing space, and yet in such a way as to make it impossible for anyone to suspect that the hay concealed a man. He also conceived another idea, with the ingenious cunning of the savage. He fetched a cat and her kittens and put them on the top of the haystack to make believe that it had not been touched for a long time. Then he carefully covered over with dust the bloodstains which he had noticed on the path near the house, and, this done, he lay down again in the sun with the utmost coolness.

Some minutes later six men in brown uniforms with yellow collars, commanded by an adjutant, stood before Mateo's door. This adjutant was a distant relative of the Falcones. (It is said that further degrees of relationship are recognized in Corsica than anywhere else.) His name was Tiodoro Gamba; he was an energetic man, greatly feared by the banditti, and had already hunted out many of them.

"Good day, youngster," he said, coming up to Fortunato. "How you have grown! Did you see a man pass just now?"

"Oh, I am not yet so tall as you, cousin," the child replied, with a foolish look.

"You soon will be. But, tell me, have you not seen a man pass by?"

"Have I seen a man pass by?"

"Yes, a man with a pointed black velvet cap and a waistcoat embroidered in red and yellow."

"A man with a pointed cap and a waistcoat embroidered in scarlet and yellow?"

"Yes; answer sharply and don't repeat my questions."

"The priest passed our door this morning on his horse Piero. He asked me how papa was, and I replied—."

"You are making game of me, you rascal. Tell me at once which way Gianetto went, for it is he we are after; I am certain he took this path."

"How do you know that?"

"How do I know that? I know you have seen him."

"How can one see passers-by when one is asleep?"

"You were not asleep, you little demon: the gun-shots would wake you."

"You think, then, cousin, that your guns make noise enough? My father's rifle makes much more noise."

"May the devil take you, you young scamp. I am absolutely certain you have seen Gianetto. Perhaps you have even hidden him. Here, you fellows, go into the house, and see if our man is not there. He could only walk on one foot, and he has too much common sense, the villain, to have tried to reach the *maquis* limping. Besides, the traces of blood stop here."

"Whatever will papa say?" Fortunato asked, with a chuckle. "What will he say when he finds out that his house has been searched during his absence?"

"Do you know that I can make you change your tune, you scamp?" cried the adjutant Gamba, seizing him by the ear. "Perhaps you will speak when you have had a thrashing with the flat of a sword."

Fortunato kept on laughing derisively.

"My father is Mateo Falcone," he said significantly.

"Do you know, you young scamp, that I can take you away to Corte or to Bastia? I shall put you in a dungeon, on a bed of straw, with your feet in irons, and I shall guillotine you if you do not tell me where Gianetto Sanpiero is."

The child burst out laughing at this ridiculous menace.

"My father is Mateo Falcone," he repeated.

"Adjutant, do not let us get into a mixup with Mateo," one of the soldiers whispered.

Gamba was evidently embarrassed. He talked in a low voice with his soldiers, who had already been all over the house. It was not a lengthy operation, for a Corsican hut consists of a single square room. The furniture comprises a table, benches, boxes, and utensils for cooking and hunting. All this time little Fortunato caressed his cat, and seemed, maliciously, to enjoy the confusion of his cousin and the soldiers.

One soldier came up to the haycock. He looked at the cat and carelessly stirred the hay with his bayonet, shrugging his shoulders as though he thought the precaution ridiculous. Nothing moved, and the face of the child did not betray the least agitation.

The adjutant and his band were in despair; they looked solemnly out over the plain, half inclined to return the way they had come; but their chief, convinced that threats would produce no effect upon the son of Falcone, thought he would make one last effort by trying the effect of favors and presents.

"My boy," he said, "you are a wide-awake young dog, I can see. You will get on. But you play a dangerous game with me; and, if I did not want to give pain to my cousin Mateo, devil take me if I wouldn't carry you off with me!"

"Bah!"

"But, when my cousin returns I shall tell him all about it, and he will give you the whip till he draws blood for having told me lies."

"How do you know that?"

"You will see. But, look here, be a good lad and I will give you something."

"You had better go and look for Gianetto in the *maquis*, cousin, for if you stay any longer it will take a cleverer fellow than you to catch him."

The adjutant drew a watch out of his pocket, a silver watch worth some thirty francs. He watched how little Fortunato's eyes sparkled as he looked at it, and he held out the watch at the end of its steel chain.

"You rogue," he said, "you would like to have such a watch as this hung round your neck, and go and walk up and down the streets of Porto-Vecchio as proud as a peacock; people would ask you the time, and you would reply, 'Look at my watch!' "

"When I am grown up, my uncle the *caporal* will give me a watch."

"Yes; but your uncle's son has one already—not such a fine one as this, however—for he is younger than you."

The boy sighed.

"Well, would you like this watch, lad?"

Fortunato ogled the watch out of the corner of his eyes, as a cat would if a whole chicken were given to it. It dares not pounce upon the prey, because it is afraid a joke is being played on it, but it turns its eyes away now and then to avoid succumbing to the temptation, licking its lips all the time as though to say to its master, "What a cruel joke you are playing on me!"

The adjutant Gamba, however, seemed really willing to give the watch. Fortunato did not hold out his hand; but he said to him with a bitter smile:

"Why do you make fun of me?"

"I swear I am not joking. Only tell me where Gianetto is, and this watch is yours."

Fortunato smiled incredulously, and fixed his black eyes on those of the adjutant. He tried to read in them how much faith could be placed in his words.

"May I lose my epaulettes," cried the adjutant, "if I do not give you the watch upon that condition! I call my men to witness, and then I cannot retract."

As he spoke, he held the watch nearer and nearer until it almost touched the child's pale cheek. His face plainly expressed the conflict going on in his mind between covetousness and the claims of hospitality. His bare breast heaved violently, almost to suffocation. All the time the watch dangled and twisted and even hit the tip of his nose. By degrees he raised his left hand towards the watch, his finger ends touched it; and its whole weight rested on his palm, although the adjutant still held the end of the chain loosely. The watch face was blue. . . . The case was newly polished. . . .It seemed blazing in the sun like fire. . . . The temptation was too strong.

Fortunato raised his right hand at the same time, and pointed with his thumb over his shoulder to the haycock against which he was leaning. The adjutant understood him immediately, and let go the end of chain. Fortunato felt himself sole possessor of the watch. He jumped up with the agility of a deer, and stood ten paces distant from the haycock, which the soldiers at one began to upset.

It was not long before they saw the hay move, and a bleeding man came out, stiletto in hand; when, however, he tried to rise to his feet his stiffening wound prevented him from standing. He fell down. The adjutant threw himself upon him and snatched away his dagger. He was speedily and strongly bound, in spite of his resistance.

Gianetto, tied up and laid on the ground like a bundle of faggots, turned his head towards Fortunato, who had come up to him.

"Son of —," he said to him more in contempt than in anger.

The boy threw to him the silver piece that he had received from him, feeling conscious that he no longer deserved it; but the outlaw took no notice of the action. He merely said in a cool voice to the adjutant:

"My dear Gamba, I cannot walk; you will be obliged to carry me to the town."

"You could run as fast as a kid just now," his captor retorted brutally. "But don't be anxious, I am glad enough to have caught you: I would carry you for a league on my own back and not feel tired. All the same, my friend, we will make a litter for you out of the branches and your cloak. The farm at Crespoli will provide us with horses."

"All right," said the prisoner; "I hope you will put a little straw on your litter to make it easier for me."

While the soldiers were busy, some making a rough stretcher out of chestnut boughs and others dressing Gianetto's wound, Mateo Falcone and his wife suddenly appeared in a turning of the path from the *maquis*. The wife came in bending laboriously under the weight of a huge sack of chestnuts, while her husband sauntered along carrying one rifle in his hand and another slung in his shoulderbelt. It is considered undignified for a man to carry any other burden but his weapons.

When he saw the soldiers, Mateo's first thought was that they had come to arrest him. But he had no ground for this fear, he had never quarrelled with the law. On the contrary he bore a good reputation. He was, as the saying is, particularly well thought of. But he was a Corsican, and mountain bred, and there are but few Corsican mountaineers who, if they search their memories sufficiently, cannot recall some little peccadillo, some gunshot, or dagger thrust, or other bagatelle. Mateo's conscience was clearer than most, for it was fully ten years since he had pointed his gun at any man; yet at the same time he was cautious, and he prepared to make a brave defence if need be.

"Wife, put down your sack," he said, "and keep yourself in readiness."

She obeyed immediately. He gave her the gun which was slung over his shoulder, as it was likely to be the one that would inconvenience him the most. He held the other gun in readiness, and proceeded leisurely towards the house by the side of the trees which bordered the path, ready to throw himself behind the largest trunk for cover, and to fire at the least sign of hostility. His wife walked close behind him holding her reloaded gun and her cartridges. It was the duty of a good housewife, in case of a conflict, to reload her husband's arms.

On his side, the adjutant was very uneasy at the sight of Mateo advancing thus upon them with measured steps, his gun pointed and finger on trigger.

"If it happens that Gianetto is related to Mateo," thought he, "or he is his friend, and he means to protect him, two of his bullets will be put into two of us as sure as a letter goes to the post, and he will aim at me in spite of our kinship!"

In this perplexity, he put on a bold face and went forward alone towards Mateo to tell him what had happened, greeting him like an old acquaintance. But the brief interval which separated him from Mateo seemed to him of terribly long duration.

"Hullo! Ah! my old comrade," he called out. "How are you, old fellow? I am your cousin Gamba."

Mateo did not say a word, but stood still; and while the other was speaking, he softly raised the muzzle of his rifle in such a manner that by the time the adjutant came up to him it was pointing skywards.

"Good day, brother," said the adjutant, holding out his hand. "It is a very long time since I saw you."

"Good day, brother."

"I just called in to say good-day to you and cousin Pepa as I passed. We have done a long tramp to-day; but we must not complain of fatigue, for we have taken a fine catch. We have got hold of Gianetto Sanpiero."

"Thank Heaven!" exclaimed Giuseppa. "He stole one of our milch goats last week."

Gamba rejoiced at these words.

"Poor devil!" said Mateo, "he was hungry."

"The fellow fought like a lion," continued the adjutant, slightly nettled. "He killed one of the men, and, not content to stop there, he broke Corporal Chardon's arm; but that is not of much consequence, for he is only a Frenchman. Then he hid himself so cleverly that the devil could not have found him. If it had not been for my little cousin Fortunato, I should never have discovered him."

"Fortunato?" cried Mateo.

"Fortunato?" repeated Giuseppa.

"Yes; Gianetto was concealed in your haycock there, but my little cousin showed me his trick. I will speak of him to his uncle the *caporal*, who will send him a nice present as a reward. And both his name and yours will be in the report which I shall send to the superintendent."

"Curse you!" cried Mateo under his breath.

By this time they had rejoined the company. Gianetto was already laid on his litter, and they were ready to set out. When he saw Mateo in Gamba's company he smiled a strange smile; then, turning towards the door of the house, he spat on the threshold.

"It is the house of a traitor!" he exclaimed.

No man but one willing to die would have dared to utter the word "traitor" in connection with Falcone. A quick stroke from a dagger, without need for a second, would have immediately wiped out the insult. But Mateo made no other movement beyond putting his hand to his head like a dazed man.

Fortunato went into the house when he saw his father come up. He reappeared shortly carrying a jug of milk, which he offered with downcast eyes to Gianetto.

"Keep off me!" roared the outlaw.

Then, turning to one of the soldiers, he said:

"Comrade, give me a drink of water."

The soldier placed the flask in his hands, and the bandit drank the water given him by a man with whom he had but now exchanged gunshots. He then asked that his hands might be tied crossed over his breast instead of behind his back.

"I prefer," he said, "to lie down comfortably."

They granted him his request. Then, at a sign from the adjutant, they set out, first bidding adieu to Mateo, who answered never a word, and descended at a quick pace towards the plain.

Nearly ten minutes elapsed before Mateo opened his mouth. The child looked uneasily first at his mother, then at his father, who leaned on his gun, looking at him with an expression of concentrated anger.

"Well, you have made a pretty beginning," said Mateo at last in a voice which, though calm, was terrifying to those who knew the man.

"Father," the boy cried out, with tears in his eyes, as if to fall at his knees.

"Out of my sight!" shouted Mateo.

The child stopped motionless a few steps from his father, and began to sob.

Giuseppa came near him. She had just seen the end of the watch-chain hanging from out his shirt.

"Who gave you that watch?" she asked severely.

"My cousin the adjutant."

Falcone seized the watch, and threw it against a stone with such a force that it broke into a thousand pieces.

"Woman," he said, "is this my child?"

Giuseppa's brown cheeks flamed brick-red.

"What are you saying, Mateo? Do you know to whom you are speaking?"

"Yes, very well. This child is the first traitor of his race."

Fortunato's sobs and hiccoughs redoubled, and Falcone kept his lynx eyes steadily fixed on him. At length he struck the ground with the butt end of his gun; then he flung it across his shoulder and started back toward the *maquis*, ordering Fortunato to follow him. The child obeyed.

Giuseppa ran after Mateo and grasped him by the arm.

"He is your son," she said in a trembling voice, fixing her black eyes on those of her husband, as though to read all that was passing in his mind.

"Leave go," replied Mateo; "I am his father."

Giuseppa kissed her son, and went back crying into the hut. She threw herself on her knees before an image of the Virgin, and prayed fervently. Meanwhile Falcone walked about two hundred yards along the path and stopped at a little ravine, into which he descended. With the butt end of his gun he sounded the ground, and found it soft and easy to dig. The spot seemed suitable to his purpose.

"Fortunato, go stand by that large rock."

The boy did as he was told, then knelt down.

"Father, father, do not kill me!"

"Say your prayers!" repeated Mateo in a terrible voice.

The child repeated the Lord's Prayer and the Creed, stammering and sobbing. The father said "Amen!" in a firm voice at the close of each prayer.

"Are those all the prayers you know?"

"I know also the Ave Maria and Litany, that my aunt taught me, father."

"It is long, but never mind."

The child finished the Litany in a faint voice.

"Have you finished?"

"Oh, father, forgive me! forgive me! I will never do it again. I will beg my cousin the *caporal* with all my might to pardon Gianetto!"

He went on imploring. Mateo loaded his rifle and took aim.

"May God forgive you!" he said.

The boy made a frantic effort to get up and clasp his father's knee, but he had no time. Mateo fired, and Fortunato fell stone dead.

Without throwing a single glance at the body, Mateo went back to his house to fetch a spade with which to bury his son. He had only returned a little way along the path when he met Giuseppa, who had run out, alarmed by the sound of firing.

"What have you done?" she cried.

"Justice!"

"Where is he?"

"In the ravine; I am going to bury him. He died a Christian. I shall have a mass sung for him. Send word to my son-in-law Tiodoro Bianchi to come and live with us."

Anton Chekhov

1873—1904

Chekhov was born in Taganrog in South Russia, studied medicine at the University of Moscow, and throughout his short life was able to harmonize his medical practice with his literary career. Aided (as he gratefully acknowledges) by his medical and scientific studies, he quite early developed habitual objectivity, restraint, understatement, and economy, qualities immensely valuable in stories that must be kept short.

Strong-willed, quietly high-spirited, gregarious, and productive, Chekhov has been misrepresented by literary modernism as a spokesman for passivity, pessimism, and futility. His unfailing comic sense in itself precluded any sort of nihilism or philosophy of despair. He did agree wholeheartedly with De Maupassant's view that the modern writer, instead of dealing in "the crises of life," should write "the history of the heart, the soul, and the intellect in their normal condition." In old, as in new Russia, the normal condition included much that was drab, coarse, and pathetic. Chekhov did not flinch from such material, but that hardly makes him a futilitarian. He even seems to go out of his way to find a comic note in the issue. Nor is it pessimism to remain an intellectually honest observer who sees plainly the difficulties of the human condition and conceives no extravagant hopes of either the individual or of collective political action. Though vaguely liberal politically, Chekhov was an artist con-

tent to remain an artist, wholly uninterested in acquiring the status of sage or visionary ideologue. Hating all presumptuousness and pretentiousness, wary of all grandiose or cosmic generalization, he usually reserved ultimate judgment in his fiction as in his life.

Most of his finest stories were written after 1885—partly, no doubt, because the circumstances of his life from the mid-1880s onward permitted him to spend more time on his writing. A great many of these stories show a similar pattern, though it is not at all mechanical: they dramatize the isolation created by the fact of human individuality, the dificulty or impossibility of mutual communication and understanding; and they end on a whisper, not a bang of surprise or revelation—end, that is, on a note that reaffirms the dominance of the ordinary and the inconclusiveness of experience. Typically the stories develop mood (Russian: nastroenie*) extensively and masterfully; and submerged in the concrete description there is often a restrained but nonetheless lyrical evocativeness. A careful student of technique and aesthetic impression, Chekhov lends no support to the oft-heard generalization that Russian writers seem so interested in ideas or "content" as to neglect the advantages of thoroughgoing craftsmanship.*

In 1901 Chekhov married the gifted actress Olga Knipper. During their brief but happy union he wrote not only short stories but two great plays, The Three Sisters *and* The Cherry Orchard.

At Home

Anton Chekhov

"Some one called from Gregorev's for a book, but I told them you were not at home. And by the way, Yevgeny Petrovitch, I really must ask you to talk seriously to Serioja. Both to-day and the day before yesterday I discovered him smoking, and when I attempted to scold him, he put his hands over his ears and shouted so loudly as to drown my voice."

Yevgeny Petrovitch Bikovsky, the district public prosecutor, who had only just returned from a sitting and was taking off his gloves in his study, looked up at his boy's governess and laughed. "Serioja smoking!" . . . He shrugged his shoulders. "I can imagine the little imp with a cigarette! How old is he?"

"Seven. Of course you may not think it serious, but smoking at his age is a bad, injurious habit, and such habits should be eradicated from the very beginning."

"I quite agree. Where does he get tobacco from?"

"From your table."

"Really? In that case you had better send him to me."

When the governess had gone, Bikovsky sat down in his armchair by the table, closed his eyes and fell to musing. His imagination pictured Serioja with a huge cigarette about a yard long, enveloped in clouds of tobacco smoke. The picture brought a smile to his lips. At the same time the anxious, serious face of the governess reminded him of a time long gone by in the half-forgotten past when smoking in the nursery or at school inspired in parents and masters a strange and somewhat puzzling feeling of horror. The word horror exactly describes it. Such boys were flogged or expelled from school; their lives were made a burden to them; yet not one of the masters nor the parents could have told you exactly what harm there was in smoking, nor why it was considered such a crime.

A great many clever grown-up people, too, fought against the tobacco habit without precisely knowing why.

Yevgeny Petrovitch recalled how the headmaster of his school, a learned and kind-hearted old man, would turn quite pale with fright if he discovered a boy smoking. He would instantly summon a council of masters, and the culprit would forthwith be expelled.

Such seems the law of everyday life! The more intangible the evil, the more fiercely it is combated.

Yevgeny Petrovitch brought to mind the cases of two or three victims, and could not help thinking that the punishment wrought consequences far more evil than did the crime. A living organism is capable of adapting itself to any environment, else otherwise human beings would realise at every turn how normal activities were based on hypotheses that could not be proved; and how little was really known of the fundamental truths in such branches as education, law, literature. . . .

These and similar thoughts, the workings of a tired brain that craved for rest, began to float through his mind. They came crowding one after another, disconnected, remaining only on the surface without penetrating the depths.

To a man whose whole time is taken up by legal affairs and whose mind is constantly set in one direction, such homely, wandering thoughts as these produce a comfortable, soothing effect.

It was nine o'clock in the evening. In the flat above, on the second floor, some one was pacing the room, to and fro, from corner to corner, and in the flat above that, two people were playing a duet on the piano. The man who was pacing the floor—judging by his nervous tread—must have been tortured by some tormenting thought, or perhaps by a toothache, while the monotonous duet imbued the evening stillness with a certain drowsiness that was conducive to lazy thinking. In the nursery Serioja and the governess were talking together. "Papa has come!" the boy sang. "Papa has come! Papa! Papa!"

"*Votre père vous appelle*, go at once!" the governess piped in a thin little voice like that of a frightened bird. "Do you hear?"

"What can I say to him after all?" Yevgeny Petrovitch asked himself. But before he had time to invent anything to say to his son, Serioja, a boy of seven, entered. It was only by his clothes that one could distinguish that he was a boy and not a girl. He was frail, fair-skinned, and fragile. He seemed like some exotic flower, and everything about him was soft and gentle; his looks, his gestures, his curly hair, even his little velvet coat. "Good evening, papa!" he said in a soft voice, climbing on to his father's knee and kissing him. "Did you want me?"

"One minute, Sergey Yevgenitch," the father began, gently disengaging the boy's arms. "Before we can think of kissing, you and I must have a serious talk. I am very angry with you and don't love you any more. Understand that I don't love you—you are no longer my son—yes . . ."

Serioja looked intently at his father, then transferred his gaze to the table and shrugged his shoulders.

"What have I done to you?" he asked in perplexity, blinking his eyes. "I did not go into your study once to-day and have not touched anything."

"Natalia Semionovna has just informed me that you smoke. Is it true? Do you smoke?"

"Yes, I smoked once. It is true!"

"There now, you are telling a lie into the bargain," the public prosecutor said, frowning in order to hide a smile. "Natalia Semionovna caught you twice. You have been discovered in three bad actions—smoking, taking another person's tobacco, and lying. Three bad faults."

"Oh, yes!" Serioja recollected, his eyes dancing. "It is quite true; I did smoke twice, once to-day and once before that."

"You see, you yourself admit it was not once but twice. . . . I am very angry with you. You used to be a good boy; and now you appear to have become bad."

Yevgeny Petrovitch rearranged Serioja's collar, thinking, "What else shall I say to him?"

"It is not right," he continued. "I did not expect it of you. In the first place you have no right to take tobacco that does not belong to you. Every man has the right of enjoying his own property, but if he takes something that is not his own, then he is a bad man! For instance, Natalia Semionovna has a trunk full of dresses. It is her own trunk, and that means that we—that is, you and I—have no right to touch it as it does not belong to us. Do you follow? Again, you have little horses and pictures . . . I do not take them, do I? Perhaps I should like to have them . . . but I know they are yours and not mine."

"You can take them if you like!" Serioja said, raising his eyebrows. "Don't mind me, papa, take them! That little dog you have on the table is mine, but I don't care . . . let it stay there!"

"You don't understand," Bikovsky said. "You gave me the dog, so now it is mine and I can do what I like with it, but I did not give you the tobacco. The tobacco is mine." (I shall never be able to make him understand this way, the public prosecutor thought. Impossible! It's quite useless!) "If I want to smoke tobacco that does not belong to me, then first of all I must ask permission." Lazily connecting his sentences, choosing childish words, Bikovsky set out to explain to his son the meaning of private property.

Serioja fixed his gaze on his father's chest, listening attentively. He loved to sit talking with his father in the evenings. Then he rested his elbows on the table, half-closed his eyes, and transferred his gaze to the paper and ink-pot. Then it wandered round the room and settled on the paste-bottle.

"Papa, what is paste made of?" he asked suddenly lifting the bottle up to inspect it.

Bikovsky took the bottle from him, put it back on the table, and continued: "And secondly, you smoke. . . . That is not good. Just because I happen to smoke, it does not mean that you may do so. I smoke, knowing that it is bad for me. I scold myself for it. . . . (What a subtle teacher I am! thought the public prosecutor.) Tobacco is bad for the health, and a man who smokes dies sooner than he would otherwise have done. Smoking is particularly bad for a little boy like you. You have a weak chest, you are not strong yet, and in delicate people tobacco causes consumption and all sorts of diseases. You remember Uncle Ignaty? Well, he died of consumption. Had he not smoked he might have been alive to-day."

Serioja gazed at the lamp pensively, touched the shade with his finger and sighed.

"Uncle Ignaty played the violin well!" he remarked. "The Gregorevs have his violin now."

Serioja put his elbows on the table, rested his head on his hands and grew thoughtful. By the expression on his face one could see that he was following the trend of his own thoughts. A look of sadness mingled with terror appeared in his large blinking eyes. No doubt he was thinking of death that had so recently taken his mother and his uncle Ignaty. Death bears mothers and uncles away to the other world, but their children and their violins remain. The dead live in heaven, somewhere near the stars, and look down on the earth. Do they feel the separation?

"What else can I say to him?" Yevgeny Petrovitch was thinking. He is not listening to me. Obviously he does not consider his action or my arguments as serious. How can I make him understand?"

The public prosecutor got up and began to pace the room.

"In my young days these questions were settled very simply," he reflected. "Every boy found smoking was whipped. This cured the poor spirited and cowardly; but the braver and more intelligent of them took to hiding their tobacco in their boots, and smoking in the sheds. When discovered there and punished a second time, they went off to the river to smoke, and so on until the small boy grew into a man. To keep me from smoking my mother used to bribe me with money and sweets. Now such methods are considered immoral and are despised."

Taking his stand at the very base of reason, the modern pedagogue strives to make the child realise the idea of "good," not as connected with fear or vanity, but as an end in itself.

While he was thus pacing up and down, Serioja knelt on his chair, and leaning over the table began to draw. Some drawing-paper and a blue pencil always lay ready for him on the table, so that he should have no temptation to touch his father's papers, or the ink.

"When cook was chopping the cabbage to-day she cut her finger," he remarked, while drawing a house. "She screamed so loudly that we were all terrified and rushed into the kitchen. She was stupid! Natalia Semionovna told her to put her finger in cold water, but she would suck it. . . . How could she put her dirty finger into her mouth! It's not nice, is it, papa?"

Then he went on telling his father how at dinner-time a barrel-organ man had come with a little girl who had danced to the music.

"He has his own thoughts," the public prosecutor mused. "He lives in his own world and sets his own standard of what is important and what is not. To fix his attention and awaken his consciousness, it is not sufficient to imitate his words, one must know and understand his way of thinking. He would have understood me easily enough had I really been sorry about the tobacco, or had I been hurt, or cried. . . . Mothers bringing up their children know unconsciously how to feel with them, to cry with them, to laugh with them. . . . You can achieve nothing with logic and moralising. Well, what shall I say to him now? What?"

And it seemed strange and absurd to Yevgeny Petrovitch that he, an experienced lawyer, who had spent half his life cross-examining and sentencing, should be at a loss what to say to the boy.

"Listen; give me your word of honour that you will never smoke again," he said.

"Word of honour!" Serioja sang out, pressing hard on his pencil and bending over his drawing. "Word—of—hon—our—word . . ."

"I wonder whether he knows what 'word of honour' means?" Bikovsky asked himself. "No, I am a bad mentor! If a teacher, or one of my colleagues, could only look into my mind just now, they would consider me soft and suspect me of too much theorising. . . . At school or in court these troublesome questions are settled much easier than at home. Here you deal with people whom you love with all your soul, and love is exacting; it complicates the question at issue. If the boy were not my own son—say a pupil, or a prisoner, I should not be afraid; my thoughts would not wander like this."

Yevgeny Petrovitch sat down by the table and pulled one of Serioja's drawings towards him. The drawing represented a house with a crooked roof and showed a column of smoke that zigzagged like forked lightning to the very top of the paper. Beside the house stood a soldier, with two dots for eyes placed in the middle of his face, and holding a gun that looked like the figure 4.

"A man cannot be taller than a house," the public prosecutor said. "Look, the roof of the house only reaches to his shoulder." Serioja climbed on to his father's knee and snuggled into a comfortable position.

"But, papa," he said, looking at his drawing. "If you draw the soldier smaller, you cannot see his eyes."

Should he correct him? From daily observation of his own son the public prosecutor was convinced that children, like savages, have their own conceptions in art, which in their various forms are quite incomprehensible to adults. Judged by adult standards, Serioja would have appeared abnormal. He thought it proper and reasonable to draw men taller than houses, and to portray by means of his pencil not only objects but also sensations. Thus he represented the sound of an orchestra as sphere and smoke; and the sound of a whistle as a spiral thread. In his mind sound was intimately connected with form and colour; thus, when colouring the letters of the alphabet, he invariably made L yellow, M red, A black, and so on.

Throwing down his drawing, Serioja settled himself comfortably once more and began toying with his father's beard. At first he smoothed it down carefully, then, parting it, he arranged it in the form of side whiskers.

"Now you look like Ivan Stepanovitch," he said. "And now you will look like our Swiss. Papa, why does a Swiss always stand by the door? Is it to frighten thieves away?"

The public prosecutor felt Serioja's breath on his face, and his beard touched the boy's cheek. A warm, gentle feeling arose in his heart, as though not only his hands but his whole soul was lying on Serioja's velvet coat. He gazed into the boy's large dark eyes, and it seemed to him that out of those deep wells there looked out at him his mother, his wife—and all that he had ever loved.

"How could I whip him?" he thought. "Of what use to think out a punishment for him? I am no good as an educationalist. At one time people were simpler, theorised less and decided things boldly. Now we think too much—logic has conquered us. . . . The more developed a man is, the more he speculates and falls into subtleties, the more undecided and doubtful he becomes, the less confidence he has; he approaches questions more timidly. And really, what courage a man must have in order to teach, judge, write ponderous tomes. . . ." The clock struck ten.

"Well, boy, time for bed!" he said. "Say good-night and go along."

"But, papa," Serioja said, making a move. "I want to stay a little longer. Tell me something. Tell me a story."

"Very well, only you must go to bed directly I have finished."

On fine evenings Yevgeny Petrovitch would often tell Serioja stories. Like most busy men he did not know a single poem or story by heart, so that he had to improvise each time. He would always begin with the formula, "Once upon a time in a certain kingdom," and then would follow some innocent nonsense or other. The scenes and characters came at random impromptu, while the plot and moral came of their own accord, so to say. Serioja loved these improvisations, and his father had noticed that the simpler the plot the more strongly it impressed itself on the boy.

"Listen," he began, raising his eyes to the ceiling. "Once upon a time, in a certain kingdom, there lived an old king with a long grey beard and . . . and such a long moustache. Well, he lived in a palace of crystal that shone and sparkled in the sun like a huge mass of clear ice. The palace, my boy, stood in a large garden where you must know grew oranges . . . figs and cherries . . . tulips, roses, lilies of the valley—and brilliantly-coloured birds sang all day. On the trees there hung little glass balls that tinkled in the wind so sweetly that it was a pleasure to listen to them. Glass gives a softer sound than metal. Well, what else was there? There were also fountains . . . you remember there was a fountain in Auntie Sonia's garden in the country? Well, the fountains in the king's garden were exactly like that, only ever so much larger, and the spray from them reached to the very top of the highest poplar."

Yevgeny Petrovitch though a moment, and then continued:

"The old king had an only son and heir to his throne—a little boy, just like you. He was a good boy. He was never cross, went to bed early, never touched anything on the table—and . . . was altogether a clever boy. He had only one fault . . . he smoked."

Serioja listened attentively, his eyes blinking as they gazed straight into his father's. "What next?" the father asked himself. Then, after a little uncertainty, ended the story thus: "Through smoking the king's son fell ill with consumption, and died when he was only twenty. The infirm and aged monarch was left alone, utterly helpless. There was none to govern the kingdom nor to protect the palace. Enemies came and killed the old king, and destroyed the palace, and now in the garden there are no longer any cherries or birds or little glass balls . . . you see, boy. . . ."

Such an end appeared to Yevgeny Petrovitch as too naîve and absurd, but on Serioja it created a great impression. Again an expression of sadness and fear came into his eyes. For a moment or two he sat gazing pensively at the dark windows, then shuddered and said in a lowered voice:

"I will not smoke any more . . ."

When the boy had bidden him good-night and had gone to bed, the father began pacing quietly up and down the room, a contented smile on his face.

"People would say it was beauty and the artistic form that affected him," he thought. "Even if that were so, it is no consolation. After all, it was not a fair means . . . why must truth and morals be presented, not in the naked form, but gilded and sugared like a pill? It is not rational. It is falsehood, deceit, trickery . . ."

He recalled how, when he had to make a speech to a jury, instead of giving them an analysis of the facts, he gave them a vivid account of the case; and how people get their ideas on life, not by reasoning and self-analysis, but by reading novels and historic romances.

Medicine must be sweet, truth beautiful. . . . Man has accustomed himself to that since the days of Adam. . . . However . . . perhaps that was natural and was as it should be. . . . There are many delusions and illusions in nature. . . . He sat down to work, but these idle homely thoughts long strayed through his mind. Above, the piano had stopped, but the inmate of the second floor was still pacing from corner to corner. . . .

The Kiss

Anton Chekhov

On the twentieth of May, at eight o'clock in the evening, six batteries of the N Artillery Brigade arrived at the village of Miestetchki to spend the night, before going to their camp.

The confusion was at its height—some officers at the guns, others in the church square with the quartermaster—when a civilian upon a remarkable horse rode from the rear of the church. The small cob with well-shaped neck wobbled along, all the time dancing on its legs as if someone were whipping them. Reaching the officers, the rider doffed his cap with ceremony and said—

"His Excellency, General von Rabbek, requests the honor of the officers' company at tea in his house near by. . . ."

The horse shook its head, danced, and wobbled backwards; its rider again took off his cap, and turning around disappeared behind the church.

"The devil!" the general exclaimed, the officers dispersing to their quarters. "We are almost asleep, yet along comes this von Rabbek with his tea! That tea! I remember it!"

The officers of the six batteries had vivid recollections of a past invitation. During recent maneuvers they had been asked, with their

Cossack comrades, to tea at the house of a local country gentleman, a Count, retired from military service; and this hearty old Count overwhelmed them with attentions, fed them like gourmands, poured vodka into them and made them stay the night. All this, of course, was fine. The trouble was that the old soldier entertained his guests too well. He kept them up till daybreak while he poured forth tales of past adventures and pointed out valuable paintings, engravings, arms, and letters from celebrated men. And the tired officers listened, perforce, until he ended, only to find out that the time for sleep had gone.

Was von Rabbek another old Count? It might easily be. But there was no neglecting his invitation. The officers washed and dressed, and set out for von Rabbek's house. At the church square they learnt that they must descend the hill to the river, and follow the bank till they reached the general's gardens, where they would find a path direct to the house. Or, if they chose to go uphill, they would reach the general's barns half a *verst* from Miestetchki. It was this route they chose.

"But who is this von Rabbek?" asked one. "The man who commanded the N Cavalry Division at Plevna?"

"No, that was not von Rabbek, but simply Rabbe—without the von."

"What glorious weather!"

At the first barn they came to, two roads diverged; one ran straight forward and faded in the dusk; the other, turning to the right, led to the general's house. As the officers drew near they talked less loudly. To right and to left stretched rows of red-roofed brick barns, in aspect heavy and morose as the barracks of provincial towns. In front gleamed the lighted windows of von Rabbek's house.

"A good omen, gentlemen!" cried a young officer. "Our setter runs in advance. There is game ahead!"

On the face of Lieutenant Lobuitko, the tall stout officer referred to, there was not one trace of hair though he was twenty-five years old. He was famed among comrades for the instinct which told him of the presence of women in the neighborhood. On hearing his comrade's remark, he turned his head and said—

"Yes. There are women there. My instinct tells me."

A handsome, well-preserved man of sixty, in mufti, came to the hall door to greet his guests. It was von Rabbek. As he pressed their hands, he explained that though he was delighted to see them, he must beg pardon for not asking them to spend the night; as guests he already had his two sisters, their children, his brother, and several neighbors—

in fact, he had not one spare room. And though he shook their hands and apologized and smiled, it was plain that he was not half as glad to see them as was last year's Count, and that he had invited them merely because good manners demanded it. The officers climbing the soft-carpeted steps and listening to their host understood this perfectly well; and realized that they carried into the house an atmosphere of intrusion and alarm. Would any man—they asked themselves—who had gathered his two sisters and their children, his brother and his neighbors, to celebrate, no doubt, some family festival, find pleasure in the invasion of nineteen officers whom he had never seen before?

A tall elderly lady, with a good figure, and a long face with black eyebrows, who resembled closely the ex-Empress Eugénie, greeted them at the drawing-room door. Smiling courteously and with dignity, she affirmed that she was delighted to see the officers, and only regretted that she could not ask them to stay the night. But the courteous, dignified smile disappeared when she turned away, and it was quite plain that she had seen many officers in her day, that they caused not the slightest interest, and that she had invited them merely because an invitation was dictated by good breeding and by her position in the world.

In a big dining room, at a big table, sat ten men and women, drinking tea. Behind them, veiled in cigar smoke, stood several young men, among them one, red-whiskered and extremely thin, who spoke English loudly with a lisp. Through an open door the officers saw into a brightly lighted room with blue wallpaper.

"You are too many to introduce singly, gentlemen!" said the general loudly, with affected joviality. "Make one another's acquaintance, please—without formalities!"

The visitors, some with serious, even severe faces, some smiling constrainedly, all with a feeling of awkwardness, bowed, and took their seats at the table. Most awkward of all felt Staff-Captain Riabovitch, a short, round-shouldered, spectacled officer, whiskered like a lynx. While his brother officers looked serious or smiled constrainedly, his face, his lynx whiskers, and his spectacles seemed to explain: "I am the most timid, modest, undistinguished officer in the whole brigade." For some time after he took his seat at the table he could not fix his attention on any single thing. Faces, dresses, the cut-glass cognac bottles, the steaming tumblers, the molded cornices—all merged in a single, overwhelming sentiment which caused him intense fright and made him wish to hide his head. Like an inexperienced lecturer he saw everything before him, but could distinguish nothing, and was in fact the victim of what men of science diagnose as "psychical blindness."

But, slowly conquering his diffidence, Riabovitch began to distinguish and observe. As became a man both timid and unsocial, he remarked first of all the amazing temerity of his new friends. Von Rabbek, his wife, two elderly ladies, a girl in lilac, and the red-whiskered youth (who, it appeared, was a young von Rabbek) sat down among the officers as unconcernedly as if they had held rehearsals, and at once plunged into various heated arguments in which they soon involved their guests. That artillerists have a much better time than cavalrymen or infantrymen was proved conclusively by the lilac girl, while von Rabbek and the elderly ladies affirmed the converse. The conversation became desultory. Riabovitch listened to the lilac girl fiercely debating themes she knew nothing about and took no interest in, and watched the insincere smiles which appeared on and disappeared from her face.

While the von Rabbek family with amazing strategy inveigled their guests into the dispute, they kept their eyes on every glass and mouth. Had everyone tea, was it sweet enough, why didn't one eat biscuits, was another fond of cognac? And the longer Riabovitch listened and looked, the more pleased he was with this disingenuous, disciplined family.

After tea the guests repaired to the drawing room. Instinct had not cheated Lobuitko. The room was packed with young women and girls, and ere a minute had passed the setter-lieutenant stood beside a very young, fair-haired girl in black, and, bending down as if resting on an invisible sword, shrugged his shoulders coquettishly. He was uttering, no doubt, most unentertaining nonsense, for the fair girl looked indulgently at his sated face, and exclaimed indifferently, "Indeed!" And this indifferent "Indeed!" might have quickly convinced the setter that he was on a wrong scent.

Music began. As the notes of a mournful valse throbbed out of the open window, through the heads of all flashed the feeling that outside that window it was springtime, a night of May. The air was odorous of young poplar leaves, of roses and lilacs—and the valse and the spring were sincere. Riabovitch, with valse and cognac mingling tipsily in his head, gazed at the window with a smile; then began to follow the movements of the women; and it seemed that the smell of roses, poplars, and lilacs came not from the gardens outside, but from the women's faces and dresses.

They began to dance. Young von Rabbek valsed twice round the room with a very thin girl; and Lobuitko, slipping on the parqueted floor, went up to the girl in lilac, and was granted a dance. But Riabovitch stood near the door with the wallflowers, and looked silently on. Amazed at the daring of men who in sight of a crowd could take unknown women by the waist, he tried in vain to picture himself doing the same. A time had been when he envied his comrades their courage and dash, suffered from painful heart-searchings, and was hurt by the knowledge that he was timid, round-shouldered, and undistinguished, that he had lynx whiskers, and that his waist was much too long. But with years he had grown reconciled to his own insignificance, and now looking at the dancers and loud talkers, he felt no envy, but only mournful emotions.

At the first quadrille von Rabbek junior approached and invited two nondancing officers to a game of billiards. The three left the room, and Riabovitch, who stood idle, and felt impelled to join in the general movement, followed. They passed the dining room, traversed a narrow glazed corridor and a room where three sleepy footmen jumped from a sofa with a start; and after walking, it seemed, through a whole houseful of rooms, entered a small billiard room.

Von Rabbek and the two officers began their game. Riabovitch, whose only game was cards, stood near the table and looked indifferently on, as the players, with unbuttoned coats, wielded their cues, moved about, joked, and shouted obscure technical terms. Riabovitch was ignored, save when one of the players jostled him or nudged him with the cue, and turning towards him said briefly, "Pardon!" so that before the game was over he was thoroughly bored, and, impressed by a sense of his superfluity, resolved to return to the drawing room and turned away.

It was on the way back that his adventure took place. Before he had gone far he saw that he had missed his way. He remembered distinctly the room with the three sleepy footmen; and after passing through five or six rooms entirely vacant, he saw his mistake. Retracing his steps, he turned to the left, and found himself in an almost dark room which he had not seen before; and after hesitating a minute, he boldly opened the first door he saw, and found himself in complete darkness. Through a chink of the door in front peered a bright light; from afar throbbed the dullest music of a mournful mazurka. Here, as in the drawing room, the windows were open wide, and the smell of poplars, lilacs, and roses flooded the air.

Riabovitch paused in irresolution. For a moment all was still. Then came the sound of hasty footsteps; then, without any warning of what was to come, a dress rustled, a woman's breathless voice whispered "At last!" and two soft, scented, unmistakably womanly arms met round his neck, a warm cheek impinged on his, and he received a sounding kiss. But hardly had the kiss echoed through the silence when the unknown shrieked loudly, and fled away—as it seemed to Riabovitch—in disgust. Riabovitch himself nearly screamed, and rushed headlong towards the bright beam in the door chink.

As he entered the drawing room his heart beat violently, and his hands trembled so perceptibly that he clasped them behind his back. His first emotion was shame, as if everyone in the room already knew that he had just been embraced and kissed. He retired into his shell, and looked fearfully around. But finding that hosts and guests were calmly dancing or talking, he regained courage, and surrendered himself to sensations experienced for the first time in his life. The unexampled had happened. His neck, fresh from the embrace of two soft, scented arms, seemed anointed with oil; near his left mustache, where the kiss had fallen, trembled a slight, delightful chill, as from peppermint drops; and from head to foot he was soaked in new and extraordinary sensations, which continued to grow and grow.

He felt that he must dance, talk, run into the garden, laugh unrestrainedly. He forgot altogether that he was round-shouldered, undistinguished, lynx-whiskered, that he had an "indefinite exterior"—a description from the lips of a woman he had happened to overhear. As Madame von Rabbek passed him he smiled so broadly and graciously that she came up and looked at him questioningly.

"What a charming house you have!" he said, straightening his spectacles.

And Madame von Rabbek smiled back, said that the house still belonged to her father, and asked were his parents still alive, how long he had been in the Army, and why he was so thin. After hearing his answers she departed. But though the conversation was over, he continued to smile benevolently, and think what charming people were his new acquaintances.

At supper Riabovitch ate and drank mechanically what was put before him, heard not a word of the conversation, and devoted all his powers to the unraveling of his mysterious, romantic adventure. What was the explanation? It was plain that one of the girls, he reasoned, had arranged a meeting in the dark room, and after waiting some time in vain had, in her nervous tension, mistaken Riabovitch for her hero. The mistake was likely enough, for on entering the dark room Riabovitch had stopped irresolutely as if he, too, were waiting for someone. So far the mystery was explained.

"But which of them was it?" he asked, searching the women's faces. She certainly was young, for old women do not indulge in such romances. Secondly, she was not a servant. That was proved unmistakably by the rustle of her dress, the scent, the voice. . . .

When at first he looked at the girl in lilac she pleased him; she had pretty shoulders and arms, a clever face, a charming voice. Riabovitch piously prayed that it was she. But, smiling insincerely, she wrinkled her long nose, and that at once gave her an elderly air. So Riabovitch turned his eyes on the blonde in black. The blonde was younger, simpler, sincerer; she had charming kiss-curls, and drank from her tumbler with inexpressible grace. Riabovitch hoped it was she—but soon he noticed that her face was flat, and bent his eyes on her neighbor.

"It is a hopeless puzzle," he reflected. "If you take the arms and shoulders of the lilac girl, add the blonde's curls, and the eyes of the girl on Lobuitko's left, then—"

He composed a portrait of all these charms, and had a clear vision of the girl who had kissed him. But she was nowhere to be seen.

Supper over, the visitors, sated and tipsy, bade their entertainers good-by. Both host and hostess apologized for not asking them to spend the night.

"I am very glad, gentlemen!" said the general, and this time seemed to speak sincerely, no doubt because speeding the parting guest is a kindlier office than welcoming him unwelcomed. "I am very glad indeed! I hope you will visit me on your way back. Without ceremony, please! Which way will you go? Up the hill? No, go down the hill and through the garden. That way is shorter."

The officers took his advice. After the noise and glaring illumination within doors, the garden seemed dark and still. Until they reached the wicket gate all kept silence. Merry, half tipsy, and content, as they were, the night's obscurity and stillness inspired pensive thought. Through their brains, as through Riabovitch's, sped probably the same question: "Will the time ever come when I, like von Rabbek, shall have a big house, a family, a garden, the chance of being gracious—even insincerely—to others, of making them sated, tipsy, and content?"

But once the garden lay behind them, all spoke at once, and burst into causeless laughter. The path they followed led straight to the river, and then ran beside it, winding around bushes, ravines, and overhanging willow trees. The track was barely visible; the other bank was lost entirely in gloom. Sometimes the black water imaged stars, and this was the only indication of the river's speed. From beyond it sighed a drowsy snipe, and beside them in a bush, heedless of the crowd, a nightingale chanted loudly. The officers gathered in a group, and swayed the bush, but the nightingale continued his song.

"I like his cheek!" they echoed admiringly. "He doesn't care *a kopek*! The old rogue!"

Near their journey's end the path turned up the hill, and joined the road not far from the church enclosure; and there the officers, breathless from climbing, sat on the grass and smoked. Across the river gleamed a dull red light, and for want of a subject they argued the problem, whether it was a bonfire, a window light, or something else. Riabovitch looked also at the light, and felt that it smiled and winked at him as if it knew about the kiss.

On reaching home, he undressed without delay, and lay upon his bed. He shared the cabin with Lobuitko and a Lieutenant Merzliakoff, a staid, silent little man, by repute highly cultivated, who took with him everywhere *The Messenger of Europe* and read it eternally. Lobuitko undressed, tramped impatiently from corner to corner, and sent his servant for beer. Merzliakoff lay down, balanced the candle on his pillow, and hid his head behind *The Messenger of Europe*.

"Where is she now?" muttered Riabovitch, looking at the soot-blacked ceiling.

His neck still seemed anointed with oil, near his mouth still trembled the speck of peppermint chill. Through his brain twinkled successively the shoulders and arms of the lilac girl, the kiss-curls and honest eyes of the girl in black, the waists, dresses, brooches. But though he tried his best to fix these vagrant images, they glimmered, winked, and dissolved; and as they faded finally into the vast black curtain which hangs before the closed eyes of all men, he began to hear hurried footsteps, the rustle of petticoats, the sound of a kiss. A strong, causeless joy possessed him. But as he surrendered himself to this joy, Lobuitko's servant returned with the news that no beer was obtainable. The lieutenant resumed his impatient march up and down the room.

"The fellow's an idiot," he exclaimed, stopping first near Riabovitch and then near Merzliakoff. "Only the worst numbskull and blockhead can't get beer! *Canaille!*"

"Everyone knows there's no beer here," said Merzliakoff, without lifting his eyes from *The Messenger of Europe*.

"You believe that !" exclaimed Lobuitko. "Lord in heaven, drop me on the moon, and in five minutes I'll find both beer and women! I will find them myself! Call me a rascal if I don't!"

He dressed slowly, silently lighted a cigarette, and went out.

"Rabbek, Grabbek, Labbek," he muttered, stopping in the hall. "I won't go alone, devil take me! Riabovitch, come for a walk! What?"

As he got no answer, he returned, undressed slowly, and lay down. Merzliakoff sighed, dropped *The Messenger of Europe*, and put out the light. "Well?" muttered Lobuitko, puffing his cigarette in the dark.

Riabovitch pulled the bedclothes up to his chin, curled himself into a roll, and strained his imagination to join the twinkling images into one coherent whole. But the vision fled him. He soon fell asleep, and his last impression was that he had been caressed and gladdened, that into his life had crept something strange, and indeed ridiculous, but uncommonly good and radiant. And this thought did not forsake him even in his dreams.

When he awoke the feeling of anointment and peppermint chill was gone. But joy, as on the night before, filled every vein. He looked entranced at the windowpanes gilded by the rising sun, and listened to the noises outside. Someone spoke loudly under the very window. It was Lebedietsky, commander of his battery, who had just overtaken the brigade. He was talking to the sergeant-major, loudly, owing to of practice in soft speech.

"And what next?" he roared.

"During yesterday's shoeing, your honor, *Golubtchik* was pricked. The regimental doctor ordered clay and vinegar. And last night, your honor, mechanic Artemieff was drunk, and the lieutenant ordered him to be put on the limber of the reserve gun carriage."

The sergeant-major added that Karpoff had forgotten the tent pegs and the new lanyards for the friction tubes, and that the officers had spent the evening at General von Rabbek's. But here at the window appeared Lebedietsky's red-bearded face. He blinked his short-sighted eyes at the drowsy men in bed, and greeted them.

"Is everything all right?"

"The saddle wheeler galled his withers with the new yoke," answered Lobuitko.

The commander sighed, mused a moment, and shouted—

"I am thinking of calling on Alexandra Yegorovna. I want to see her. Good-by! I will catch you up before night."

Fifteen minutes later the brigade resumed its march. As he passed von Rabbek's barns, Riabovitch turned his head and looked at the house. The Venetian blinds were down; evidently all still slept. And among them slept she—she who had kissed him but a few hours before. He tried to visualize her asleep. He projected the bedroom window opened wide with green branches peering in, the freshness of the morning air, the smell of poplars, lilacs, and roses, the bed, a chair, the dress which rustled last night, a pair of tiny slippers, a ticking watch on the table—all these came to him clearly with every detail. But the features, the kind, sleepy smile—all, in short, that was essential and characteristic—fled his imagination as quicksilver flees the hand. When he had covered half a *verst* he again turned back. The yellow church, the house, gardens, and river were bathed in light. Imaging an azure sky, the green-banked river specked with silver sunshine flakes was inexpressibly fair; and, looking at Miestetchki for the last time, Riabovitch felt sad, as if parting forever with something very near and dear.

By the road before him stretched familiar, uninteresting scenes; to the right and left, fields of young rye and buckwheat with hopping rooks; in front, dust and the napes of human necks; behind, the same dust and faces. Ahead of the column marched four soldiers with swords—that was the advance guard. Next came the bandsmen. Advance guard and bandsmen, like mutes in a funeral procession, ignored the regulation intervals and marched too far ahead. Riabovitch, with the first gun of Battery No. 5, could see four batteries ahead.

To a layman, the long, lumbering march of an artillery brigade is novel, interesting, inexplicable. It is hard to understand why a single gun needs so many men; why so many, such strangely harnessed horses are needed to drag it. But to Riabovitch, a master of all these things, it was profoundly dull. He had learned years ago why a solid sergeant-major rides beside the officer in front of each battery; why the sergeant-major is called the *unosni*, and why the drivers of leaders and wheelers ride behind him. Riabovitch knew why the near horses are called saddle horses, and why the off horses are called led horses—and all of this was uninteresting beyond words. On one of the wheelers rode a soldier still covered with yesterday's dust, and with a cumbersome, ridiculous guard on his right leg. But Riabovitch, knowing the use of this leg guard, found it in no way ridiculous. The drivers, mechanically and with occasional cries, flourished their whips. The guns in themselves were unimpressive. The limbers were packed with tarpaulin-covered sacks of oats; and the guns themselves, hung round with teapots and satchels, looked like harmless animals, guarded for some obscure reason by men and horses. In the lee of the gun tramped six gunners, swinging their arms, and behind each gun came more *unosniye*, leaders, wheelers; and yet more guns, each as ugly and uninspiring as the one in front. And as every one of the six batteries in the brigade had four guns, the procession stretched along the road at least half a *verst*. It ended with a wagon train, with which, its head bent in thought, walked the donkey Magar, brought from Turkey by a battery commander.

Dead to his surroundings, Riabovitch marched onward, looking at the napes ahead or at the faces behind. Had it not been for last night's event, he would have been half asleep. But now he was absorbed in novel, entrancing thoughts. When the brigade set out that morning he had tried to argue that the kiss had no significance save as a trivial though mysterious adventure; that it was without real import; and that to think of it seriously was to behave himself absurdly. But logic soon flew away and surrendered him to his vivid imaginings. At times he saw himself in von Rabbek's dining room, *tête-à-tê* with a composite being, formed of the girl in lilac and the blonde in black. At times he closed his eyes, and pictured himself with a different, this time quite an unknown, girl of cloudy feature; he spoke to her, caressed her, bent over her shoulders; he imagined war and parting . . . then reunion, the first supper together, children. . . .

"To the brakes!" rang the command as they topped the brow of each hill.

Riabovitch also cried "To the brakes!" and each time dreaded that the cry would break the magic spell, and recall him to realities.

They passed a big country house. Riabovitch looked across the fence into the garden, and saw a long path, straight as a ruler, carpeted with yellow sand, and shaded by young birches. In an ecstasy of enchantment, he pictured little feminine feet treading the yellow sand; and, in a flash, imagination restored the woman who had kissed him, the woman he had visualized after supper the night before. The image settled in his brain and never afterward forsook him.

The spell reigned until midday, when a loud command came from the rear of the column.

"Attention! Eyes right! Officers!"

In a *calèche* drawn by a pair of white horses appeared the general of the brigade. He stopped at the second battery, and called out something which no one understood. Up galloped several officers, among them Riabovitch.

"Well, how goes it?" The general blinked his red eyes, and continued, "Are there any sick?"

Hearing the answer, the little skinny general mused a moment, turned to an officer, and said—

"The driver of your third-gun wheeler has taken off his leg guard and hung it on the limber. *Canaille!* Punish him!"

Then raising his eyes to Riabovitch, he added—

"And in your battery, I think, the harness is too loose."

Having made several other equally tiresome remarks, he looked at Lobuitko, and laughed.

"Why do you look so downcast, Lieutenant Lobuitko? You are sighing for Madame Lopukhoff, eh? Gentlemen, he is pining for Madame Lopukhoff!"

Madame Lopukhoff was a tall, stout lady, long past forty. Being partial to big women, regardless of age, the general ascribed the same taste to his subordinates. The officers smiled respectfully; and the general, pleased that he had said something caustic and laughable, touched the coachman's back and saluted. The *calèche* whirled away.

"All this, though it seems to me impossible and unearthly, is in reality very commonplace," thought Riabovitch, watching the clouds of dust raised by the general's carriage. "It is an everyday event, and within everyone's experience. . . . This old general, for instance, must have loved in his day; he is married now, and has children. Captain Wachter is also married, and his wife loves him, though he has an ugly red neck and no waist. . . . Salmanoff is coarse, and a typical Tartar, but he has had a romance ending in marriage. . . . I, like the rest, must go through it all sooner or later."

And the thought that he was an ordinary man, and that his life was ordinary, rejoiced and consoled him. He boldly visualized *her* and his happiness, and let his imagination run mad.

Towards evening the brigade ended its march. While the other officers sprawled in their tents, Riabovitch, Merzliakoff, and Lobuitko sat round a packing case and supped. Merzliakoff ate slowly, and, resting *The Messenger of Europe* on his knees, read on steadily. Lobuitko, chattering without cease, poured beer into his glass. But Riabovitch, whose head was dizzy from uninterrupted daydreams, ate in silence. When he had drunk three glasses he felt tipsy and weak; and an overmastering impulse forced him to relate his adventure to his comrades.

"A most extraordinary thing happened to me at von Rabbek's," he began, doing his best to speak in an indifferent, ironical tone. "I was on my way, you understand, from the billiard room. . . ."

And he attempted to give a very detailed history of the kiss. But in a minute he had told the whole story. In that minute he had exhausted every detail; and it seemed to him terrible that the story required such a short time. It ought, he felt, to have lasted all the night. As he finished, Lobuitko, who as a liar himself believed in no one, laughed incredulously. Merzliakoff frowned, and, with his eyes still glued to *The Messenger of Europe*, said indifferently—

"God knows who it was! She threw herself on your neck, you say, and didn't cry out! Some lunatic, I expect!"

"It must have been a lunatic," agreed Riabovitch.

"I, too, have had adventures of that kind," began Lobuitko, making a frightened face. "I was on my way to Kovno. I traveled second-class. The carriage was packed, and I couldn't sleep. So I gave the guard a *rouble*, and he took my bag, and put me in a *coupé*. I lay down, and pulled my rug over me. It was pitch dark, you understand. Suddenly I felt someone tapping my shoulder and breathing in my face. I stretched out my hand, and felt an elbow. Then I opened my eyes. Imagine! A woman! Coal-black eyes, lips red as good coral, nostrils breathing passion, breasts—buffers!"

"Draw it mild!" interrupted Merzliakoff in his quiet voice. "I can believe about the breasts, but if it was pitch dark how could you see the lips?"

By laughing at Merzliakoff's lack of understanding, Lobuitko tried to shuffle out of the dilemma. The story annoyed Riabovitch. He rose from the box, lay on his bed, and swore that he would never again take anyone into his confidence.

Life in camp passed without event. The days flew by, each like the one before. But on every one of these days Riabovitch felt, thought, and acted as a man in love. When at daybreak his servant brought him cold water, and poured it over his head, it flashed at once into his half-awakened brain that something good and warm and caressing had crept into his life.

At night when his comrades talked of love and of women, he drew in his chair, and his face was the face of an old soldier who talks of battles in which he has taken part. And when the rowdy officers, led by setter Lobuitko, made Don Juanesque raids upon the neighboring "suburb," Riabovitch, though he accompanied them, was morose and conscience-struck, and mentally asked *her* forgiveness. In free hours and sleepless nights, when his brain was obsessed by memories of childhood, of his father, his mother, of everything akin and dear, he remembered always Miestetchki, the dancing horse, von Rabbek, von Rabbek's wife, so like the ex-Empress Eugénie, the dark room, the chink in the door.

On the thirty-first of August he left camp, this time not with the whole brigade but with only two batteries. As an exile returning to his native land, he was agitated and enthralled by day-dreams. He longed passionately for the queer-looking horse, the church,the insincere von Rabbeks, the dark room; and that internal voice which so often cheats the lovelorn whispered an assurance that he should see *her* again. But doubt tortured him. How should he meet her? What must he say? Would she have forgotten the kiss? If it came to the worst—he consoled himself—if he never saw her again, he might walk once more through the dark room, and remember. . . .

Towards evening the white barns and well-known church rose on the horizon. Riabovitch's heart beat wildly. He ignored the remark of an officer who rode by, he forgot the whole world, and he gazed greedily at the river glimmering afar, at the green roofs, at the dove-cote, over which fluttered birds dyed golden by the setting sun.

As he rode towards the church, and heard again the quartermaster's raucous voice, he expected every second a horseman to appear from behind the fence and invite the officers to tea. . . . But the quartermaster ended his harangue, the officers hastened to the village, and no horseman appeared.

"When von Rabbek hears from the peasants that we are back he will send for us," thought Riabovitch. And so assured was he of this, that when he entered the hut he failed to understand why his comrades had lighted a candle, and why the servants were preparing the samovar.

A painful agitation oppressed him. He lay on his bed. A moment later he rose to look for the horseman. But no horseman was in sight.

Again he lay down; again he rose; and this time, impelled by restlessness, went into the street and walked towards the church. The square was dark and deserted. On the hill stood three silent soldiers. When they saw Riabovitch they started and saluted, and he, returning their salute, began to descend the well-remembered path.

Beyond the stream, in a sky stained with purple, the moon slowly rose. Two chattering peasant women walked in a kitchen garden and pulled cabbage leaves; behind them their log cabins stood out black against the sky. The river bank was as it had been in May; the bushes were the same; things differed only in that the nightingale no longer sang, that it smelt no longer of poplars and young grass.

When he reached von Rabbek's garden Riabovitch peered through the wicket gate. Silence and darkness reigned. Save only the white birch trunks and patches of pathway, the whole garden merged in a black, impenetrable shade. Riabovitch listened greedily, and gazed intent. For a quarter of an hour he loitered; then hearing no sound, and seeing no light, he walked wearily towards home.

He went down to the river. In front rose the general's bathing box; and white towels hung on the rail of the bridge. He climbed on to the bridge and stood still; then, for no reason whatever, touched a towel. It was clammy and cold. He looked down at the river which sped past swiftly, murmuring almost inaudibly against the bathing-box piles. Near the left bank glowed the moon's ruddy reflection, overrun by ripples which stretched it, tore it in two, and, it seemed, would sweep it away as twigs and shavings are swept.

"How stupid! How stupid!" thought Riabovitch, watching the hurrying ripples. "How stupid everything is!"

Now that hope was dead, the history of the kiss, his impatience, his ardor, his vague aspirations and disillusion appeared in a clear light. It no longer seemed strange that the general's horseman had not come, and that he would never again see *her* who had kissed him by accident instead of another. On the contrary, he felt, it would be strange if he did ever see her again. . . .

The water flew past him, whither and why no one knew. It had flown past in May; it had sped a stream into a great river; a river, into the sea; it had floated on high in mist and fallen again in rain; it might be, the water of May was again speeding past under Riabovitch's eyes. For what purpose? Why?

And the whole world—life itself—seemed to Riabovitch an inscrutable, aimless mystification. . . . Raising his eyes from the stream and gazing at the sky, he recalled how Fate in the shape of an unknown woman had once caressed him; he recalled his summer fantasies and images—and his whole life seemed to him unnaturally thin and colorless and wretched. . . .

When he reached the cabin his comrades had disappeared. His servant informed him that all had set out to visit "General Fonrabbkin," who had sent a horseman to bring them. . . . For a moment Riabovitch's heart thrilled with joy. But that joy he extinguished. He cast himself upon his bed, and wroth with his evil fate, as if he wished to spite it, ignored the invitation.

Charles Dickens
1812—1870

In energy and in the "infinite variety" of his imagination, Dickens resembles Shakespeare; and like his predecessor he had the right talent and ambition at the right time. Available to him when he started his literary career in the mid-1830s was an expressive medium—prose suitable for fiction—and a genre—the novel—congenial to his particular genius and propitious for his financial ambitions. Defoe, Richardson, Smollett, Fielding, Scott, and Austen had shown the way; yet the novel was still as fresh in 1835 as the vigorous new secular drama was to the audiences of Marlowe and Shakespeare. The novel had flourished to meet the demands of an increasingly literate middle class; and the quality of the product had constantly fed the fires of the demand. By Dickens's time the size of the potential audience made the publishing of fiction, whether in book or magazine serial form, an attractive prospect. Revelling like an Elizabethan in spirited, earthy dialogue, and driven by a vivacious and expansive imagination, Dickens was in his element in the full-dress novel.

Spiritually scarred by the poverty that had placed him among the child laborers of the Victorian work force and consigned his father John to the Marshalsea debtor's prison, he was determined to amass money. Here, it was the novel that would answer. Short fiction of the "well made" variety, achieving "unity of impression," was, both in England and on the continent, only just beginning to come into its own. Addicted to vividness, dialogue, and dramatic incident, Dickens wrote plays and was consistently interested in theatre. But theatre was, as it still is, risky business; and drama demands tight structure, a requirement the exuberant and unmeticulous Dickens assented to only grudgingly even in the novel.

Yet from mid-career onward he did make the accommodation. He never became devoted to structure, or technique, or interested in it theoretically, but Dombey and Son *(1848),* Blreak House *(1853),* Great Expectations *(1861), and most of his other later novels reveal a writer who has come to sense the advantages of working out a careful plan and of building it around the inward development of character, especially around its change and maturation through suffering.*

This slowly-evolved constraint of style is evident in "The Signal-Man," a late story whose technique would have satisfied Poe on every point. Dickens travelled much on the rails and had long been given to brooding on them both as immediate experience and as enterprises of the spoliative industrialism that roused him to such indignation and exasperation. In Dombey and Son *he had long ago dealt with railroad entrepreneurship and depicted a railway accident. More recently, in 1865, returning from Paris with his mistress, Ellen Terney, he had survived a terrible derailment at Staplehurst in Kent and had been permanently weakened by the shock and strenuous physical effort of rescuing and ministering to many injured or trapped passengers. Personal encounter no doubt did something to lend the feeling of authenticity and to create the soberness of style that mark "The Signal-Man." Dickens died on June 9, 1870, five years to the day after the Staplehurst wreck.*

The Signal-Man

Charles Dickens

"Halloa! Below there!"

When he heard a voice thus calling to him, he was standing at the door of his box, with a flag in his hand, furled round its short pole. One would have thought, considering the nature of the ground, that he could not have doubted from what quarter the voice came; but, instead of looking up to where I stood on the top of the steep cutting nearly over his head, he turned himself about and looked down the Line. There was something remarkable in his manner of doing so, though I could not have said for my life what. But I know it was remarkable enough to attract my notice, even though his figure was foreshortened and shadowed, down in the deep trench, and mine was high above him, so steeped in the glow of an angry sunset, that I had shaded my eyes with my hand before I saw him at all.

"Halloa! Below!"

From looking down the Line, he turned himself about again, and, raising his eyes, saw my figure high above him.

"Is there any path by which I can come down and speak to you?"

He looked up at me without replying, and I looked down at him without pressing him too soon with a repetition of my idle question. Just then there came a vague vibration in the earth and air, quickly changing into a violent pulsation, and an on-coming rush that caused me to start back, as though it had force to draw me down. When such vapour as rose to my height from this rapid train had passed me, and was skimming away over the landscape, I looked down again, and saw him refurling the flag he had shown while the train went by.

I repeated my inquiry. After a pause, during which he seemed to regard me with fixed attention, he motioned with his rolled-up flag towards a point on my level, some two or three hundred yards distant.

I called down to him, "All right!" and made for that point. There, by dint of looking closely about me, I found a rough zigzag descending path notched out, which I followed.

The cutting was extremely deep, and unusually precipitate. It was made through a clammy stone, that became oozier and wetter as I went down. For these reasons, I found the way long enough to give me time to recall a singular air of reluctance or compulsion with which he had pointed out the path.

When I came down low enough upon the zigzag descent to see him again, I saw that he was standing between the rails on the way by which the train had lately passed, in an attitude as if he were waiting for me to appear. He had his left hand at his chin, and that left elbow rested on his right hand, crossed over his breast. His attitude was one of such expectation and watchfulness, that I stopped a moment, wondering at it.

I resumed my downward way, and stepping out upon the the level of the railroad, and drawing nearer to him, saw that he was a dark sallow man, with a dark beard and rather heavy eyebrows. His post was in as solitary and dismal a place as ever I saw. On either side, a dripping wet wall of jagged stone, excluding all view but a strip of sky; the perspective one way only a crooked prolongation of this great dungeon; the shorter perspective in the other direction terminating in a gloomy red light, and the gloomier entrance to a black tunnel, in whose massive architecture there was a barbarous, depressing, and forbidding air. So little sunlight ever found its way to this spot, that it had an earthy, deadly smell; and so much cold wind rushed through it, that it struck chill to me, as if I had left the natural world.

Before he stirred, I was near enough to him to have touched him. Not even then removing his eyes from mine, he stepped back one step, and lifted his hand.

This was a lonesome post to occupy (I said), and it had riveted my attention when I looked down from up yonder. A visitor was a rarity, I should suppose; not an unwelcome rarity, I hoped? In me he merely saw a man who had been shut up within narrow limits all his life, and who, being at last set free, had a newly awakened interest in these great works. To such purpose I spoke to him; but I am far from sure of the terms I used; for, besides that I am not happy in opening any conversation, there was something in the man that daunted me.

He directed a most curious look towards the red light near the tunnel's mouth, and looked all about it, as if something were missing from it, and then looked at me.

That light was part of his charge? Was it not?

He answered in a low voice, "Don't you know it is?"

The monstrous thought came into my mind, as I perused the fixed eyes and the saturnine face, that this was a spirit, not a man. I have speculated since whether there may have been infection in his mind.

In my turn, I stepped back. But, in making the action, I detected in his eyes some latent fear of me. This put the monstrous thought to flight.

"You look at me," I said, forcing a smile, "as if you had a dread of me."

"I was doubtful," he returned, "whether I had seen you before."

"Where?"

He pointed to the red light he had looked at.

"There?" I said.

Intently watchful of me, he replied (but without sound), "Yes."

"My good fellow, what should I do there? However, be that as it may, I never was there, you may swear."

"I think I may," he rejoined. "Yes; I am sure I may."

His manner cleared, like my own. He replied to my remarks with readiness, and in well-chosen words. Had he much to do there? Yes; that was to say, he had enough responsibility to bear; but exactness and watchfulness were what was required of him, and of actual work—manual labour—he had next to none. To change that signal, to trim those lights, and to turn this iron handle now and then, was all he had to do under that head. Regarding those many long and lonely hours of which I seemed to make so much, he could only say that the routine of his life had shaped itself into that form, and he had grown used to it. He had taught himself a language down here,—if only to know it by sight, and to have formed his own crude ideas of its pronunciation, could be called learning it. He had also worked at fractions and decimals, and tried a little algebra; but he was, and had been as a boy, a poor hand at figures. Was it necessary for him when on duty always to remain in that channel of damp air, and could he never rise into the sunshine from between those high stone walls? Why, that depended upon times and circumstances. Under some conditions there would be less upon the Line than under others, and the same held good as to certain hours of the day and night. In bright weather he did choose occasions for getting a little above these lower shadows; but being at all times liable to be called by his electric bell, and at such times listening for it with redoubled anxiety, the relief was less than I would suppose.

He took me into his box, where there was a fire, a desk for an official book in which he had to make certain entries, a telegraphic instrument with its dial, face, and needles, and the little bell of which he had spoken. On my trusting that he would excuse the remark that he had been well educated, and (I hoped I might say without offence) perhaps educated above that station, he observed that instances of slight incongruity in such wise would rarely be found wanting among large bodies of men; that he had heard it was so in workhouses, in the police force, even in that last desperate resource, the army; and that he knew it was so, more or less, in any great railway staff. He had been, when young (if I could believe it, sitting in that hut,—he scarcely could), a student of natural philosophy, and had attended lectures; but he had run wild, misused his opportunities, gone down, and never risen again. He had no complaint to offer about that. He had made his bed, and he lay upon it. It was far too late to make another.

All that I have here condensed he said in a quiet manner, with his grave dark regards divided between me and the fire. He threw in the word "Sir" from time to time, and especially when he referred to his youth,—as though to request me to understand that he claimed to be nothing but what I found him. He was several times interrupted by the little bell, and had to read off messages and send replies. Once he had to stand without the door, and display a flag as a train passed, and made some verbal communication to the driver. In the discharge of his duties, I observed him to be remarkably exact and vigilant, breaking off his discourse at a syllable, and remaining silent until what he had to do was done.

In a word, I should have set this man down as one of the safest of men to be employed in that capacity, but for the circumstance that while he was speaking to me he twice broke off with a fallen colour, turned his face towards the little bell when it did not ring, opened the door of the hut (which was kept shut to exclude the unhealthy damp), and looked out towards the red light near the mouth of the tunnel. On both of those occasions he came back to the fire with the inexplicable air upon him which I had remarked, without being able to define, when we were so far asunder.

Said I, when I rose to leave him, "You almost make me think that I have met with a contented man."

(I am afraid I must acknowledge that I said it to lead him on.)

"I believe I used to be so," he rejoined in the low voice in which he had first spoken; "but I am troubled, sir, I am troubled."

He would have recalled the words if he could. He had said them, however, and I took them up quickly.

"With what? What is your trouble?"

"It is very difficult to impart, sir. It is very, very difficult to speak of. If ever you make me another visit, I will try to tell you."

"But I expressly intend to make you another visit. Say, when shall it be?"

"I go off early in the morning, and I shall be on again at ten to-morrow night, sir."

"I will come at eleven."

He thanked me, and went out at the door with me. "I'll show my white light sir," he said in his peculiar low voice, "till you have found the way up. When you have found it, don't call out! And when you are at the top, don't call out!"

His manner seemed to make the place strike colder to me, but I said no more than, "Very well."

"And when you come down to-morrow night, don't call out! Let me ask you a parting question. What made you cry, 'Halloa! Below there!' to-night?"

"Heaven knows," said I. "I cried something to that effect—"

"Not to that effect, sir. Those were the very words. I know them well."

"Admit those were the very words. I said them, no doubt, because I saw you below."

"For no other reason?"

"What other reason could I possibly have?"

"You had no feeling that they were conveyed to you in any supernatural way?"

"No."

He wished me good night, and held up his light. I walked by the side of the down Line of rails (with a very disagreeable sensation of a train coming behind me) until I found the path. It was easier to mount than to descend, and I got back to my inn without any adventure.

Punctual to my appointment, I placed my foot on the first notch of the zigzag next night as the distant clocks were striking eleven. He was waiting for me at the bottom, with his white light on. "I have not called out," I said when we came close together; "may I speak now?" "By all means, sir." "Good night, then, and here's my hand." "Good night, sir, and here's mine." With that we walked side by side to his box, entered it, closed the door, and sat down by the fire.

"I have made up my mind, sir," he began, bending forward as soon as we were seated, and speaking in a tone but a little above a whisper, "that you shall not have to ask me twice what troubles me. I took you for some one else yesterday evening. That troubles me."

"That mistake?"

"No. That some one else."

"Who is it?"

"I don't know."

"Like me?"

"I don't know. I never saw the face. The left arm is across the face, and the right arm is waved,—violently waved. This way."

I followed his action with my eyes, and it was the action of an arm gesticulating, with the utmost passion and vehemence, "For God's sake, clear the way!"

"One moonlight night," said the man, "I was sitting here, when I heard a voice cry, 'Halloa! Below there!' I started up, looked from that door, and saw this Someone else standing by the red light near the tunnel, waving as I just now showed you. The voice seemed hoarse with shouting, and it cried, 'Look out! Look out!' And then again, 'Halloa! Below there! Look out!' I caught up my lamp, turned it on red, and ran towards the figure, calling, 'What's wrong? What has happened? Where?' It stood just outside the blackness of the tunnel. I advanced so close upon it that I wondered at its keeping the sleeve across its eyes. I ran right up at it, and had my hand stretched out to pull the sleeve away, when it was gone."

"Into the tunnel?" said I.

"No. I ran on into the tunnel, five hundred yards. I stopped, and held my lamp above my head, and saw the figures of the measured distance, and saw the wet stains stealing down the walls and trickling through the arch. I ran out again faster that I had run in (for I had a mortal abhorrence of the place upon me), and I looked all round the red light with my own red light, and I went up the iron ladder to the gallery atop of it, and I came down again, and ran back here. I telegraphed both ways, 'An alarm has been given. Is anything wrong?' The answer came back, both ways, 'All well.' "

Resisting the slow touch of a frozen finger tracing out my spine, I showed him how that this figure must be a deception of his sense of sight; and how that figures, originating in disease of the delicate nerves that minister to the functions of the eye, were known to have often troubled patients, some of whom had become conscious of the nature of their affliction, and had even proved it by experiments upon themselves. "As to an imaginary cry," said I, "do but listen for a moment to the wind in this unnatural valley while we speak so low, and to the wild harp it makes of the telegraph wires!"

That was all very well, he returned, after we had sat listening for a while, and he ought to know something of the wind and the wires,—he who so often passed long winter nights there, alone and watching. But he would beg to remark that he had not finished.

I asked his pardon, and he slowly added these words, touching my arm:—

"Within six hours after the Appearance, the memorable accident on this Line happened, and within ten hours the dead and wounded were brought along through the tunnel over the spot where the figure had stood."

A disagreeable shudder crept over me, but I did my best against it. It was not to be denied, I rejoined, that this was a remarkable coincidence, calculated deeply to impress his mind. But it was unquestionable that remarkable coincidences did continually occur, and they must be taken into account in dealing with such a subject. Though to be sure I must admit, I added (for I thought I saw that he was going to bring the objection to bear upon me), men of common sense did not allow much for coincidences in making the ordinary calculations of life.

He again begged to remark that he had not finished.

I again begged his pardon for being betrayed into interruptions.

"This," he said, again laying his hand upon my arm, and glancing over his shoulder with hollow eyes, "was just a year ago. Six or seven months passed, and I had recovered from the surprise and shock, when one morning, as the day was breaking, I, standing at the door, looked towards the red light, and saw the spectre again." He stopped with a fixed look at me.

"Did it cry out?"

"No. It was silent."

"Did it wave its arm?"

"No. It leaned against the shaft of the light, with both hands before the face. Like this."

Once more I followed his action with my eyes. It was an action of mourning. I have seen such an attitude in stone figures on tombs.

"Did you go up to it?"

"I came in and sat down, partly to collect my thoughts, partly because it had turned me faint. When I went to the door again, daylight was above me, and the ghost was gone."

"But nothing followed? Nothing came of this?"

He touched me on the arm with his forefinger twice or thrice, giving a ghastly nod each time.

"That very day, as a train came out of the tunnel, I noticed, at a carriage window on my side, what looked like a confusion of hands and heads, and something waved. I saw it just in time to signal the driver, Stop! He shut off, and put his brake on, but the train drifted past here a hundred and fifty yards or more. I ran after it, and, as I went along, heard terrible screams and cries. A beautiful young lady had died instantaneously in one of the compartments, and was brought in here, and laid down on this floor between us."

Involuntarily I pushed my chair back, as I looked from the boards at which he pointed to himself.

"True, sir. True. Precisely as it happened, so I tell it you."

I could think of nothing to say to any purpose, and my mouth was very dry. The wind and the wires took up the story with a long lamenting wail.

He resumed. "Now, sir, mark this, and judge how my mind is troubled. The spectre came back a week ago. Ever since, it has been there, now and again, by fits and starts."

"At the light?"

"At the danger-light."

"What does it seem to do?"

He repeated, if possible with increased passion and vehemence, that former gesticulation of, "For God's sake, clear the way!"

Then he went on. "I have no peace or rest for it. It calls to me, for many minutes together, in an agonised manner, 'Below there! Look out! Look out!' It stands waving to me. It rings my little bell—"

I caught at that. "Did it ring your bell yesterday evening when I was here, and you went to the door?"

"Twice."

"Why, see," said I, "how your imagination misleads you! My eyes were on the bell, and my ears were open to the bell, and, if I am a living man, it did not ring at those times. No, nor at any other time, except when it was rung in the natural course of physical things by the station communicating with you."

He shook his head. "I have never made a mistake as to that yet, sir. I have never confused the spectre's ring with the man's. The ghost's ring is a strange vibration in the bell that it derives from nothing else, and I have not asserted that the bell stirs to the eye. I don't wonder that you failed to hear it. But *I* heard it."

"And did the spectre seem to be there when you looked out?"

"It was there."

"Both times?"

He repeated firmly: "Both times."

"Will you come to the door with me, and look for it now?"

He bit his under lip as though he were somewhat unwilling, but arose. I opened the door, and stood on the step, while he stood in the doorway. There was the danger-light. There was the dismal mouth of the tunnel. There were the high, wet stone walls of the cutting. There were the stars above them.

"Do you see it?" I asked him, taking particular note of his face. His eyes were prominent and strained, but not very much more so, perhaps, than my own had been when I had directed them earnestly towards the same spot.

"No," he answered. "It is not there."

"Agreed," said I.

We went in again, shut the door, and resumed our seats. I was thinking how best to improve this advantage, if it might be called one, when he took up the conversation in such a matter of course way, so assuming that there could be no serious question of fact between us, that I felt myself placed in the weakest of positions.

"By this time you will fully understand, sir, " he said, "that what troubles me so dreadfully is the question, What does the spectre mean?"

I was not sure, I told him, that I did fully understand.

"What is its warning against?" he said, ruminating, with his eyes on the fire, and only by times turning them on me. "What is the danger? Where is the danger? There is danger overhanging somewhere on the Line. Some dreadful calamity will happen. It is not to be doubted this third time after what had gone before. But surely this is a cruel haunting of *me*. What can *I* do?"

He pulled out his handkerchief, and wiped the drops from his heated forehead.

"If I telegraph Danger on either side of me, or on both, I can give no reason for it," he went on, wiping the palms of his hands. "I should get into trouble, and do no good. They would think I was mad. This is the way it would work,—Message: 'Danger! Take care!' Answer: 'What Danger? Where?' Message: 'Don't know. But, for God's sake, take care!' They would displace me. What else could they do?"

His pain of mind was most pitiable to see. It was the mental torture of a conscientious man, oppressed beyond endurance by an unintelligible responsibility involving life.

"When it first stood under the danger-light," he went on, putting his dark hair back from his head, and drawing his hands outward across and across his temples in an extremity of feverish distress, "why not tell me where that accident was to happen,—if it must happen? Why not tell me how it could be averted,—if it could have been averted? When on its second coming it hid its face, why not tell me, instead, 'She is going to die. Let them keep her at home'? If it came, on those two occasions, only to show me that its warnings were true, and so to prepare me for the third, why not warn me plainly now? And I, Lord help me! A mere poor signal-man on this solitary station! Why not go to somebody with credit to be believed, and power to act?"

When I saw him in this state, I saw that for the poor man's sake, as well as for the public safety, what I had to do for the time was to compose his mind. Therefore, setting aside all question of reality or unreality between us, I represented to him that whoever thoroughly discharged his duty must do well, and that at least it was his comfort that he understood his duty, though he did not understand these confounding Appearances. In this effort I succeeded far better than in the attempt to reason him out of his conviction. He became calm; the occupations incidental to his post as the night advanced began to make larger demands on his attention; and I left him at two in the morning. I had offered to stay through the night, but he would not hear of it.

That I more than once looked back at the red light as I ascended the pathway, that I did not like the red light, and that I should have slept but poorly if my bed had been under it, I see no reason to conceal. Nor did I like the two sequences of the accident and the dead girl. I see no reason to conceal that either.

But what ran most in my thoughts was the consideration, how ought I to act, having become the recipient of this disclosure? I had proved the man to be intelligent, vigilant, painstaking, and exact; but how long might he remain so, in his state of mind? Though in a subordinate position, still he held a most important trust, and would I (for instance) like to stake my own life on the chances of his continuing to execute it with precision?

Unable to overcome a feeling that there would be something treacherous in my communicating what he had told me to his superiors in the Company, without first being plain with himself and proposing a middle course to him, I ultimately resolved to offer to accompany him (otherwise keeping his secret for the present) to the wisest medical practitioner we could hear of in those parts, and to take his opinion. A change in his time of duty would come round next night, he had apprised me, and he would be off an hour or two after sunrise, and on again soon after sunset. I had appointed to return accordingly.

Next evening was a lovely evening, and I walked out early to enjoy it. The sun was not yet quite down when I traversed the field path near the top of the deep cutting. I would extend my walk for an hour, I said to myself, half an hour on and half an hour back, and it would then be time to go to my signalman's box.

Before pursuing my stroll, I stepped to the brink, and mechanically looked down, from the point from which I had first seen him. I cannot describe the thrill that seized upon me when, close at the mouth of the tunnel, I saw the appearance of a man, with his left sleeve across his eyes, passionately waving his right arm.

The nameless horror that oppressed me passed in a moment, for in a moment I saw that this appearance of a man was a man indeed, and that there was a little group of other men, standing at a short distance, to whom he seemed to be rehearsing the gesture he made. The dangerlight was not yet lighted. Against its shaft, a little low hut, entirely new to me, had been made of some wooden supports and tarpaulin. It looked no bigger than a bed.

With an irresistible sense that something was wrong,—with a flashing, self-reproachful fear that fatal mischief had come of my leaving the man there, and causing no one to be sent to overlook or correct what he did,—I descended the notched path with all the speed I could make.

"What is the matter?" I asked the men.

"Signal-man killed this morning, sir."

"Not the man belonging to that box?"

"Yes, sir."

"Not the man I know?"

"You will recognise him, sir, if you knew him," said the man who spoke for the others, solemnly uncovering his own head, and raising an end of the tarpaulin, "for his face is quite composed."

"Oh, how did this happen, how did this happen?" I asked, turning from one to another as the hut closed in again.

"He was cut down by an engine, sir. No man in England knew his work better. But somehow he was not clear of the outer rail. It was just at broad day. He had struck the light, and had the lamp in his hand. As the engine came out of the tunnel, his back was towards her, and she cut him down. That man drove her, and was showing how it happened. Show the gentleman, Tom."

The man, who wore a rough dark dress, stepped back to his former place at the mouth of the tunnel.

"Coming round the curve in the tunnel, sir," he said, "I saw him at the end, like as if I saw him down a perspective-glass. There was no time to check speed, and I knew him to be very careful. As he didn't seem to take heed of the whistle, I shut it off when we were running down upon him, and called to him as loud as I could call."

"What did you say?"

"I said, 'Below there! Look out! Look out! For God's sake, clear the way!' "

I started.

"Ah! it was a dreadful time, sir. I never left off calling to him. I put this arm before my eyes not to see, and I waved this arm to the last; but it was no use."

Without prolonging the narrative to dwell on any one of its curious circumstances more than on any other, I may, in closing it, point out the coincidence that the warning of the engine-driver included, not only the words which the unfortunate signal-man had repeated to me as haunting him, but also the words which I myself—not he—had attached, and that only in my own mind, to the gesticulation he had imitated.

Notes on the Stories

OLALLA

the good cause: the alliance against Napoleon
bartizan: a small overhanging turret on a tower or wall, common in Spanish architecture
kirkton: the church or cathedral town

GOD SEES THE TRUTH BUT WAITS

Nijni Fair: annual summer fair at Nijni (Nizhny) Novgorod (now Gorki) at the junction of the Volga and Oka rivers; lasting from mid-July to mid-September, it was the world's largest annual fair
samovar: a tea urn in which the water is kept hot by charcoal
troika: a sleigh vehicle drawn by three horses abreast

THE SENTRY

the Winter Palace on the Neva: the traditional winter residence of the Czar at St. Petersburg (now Leningrad), where the river Neva flows into the Baltic
the Emperor Nikolai Pavlovich: Czar Nicholas I (reigned 1825-1855); Pavlovich means son of Paul
Gogol, *The Government Inspector:* a play (1835) by Nikolai Gogol (1809-1852) satirizing government bureaucracy

MADEMOISELLE FIFI

The setting is the Franco-Prussian War (1870-1871); the Chateau d'Urville on the Andelle River near Rouen, the principal city of Normandy.
Graf: Count
fi, fi donc: a French expression of utter scorn
Le Devoir: "Duty"
Belfort and Strassburg: two cities of Alsace fiercely contested during the War; the French retained Belfort

MOONLIGHT

The Abbé Marignan bore his fighting title well: Marignano (Melegnano), a town near Milan, was famous as the site of important military victories by François I in 1515 and by Napoleon III in 1859.

DUCK SHOOTING

Saint Nazaire: a village at the foot of the Pyrenees on the Mediterranean
Canigou: a high peak of the Pyrenees behind Saint Nazaire
Albères: a chain of the Pyrenees, of which Canigou is one of the major peaks
crosier shape: The boat's prow is curled like a bishop's crozier.
Catalanian: the ancient language of the Catalan area (northeast Spain) and of the contiguous region of France

A PASSION IN THE DESERT

General Desaix: commander of Napoleon's army in Egypt
Maugrabins: Arab brigands
Arles: a principal city of Provence, on the Rhône
petite maîtresse: little mistress
Mignonne: sweetheart, darling; the French word implies a person of docility, gentleness.
ma petite blonde: my little blonde
the soul of Virginie: refers to the heroine of *Paul et Virginie* (1784), a romantic and exotic novel by Bernardin de Saint-Pierre, a disciple of Rousseau
simoom: a hot, suffocating, sand-laden wind

THE RED INN

Five or six words in this translation by Clara Bell have been modernized.
Carême: (1784-1833), Napoleon's chef; author of works on culinary art
Gymnase: German secondary school
Brillat-Savarin: (1755-1826), French gastronomist, author of *The Physiology of Taste*
diorama: a miniature three-dimensional scene
take the news to Pekin: refers to the time when Pekin (Peking) was administered jointly by the French and English
in anima vili: on an unworthy subject, on a vile person
Vendémiaire . . . year VII: refers to the calendar devised during the French Revolution but eventually discarded
diligence: a public stagecoach
Turenne: Marshal of France, commander of the army of Louis XIV in the Thirty Years' War (1618-1648)
Beauvais: a town in Picardy, in north-east France
louis: louis d'or; gold coins, a basic unit of French money, 1640-1795
assignats: monetary notes, usually quick to depreciate
Aix-la-Chapelle: French name of Aachen in Germany, once Charlemagne's capital
hoc erat in votis: a heart's desire
The whole eighteenth century . . .: refers to the notorious skepticism of the Enlightenment
Peace of Amiens: the truce between England and Napoleonic France, 1802
Court of Assize: French criminal court
Sanhedrin: Jewish tribunal
General Foy: one of Napoleon's generals
Edict of Nantes: a law, promulgated by Henri IV, which granted freedoms to Huguenots (French Protestants), 1598; revoked by Louis XIV in 1685

Aceldama: any place of human slaughter; originally the "field of blood" near Jerusalem, purchased with the bribe Judas Iscariot took for betraying Jesus (*Acts*, 1:19)
Rossini: (1792-1868), Italian composer of *William Tell, The Barber of Seville*, etc.
Jeanie Deans: peasant heroine of Sir Walter Scott's novel *The Heart of Midlothian*

SUNSTROKE

Samara: a port on the Volga
Anapie: a resort town on the Sea of Azov
Sebastopol: a city at the juncture of the Sea of Azov and the Black Sea
Kertch: a port on the narrows of the Sea of Azov

IMMENSEE

The setting of this story is the dyke country of north-west Germany on the North Sea.
Tyrolese: dialect of the Tyrol, an alpine region of western Austria and northern Italy

THE BRACELET

Dresden plates: Dresden, East Germany, famous for china manufacture
Alençon lace: Alençon, a lace-making center in Normandy
Calville apples: succulent apples with textured skins

THE LITTLE BOUILLOUX GIRL

Sundays and Thursdays: traditional days of leisure for European schoolchildren
figure of eight: the characteristic shape of a chignon hair style
a Greuze: refers to a typical painting by Jean Baptiste Greuze, a genre and portrait painter of the late 18th century, noted for pretty compositions of young girls
a steel châtelaine: a decorative belt of metal loops
St. John's Eve: June 24, Feast of the Nativity of John the Baptist, patron of France; a traditional national holiday

THE LAST CLASS

Franco-Prussian War: commenced in 1870, concluded in 1871, with the defeat of France
Alsace and Lorraine: provinces perennially contested between France and Germany
the Soar: a river of Lorraine
Vive la France: Long live France

TEARS, IDLE TEARS

The story is set in London during World War II.
Regent's Park: large park in north-central London known for its woods and zoological gardens
red may: the red hawthorn tree

MATEO FALCONE

Porto-Vecchio: city near the south-east point of Corsica
the island: Corsica
Bastia, Corte: towns in eastern Corsica
caporal: formerly the chief officer of the Corsican commune after the revolt against the feudal landlords

AT HOME

votre père vous appelle: "Your father is calling you." French was traditionally spoken in nurseries in Russia (and other European countries) so that children would acquire an early knowledge of the language.
our Swiss: Swiss Guards, hired by European governments to protect public officials as, here, a public prosecutor

THE KISS

cob: a thick-set, short-legged horse, often with an unusually high gait
verst: Russian measure of distance, 2/3 mile
in mufti: civilian clothes worn by men normally in uniform
ex-Empress Eugénie: wife of Louis Napoleon (Napoleon III)
quadrille: a five-part square dance for four couples
mazurka: lively traditional dance, originally Polish, in triple rhythm
kopek: small-denomination Russian coin
The Messenger of Europe: popular nineteenth-century journal
canaille: riffraff, the rabble
limber: the detachable portion of a gun carriage
calèche: a carriage
tête-à-tête: (literally head-to-head); a private conversation
Kovno: (Kaunas); a city in Lithuania, near the (then) Prussian border
ruble: the basic Russian monetary unit; a coin (formerly silver) equivalent to 100 kopeks
coupé: as used here, a railway sleeping car